Not Our Own

The Portal in the Picture—Passing through a portal in time and space, Eddie Burton discovered a bizarre twin city to his own New York, a city where priests ruled in the name of a religion called Alchemy—and a man from our Earth could start a revolution with one little flame...

★   ★   ★

Valley of the Flame—In search of a legendary radioactive fire, Brian Raft stumbles upon a nightmare land where monsters rule, guarding the cosmic power that may someday create new life—or destroy all that lives...

★   ★   ★

The Dark World—A fateful visit from a giant wolf and a mysterious hooded figure catapults Edward Bond into a dangerous alternate world—and a deadly battle between the forces of science and sorcery...

THE STARTLING WORLDS OF HENRY KUTTNER

HENRY KUTTNER was one of the finest writers of the "pulp" era of science fiction, a man whom author and critic Anthony Boucher called: "among the most imaginative, technically skilled and literarily adroit science fantasy writers." Henry Kuttner more than lived up to that praise. Writing both alone and in collaboration with his wife, C.L. Moore, and using countless noms de plume, Henry Kuttner produced a vast body of truly remarkable tales including his classic novel *Fury*, his delightful stories about "Galloway Gallegher," a drunken inventor with a robot companion, and stories dealing with everything from undersea cities to mutant telepaths to life after nuclear war. A writer whose influence on the field spans more than two decades, Henry Kuttner died in 1958, leaving behind a legacy of some of the finest fiction written in science fiction's golden age.

THE STARTLING WORLDS of HENRY KUTTNER

BY HENRY KUTTNER

POPULAR LIBRARY

An Imprint of Warner Books, Inc.

A Warner Communications Company

Contents

Henry Kuttner and
Startling Stories
(and C.L. Moore)

Forty years ago if you wanted to read science fiction and/or fantasy, you didn't go to a bookstore or a library. You popped round to your neighborhood newsstand and if you were lucky, you'd find one or more of about a dozen magazines devoted to "that Buck Rogers stuff" or related genres. They had alluring names such as *Famous Fantastic Mysteries*, *Thrilling Wonder Stories*, *Weird Tales*, and *Startling Stories*.

Of those magazines, the one that has gone down in history is *Astounding Stories*, which still exists under the name of *Analog*. And that was because under its editor, John W. Campbell, Jr., it brought a new sensibility to science fiction. Its authors and many of its stories have become classics of the field and rightfully so. But another of the magazines was also much more quietly establishing important links to the future without being quite so revolutionary about it. This was *Startling Stories*, under the editorship of Samuel Merwin. It was much more traditional than Campbell's magazine. The covers almost always had a Bug-Eyed Monster (which were affectionately known as BEMs) and a seminaked lady, whose seminakedness was usually covered in such interesting examples of *haute couture* as a brass brassiere. (A seminaked lady on *Astounding* was as rare as a hobbit in Trantor.)

Startling Stories continued the older tradition of science fantasy and space opera, but with more and more variation from the old formulas. The result was what might be called soft SF (as opposed to the high-tech "hard" SF of *Astounding*), on the literary spectrum leaning more toward fantasy. For example, one of Merwin's discoveries was a brilliant young author who wrote under the name of Jack Vance, whose work was undoubtedly much too fanciful for Campbell. And Arthur Clarke's beautiful *Against the Fall of Night* (which was to be rewritten as *The City and the Stars*) first appeared in *Startling*.

In short, Merwin and *Startling* carried on the tradition of nontechnical SF, which, combined with fantasy, is much closer to today's taste.

By all odds, the most popular writer in *Startling Stories* was Henry Kuttner, whose "novels" (a pulp magazine novel was much closer in length to a novelette in today's terms) were begged for in the letters column and greeted with joy when they appeared.

Kuttner was the pulp writer par excellence. He could write *anything*, any style, and did so: tales of the supernatural (his first published story had the engaging title of "The Graveyard Rats"), sword and sorcery, soft SF, and hard SF. (Some of his best work indeed appeared in *Astounding*, but he was not one of Campbell's "stable.") But he also wrote well, with wondrously imaginative concepts. He wrote so well, in fact, that any SF reader of the '40s, if asked his favorite writer, would have been as likely to say Kuttner as Asimov or Heinlein or Van Vogt.

His prodigious and varied output was complicated by appearing under any number of pen names (there was a persistent rumor that Jack Vance was one of these), and further complicated when he married the equally talented writer C. L. Moore (in 1940). The two, more often than not, collaborated on their stories thereafter, which might then appear under either name or yet another nom de plume.

But of all this bewildering oeuvre, the most exciting and the most popular were the science fantasies he (they) wrote for *Startling Stories*. Vaguely akin to the earlier works of A. Merritt, they usually placed the hero *elsewhere*, in other worlds—planes?—dimensions?—that infringed somehow on ours, and that (given the vaguest of scientific rationales) were full of wonderfully exotic beings, beasts, and things. Speed was of the essence in SF-magazine writing, and Kuttner's novels were very speedy indeed; a thrill a minute was the rule. Reading them today is a marvelous antidote to the verbose trilogies with which we're currently afflicted. But there is somehow always room for Kuttner (and Moore) to inject liberal amounts of colorful atmosphere. Curiously enough, there are few, if any, contemporary writers whose work seems so cinematic, so close to the dazzling special effects that the movies have developed. What visions Kuttner (and Moore) evoked in the mind's camera lens!

So welcome to three of Henry Kuttner's (and C. L. Moore's) most startling worlds: Paititi, lost in the South American jungle, where time does strange things; Malesco, an alternate Earth based loosely (and a little giddily) on the science of alchemy; and the most famous and popular of all, the Dark World, where the legends live.

—Baird Searles

THE
PORTAL
IN
THE
PICTURE

Prologue

SHE called herself Malesca. Her agent called her the "Loveliest Girl in the World" and I suppose he wasn't far wrong, at that. If I'd known she was playing the Windsor Roof that night I'd have gone somewhere else.

But by the time I was at the table, having a sandwich and a highball, it was too late. The lights dimmed, the spot went on and there stood Malesca, bowing to the storm of applause. I wasn't going to let her spoil my drink. I could always look somewhere else while she was on. I ate white meat of chicken, drank my highball and thought about other things—until the famous velvet voice began to sing.

I listened to her sing. A chair creaked. In the dimness someone sat down beside me. I peered through the gloom, recognizing the man, a top figure in show business.

"Hello, Burton," he said.

"Hello."

"Mind if I join you?"

I waved my hand and he gave his order to the waiter who slid up noiselessly. Malesca was still singing.

The man beside me watched her, as rapt and intent as everybody else in the club except me.

Two encores later, when the lights went up, I realized that he was staring at me curiously. My disinterest in the singer must have been pretty obvious.

"No like?" he asked in a puzzled voice.

Even before Korzybski that particular question would have been meaningless. I couldn't answer him and I knew it. So I didn't bother. I just didn't say anything. I could see Malesca from the corner of my eye, hear the rustle of her stiff skirts as she came through the tables toward me. I sighed.

She was wearing some light flowery scent I knew she hadn't picked out for herself. She put her hand on the table edge and leaned toward me.

"Eddie," she said.

"Well?"

"Eddie, I haven't seen you for ages."

"That's right."

"Listen, why don't you wait around? Take me somewhere after my last show. We could have a drink or something. How about it, Eddie?"

Her voice was pure magic. It had been magic on radio and records and video. It would soon be magic in the movies. I didn't say a word.

"Eddie—please."

I picked up my glass, emptied it, brushed crumbs off my coat, laid the napkin beside the plate.

"Thanks," I said. "Wish I could."

She stared at me, the familiar, searching stare full of incomprehension. I could hear the applause still echoing.

"Eddie—"

"You heard me," I said. "Take a walk. Take an encore. Go on, beat it."

Without a word she turned away and went back to the floor, her skirts frothing and hissing as she squeezed between the tables. The man beside me said: "Eddie, are you crazy?"

"Probably," I said. I wasn't going to explain to him.

"All right, Eddie. You know the answers, I suppose. But something must be wrong. The most beautiful woman in the world throwing herself at your feet—and you won't even look at her. That just isn't sensible."

"I'm not a very sensible guy," I told him. It was a lie, of course. I'm the most sensible guy in the world—in any world.

"Don't give me clichés," he said. "That's no answer."

"Clichés!" I said and choked in my glass. "Okay, okay, never mind. Nothing wrong with clichés, you know. They're just truths that happen so often they're trite. It doesn't make them any less true, does it?" I looked at Malesca squaring off at the mike, getting ready to sing again.

"I knew a man once who tried to discredit clichés," I went on thoughtfully, knowing I was probably saying too much. "He failed. He had quite a time, that guy."

"What happened?"

"Oh, he found a fabulous land and rescued a beautiful goddess and overthrew a wicked high priest and—forget it. Maybe it was a book I read."

"What fabulous land was that?" my friend inquired idly.

"Malesco."

He lifted an eyebrow at me and glanced across the room at the Most Beautiful Girl in the World.

"Malesco? Where's that?"

"Right behind you," I said.

Then I picked up my fresh highball and buried my nose in it. I had nothing more to say—to him. But a chord in the music just then woke a thin shivering wire of sound at the back of my brain, and for an instant the barrier between this world and the worlds outside was as thin as air.

Malesco, I thought. I shut my eyes and tried to make the domes and towers of that rose-red city take shape in the darkness while the chord still sounded in my ears. But I couldn't do it. Malesco had gone back into the fable again and the gates were shut forever.

And yet, when I think about it now even the sense of wonder and disbelief is suspended and I have no feeling at all that it was in some dream I walked those streets. They were real. I've got the most convincing kind of proof that they were real.

It all happened quite a while ago . . .

Chapter I

REMEMBER the story of the blind men and the elephant? Not one of them ever found out it was an elephant. That's the way it was with me. A new world was opening right in front of me and I put it down to eyestrain.

I sat there in my apartment with a bottle and watched the air flicker.

I told myself to get up and switch off the lights because Lorna had got in the habit of dropping by if I didn't show up at the ginmill where she worked, and I didn't want to talk to her. Lorna Maxwell was a leech. She had attached herself to me with all the simple relentlessness of her one-track mind and short of killing her I knew no way to pry her loose.

It all seemed so easy to Lorna. Here I was, rising young actor Eddie Burton with a record of three straight Broadway hits and a good part in something new that all the critics liked. Fine.

Here she was, that third-rate young ginmill singer Lorna Maxwell with no record at all that she admitted to. Don't ask me how we met or how she got her hooks into me. I'm a born easy mark. Children, animals and people like Lorna can spot people like me a mile away.

She'd got it into her addled little head somehow that all I had to do was say the word and she'd be right up there beside me, a success, the darling of the columnists. Only selfishness kept me from saying the magic word to somebody in authority and turning her into Cinderella. Arguments wouldn't move her. It seemed simpler to turn off the lights when I was at home alone and not answer the door.

The air flickered again. I squinted and shook my head. This was getting a little alarming. It couldn't be the Scotch. It never happened outside the apartment. It never happened unless I was looking at that particular wall.

There was a Rousseau picture on it, *Sleeping Gypsy*, something Uncle Jim had left me along with the apartment. I made a great effort to focus on the blue-green sky, the lion's blowing mane, the striped robe of the black man on the sand.

But all I got was a blur. And then I knew I must be drunk because a sound seemed to go with the blur, a roaring that might have been the lion except that the lion had entirely vanished and I seemed to be seeing a dome of shining rosy-red light that moved like water.

I squeezed my eyes shut. This was crazy.

Uncle Jim had left me the apartment in his will. It was one of those deals where you pay a fabulous sum down and a high rental for life and call the apartment yours. I wouldn't have got into it myself, but Uncle Jim did and it was nice to have a place the landlord couldn't throw me out of when somebody offered him a higher bribe.

This is probably the place for a word about Uncle Jim Burton. He was a Character. He had red hair, freckles and a way of losing himself in foreign parts for months at a stretch. Sometimes for years.

He used to visit us between trips when I was a kid, and of all the people I knew in those days he was my favorite because he took me in on a secret.

It started out as bedtime stories. All about a marvelous land called Malesco that followed the pattern for all marvelous lands. There was a beautiful princess and a wicked high priest and a dashing young hero whose adventures kept me awake for all of fifteen minutes sometimes after the lights were put out.

Those were the pre-Superman days, so I didn't picture myself soaring through Malesco in a red union suit. But sometimes I wore a lion skin like Tarzan and sometimes the harness of an intrepid Martian warrior who looked like John Carter.

I even learned to speak Malescan. Uncle Jim made it up, of course. He had a restless mind, and he was recovering from some sort of illness during those months he stayed with us when the Malesco stories began. He made up a vocabulary of the language. We worked out a sort of primer together and jabbered away to each other in Malescan with a good deal of fluency before the episode came to an end and he went away again.

I sat there, watching the wall flicker, looking at the blurred rose-red globe on the wall and something like roofs beyond it, lit with a brilliant sunset. I knew I was imagining most of it. What I saw was the red blur you get when you rub your eyes hard and my imagination was making it into something very much like the tales of Malesco Uncle Jim used to tell.

The whole thing had sunk far back into my mind in the many years since. But when I groped I seemed to dredge up a memory of a city lit with crimson sunsets. In the center of the city was a great dome from which reflected the light from a surface of—had it been water? Had it been—

The doorbell rang.

"Eddie!" Lorna's voice called loudly. "Eddie, let me in a minute."

I knew if I didn't she'd rouse the neighbors with her knocking and shouting. I heaved myself out of the chair and sidled cautiously around that blur which was pure imagination between me and the wall where the Rousseau hung. It was odd, I thought, that the hall wasn't blurred, or the front door, or even Lorna's pretty, cheap little face when I let her in.

"I waited for you, Eddie," she said reproachfully, slipping in fast before I could change my mind. "What kept you? Eddie, I had to see you. I've got a new idea. Look, how would it be if I could dance a little too? Would that help? I've worked out a sort of routine I wish you'd—"

"Have a drink," I said wearily. "Let's not talk about it now, Lorna. My head aches. I think I've got eye trouble. Things keep blurring."

"—look while I just run through it," she went right on as soon as I finished speaking. It was one of her less endearing tricks.

I shut my ears and followed her back into the living room, hoping she'd go away soon. The Rousseau Gypsy had come back anyhow. That was a comfort. The red blur which my imagination made into a vision of Malesco was entirely gone. I sat down in the same chair, sipped my Scotch and looked morosely at Lorna.

It doesn't matter what she was saying. I heard about every tenth word. She fixed herself a drink and perched girlishly on the arm of a chair, making graceful gestures with her glass, telling me all about how I was going to help her become a great dancer if I'd only say the right word to the right man.

I'd heard it all before. I yawned, looked crosseyed at the ice in my glass, drained the last of the Scotch and glanced up at the opposite wall.

This time it was pure hallucination. Instead of the Rousseau it was another kind of picture on the wall and it moved as though I were looking at a pull-down movie screen, stereoscopic, technicolored.

There it all was, clear and perfect. No imagination about it this time. Malesco—exactly as Uncle Jim had told me. A black line that looked like an iron bar ran across one corner of the picture. Beyond it, small and far away, was the city lit with sunset.

Domes, soaring columns, a shining globe that moved like

water in one enormous sphere, surrounded by curved arches that seemed to support it though they too had a flowing upward motion. And all the intricate pattern of arches and bubbles was on fire with reflected light.

A *rose-red city, half as old as time*.

"Eddie, look at me!"

I didn't stir. This was like hypnosis. I couldn't turn my eyes away from that incredible hallucination. I knew Lorna hadn't seen it, for the pitch of her voice didn't change.

Maybe she couldn't see it. Maybe I was crazy. Or maybe she just hadn't glanced that way.

She was babbling something about taking her shoes off so she could show me the dance and I realized vaguely that she was thumping heavily about the floor. I knew I ought to rub my eyes and try to make that vision go away.

"Eddie, look at me!" she insisted.

"All right, all right," I said, not looking. "It's fine."

I rubbed my eyes.

Then Lorna screamed.

My head jerked up. I remember the coldness of ice spilling across my hand, I stared at the spot where she should have been and all I could see across the room was that picture: the sunset city with its globe of burning water and the black bar across the foreground. The whole city quivered.

I heard her scream fade. It diminished and grew thin and ceased so gradually it still seemed to ring in my ears long after I thought it had stopped. Then the air's flickering steadied. The rose-red city blurred again and in the next moment the lion crouched above the sleeping gypsy and the Rousseau painting was unchanged there on the solid wall.

"Lorna," I said. No answer. I stood up, dropping the glass. I took a step forward and stumbled over her shoes. I ran across to the door and jerked it open. The corridor was empty outside. No footsteps sounded.

I came back and tried the kitchen, the bedroom. No Lorna.

An hour later I was down at police headquarters, trying to tell the cops I hadn't murdered her. An hour after that I was in jail.

Chapter II

I'D RATHER deal with a crook than a fanatic any day. The Assistant D.A. was a fanatic about his own theories, and I found myself in a difficult spot in less than no time. This isn't the story of how circumstantial evidence can make mistakes and I won't go into detail. It was just that Lorna had left a friend waiting in the lobby, the neighbors heard Lorna call and heard me let her in—and where was she?

I didn't try to tell the truth. I said she'd gone out. I was too rattled to remember the shoes and that was a strong point against me. The Assistant D.A. was bucking for his boss' job, and he got himself so thoroughly convinced of my guilt that toward the end I think he'd have been willing to stretch a point or two, legally speaking, if he could bring a murderer to justice—me.

Maybe you remember the newspaper stories about it. I lost my part in the hit play. I got a lawyer who didn't believe me because I couldn't tell him the truth. Time went by and all that saved me was the fact that Lorna's body never did show up. Eventually they let me go.

What would you have done in my spot? In the movies I'd instantly have gone to see Einstein, and he'd have figured it all out and whipped up a super-machine that would bring Lorna back or send me into a world like King Kong's.

Or in another kind of movie there'd have been gangsters hammering at the door while I climbed down the fire escape, looking like Dick Powell. Or there'd have been sliding panels or something to explain things at the end of the movie. But Lorna had vanished into a picture on the wall, and I was beginning to worry about my own sanity.

The only hope was that the shimmer in the air might come again and I could somehow lean through and haul Lorna back. I'd come to accept that hope definitely by the time a few months had gone by. I'd thought it all over and been to an optometrist and a psychiatrist and found out all the things it couldn't have been. Not hallucination. Not visual disturbance. Not madness.

No, it had simply been—Malesco.

I went through Uncle Jim's books and papers after that. I found a lot of notes in a shorthand I never was able to read, then or later. I found quite a lot of stuff on alchemy, of all odd things. And I found the old Malescan primer and vocabulary. This was the one thing I really got some good out of—but not then.

That came much later when everything broke at once. It was night again. I was sitting at home drinking Scotch again. And again a bell rang, but this time it was the phone. It was my attorney. He talked fast and carefully.

"Listen, Burton," he said. "A body's been picked up in the Sound. A floater. Your friend Thompson's got the lab working on it. He thinks it's the Maxwell woman."

"Lorna's not dead," I said stupidly. "At least not—"

"All right. Take it easy. It's just that I'm a little worried. This is what Thompson's been waiting for, you know."

"They can't possibly identify—"

"After this long it's mostly guesswork anyhow. But Thompson's got the experts working for him, and juries have a way of believing experts. They might—just might—make it stick, Burton."

So that was that—crisis. And what could I do? If I ran they'd pick me up. If I stayed, they'd probably convict me. I hung up the phone and went back to my chair, pausing on the way to tap with insane hopefulness at the Rousseau. If I tore my way through that wall would I come out on the other side into Malesco? Would Lorna be there or was she that floater after all?

"Lorna?" I said inquiringly into the empty air. "Lorna?"

I waited. No answer. And yet there was something more than silence. My voice had a curious echoing quality as if I'd spoken in a tunnel. Malesco, of course, didn't exist. It was a fairy-tale land like Oz and Wonderland out of a childhood story. But I had a sudden, compelling certainty that my voice echoed when I called to Lorna and echoed in Malesco.

"Lorna!" I said it louder. *"Lorna!"* This time it was a shout. But it was a hollow and ghostly shout, echoing and reechoing down a long invisible tunnel, dying away at the far end—in Malesco.

"Lorna!"

The shrill hum of the doorbell cut through the echoing of my voice. The police? I spun around. But as I moved, the walls tilted sickeningly. Either I couldn't stop turning or the room was falling sidewise—no, collapsing in a direction I didn't understand.

The doorbell sang its thin, shrill summons, over and over, farther and farther away . . . For I was falling.

I saw a man's face whirl by in darkness. He wore a queer headdress and his mouth was wide open with a look of surprise and terror. He was pointing a weapon at me.

He slid sidewise and vanished. I slipped down a wire of singing sound, clinging to it as to a lifeline, pausing, falling, sliding into an abyss. Then the ringing wire of sound grew thinner. It began to fade. It no longer supported me.

I was falling.

A black horizontal line whipped up, vertical bars appeared. And I saw suddenly that my hands were gripping them, sliding down slowly. Instinct had sent its red warning flashing through my body: "Grab! Hang on! *Hang on!*"

This was real. There was no singing void around me any more. But there was a very real void under me and a terribly real pavement a million feet straight down. I was clutching the outside of a balcony rail with both hands and dangling over a drop I couldn't let myself think about.

Was this, I wondered frantically, the usual method of entering Malesco? If it was the way Lorna came then I was wasting my time. Lorna would be a long time dead by now, down there on that horribly distant, horribly hard-looking pavement, in the pink sunset light.

I couldn't see anything except the bars I clung to, the wall in front of me and a sickening angle of vertical building ending in pavement far down. I didn't see the city. The only important things were very near ones—real, vital, beautiful things like a ledge in the wall or a cornice I could brace my foot against.

If I'd been sent back to New York right then I'd have had exactly this to say about Malesco: one, railings are made of some hard slick metal too thin and slippery to hold on long. Two, building walls are stone or plastic or metal or something, maybe pre-fab, and there aren't any joints or cracks and it's a very poor way to build a wall.

I simply didn't have the strength to get over that balcony rail. But I got over it. My simian progenitors sent me a cable along the instinct channel, my feet became prehensile in spite of my shoes. And the ancient basic terror of the long drop spurred me on. I don't like to think about it even now. I don't know how I did it.

But eventually I levered myself over and felt the balcony floor under my feet. The simian strength went back where it came from, millions of years in my biological past. My remote ancestor, Bandar-Log Burton, returned to hunting his antediluvian fleas and a still older ancestor, a mere blob of protoplasm, became dominant.

I felt like jelly. My protoplasm carried me with reeling rapidity across the balcony and through an open window. I found myself in a medium-sized room with the guy who had tried to shoot me.

Chapter III

THE room was empty except for my new acquaintance. I mean empty. There wasn't a thing in it except that in the four upper corners were good-sized cups of corroded steel or iron. The walls were blue-green, and the floor was darker green and gave slightly underfoot. The pink light of sunset cast my shadow ahead of me across the walls.

There were two doors. At one of them was my friend with the odd headdress, which was perched at a drunken angle so that one flap hung over his eye and the other at the back of his head. He had his ear against the door panel, listening, paying no attention to me.

I got an impression of a thin middle-aged face alert with apprehension, a shirt with what looked like a coffee stain on it and long red-flannel drawers. I had just time to realize that it was the sunset light which made them look so crimson. Then the man heard my footstep, twisted around, saw me and fell into a fit of violent indecision.

He tried to do several things at once. He seemed to want to open the door and run. He wanted to yell for help. He wanted to pull out his equivalent of a Police Positive and kill me.

What he did was run at me, grip me around the waist and shove me back on the balcony. Before I knew what was happening, the guy had stuffed me halfway over the rail again. Don't think I wasn't resisting. I was. But what can an amoeba do?

A couple of times he could simply have let go and I'd have fallen. But he didn't let go. To him, it seemed, I was a square peg and he was frantically trying to find a square hole in space to fit me. He was trying to hit the lucky number on a punchboard and using me to do it.

All the while he was looking around in a worried fashion, glancing down, trying to prevent my falling, looking over his shoulder, up at the sky and shaking at the flap of his headdress, which had twisted around even farther so that he could scarcely see at all.

As for me, I was in a nightmare. There was a ridiculous temptation to stay passive and wait till I'd been stuffed into that square hole in space. Maybe *he* could find it, I thought. I never had exactly in thirty-odd years. All I'd found were round holes.

On that philosophical point I got a grip on myself. I grabbed my friend around the neck and hauled myself back to safety. Neither of us was in a state suitable for a ten-round scrap. I hit him somewhere. He snatched at his belt and brought up a weapon that looked like a little dumbbell and I hit him again.

He gripped the ends of the dumbbell in each hand and pulled it apart. A silent flash of blue light streamed between his clenched fists. He looked at me. I could see only half his face because of that striped flap, but in his one visible eye there was desperation. Then it looked past me. A shadow fell on us. The man hesitated.

I knocked the weapon out of his hand. As the two globes fell they snapped together and the blue light was gone. My opponent must have gone crazy, because he stooped to pick up his gadget and I gave him a fast rabbit punch. I had just enough strength left me to make it effective. He kept on stooping until he lay flat on his face, motionless.

I looked around and saw some kind of aircraft moving between me and what was left of the sun. It was a good distance away and for an instant it reminded me of a galleon. It had a cobwebby filigree appearance as it slid across the red bisected sphere.

Beneath it lay the city with its domes and swooping roads and spires. And there was the fiery ball of moving light or water, supported by its shifting arches. So this was Malesco.

I knew Malesco. Uncle Jim had told me about it too often for me not to know the place when I saw it.

I was just glancing shudderingly down at a formal garden below, in a sort of clear, shadowy well of air lit by sunset, when a deep sigh from my fallen enemy made me turn abruptly.

He hadn't moved. But I went rapidly back into the room and stood listening. Once I thought I heard footsteps outside, but they ceased and there was only silence except for an occasional muffled distant murmur of voices. I opened the door, the one my murderous friend had been listening at, and peered out through a narrow crack. I saw a hall well lighted.

I closed that door and tried the other one across the room. Beyond was another chamber of the same size with the same rusty cups in the upper corners. The wall opposite the door was a machine. At any rate it was solid with dials and panels and levers and things. It had a round flat face about as tall as I was. I looked at it. It looked at me. Nothing happened.

For the rest of the room, there was a curtain across one corner that screened a sort of clothes closet. In the middle of the floor was a small table. On the table was the remnant of a meal. There was a crust of bread, the green dregs of liquid in a cup and a fruit or vegetable the size of a radish with a wormhole in its pink skin.

On the floor by the table, lying as if someone had dropped it, was a crumpled black robe. Beside the bread crust lay a tablet with circles drawn on it, most of them connected by straight lines, and the whole thing irritably crossed out with a few heavy strokes. I don't know why I thought of tic-tac-toe.

I walked back and forth, studying the machine hopefully from several angles. It made not the slightest sense to me.

However, it would have made just as much sense if it had been a Ford motor or a vacuum cleaner, so I let it go and went back to see if my victim had wakened.

He hadn't. I rolled him over and investigated. He wore a light tunic, heavy brown sandals, tight ankle-length trousers, pure white except for the dirt, and the striped headdress.

Oh, yes—he wore a bracelet and a ring on his left wrist and middle finger, and they were connected by a flexible band of the same metal—bluish-green. There was a pouch in his belt and, as I touched it—just before I touched it—the thing made a noise at me, like a rattlesnake giving warning.

Then it said something in a language I automatically translated and understood before I realized what that language was.

"Temple Headquarters," it remarked. *"From the Priest of the Night. Falvi!"*

Two thoughts collided inside my head. One of them brought my gaze down to my victim's striped headdress and the other made my lips move silently as I repeated the words I had just heard spoken. One and one are two. One and one are—Malesco.

All of a sudden, I was remembering Uncle Jim's bedtime stories and how striped headdresses had occasionally figured in those tales. Those who wore them bore the rank of—what had it been? Priest. And that meant—

My mind clamped down and rejected such an impossibility. I stood up, took a deep breath and wished I hadn't.

For this was the moment I'd been avoiding—the moment when I couldn't keep moving and would have to start thinking and realizing. I was in another world. (What world? Oh, no! I wasn't quite ready to believe *that* yet.)

The only other explanation was that I'd gone crazy and was really in a bed in Bellevue with doctors looking at me thoughtfully and remarking, "Obviously a hopeless case. Shall we try shock treatment, or should we experiment with that new method, the one that killed all the Rhesus monkeys?"

Meanwhile at my feet was an unconscious priest and beyond the railing lay the city, no longer rose-red, but darkening into evening. The sun had gone. Night came quickly here. I looked out over the eerily familiar view I'd dreamed of so often as a child.

The sense of wonder hadn't hit me yet. I wasn't even incredulous—yet. Anybody pitched headforemost into Oz or Graustark or any other familiar unreal world and finding it a real place after all would expect to be half-stunned by disbelief. I wasn't. There was no use disbelieving in Malesco—here it was. After a while, I told myself, I'll start being surprised. Then, there wasn't time.

The thing that I wanted to think about most when I got a moment was Uncle Jim. It had been no series of bedtime tales he'd told me then. He *knew* Malesco. All right—had he been here in person?

Had he just found some way to open the door betwen the worlds and look through, maybe listen, since he'd learned the language? I wanted time to think about it, but I hadn't any to spare right now. Too much was going on.

One thing was certain: the Malesco that Uncle Jim described to me had been the description of an eyewitness. There was the great flowing dome with its spires of bright water. He hadn't mentioned the patterns of lights visible all over the city after dark, though. Some of them were colored, some of them formed words. I could read Malescan. I knew advertising when I saw it.

This isn't happening, this isn't real, this is a dream I'm having and I'm ten years old again and Uncle Jim made the whole thing up.

The pouch at the priest's belt buzzed. Then it said something in a thin, inquiring voice.

"Falvi! Responde!"

Responde was pronounced the way it was written. I knew what it meant. *Falvi* I didn't know. It might be a proper noun. It might be the name of my priest. If so, Falvi wasn't going to *responde* and I guessed what would probably happen.

I thought I might be safer, somehow, out there in the city. Since there were lights, there would be darkness, too.

Chapter IV

BECAUSE I was in a hurry, I probably wasn't too logical. I'd wasted time. Since the priest had tried to kill me at sight—or at least to stuff me back where I came from through a hole in space and had not seemed to care much whether I fell to the pavement below in the process—I could probably expect similar treatment from other priests. At any rate it was hardly safe to assume I wouldn't get similar treatment.

I went into the room where the machine was, gazed up stupidly at its enigmatic round flat face and turned away, looking for that black cloak. I shook it out, snapped it around my throat, and discovered there were little magnetic clasps all along the front of it, so that when I pulled it down it fell neatly shut.

Then sudden panic seized me. What was I doing here anyway? What were my chances of finding Lorna in a bedtime-story world which I was probably dreaming up as I went along? The place for me was back in New York, where I came from. I turned rapidly and trotted back to the balcony, the cloak flapping at my heels.

I leaned out over the rail and the emptiness and began to grope in the air. But I didn't feel New York. What a hole in space would feel like was uncertain, of course. Rather like the hole in a doughnut, maybe. I had no real hope that I could get hold of something in my own apartment that was solidly anchored and haul myself home that way. It was too much like trying to lift myself by my bootstraps.

And yet I found myself violently reluctant to leave that balcony and go out in a world I didn't know at all. In a curious sort of way I'd been born into Malesco at this spot and I was too young in Malescan experience to like the prospect of seeking fame and fortune in a world I never made.

I was a stranger and afraid—in a world I never made . . .

I had made Earth, you know. Everyone shapes a little part

of his environment, and his parents and ancestors shaped other parts. Maybe that's why it will take a long time for people to get used to living on Venus or Mars. Anyhow, there was a queer sort of silver-cord feeling that held me to the balcony.

Suddenly I thought with some bitterness of the tales written about just such miracles as the one I was undergoing. Burroughs, in particular, and Haggard. But I wasn't on Barsoom now and I wasn't John Carter. He was made of the stuff of mythical heroes. He was indestructible.

I didn't feel specially heroic, but of course one never knows. And the heroism of one society is the rank cowardice of another. Malescan ethics might differ considerably from terrestrial ones. I didn't really think they would, but you never know.

My trouble was that I could be killed.

I hadn't thought much about such things back home. You don't lean too far out of high windows, you don't step in front of speeding cars and you don't touch hot wires because you've heard of electricity. Okay. In Malesco there was gravity and it seemed the usual kind. I could allow for that. But what about the unknown forces like electricity?

A Malescan in a subway in New York might very well sit on the third rail because it looked innocuous. In Malesco, I might sit on an atomic power plant without recognizing it. The priest's dumbbell-shaped weapons seemed to indicate some non-electrical force activating it, and the machine in the other room might operate on some power I'd never heard of. Luckily I could read Malescan. I decided to keep my eyes open for signs reading CAVE! No, that was Latin—Malescan would be CAVEO.

I wasn't getting very far, leaning over this rail searching the air. The priest might wake up at any moment, and I would have to make up my mind whether to run, hide or throw myself on his mercy, such as it was.

I went back thoughtfully into the room and looked down at him. He was starting to twitch a little. Even in repose his face looked irritable and impulsive. It had better be either run or hide, I told myself. Preferably hide—but where?

There was the alcove with a rack of cloaks and robes behind a curtain. There wasn't any other cover I could think of, and I didn't dare go out into the hall and take a chance on other priests coming at me with dumbbells flashing blue fire.

This was the point at which the heroes of the conventional tales perform some miracle of physical or mental prowess and get the upper hand with the ease of long practice. But it was all new to me. I didn't feel heroic and I had no resources whatever.

In the room where the priest lay I heard a thin voice call, "*Falvi!*" again. A groan answered it. The prostrate priest moved his hand. I was as good as caught and I knew it. This was the spot where John Carter would have sprung easily to the top of a ten-foot wall that providentially didn't quite reach the ceiling, there to lie hidden while his enemies searched in vain.

In the tales the enemies never looked up, of course. But all the walls here reached to the ceiling, and even if they hadn't I gravely doubted my ability to dart up them like a startled cat. I wasn't as resourceful as Carter. The best thing that occurred to me was to dive into that clothes closet and burrow my way among the robes into the corner. If I squatted down, the black cloak I was wearing would hide my feet.

It wasn't very good. Fortunately for me it didn't have to be. If I wasn't a resourceful hero, neither was my adversary a very resourceful villain. He was just an ordinary guy who'd been knocked out and felt rattled and confused when he finally came to.

Between two garments and the edge of the curtain I saw him sit up, groan and put his head in his hands. The voice at his waist said irritably, "*Falvi! Responde!*"

He shook his head a couple of times, looked dizzily around, and then suddenly muttered something and scrambled to his feet. His face was frightened. It was worse than frightened. For some reason he was on a spot so bad that things couldn't possibly get worse and somehow or other I was responsible.

I knew that. I knew by the way he looked around the room, obviously searching for me. I was very glad I wasn't in plain sight. My refuge seemed pitiably inadequate now, but it was too late to change it. Luckily the priest seemed to be an amateur too at this sort of thing.

He scuttled out on the balcony, and I watched his back as he bent over the edge and peered hopefully downward. Since I wasn't visible, either climbing down the wall or spread out on the pavement below, he came back again and this time his eye caught the half-open door to the hall.

It was sheer luck that I had left it open. He must have jumped to the conclusion that I had fled. Of course he had no way of knowing how long he'd been unconscious. It might have been hours and I might have got clear away a long time ago.

He hurried to the door and I heard him take a few uncertain steps outside. But he came back in a moment and shut the door firmly. By the look on his face I was sure he had ulcers. He was the kind of guy who always does have ulcers.

The little voice at his belt called again and this time he took a thing like a white waffle out of his pouch and did something very odd. He yawned into it. That is, he made the noises a man makes when he's slowly waking out of deep sleep.

I was surprised, but not entirely, by the yawn. A light had gone on beyond his shoulder, out there in the slowly lighting city. Sheer astonishment made me blank to everything but the thing I saw spread across the whole side of a building about a block away.

It was a picture of Lorna's face.

It must have been huge, though from where I crouched I could see it all and it looked small in perspective. The picture was illuminated and was on something like stained glass, though not formalized the way stained glass pictures usually are. I knew it was Lorna's face, but for a long moment I just didn't believe it.

It was Lorna's face, all right, but glamorized as though Arden had collaborated with Rubinstein and then turned it over to a Romney who's become a religious idealist. Just as Romney had on canvas given Lady Hamilton qualities that essentially bird-brained woman never possessed, so this super-electric sign changed Lorna Maxwell into a very beautiful woman with a strangely etherealized appearance.

Over the portrait head was a huge golden A—a rather mystifying letter which I noticed standing alone in gold lights elsewhere here and there through the city. It seemed to mean something. Under Lorna's portrait was the word or name CLIA.

"Falvi!"

I'd almost got used to that thin urgent voice. It was the answering voice that brought my attention back—a drowsy startled murmur, then the falsely brisk tone of a man suddenly awakened.

"In the name of the Phoenix. Falvi to the Hierarch. There is peace in the Earth-Gates watchroom."

"Were you asleep?"

"I—ah—I was contemplating the mysteries."

"You'll have a chance to contemplate the mysteries in solitude when I report this to the Hierarch." There was a pause. Then: "Falvi, if you're sleepy I'll put someone else on. But I'm supposed to be responsible tonight. If there's trouble the Hierarch will devour my—" There followed a word I didn't understand.

"Sorry," Falvi said. "Could you get some other priest to take over? I—I think I'm sick."

"Right away," the thin voice agreed and there was silence, in which I could hear Falvi's hard breathing.

I stood perfectly motionless, waiting. Curiously, though Falvi and his communicant sounded nothing at all like Uncle Jim, I'd had a ghostly feeling that it was Uncle Jim who spoke. For their language was Malescan and it was only in his voice that I had ever heard that tongue spoken before.

Of course I hadn't understood every nuance of meaning. But obvious shades of inflection in the voices made the sense unmistakable. Malescan is a simple language, though until now I had never realized just how simple it really was. I'd never questioned it any more than you question pig-Latin or any childhood memory of a code.

Malescan is pronounced the way it's spelled, or at least the way Uncle Jim spelled it in his notes. And the illuminated signs I'd seen confirmed most of his spelling. Then too it seemed based on Latin and anybody who remembers his high-school Latin can make a good guess at the meanings of any language that stems from it.

Falvi came to the doorway and looked out across the city. He said a low word under his breath. Then I realized that Malescan stems partly from Anglo-Saxon, too.

"Obscenity New York!" Falvi said furiously, and before I could realize the full implications of that reference, he turned back into the room and disappeared.

New York—he *had* said New York.

* * *

I gazed across the city at the beautiful transfigured face of Lorna Maxwell and longed for the safe familiar environment of Barsoom.

Falvi was speaking again.

"Coriole," he said quietly. "Dom Coriole!"

There was a wild buzzing which ended in a squeaky voice that said "—wanted me to make the robe for her and I'm just too good-natured to say no, but where I'll get time to—"

"Private beam!" Falvi snapped—or perhaps it was "line" or "circuit." I couldn't translate literally. But I got the sense of the words and heard them as colloquial rather than formalized because I was used to thinking colloquially myself.

There was a pause during which Falvi's gaze moved uneasily about the room. I shrank back shyly among the cloaks. Then an oily giggle sounded.

"I am in spasms," said a thin voice. "Yes, positively in spasms. Purdelor has told me the funniest quip I've heard in years. I nearly split myself laughing. I laughed till I cried. Do you remember Dom Pheres? He always insisted—"

"Coriole, listen! This is Falvi. Somebody else has come through."

"—insisted that his name ought to be pronounced Peres—don't interrupt, I must tell you this."

Falvi was trying to mention somebody named or called the Hierarch.

"Be quiet," Coriole said with thin cheerfulness. "Insisted that his name ought to be pronounced Peres—you have that? So Morander, one evening over dinner, said, 'If you please, Dom Peres, will you hand me the *paselae?*' Paselae! Oh, ha, ha, ha, ha!" There were wild giggles.

"*Damnatio!*" Falvi said, presumably seeing no more point to the joke than I did. I felt a twinge of sympathy for the harassed priest. What Coriole needed was an appreciative studio audience, I thought. But I was underestimating the man.

Falvi said with furious patience, "I was guarding the Earth-Gates tonight and another one came through—a man, this time—and he knocked me out and got away. Ha, *ha*."

Coriole's chuckles died.

"Well," he said, "I suppose you were playing with the Earth-Gates—"

"I never touched them."

"Lie to the Hierarch if you like but don't try it with me, Falvi. What was the man like, eh?"

It was a curious sensation to me, cowering in the clothes closet, hearing myself accurately described. I had a momentary sense of having been discovered, as though the shadows had been driven away by a bright light. I stared at Lorna's face beyond Falvi and the balcony. That steadied me.

Very often in Malesco I needed that steadiness. I kept finding myself inclined to slip over into an odd state in which everything seemed quite unreal and it was difficult for me to move or even think.

A touch of that helpless passivity gripped me now, and for a second Falvi seemed unimportant and unreal. The fact that he was announcing his decision to find and kill me had an abstruse interest, no more than that.

"If you harm him I'll break your neck," Coriole said. "You hear me?"

"All right, I won't touch him," Falvi said in an unconvincing tone. "If any of the other priests have found him he may be dead already. I don't know."

"He sounds like the man you say Clia described. Well, meet me at the Baths immediately."

"But this is the night the—"

"Bless me, this is the night I thought I was on horseback," Coriole said and chuckled again. A humorist, part of my mind said. The other part was considering Lorna's face a block away and the name CLIA under it. So I sounded like the man Clia described, did I? That meant Clia was Lorna, a deduction which required little brilliance on my part.

"It's nothing to joke about," Falvi said. "The Hierarch won't believe I didn't touch the Earth-Gates."

"Naturally he won't," Coriole said. "He knows you're a liar. Meet me at the Baths immediately. Hurry along. This man who came through may be exactly what we need. If you harm him I'll be inclined to wash my hands of you."

"Listen, if he's wandering through the Temple in the clothes he had on he'll be stopped before—"

"There's been no alarm yet, has there? Come along. Leave the thinking to me. I'm qualified for it. And don't try to act on your own. You're not indispensable."

"Perhaps you're not either."

At this Coriole burst into wild thin giggles, sounding rather like a disembodied goblin, and gasped, "Saturn mend you, indeed! It would be less trouble to make a new one. Oh, hurry along. When I explain you'll see why we need this man alive. Less trouble to make—" The giggling died.

"Damned comedian," Falvi said under his breath, then, louder, "Your jokes smell. You're a fool, Coriole. Nobody thinks you're funny. And if I find that man I'll kill him so fast he won't even notice. Maybe it doesn't matter to you whether or not I get in trouble but—"

His words became mutters. I gathered that the "walkie-talkie" had been turned off before Falvi began his diatribe. This seemed to indicate that Falvi was both sensible and cautious.

Then a door slammed and it was time for me to decide what to do next.

Chapter V

THAT was not difficult to figure out but the trouble was to put any sort of plan into action. Any move I made might reveal my identity to enemies. And I had excellent reason to suspect that this temple, or palace, or skyscraper was full of potential enemies—all quite willing to kill me on sight once they discovered I was no Malescan.

So I had to find Lorna. I was completely blindfolded. What I needed most of all was information. What I most wanted was information about how to get home. Meanwhile I badly needed to be briefed. Lorna—going under the name of Clia, I gathered—had found a safe spot in Malesco. I couldn't tell how she'd done it nor, naturally, did I know exactly how safe that spot might be. But if some sesame existed I wanted to know it.

It was quite simple: I was in a dark labyrinth, full of pitfalls and traps, and there was a gleam of light in the distance. So I had to reach that light, which meant information and perhaps help. My immediate goal was Lorna, and I didn't dare think beyond that. While I hated the idea of leaving the room which connected, somehow, with my New York apartment, finding Lorna would mean a very real contact with my own world.

It took me no time at all to make sure the room was empty, cautiously emerge from the closet and, on second thought, dive back into it and search till I located a headdress with flaps such as Falvi wore. It had blue stripes and shadowed my face effectively when I donned it. Then I went to the outside door and peeped out in time to see Falvi walk through a doorway down the hall and disappear.

That left the hall quite empty. I stepped boldly out and hurried after Falvi, passing a few closed doors. Along the ceiling there were more of the metal cups, pouring out light, a milky flowing glow that dissolved in the air and gave a gentle daylight illumination.

Several I passed were burned out and another one was flickering wanly. On the doors themselves I noticed symbols engraved: a formalized bird and a trident on each one and Roman numerals, XVI, XVII, and so forth.

Where Falvi had vanished was an opening in the wall, as large as a doorway. It seemed to be a small elevator shaft, lighted from within. A foreshortened Falvi was twenty feet below, floating down very gently.

I supposed it was Falvi, but all I could see were the headdress and his feet. He resembled a squashed dwarf. He didn't look up and I laid one hand on the wall to brace myself and stared down at him.

There seemed to be no cables nor other mechanical elevator devices, though of course Falvi might be standing on a perfectly transparent floor that was slowly sinking beneath him. I noticed his shadow appear on the wall behind him and vanish as he went on down.

When I looked up I saw part of my own shadow—the deformed head startled me till I remembered the flaps of my headdress—across the shaft, so I understood that Falvi was dropping past similar openings on other floors.

I leaned farther out and counted the brighter patches of illumination. Falvi went down seven levels before he stepped out. Then the shaft was empty and it seemed to go on down for quite a distance.

I was considering the possibility of tossing something into

the shaft as a test to see if it would float or plunge when my shadow on the opposite wall blurred slightly and became suddenly double. My state of mind by now was such that I found myself seriously considering whether I could possibly have two heads. In the same instant I turned to see what had cast the second shadow.

I found myself looking into a pair of very bright expectant eyes on a level with mine. Another priest had come up behind me without a sound and was watching me with a look that reminded me uncomfortably of a cat watching a mouse.

There were extraordinary alertness and anticipation in the face between the flaps of the priestly headdress. He was young and there was a faintly dissipated air about him as though he'd had a big night recently. He wore his robes with a certain negligent elegance that was far from ecclesiastic.

I went into a state of concealed shock. How long had he been following me? From Falvi's door? And why? That expectancy on his face was frightening. He was so clearly waiting for me to do something. But what? From the penetrating interest of his eyes I was ready to believe that he was reading my innermost thoughts and finding them, on the whole, rather amusing.

I had no idea what one priest did when he met another. Before I could come to any decision about how to save my hide, though, he saved it for me by murmuring, "*Pardae-se*," in a polite voice and squeezing past me into the shaft, still not taking that ironic gaze from mine.

I had a strong impression that he knew exactly what had been happening and was simply waiting for me to give myself away. He lifted one eyebrow at me as he slowly sank, a quizzical look that seemed to ask what I was waiting for.

That decided me. After all, what would John Carter have done? The priest was about ten feet down, his head still tilted back to watch me and a grin was beginning to broaden upon his face. I took a deep breath and stepped out into emptiness, confidently expecting a sort of antigravity skyhook to grip me and lower me gently down the shaft.

This did not happen. I dropped like a bullet, head over basket, with the full velocity and acceleration of a freefalling body. I had a glimpse of the priest floating down calmly beneath me—he seemed to be standing still—and then I hit him and we were in a wild Laocoon group, with me playing the python.

He grabbed me, not that it was necessary, because I was hanging on to him like a frantic cat. There was a brief, mad scuffle, which subsided gradually. Clinging together, we drifted slowly downward.

Our faces were quite close now, naturally enough, and the priest's was full of triumphant excitement. I had an idea that I had given myself hopelessly away and that this was just what he'd expected. The look on his face said he knew I was from New York, knew I'd come through Falvi's forbidden Earth-Gates, whatever they were, and the next stop would be the ecclesiastical firing squad.

Just to clinch the matter he spoke to me. It was, of course, Malescan and it meant nothing at all. My ears were ringing anyhow and I was shaking all over with shock and sheer un-heroic fright. The shaft below us looked bottomless. I breathed hard and stared into the bright triumphant eyes about six inches from mine.

He repeated himself more slowly and this time I understood.

"You're lucky I caught you," he said. "You might get re-ported."

I had heard enough of the spoken Malescan tongue to catch the right emphasis and accent. But I still wasn't sure I could speak it naturally. I had to try though. My words came out in a series of gasps—an excellent way of disguising unfamiliarity with a language, by the way.

"I was thinking of something else," I said.

The effect on him was tremendous. I think if I hadn't been clutching him so tightly he might have let me drop in his surprise. For a moment I wondered if I'd made some astounding error in speech. Then I realized that the fact I'd spoken at all—in Malescan—was what startled him so much. He hadn't ex-pected it. His face went perfectly blank for a moment.

When expression came back to it he allowed only the slight-est glimmer of what must have been great disappointment to show through before he pulled himself together and spoke again. This time the malicious expectancy and the penetrating intentness of his look had vanished.

"What did you say?" he asked politely.

"I said I was thinking of something else."

A flicker of the keen suspicion came back into the quick gaze he turned on me. I realized then that I simply didn't know Malescan well enough to pass as a native.

"Well, you'd better think of the Hierarch next time," the priest said, his eyes never swerving from mine. "What are you talking like that for?"

"I bit my tongue," I said hastily.

"Bit your nose?" he asked. "How could you do that? Oh, your *tongue*."

I met his bright stare briefly and then glanced aside at the walls, slipping up slowly around us. Was he simply amusing himself with me? I wasn't sure and I didn't think he was either. Certainly he was suspicious, but he had nothing definite to go on. The fact that I could speak Malescan even passably seemed to knock the bottom out of whatever theory he had formulated about me. Still . . .

"Where do you want out?" he asked, still politely, his tone making a rather insolent contrast to the look on his face.

"I'm going to the Baths," I hazarded.

"Oh, are you? I'll let you off at the main floor, then. I don't know you, do I? You must be fresh from the Crucible."

I nodded.

"No?" the priest said. "But—"

"I mean yes," I corrected, making a mental note on the permutations of symbolic gestures in various cultures. "I'm still fresh from the Crucible."

"A little too fresh," he told me. "You must be from Ferae. Nothing personal but the Feraen dialect is suitable only for talking to dogs. I'm Dio and I know the best"—he used a word I didn't catch—"in the city if you need advice."

"Thanks," I said, wondering if I should tell him my name and finding my mind totally blank when it came to choosing a Malescan *nom-de-guerre*. I didn't know enough about proper nouns. I might ignorantly call myself the equivalent of Santa Claus or Little Bo Peep.

I grimaced and said my tongue hurt.

He seemed to be thinking. "Did *I* bite your nose?" he asked suddenly. "I don't remember doing it. But when you fell on me that way—"

"It's all right," I said.

"Where's your pouch?"

"I forgot it."

"Don't they teach you anything at the Ferae Crucible?" He glanced up the shaft. "Here we are." He lunged forward, carrying me, and we found ourselves standing in a room the size of Grand Central, quite as noisy and crowded and busy. To the left was a great open archway with darkness beyond. The fresh wind blowing in told me it was the open air.

"No use going back for your pouch now," the priest Dio said, reaching toward his belt. "I'll lend you some grain." He put a few coins into my hand. "Don't forget to pay it back. I'm Dio, remember, on the twenty-third Goose of Hermogenes at the fifth Cherub."

"Well—thanks," I said. He looked at me blandly. His dissipated young face had lost its brilliant intentness now and was a little sleepy, as if with satisfaction. Sometime during our brief conversation he had come to a decision about me.

I couldn't understand him at all. If Falvi's prognosis were right any priest who recognized me for a newcomer from Earth was pretty certain to shoot first and ask questions later. Why, I didn't know yet.

Dio's behavior was simply confusing the issue still further. If he knew me for a stranger, he ought to report me. If he didn't, why was he looking so complacent now? He was the cat that had swallowed the canary, and found it more than satisfying.

"I hope they taught you honesty at the Ferae Crucible," he said.

Was he really going to let me go? I could hardly believe it. There might even be time to catch up with Falvi, given a little luck.

"I'll pay you back," I said. "Don't worry."

He shrugged and I started to turn away, hardly believing my own good fortune. Either Falvi had exaggerated the danger that waited me from the priests or—

"Just a minute, you," Dio's voice hailed me over the half-dozen steps that parted us. I knew by the tone of it, even before I turned, that he was grinning. The bright malice was on his face again as our eyes met.

"I think there's something you ought to know," he said. "There haven't been any Crucibles in Ferae for thirty years."

He beamed at me. "Well, good night," he said and stood there, smiling.

I felt exactly as if he'd kicked me in the stomach. There *was* danger. If I'd ever seen danger in my life I saw it in his face. He knew all about me or enough about me to get me killed. And yet he was still standing there, still smiling, waiting for me to go.

I took a tentative backward step as soon as I could breathe again. He was perfectly capable of letting me get to the very door before he raised a shout and set the pack on me. It was open season for Earthmen, all right, and Dio liked the idea.

I thought, "He'll give me sixty seconds, then he'll yell," and I turned and walked toward the door with long, firm steps. The best I could hope for was to get out into the dark before he started the alarm. It wasn't much, but it offered a better chance than this crowded hall.

I glanced around nervously at the thronging priests. They were all dressed alike here except that some didn't wear the outer robes and others were bareheaded. Even in my alarm I noticed the surprisingly atypical haircuts of Malesco.

One priest had a ruff of red hair rising up like a rooster's comb, another had the front of his head shaved and long ringlets hanging down the back. A third had a shaved parting down the center, more than an inch wide. They looked funny to me then, but if Dio raised the alarm before I got to the door they'd probably cease to look funny and become wholly frightening.

I was six steps from the door. I was one step from the door. I stepped out under it onto the lighted steps. I couldn't help glancing back as I hurried down into the darkness. Dio's glance had flicked away from me as he lifted a hand and nodded casually to a passing priest. As I turned I saw his eyes come back to me, and he stroked his jaw in an affectionate way.

I kept going, heading toward the open archway ahead. I was feeling foolish again in the uncertain letdown. Was there any danger, after all? *Had* Falvi known what he was talking about? Certainly Coriole, whoever he was, seemed to take my danger seriously. If I could find Falvi and follow him to Coriole, maybe I could find out the truth.

Beyond the arch was a formal garden, stretched out into a park that ended at a high wall. But from the threshold itself a paved road ran straight to another gate in the wall, and a line had formed there. I hurried in that direction, trying to accustom my eyes to the night.

Just at the gate was a splash of light from one of the overhead metal cups. I saw a priest standing casually behind a tall crystal vase as high as his waist. As the line moved forward and each priest came abreast of the vase he tossed a coin into it. The cashier seemed too bored to pay much attention to his job though he kept one steady eye on the vase.

I joined the line, looking back. Through the open arch leading into the great hall I could see the moving throngs, but I couldn't see Dio now. That didn't mean anything. I felt very very anxious to get on the other side of the temple wall. What I would do there I didn't know yet but...

There were a dozen priests ahead of me, moving forward slowly. I heard the clink of coins. How much should I contribute? Why had Dio given me the—grain? Most of all, who was he? How much did he know and what was his game?

Someone pushed me roughly from behind. I started to swing around and one of the flaps of my headdress swung across my face so that I was momentarily blinded. In that second of darkness, I heard Falvi's familiar voice say, "Keep moving, will you?"

I turned my head back again toward the front, faster than I'd turned it toward Falvi. He was standing right behind me. I hurriedly moved forward, closing the gap between me and the next priest. I heard Falvi's feet scuffle behind me.

Fine—wonderful! Of course it was a lucky break that I hadn't lost Falvi after all, that I could still depend on him to lead me to Lorna. But my back felt singularly unprotected. I could feel rings being drawn concentrically on the back of my robe, with a bull's-eye just in the center, where a knife would be most effective. Inevitably I was moving closer to the splash of light by the cashier.

There were six priests ahead of me... five... four. I looked rigidly ahead, the coins clutched in my hot little palm. Automatically, I noted the size and shape of the "grain" being tossed into the vase. Automatically, I opened my hand and selected a coin that seemed identical. Then there were two men ahead of me... one... nobody at all.

I bent my head forward, so that the flaps fell forward too, and hoped my profile wouldn't be visible to Falvi. I dropped a coin in the vase. The cashier glanced at me sharply, ran his eyes down toward my legs—*my shoes and trousers!*

"Wait a bit!" he said, meeting my eyes again. "You're out of uniform." That wasn't his exact phrase, but the meaning was identical.

And then Falvi yelled in my ear,

"Blast it, Vesto, keep your nose clean! I'm in a hurry! Step it up, step it up."

He shoved me through the gate and as I hastily moved to one side, I heard a violent altercation begin between Vesto and Falvi. It ended in a perfect scream of rage from Falvi, and the next thing I knew he was through the gate too and hurrying into the shadows.

Vesto appeared briefly and swore after him. I moved away in the opposite direction. When Vesto retreated I circled and began to trail Falvi, being doubly careful till we were both past the huge brightly lit open square that faced the temple.

Chapter VI

IT'S no more difficult than a Chicago man suddenly finding himself in Bombay, or Lhasa, or Moscow, dressed in the appropriate local costume. But the boy from State Street has seen newsreels of those places, he's read about them and he knows there are French and English in Bombay. And, anyway, there's not much basic difference between a rickshaw and a Dynaflow.

All the same he'll get a queer picture of Bombay, just as I did of this Malescan city. One reason was that I was afraid to try anything new that might unmask me by revealing my ignorance. A Martian might follow the crowds down a B.M.T. subway entrance and he'd get along fine till he ran up against the coin-operated turnstile. Then he'd start frantically wondering what peculiar ritual was required.

He might figure out how the change booths worked; but unless he had some U.S. currency, he'd be sunk. Even if he spoke English there'd still be trouble, since nobody in one of

those New York subway change booths has ever been known
to speak in human tongues.

I certainly couldn't make much of the coins Dio had loaned
me. I took them out and examined them as I went along. They
all bore Roman numerals—I, II, V, XX—as well as puzzling
symbols like those I had seen on the doors in the Temple. But
none was of a recent enough mintage for me to make out details.
They all had ornamental curlicues on the edges, like our own
milled edges, so I guessed that Malesco had its coin shavers
too.

Malesco—oh, it was a rose-red city, all right. But some of
the walls had graffiti scrawled on them—words my uncle
hadn't listed in his vocabulary, though it was easy to figure
some of them out—and the streets weren't especially clean.

The city wasn't crowded, though. I didn't see any throngs
except once. A gang of people had got a man in gray coveralls
backed up against a building and were yelling at him. That
should have been my cue to spring to the victim's aid. He
could have been the prince of some neighboring country and
have been suitably grateful for my help.

But when an air-car swooped down and grounded gently
not far away, I hastily joined the crowd and yelled with them.
Men in uniform were getting out of the air-car, which was built
like a chariot, ornately decorated with scrolls and gilded curlicues.

The police dragged their victim away and, from what I
overheard, I decided the "prince" was a pickpocket who'd been
caught. So that was all right.

Falvi seemed to know where he was going. I never lost
sight of that hurrying figure with its flapping headdress. I had
a sense of immediate urgency for I remembered Dio very clearly.
He knew who I was. Or did he?

I didn't form a complete picture of the city as I trailed Falvi.
All I got were flashes, like the way a moving light slipped
along one of the overhead causeways, the luminous jewelry
some of the people wore, men and women both, and a flutter
of confetti that blew past me down the street. One coil wrapped
itself around my neck and as I pulled it free I saw lettering on
the paper. COME TO THE BATH OF THE DIVINE WATER, it said
in Malescan.

Well, that was what I meant to do if I could find the place.

A few aspects of the city stood out even above my preoccupation: one was the curious attitude of the populace toward the priests. The first time a man stepped off the sidewalk into the gutter and bowed to me, with a touch of masochistic abasement in the gesture, I almost stopped in my tracks.

My first thought was that he'd seen through my disguise and was staging some elaborate joke before he hit me over the head and dragged me back to my doom. Then I saw he meant it. But what was expected of me in response I had no idea.

I looked ahead at Falvi. All I could see was the top of his head bobbing along in a straight hasty course. If this were happening to me, maybe it was happening to him too and he seemed to pay no attention. I took a chance and stalked haughtily by the bowing man. I didn't dare look back to see what his reaction was. Nothing happened, so that was all right too. And luckily not every person I passed felt quite that pious.

But they did get out of my way with respectful glances. I began after a while to check on the expression they turned on me, trying to figure out what was going on. Most of them looked just respectful—stupid and awed. Some glowered but stood aside. Some gave me looks of sheer hatred.

Now and then somebody would all but throw himself at my feet in the same abject deference the first man had shown. Maybe it was consciousness of sin. Maybe these men had some guilt on their minds they thought I could read in their faces and were showing penitence by groveling in the gutter when I passed.

I didn't like it, and I didn't like the idea of a priesthood that would encourage such an attitude, but, after all, Malesco wasn't my responsibility. All I wanted was to get out of it, and take Lorna with me if I could find her.

I can't begin to tell you all the mystifying things I saw in that quick walk through the streets of Malesco. It wasn't like our cities. If it wasn't a place out of the Arabian Nights, neither was it the equivalent of New York and Chicago. There were shops, but their displays were mostly hidden and what I could see was arranged in ways that didn't make sense to me.

There were vehicles in the streets, but they didn't make much sense either beyond the fact that they moved, carried passengers and seemed to obey traffic laws of a sort. Once in a while I saw moving lights in the sky and remembered the aircraft I'd already encountered.

There were no newspapers. You'd be surprised how you can miss commonplace things like that. Until you do miss them you don't realize what a big part newspapers play in normal city life. There was no litter of torn printed pages in the gutter, no noisy newsboys yelling on corners, no stands of magazines and dailies, nobody with a folded paper under his arm.

But what I did see every few blocks, which as I later learned was the equivalent, was a long rack against buildings which held on slanting shelves rows of big looseleaf paper volumes about the size of the average tabloid. Each rack had several people reading with their elbows on the shelf, turning the pages.

You paid a penny and read your daily news right out in public. I wished for time to stop and see what was new in Malesco myself, but Falvi was moving fast ahead of me. There was no time to do more than steal a glance as I passed the stands, earning a look of resentment from the penny collector when I did so.

If I had known my rights as a priest I could simply have put one of the volumes under my arm and walked off and nobody would have dared to complain. But I didn't know that and I hadn't time then anyhow.

I went on after Falvi.

Strange things continued to happen all around me. I was getting used to the looks of awe, hatred or abject deference on the faces I passed. But I had a lot of other things to get used to, too. For instance, a voice suddenly and urgently whispered in my ear, "*Listen!*"

I halted where I was. I looked around over my shoulder, but there was no one near me. The only suspicious sight was a man in the priestly robe and headdress across the street, hurrying in the same direction that I was. But he was too far away to be the—

"Listen!" the whisper came again. "It's important! Your life may depend on it!"

For a second I dithered like a skeleton hung on wires. There just wasn't anyone near enough to me to whisper in my ear. And the whisper had a strange fading quality like a voice on the radio when you play with the dial.

"This is the secret," said the voice, brightening. "Drink

Elixir, the refreshing tonic that makes you live longer." Then it broke into song. "Elixir, Elixir, Mother Ceres' fixer," it caroled and changed to a conspiratorial whisper again. "Listen! Listen! It's important—"

I cursed quietly and took up the trail again. Falvi was just turning a corner. I walked faster, occasionally running into a gust of auditory advertising that seemed to blow invisibly past me like confetti streamers. My first glimpse of Malesco, with the glamorous rose-red city gleaming in the sunset, hadn't prepared me for the uses of publicity as practiced there.

I rounded the corner and there was Falvi, safely ahead. He hadn't once looked back. He was hurrying along the curving street, moving from dimness to brightness as light from shop windows irregularly shone on him.

I remembered what I'd seen when I'd looked around a moment ago. I'd seen a priest on the opposite side of the street. It meant nothing, of course, but I couldn't help glancing around again. And there, turning the corner, was Dio.

He was dodging a group of adolescents walking arm in arm across half the sidewalk and he didn't seem to see me looking back at him. He didn't seem to see the adolescents either except as objects to be avoided. I had a clear view of his face through the pedestrians, and I saw with unpleasant clarity the fierce anticipatory joy he was not even trying to conceal.

I spun back again, remembering Falvi, wondering how much of that anticipating triumph applied to Falvi and how much to me. The thin priest was just vanishing around a corner ahead and I hurried after him, feeling those concentric rings making a target of my back again. I knew Dio was behind me and I knew he meant me anything but good.

Yet what could I do about it? I couldn't lose him without losing Falvi and my only hope of reaching a potential friend. And yet I was leading Dio straight to Coriole. I couldn't get to Coriole at all unless I led Dio, too.

And from what I'd overheard I suspected Coriole's safety depended on secrecy. Coriole discovered might be Coriole liquidated for all I knew. What good would he be to me liquidated? There didn't seem any way out of the noose I was running my neck into.

So we all trudged on through the rose-red city in our little game of follow-the-leader. Meanwhile, I was busily turning over schemes for thwarting Dio, by-passing Falvi and joining forces with Coriole.

The smart thing would have been to warn Falvi about our mutual follower. No doubt he would have some resource at his fingertips for dealing with spies. I could catch up with him easily. I could tap him on the shoulder and say:

"Listen! It's important! Drink Elix—" No, that was something else entirely. I felt a little drunk. I was not made of the indestructible stuff of heroes. Already I was getting tired, my head ached and I was wondering where my next meal would come from. If I warned Falvi of our mutual follower, he could fix Dio easily enough. But first he'd fix me. So the two of us diligently led Dio directly toward Coriole.

After about three turns, Falvi hit a broad thoroughfare that led straight to a familiar sight. Now I could see a sign glowing in colored lights ahead of us that said BATH OF THE DIVINE WATERS, in crawling Malescan letters and I knew I couldn't miss the place. You could see the Divine Water for miles. It was that huge globe of fiery liquid movement I had first glimpsed from my apartment—the rose-red globe that had formed a background for Lorna's fall into another world.

Lorna, I thought, Lorna Maxwell. It had to be Lorna I had got myself into Malesco to find—not a beautiful princess dripping with jewels. Not a lovely heiress from an old titled family whose life hung on my dashing accomplishments with sword and pistol. No, I was here to find Lorna Maxwell. It confirmed still further my uneasy suspicion that I was not the hero of this drama.

We were halfway down the thoroughfare to the Baths when a minor miracle happened. A chord of music sounded from nowhere, almost inaudible at first and then swelling upon the air until every other sound of the city was temporarily drowned out. Everybody stopped dead still in the streets. Everybody looked up.

I looked up, too, in time to see an expanding circle of light dawn like a ghostly sun upon a cloud straight overhead. It was full dark by now and there was no moon. But the sky was full of stars, though I could see only the brightest of them because the city's illumination drowned out all the rest.

I was a little startled to see the Dipper, practically the only constellation I know. Things hadn't changed as much as I'd thought if the stars were still in their familiar places over Malesco.

Then a face began to take shape in the luminous sun that glowed upon the cloud. An enormous sigh breathed up from the city, almost inaudible, a breath from every man and woman of all these thousands around me in the streets. The face grew clearer. It took on familiar features.

Another few seconds and Lorna Maxwell was smiling down at me from the clouds, a vast luminous Lorna idealized like the poster I'd seen on the side of a building. She looked lovely. She looked tender and sweet. Her smile was exquisite. She just couldn't be Lorna Maxwell.

The smile faded slowly. This was no poster, it was a reflection on the cloud of the woman herself, whoever she was. The vast, shining blue eyes, each as large as a good-sized swimming pool, beamed softly down upon Malesco. The music fell silent and the lovely lips on the cloud parted. Lorna's voice spoke to the breathless city.

It was Lorna, all right. The voice, like the face, was idealized almost out of all recognition—but not quite. Just enough of the old Lorna's inflection and tonal qualities remained to make me sure I knew her. Down from the sky the gentle music of the voice floated softly.

"It is the hour for my withdrawal now," Lorna informed the city. "Now I go to my meditation and all of you, my faithful friends, go out to your evening's pastimes. Go with my blessing, Malescans. Remember your priests and their teachings.

"Drop your tithe without fail into the Temple box when you pay your entrance fees tonight. Be virtuous, be happy. Ensure your reincarnation into higher calling by your conduct tonight and every night. I will await you in Paradise, my friends. I will await you in the sacred pathways of New York."

I heard a tremendous breath of murmured response all around me as the image began to fade. I couldn't believe what the words were that every man and woman within hearing said as Lorna grew dimmer upon the cloud. And yet I couldn't mistake it. What everyone in the city was murmuring in hushed devout accents was an echo of Lorna's last words.

"New York! New York!" all Malesco whispered, and the light faded from overhead.

Chapter VII

FALVI hurried up the broad steps under the dome of the Baths. The colored lights that said BATH OF THE DIVINE WATERS cast changing reflections on the street and shimmered in the glass of the change-maker's booth beside the entrance. I saw Falvi drop a coin in the glass bowl on the side of the booth and the man at the door clicked a turnstile and let him in.

In a daze I followed him up the steps, fumbling for the "grain" Dio had lent me. I felt both bewildered and heartened by what I had seen in the sky. It still made no sense, but I felt much more important than I had fifteen minutes earlier.

It didn't add up, of course. One person fell through into Malesco from Earth and was given some sort of super-beauty treatment and enthroned as a goddess mouthing what I couldn't help regarding as rather chauvinistic gibberish from the clouds. Another person fell through—me—and was instantly set upon by priests and hounded like a criminal through the streets.

The New York angle of this very materialistic religion in Malesco I wouldn't let myself think about. It was too entirely impossible. Later, maybe someone would explain it to me. Until then I couldn't allow myself to speculate. I would pretend it never happened. The sacred pathways of New York!

The effect of that vision on the clouds had been enormous. When it faded the city had buzzed with awed murmurings, and even now the normal noises of crowds and traffic were not yet back to their previous volume. I overheard enough on the streets to realize that Lorna's visitation was accepted as something like a miracle. Nobody understood or attempted to understand how such a thing could be achieved mechanically.

This confused me still more. A city of the technological level that Malesco seemed to enjoy ought not to be rendered speechless with awe at the projection of a television image or the broadcasting of a human voice.

Naturally I didn't know how the priests had done the job.

Maybe by drawing a pentagram and working black magic. But I knew how it *could* be done, so the only awe I felt was amazement at the change in Lorna.

Falvi vanished under the great arched entrance above me. He was certainly an inefficient conspirator. It seemed to me anybody who glanced at him would know without looking twice that here was a spy on the way to plot with a mastermind ringleader for the overthrow of the government.

The way he kept looking nervously over his shoulder was in itself a complete giveaway. He glanced again without seeing me—even that showed what a failure he was as a secret agent—and then disappeared into the building.

I wasn't any too sure of myself. My trouser cuffs and shoes showing under the priestly robes made me nervous. If they'd been lit up with neons I couldn't have felt any more conspicuous. I was afraid of losing Falvi, but I just didn't dare walk up to that booth and try to bluff my way in.

So I waited until a group of five or six men came along, just cheerful enough to be careless, and fell in behind them as they climbed the steps. One of the men threw several coins in the glass bowl beside the booth.

They started to file in through the turnstile and the man in the booth called something after them that I didn't hear very clearly. But the head man looked back, grinned sheepishly, then threw another coin into a box on the wall.

The Temple box, I thought—the priestly jackpot that Lorna had plugged in her commercial from the clouds. I wondered wildly how much was due bowl and box. Then I remembered that Falvi hadn't contributed to the box. The flapping of my headdress against my cheek reminded me why. I was a priest too. We didn't have to contribute to our own support.

I tossed a coin at random into the glass bowl and shoved through the turnstile after the party ahead. Nobody stopped me. Nobody paid me any attention. I couldn't help looking back as I passed the turnstile and, sure enough, Dio was just starting up the steps from the street.

When I got into the vast rotunda inside, Falvi was nowhere in sight. I had lost him.

It seemed unnecessarily ironic. I had managed to keep him in sight from the moment of my entrance into Malesco, only to lose him about five minutes short of Coriole. The big hall

was full of people, all of them in the brightly colored tunics
and short cloaks which the well-dressed man was wearing in
Malesco that night. If there were women here they must have
had a separate entrance. This crowd was exclusively male.

Because I had no alternative I let myself drift with them.
The newcomers seemed to be heading in a steady stream for
a row of arches on the far side of the room. Hoping Falvi had
gone that way too, I drifted with them. Under easier circumstances I'd have enjoyed the experience.

The big room was cool and pleasant. Music was floating
through the air from some Malescan version of Muzak; colored
lights made layers of rose and green and violet above us,
sinking on what looked like drifts of fog in the air overhead.

Row upon row of balconies climbed the high dome of the
rotunda, and laughter and music and the clink of dishes and
glasses drifted down from above. Now and then a slow shower
of the advertising confetti sprinkled down through the air or
streamers of coiling serpentine spiraled gently downward among
the colored mists.

I wondered why my uncle had never told me about the Baths
of the Divine Water. The outer shell of it I remembered from
his bedtime tales. Maybe he had never been here. Maybe the
Baths were new since his time, though the outer globe of
shining fire was not.

Again I wondered, with consuming curiosity, just what had
been his part in Malescan history, whether he'd really entered
the place. It was rather like walking through Wonderland and
looking for a handkerchief Alice had dropped seventy years
ago or the print of her foot on the path through the woods
where the Cheshire Cat sat waiting in a tree.

The Baths were enormous. I knew it was going to be hopeless to run across Falvi by accident or to find Coriole without
being actually led up to him and introduced. All I could do
was stroll with the crowd and try to ignore the occasional
curious glance cast my way.

A streamer of purple paper wound round my face and commanded me to CALL FOR ALIETTE IN THE CRYSTAL GROTTO.
I wondered if Aliette were a girl, a drink, a song or something
completely Malescan and strange to me.

Beyond the arches was a long narrow hall which looked
glamorous for a moment and then on second glance turned into

a fairly commonplace locker room. The lockers were a wall of shining green stone checkered with white squares, and instead of benches there were rows of individual padded stools. As I stood hesitating, the crowd parted for a moment and there, halfway down the room, I saw a familiar flapped headdress and Falvi's anxious thin nose in profile.

It seemed too good to be true for a moment. Then common sense took over and I realized that if everyone who entered came first to the locker room it was no miracle that I had found Falvi.

I edged down the room toward him. He was sitting on a padded stool, one ankle crossed over his knee, working on the lacings of a calf-high boot, and he was talking earnestly to the man on the next stool. The man wore nothing but an orange towel knotted around his waist.

But he was clothed permanently in a head-to-foot garment of freckles that patterned every inch of his skin as if he had been tattooed with them. He had characteristic stiff reddish hair, cut in a sort of brush on top of his head, and the orange towel looked hideous on him.

The freckled man laughed, a thin giggle that struck a responsive chord in my mind. Coriole! But I couldn't get near enough to eavesdrop without some better disguise than a priest's robe and headdress. Falvi would know me.

What better disguise, I realized suddenly, than nothing at all? Clothes make the Malescan, but nakedness in a public bath ought to break down all barriers of fashion. Without my clothing I would be as good a Malescan as anybody so long as I kept my mouth shut.

I watched what the others were doing, found out and walked along till I located an empty locker. There was a three-inch square of white on the front of it, a blank square. I pushed my thumb against it and the locker slid open. When I took my thumb away, there was a black indentation of whorls and lines left on the white square.

I stripped in a hurry, having a little difficulty because I wanted to keep my robe on till last. If anyone noticed my garments weren't Malescan, I suppose my entirely fallacious air of self-assurance got me over that hump. Stripped, I stopped feeling conspicuous.

There was a large sheet of toweling hanging in the locker

and, following the precedent I saw around me, I draped myself in the thing before I pushed the locker door shut and heard it click briskly into palce. I realized that only my thumb, pressed into the indented print, would unlock it again. My towel was blue, a more fortunate color than Coriole had drawn.

When I looked again for Falvi I saw him just putting his headdress into the locker. There was a purple towel around his thin shoulders and his thin shanks were meager beneath its lower edge. He was alone.

In momentary panic I looked around the room, finally spotting an orange towel and a freckled back receding down the hall toward an archway at the end through which steam drifted fragrantly now and then. My job, I realized, was to get to Coriole now and introduce myself before Falvi could intervene.

If he recognized me, Falvi was perfectly capable of doing something disastrous to us both out of sheer nervous inefficiency. For all I knew he had some deadly weapon hidden in his locker or carried in a fold of the purple towel. Why he was so anxious to kill me I wasn't quite sure, but the fact that he was seemed evident. It was not mine just then to question why.

I was about to follow Coriole and trust to luck when from the corner of my eye I caught a flash of striped and flapping headdress near the entrance by which I had come. Dio stood there, boldly surveying the hall. I turned my back hastily, thanking heaven for my protective coloration in this hall of nakedness and colored towels.

Dio would not, I thought, know me unless I were careless. But I was fairly sure he would know Falvi. And then a flash of brilliant wisdom shot through my head and I conceived the perfect scheme for getting rid of both Dio and Falvi.

Barefooted, I pattered down the warm tiled floor after Falvi, who was now making for the far archway. I caught up with him about where I'd intended, beyond that misty threshold. The room beyond might have been any size, for it was filled with a dry tingling kind of steam or smoke, hot and perhaps electrically charged. My hair stirred a little and a vibration ran along my skin.

Shapes moved dimly in that curtained dimness. Falvi had blurred to a skinny shadow and I walked faster, timing myself carefully. I had to say something to him, but I didn't want to give him time enough to recognize my face.

Just behind him, I hissed in his ear, "Listen! It's important! Your life may depend on it!"

He kept right on walking. As I'd hoped he was thoroughly conditioned to Malescan commercials.

I spotted a group of shadows near me and just before I drifted toward them I whispered, "Dio's following you, Falvi!"

He did a double-take. It wasn't what he'd been expecting to hear. Probably his mind assumed for a second or two that he was being ordered to drink Elixir. Then he snapped to a halt and turned round wildly.

But by then I was safely concealed among that shadowy group of Malescans. I could see Falvi, though not clearly. But he couldn't see me because he didn't know where to look. In that dim room one figure was exactly like another.

I saw the vague shape that was Falvi hesitate, take a few steps in one direction, pause again. Then the priest made an indistinct gesture with his arms and plunged away, back toward the locker room. I drifted in that direction, but I didn't leave the concealment of the dry steam. There was no sign of Dio, but Falvi was getting dressed again with furious haste.

I retreated into the mist. I started looking for Coriole. There are few red-haired, freckled men in any single social group. At least, I found only one in the series of interlocking steam rooms here—and that one, of course, was Coriole.

I located him after a rather nightmarish sequence in which I floated in ghostly fashion through what gradually became an Elysian Fields, peopled with apparitions. I was considering following Ulysses' example and opening a vein in my arm to attract the ghosts when I unexpectedly saw a pair of freckled legs. They were covered with red hair, floating in the fog, the soles of two feet staring up at me with an odd air of black expectancy.

Luckily the air was thicker than ever here. All I could see was Coriole's legs, but the rest of him was presumably reclining on a couch. I clutched the towel around me and dithered slightly for a bit. Now that I'd found the man, I didn't know what came next.

I was going on a very tenuous assumption after all. Maybe it would be better to feel him out a little before I gave myself away. I saw the dim outlines of an empty couch beside Coriole's and I sat down on it tentatively. It had a firmly yielding surface, slick and warm. I sat staring at Coriole's dim outlines, revolving opening lines in my mind and discarding them. There was a long pause. Then Coriole stirred.

"Falvi?" he asked. "Is that you?"

It was all the cue I needed. I tried to remember what little I heard of Falvi's intonation. I pitched my voice to the front of my mouth, spoke thinly and a little through my nose like Falvi and ventured one brief word.

"Yes."

Then I held my breath. Apparently it worked for Coriole rolled over to face me and said, "Lie down then. Relax and tell me what happened."

Willingly I lay down because it hid my face better. However, my scheme was not to do the talking but to get Coriole started. I said experimentally, "Well—"

Somebody blundered past us in the steam. Coriole laughed the already familiar thin chuckle and said loudly:

"Did you hear the story about Blandus? He was complimented on his stable and he said it was because his horses ate such fine pargani. Even the Hierarch didn't get anything better. The joke was of course, that it's exactly what *did* happen on Tuesdays!"

I forced a polite laugh. The blunderer stubbed his toe, swore and receded. Coriole, an orange-shrouded ghost in the steam, got up and nudged me.

"There's an empty clear-room at the end of the row," he said. "This is too public. Come on."

I made a great effort to put myself in Falvi's mental shoes and said in Falvi's voice, as we stumbled through the dimness:

"Coriole, what am I going to do?" I put some of Falvi's panic into the query.

"Do what Dom Corbi did," Coriole said with dreadful joviality. "Call it a *nolli secundo* and the second race won't be run today."

I was silent, wondering just how well I really understood Malescan.

"The first thing I want you to do," my guide said in a lower voice, "is to find that man from New York. The second thing is to stop playing with fire. You had no business fiddling with the Earth-Gates and you ought to know it by now. For a man as timid as you, Falvi, you do run the most terrible risks."

"I meant to kill him," I said, remembering Falvi's defense on the communicating waffle I had watched him use.

"I know you did. I'm inclined to have *you* killed if you do. Fortunately for me he did get away. The next thing's to find him."

"Why?" I asked.

"He needs me and I need him," Coriole said illuminatingly, taking me by the arm. He paused for a moment. Then he said, "Here's the passage. Look out!" He stumbled heavily and fell against me, gasping an apology as we both reeled.

"Sorry," I said mechanically as I regained my balance.

Coriole stood perfectly still in the mist. He did not speak and he did not move. I couldn't even hear him breathing. There was something terrifying about that sudden immobility. I didn't understand it for a long moment. Then it came to me. I heard the echo of my own apology still hanging in the air, and it was not in Malescan I had spoken.

I had spoken English.

Coriole laughed very softly. My mind went blank with dismay. Why had I done it? The answer was slow in coming, but when I realized what it was I felt my jaw drop and I gaped stupidly at the dim outlines of my companion. I'd had a good reason for speaking in English, after all. Coriole had spoken in English too. When he said "Look out!" he'd said exactly that, no "*Se-garde*," which is the Malescan equivalent.

Coriole was still laughing, still almost silently. Now he said, "Name of Burton, by any chance?" and this time he spoke Malescan again.

There wasn't any use in trying to keep up the game any longer. I said, "That's good. How did you know?"

"Falvi talked to Clia. And not all the priests idolize Hierarch."

"Do I know Clia?"

"You knew her as Lorna Maxwell."

"Oh," I said. "Did—who taught you English? Falvi?"

"No, my father taught me that. I don't know much of it—he went away when I was only ten. Here, come on in where we can look at each other."

He groped forward, guiding me by the arm.

"My Falvi wasn't so good, eh?" I inquired, rather hurt, as I followed him.

"On the contrary, my friend. You took me in until I touched
your arm." He slapped me gently on the shoulder. "If you'd
ever taken Falvi by the arm you'd know the difference. Falvi
worries too much. Your arm would make two of his. I didn't
know you weren't a spy from the Hierarch, of course, but I
had a strong conviction and it's proved itself. Here we are.
Come along."

The room was small. Coriole shut the door behind us and
locked it while I glanced at the furnishings of the place. There
was no fog here though the air tingled as it had done outside.
There were two low couches with the same slick warmish
padding on them.

There was a table between them. Above it on the wall was
a large blank screen with dials set in a row across the bottom,
each stamped in gilt with Roman numerals. I think I realized
then for the first time that I hadn't seen Arabic numbers anywhere in Malesco, only the angular and, to me, confusing
Roman numerals.

Then I turned around and saw Coriole's face. For a second
or so the bottom dropped out of my stomach and I could only
stare. After a while I heard myself murmuring tentatively,
"Uncle Jim? Uncle Jim?"

Coriole grinned blankly at me. He didn't understand. And
of course he wasn't really Uncle Jim. But the likeness was so
strong it couldn't be coincidence Most red-headed men with
freckles look alike—it's a familiar mold of countenance that
seldom varies much. But this was a closer likeness than you
could explain that way.

Coriole had the same long-jawed, raw-boned face, the same
heavy freckling, the same pale blue eyes, the same bristle of
red hair growing to the same line on the forehead. He was
younger than I by a few years, I thought. I counted back rapidly
and the idea that struck me then has probably been obvious
for some time now in this narrative. But at the moment it
rocked me back on my heels.

"What was your father's name?" I demanded.

"Jimmerton," he said promptly. "He came from Paradise."

I sat down heavily on the nearer couch. "His name," I said,
"was Jim Burton, and he came from New York."

"I *said* he came from Paradise," Coriole nodded agreeably.

"Jim Burton? *Burton?* But you—"

"That's right," I said numbly. "He was my uncle."

Coriole sat down heavily too and we stared at each other in silence. After a while he shook his head dubiously. He had more reason than I for doubts. After all, I had the likeness to go on and Uncle Jim's tales. Coriole had nothing but my word. I offered what facts I could.

"Jim Burton looked just like you. He disappeared about thirty years ago and was gone for ten years. When he came back he lived with us for a while, quite a few years, in fact. He taught me Malescan, when I was a kid. How else could I be speaking it?

"He never had much to say about where he'd been, but he was ill for a long time and I think he'd had a lot of trouble during the time he'd been away. He died three years ago. He left me his apartment. That was how—"

"Of course!" Coriole said suddenly. "Jimmerton came through the Earth-Gates from his own library in New York. I remember that much. It was how you came too and Clia. What a fool I am! I never connected her with Jimmerton at all. She didn't know the name and I supposed the entry between the worlds— the nexus—had shifted since my father's day. But it didn't! And you—we're cousins, aren't we?"

"I guess so," I agreed, looking at him in a dazed way. Malesco was real, of course. I couldn't doubt that any more. But somehow this finding of relatives in the place brought it a lot closer than I'd been able to realize before. It was like finding cousins in Graustark or through the looking glass. Coriole was staring at me with the same dazed wonder.

"Think of that!" he murmured, scanning my face. "*Think* of it! A cousin from Paradise!"

"Look," I said firmly, "let's get this straight right now. What makes you people think New York is Paradise? Believe me, I know better!"

Coriole grinned crookedly. He glanced at the locked door.

"Yes, I know better too. But if anybody else hears you saying so you'll find your head off your shoulders before you finish speaking. The Hierarch doesn't encourage heresy, you know."

I leaned back on the couch, settled the blue towel comfortably around me, and crossed my legs. "I don't know anything," I said. "You've got a long session of explaining before you. But first—I'm hungry. Have I got enough money here to buy myself a meal?"

I held out the handful of coins Dio had given me. Coriole smiled and punched a button in the wall without rising.

"Refreshments go with the admission fee," he said. "I want to know a few things, too, such as where you got that grain and how you found your way here to start with. I ought to warn you—" He gave me a pale blue stare, quite coldly.

"I'm not taking you entirely at your word. I think you're telling me the truth, but if you are you can't prove it. You fooled me back there in the steam-hall into saying enough to hang me if you're a spy, so I've got to go on the assumption you aren't. We'll pretend we believe each other, shall we?"

"Play it from there," I said. "Maybe something will come out that will convince you. I can't blame you for suspecting the worst, I suppose. My speaking the language ought to be the best convincer I can offer."

"It is. I'll admit that had me puzzled for a moment. But—"

A tap at the door interrupted him. He gave me a wary glance.

"You answer it," he said.

"I can't work the lock."

He reached out to slip the handle of the door sidewise, then sank back. I opened the door. Fog drifted in. There was a man in pink shorts outside, pushing a three-tiered cart that jingled.

"Refreshments, sir," he said. "You rang?"

"Oh yes," I said and accepted the tray he handed me. Coriole silently shut and locked the door as I set down the tray.

There was a basket of rolls that looked very much like the bread I was accustomed to. There was a dish of boiled eggs differing from Earthly eggs only in the bluish pattern on the shells. There was a pot of cheese and a pot of something steaming that smelled like tea and a big bowl of some chopped-up stuff that smelled pungent.

There was a tray of apples, peaches, some bunches of bright red grapes and two other fruits I didn't recognize. It was not what I'd have ordered, but it looked good and I was hungry. We helped ourselves, munching away from opposite couches, glancing warily at each other from time to time, talking as we ate.

And I found out at last under what circumstances New York could be Paradise.

Chapter VIII

BEFORE the wall opened to pitch me through into another world, Malesco had in my mind been one with Graustark, Ruritania, Oz, Islandia, Gormenghast, Erewhon, the Utopias of Plato, Aristotle and Sir Thomas More, all the other imaginary worlds I had assumed existed only in human minds. Now—I wonder.

It may be that every one of them is as real as Malesco or only a little less real, in the plane of what Coriole called the *mundi mutabili*. He also referred to the same theory under the name of *orbis inconstans* and *probabilitas-universitas-rerum*. But with Malescans it was no theory—it was fact.

I'd read enough about the alternative futures theory to understand him without much trouble, though he took it for granted I knew somewhat more than I did. I had to pull him up now and then and get a fuller explanation. But briefly, this is what happened at the point of split-off between Earth and Malesco, away back in the Claudian times of first-century Rome.

Up to the end of the reign of Caligula there was no Malesco. As a world it had never existed, never even been thought of. Our past and its were identical. But when Caligula died something definitive happened and there was a split between Malesco and Earth. Instead of Claudius a man named Rufus Agricola mounted the Roman throne. After that men with unfamiliar names ruled Rome until it fell to the barbarian invaders and its own inept policies.

In our world a religion which Caligula had persecuted spread until it controlled all of Europe. In Malesco a religion Caligula had encouraged spread instead like wildfire until it submerged every other faith. It was an extremely practical religion, originating in Egypt, and it had ruled all Malesco ever since until the present day.

Its name was Alchemy.

Alchemy had made a utopia of Malesco and there is nothing worse than a utopia, though very few people seem to realize it. Only in Butler's Erewhon and Huxley's Brave New World is it suggested that the standard utopia can be a version of hell itself.

For in most utopias it's taken as a matter of course that the stability of the community is the goal of mankind. Private happiness is unimportant, rigid caste systems are enforced and total paralysis of society is the prime condition without which the utopia wouldn't last half an hour.

Maybe Alchemy's coming out of Egypt had some connection with what happened to Malesco because Egypt for two thousand years was the most rigid "utopia" in history. Like Egypt, Malesco reached a peak of growth early in its career. And like Egypt its priesthood got so firm a hold upon the government that though all growth ceased long before, the society continued in a sort of deathless rigor mortis far beyond the normal life-span of a civilization.

Malesco for the past five hundred years had stood dead still, a society frozen into stasis and operated solely for the benefit of the priesthood and that of whatever conqueror briefly seized control. The priests let the tides of rebellion wash over the country, carry a conqueror to a throne and maintain him there until somebody else pushed him off—but it was the priests who manipulated all the wires and collected all the benefits.

There was conflict between church and state, of course. But in Malesco the powers of science were with the church, for Alchemy was based on practical science. In Malesco, Galileo would have been a priest, not a heretic. Gunpowder once conquered vast countries. In Malesco, only priests of Alchemy could possibly have discovered the uses of gunpowder; the only textbooks on chemistry were in the temples.

As in Egypt, for a long, long time there was no promise of relief even in the hereafter for the hoi polloi. Only the priests and the kings could expect to survive and enjoy the benefits of heaven.

About three hundred years ago, while in our world America was being colonized and Shakespeare was getting drunk at the Mermaid Tavern and Eastern Europe was falling piece by piece into the hands of the Turks, Malesco had a worldwide revolution. The priests for the first time found themselves face to face with a real problem.

Malesco is a smaller world than ours. A lot of it is ocean and a lot more unexplored wilderness. But on every inhabited continent there were tremendous waves of terrorism as the common man got mad enough to let himself go. They weren't very wise or intelligent men because they'd never been allowed to be.

They had no more knowledge of self-control than so many angry children because they'd never been trusted with self-control. When they ran wild they instituted a reign of terror all over Malesco, taking out their anger and frustration on each other when no priests were handy.

It was just what you'd expect—look at the French Revolution—and it made a very ugly blot in Malescan history. The blame was all the priests' and they easily managed to shift it right back on the revolutionists.

And the priests, as usual, found a clever way to pacify the people and still get their own way. The same thing happened in Egypt. A profound social revolution was neatly transferred to the plane of religion and solved there without making a ripple in the course of real human living. If it hadn't actually happened in Egypt, you'd find it hard to believe it could happen anywhere outside the pages of romance.

The priests simply promised the people that if they would be good and go home they could look forward to seeing Paradise, too, some day after they were dead. It worked. The Egyptians accepted the Osiris cult without a murmur and went on building pyramids. The Malescans went right on under the heavy yoke of the Alchemic priesthood and accepted the promise of New York as their future Paradise.

At that point in the story I choked over my supper and Coriole had to pound me on the back. He also showed symptoms of telling me another joke which my contretemps reminded him of, but I shut him off quickly.

"Go on," I urged. "I want to hear more about Paradise."

Coriole went back to the egg he'd been eating. The blue patterns on the shell gave it a festive Easter-egg look and apparently the shell was edible too. He was crunching it between his teeth in a way that gave me gooseflesh.

"You're sure," he inquired, crunching, "that nobody in your

world knows about Malesco? Because from the very first we've known about Earth. The split wasn't very sharp at first. The priests, the clairvoyants and oracles and people like that made contact very easily.

"We figured out about what happened long ago. From then on the priests kept telling us that Earth had taken the right path and we'd taken the wrong one and were going to be punished for our sins."

He dipped the egg in sugar and tossed what remained of it in his mouth with a flourish.

"The letter A," he said, "is the symbol of the *mundi mutabili*, the variable worlds. You've noticed it in the city, I expect. The priests make an A with their fingers and thumbs when they talk about New York. The apex of the letter represents the point where Malesco and Earth divided.

"The two shanks are the separate, diverging paths as the worlds draw apart. The crossbar, of course, represents the bridge by which the virtuous go to their reward in Paradise. It's also the bridge by which you and Clia and Jimmerton came to Malesco."

He grinned at me suddenly. "Would you like to see Paradise?" he asked.

"I would."

Coriole got up, shaking crumbs from his orange towel and fiddled with one of the gilt-numbered dials under the screen.

A large glowing A dawned slowly on the wall. Then it faded, music swelled impressively in the little room and a priest's voice began to chant some solemn words I couldn't understand very well. I imagine it was archaic Malescan, but I caught the name of New York repeated several times.

Then the clouds which had been rolling luminously over the screen cleared and a shining city took place. I leaned forward. We were looking down at an angle from several thousand feet up and, sure enough, we were looking at New York.

I could see the Battery and the fringe of wharves lying out in the rivers all around the lower edges of the city. I could see Central Park making a flat rectangle of green in the distance and the tall midtown buildings stuck up like monoliths above the patterned streets.

I could even see the angle Broadway makes out of the welter of the Village, and down at the tip of the island a magnificent cluster of dazzling white skyscrapers shot out continuous streamers of gold light.

It seemed a little odd that the Eiffel Tower should be standing in the vicinity of Chatham Square and something like the Pyramid of Cheops cast a huge triangular shadow across the approaches to the Brooklyn Bridge. But otherwise the city was unmistakable.

"I don't seem to remember," I told my cousin dubiously, "that the City Hall has a halo like that. And the Empire State isn't really gold-plated, you know. And—"

"I believe you," Coriole said. "This isn't a real reflection of New York. It's something the priests worked up for public release."

"But how did the Eiffel Tower get there?" I asked. "That's in Paris."

"Don't quibble. It's sacrilege to question the Alchemic version of Paradise."

"As a matter of fact," I said, eying the streets of Paradise with fascinated attention, "I've been wondering why they picked New York at all. It's such a young city, historically speaking. Why, three hundred years ago when you had your uprising it wasn't even called New York."

"Oh, Paradise used to be London," Coriole explained. "Then there was a shake-up in the priesthood and after that all the best people went to New York when they died. Only the priests are reincarnated in Paradise, you know. Did I tell you that?

"Reincarnation is the keystone of the religion. You've got to work your way up by virtuous living until you get reborn a priest. When a priest dies—*flash!*—he finds himself driving up Fifth Avenue in a golden chariot drawn by dragons. It's a fact!"

I looked at him narrowly, wondering if this were another of his terrible jokes.

"You'd like to see it?" he asked, leaning toward the screen.

"No, no, I don't think I could stand that," I told him hastily.

"All right," Coriole said. He paused and his grin faded. "It's funny when you look at it objectively like this," he went on, "but it's tragic when you consider how many generations have lived and died in what amounts to slavery, with no more reward than the prospect of an impossible after-life like that to keep them quiet. In one way maybe the Alchemists are right, though. Earth can't have gone any farther astray than we. Perhaps theirs was the better course after all."

"I doubt it," I said. "The Industrial Age was bad enough but the Atomic Age looks pretty grim too, from where I sit." It reminded me of something. "What about industrialism in Malesco?" I asked. "You've got a mechanistic civilization, but the people seem to take some perfectly obvious gimmicks awfully seriously. That projection of Lorna on the clouds, for instance—"

"You know how it was done?" Coriole leaned forward suddenly, his pale blue eyes shining. "Do you *know?*"

"I know one way. There may be others."

"Then it was no miracle?"

I snorted. Coriole's freckled face wreathed itself in smiles.

"We need you, cousin," he said. "The priesthood has controlled all the devices for what you call 'mechanistic society' ever since they began to appear. These things are officially known as miracles. Everything a man can't do with his own bare hands or tools he can make himself out of raw materials is classed as a miracle.

"If you punch a button and a hidden bell rings—that's a miracle. This screen that brings pictures out of the air is a miracle. Nobody but an Alchemist is allowed to question how they work. You see?"

I sat back and tried to picture life in New York operating by miraculous subway, miraculous taxis, miraculous electric power. I couldn't do it.

"And the people put up with that?" I asked incredulously. Coriole shrugged.

"People put up with a lot," he said. "Now and then they stage a revolution and thrones change hands, but it never shakes the hold the priests have. That revolt three hundred years ago came nearest to it, and you know what happened then.

"The people have been trained to be fools for too long to outwit the priesthood. About a generation ago, though, something did happen that had the Hierarch worried for a while." He paused and looked at me quizzically.

"What happened?"

"My father came to Malesco," Coriole said. "He must have been a great man, Jimmerton. I wish I'd known him better."

I looked at him in silence, thinking of the red-headed boy

who had been growing up in Malesco all the while I was growing up in Colorado, each of us learning the language and customs of Malesco and cherishing the memories we had of Jim Burton, who had vanished out of both our lives.

"Go on," I said. "What happened?"

"He came through from Earth during one of the Equinoctial Ceremonies. Stepped right through the Earth-Gates into the Temple while the Hierarch was chanting about New York. The people were all worked up to a great pitch of emotion and they were ready to accept Jimmerton as a god from another world.

"If the Hierarch had had any sense he'd have let them do it. But he began yelling about red-haired devils and the priests dragged Jimmerton off to jail."

Coriole looked wistful. "Those were the days," he said. "I wish I'd been alive then. I wish somebody'd been ready to grab the opportunity when it came. The people of Malesco were wild. They'd have risen against the Alchemists in one mass if they'd had any leadership at all. But they didn't.

"There were people among the jailors who weren't afraid of the consequences, though. My grandfather was one of them. So was my mother. They smuggled Jimmerton out and took him to one of the East Bay villages and people made pilgrimages to see him. Oh, those were great days!

"The priests couldn't keep the news quiet. And they couldn't catch Jimmerton, either. They tried hard. They tried for ten years. Jimmerton lived in the mountains and organized his followers for an all-out attack on the Alchemists. They say he never slept twice in the same place for months at a time.

"My mother traveled with him and helped with the organization and training. I was born in a fishing boat on the Gonwy within sight of the Alchemists' campfires at the height of a campaign against the revolutionaries."

He paused again, his face darkening with introspection in the way I'd seen Uncle Jim's face darken so many times when he sat silent, thinking about things I couldn't imagine. Now I knew. And this time I realized that all my wild fancies about the hero from Earth battling against fearful odds were not so wild and fanciful after all.

I'd just got at them from the wrong end. Things like that do happen, in just the way Coriole was recounting. You don't often find the dashing hero with the muscles of a giant, swing-

ing a six-foot sword against overwhelming odds while the
heroine quails lushly in the background, inspiring him to superhuman efforts. That much was phony.

But entirely unromantic-looking men like Jim Burton actually do find themselves in desperate situations sometimes and
engage in pure melodrama to escape. I was glad the heroine
had been a brave and intelligent woman who didn't waste her
time quailing in corners. I didn't think Uncle Jim had indulged
in any fake heroics, either.

Our own segment of current history is full of tales like his,
men who lead guerrilla warfare against intolerable situations
and strike no dramatic poses while they're doing it. I couldn't
imagine Uncle Jim striking poses.

"What happened then?" I asked again.

"Oh, Jimmerton was defeated, of course," Coriole said, and
sighed. "What did you suppose? They caught up with him
finally. I was just old enough to remember him afterward. He
and my mother were resting in a mountain village after a long
campaign. I was having a nap that afternoon under a tree by
a spring behind the house. I remember it very well, really."

He sighed again.

"There was a miracle," he said bitterly. "The whole village—well, no use going into all that. The real miracle was
that both Jimmerton and I did escape. But he never knew about
me. I was badly burned and buried under a sort of avalanche
the explosion started.

"An old shepherd dug me out and brought me back to life
three days after I was buried. When I could ask questions again
I learned Jimmerton had gone back to Paradise. What really
happened, do you know?"

I shook my head. "He never talked about it. He taught me
Malescan and told me a little about the city, how it looked,
what the people were like— not much. He was ill for a long
time, you know. Maybe he was injured in the—miracle."

"I suppose he was. My mother was killed and of course he
thought I was dead, too. He must have given up after that. If
he'd come back——" Coriole was silent a while.

Then he said heavily, "Well, maybe I'll finish the job he
started. Maybe you and I together can do it. What do you say,
Burton?"

I blinked at him stupidly. "How do you mean?"

He made an impatient gesture. His pale eyes were cold and eager.

"You know the things we need to know. You're from Paradise too, but you're not a puppet like Clia. You could teach us—"

"I'm an actor, Coriole," I said firmly. "That's all—just an actor. I don't know how to whip up an atom-smasher out of an old washtub and a jury-rigged cigarette lighter. There's nothing I could teach you."

"You can count, can't you?" he demanded in a sort of desperation. "You know the Arabic numerals through zero, don't you?"

I nodded mutely, staring at him.

"I don't," he said. "I can't. We aren't allowed to use Arabic numerals. It's a treasonable offense to learn them. All we have are Roman numerals and you can't work out anything but the simplest types of problems with that clumsy system. Do you have any idea what that means?"

I did, dimly. I nodded again, remembering what I'd read about the invention of zero and all the mathematical intricacies it had led to. With the old numerals multiplication and division themselves had been tremendous undertakings. With Arabic numerals the man in the street could learn arithmetical tricks only Roman scholars could perform—and that laboriously.

"I see what you mean," I said. "I don't know much about modern technology, but I do know how closely the development of physics, for instance, ties in with mathematics. I can see your problem. Those Alchemists are pretty smart boys."

"I've got a good organization now," Coriole said, still with the strange cold eagerness that rather repelled me. "Here's the setup. I won't go into details but I got in touch with a lot of Jimmerton's old lieutenants and we learned by his mistakes.

"We've got to strike at the heart of the Alchemists—at the Hierarch himself. We can't win by nagging at the outskirts, the way Jimmerton had to. I've got men in key positions everywhere. Like Falvi, you know. He's one of the top men in Alchemy."

I nodded dubiously. For my money Falvi was a broken reed so far as conspiracy went. But it wasn't for me to say so.

"The people are with us," Coriole went on, his cold violence making every word crackle. "Clia's coming was a setback. For a while we hoped we could use her, but the priests got there first. They're terribly cunning. They never miss a bet. And they'd learned their lesson when Jimmerton came through."

"What happened?" I asked yet again. "With Lorna—Clia?"

"I'll show you," Coriole said, reaching for another gilt dial below the screen.

Chapter IX

AGAIN the golden A began to glow slowly before us. The voice chanted again in the same archaic Malescan I couldn't follow. After a moment or two fog began to roll across the screen and music swelled majestically.

The music sank and an echoing hum and buzz of voices replaced it. We were looking down a long room, enormous, crowded with men and women, at a high dais at the far end. It was the voices of the people that hummed above the music.

"That's the Alchemic Temple," Coriole said.

It was a vast room and, curiously, you could see very little of it. The upper walls and all the ceiling were hidden by rolling fog, no doubt accepted by the congregation as a minor miracle though it was obvious that concealed pipes must be puffing it out at intervals. You could even see the disturbances in the clouds now and then where fresh fog came in.

It gave an air of tremendous mystery to the Temple. Through the shifting veils of it you could once in a while catch a glimpse of the walls and you could then see the great colored and gilded images on them. There were stylized animals, lions in red, green and yellow. There were black eagles, red eagles, sala-manders in gold, all the planets labeled in luminous characters.

I had a vague memory of the alchemic symbolisms and knew that these figures represented chemical terms. But to the people they obviously represented only mysterious secrets of the priesthood. The people were watching the dais.

On the wall at its back there was a vast round window looking out over the city. I saw the great globe of water with the fiery fountains playing around it, the roofs and streets beyond. It was the same view of Malesco I had first glimpsed through the shimmering air in my apartment. I watched with great interest.

"This is part of the usual Equinoctial Ceremony," Coriole said, reaching for another egg. "They give us a glimpse of Paradise and a lecture about how to get there. Only this time, something went wrong. Watch."

On the dais a great deal of ceremonial arm-waving was going on. Enormous coiled horns were being blown with solemn hootings, priests in brilliant robes did some kind of a trudging little dance before the window and the glass in it began to cloud. Then right down the middle the cloud quivered and opened like a cat's pupil dilating—and there was New York.

The horns blatted triumph. The people gave one enormous emotional sigh. The priests sang out all together on a single sustained note and then let it quaver down the scale to silence. We all looked at Paradise

This was the real thing. There was no Eiffel Tower or Great Pyramid in this New York. The camera appeared to be moving rapidly up Fifth Avenue from a considerable height. It was a foggy evening in Manhattan and the lights of the city shimmered and twinkled spectacularly.

On the far side of the Park the diamond-studded apartment house peaks floated on a sea of mist with black treetops silhouetted against its base. I felt impressed and strangely homesick. I could see what a conviction of Paradise a sight like that might give people who didn't know New York.

The vision floated swiftly away beneath us. Traffic made streaks of bright gold through the fog—sainted priests no doubt, driving fiery dragons along Fifth Avenue. I could see what they meant.

"This is only visual, you know," Coriole was explaining at my elbow, crunching blue eggshell between his teeth as he talked. "They thought it was perfectly safe. They didn't know about the flaw Jimmerton came through. Look now—they're going to strike it in a minute. There! You see?"

New York reeled dizzily sidewise in the temple screen. It was an immensely unsettling feeling. The whole congregation screamed and appeared to stagger. The horns gave a series of disorganized hoots.

Fifth Avenue soared straight up the sky and turned upside down and the priests in Paradise could be seen calmly driving their dragons across the firmament. Then the whole city blurred like rain on a window and there was an uncanny moment when I could hear Lorna's voice, very thin and small.

"Eddie, look at me! Eddie!"

Then far away I heard my own voice, growling at her. It was a shocking moment of *déjà vu*. Shadows whirled in the screen. It must have been a quick glimpse straight into my apartment and my own past, but it happened too fast to mean anything from this angle.

A scream welled out of the spinning shadows, a scream that began thin and distant and swelled like a siren wailing. It was the same scream I had heard diminishing into nothing from the other side as Lorna fell through the gap between worlds and vanished from Earth.

The shadows seethed. Then very clearly I saw Lorna's face, distorted with terror, spin quite slowly and vanish behind a screen of her swirling hair. There was a high vibrant note like music that made the eardrums ache. Lorna tumbled out of the chaos on the screen and sprawled on the dais face down, her hair fanning across the gilded floor.

"Look!" Coriole said quickly. "Watch—everything will flicker for a second. There—see that? It's where the priests cut out a bit from the records. You know why? Can you guess? Because every man and woman in the congregation breathed one word when they saw the figure come through. *Jimmerton!*" He sighed.

"I wish they'd tried to arrest her and get rid of her. Things would have been easy for us then. But the Hierarch was too smart for us. That's the Hierarch, in the gold robes—the fat man. Watch."

A broad, squat figure, built like Friar Tuck or Santa Claus without the beard, trundled importantly forward and bent above Lorna. Then he turned and raised both arms toward the people. The rising murmur of the congregation had a note of menace in it, I thought, but they quieted to hear what he would say.

"An angel has come down to us from Paradise," the Hierarch

announced importantly in a voice so amplified that I felt sure he had a mike somehow concealed in his golden bib.

Lorna lay quiet on the dais. I could see now that she must have struck her head against something when she fell. It wasn't like Lorna to stay quiet more than fifteen seconds at a time, especially when she had the chance of a lifetime to attract attention from a crowd.

"The shock of emerging in our troubled and sinful world," the Hierarch went on with unction, "has proved too great for the delicate nerves of this heavenly being. We must pray that she survives the grossness of our sphere—"

The picture flickered again. Coriole crunched eggshell and said, "A little more came out there. That was when the congregation began to roar. They remembered what happened to Jimmerton. Probably the Hierarch did have some such thing in mind, but he knuckled under fast enough when he heard the people protest. He didn't dare risk another uprising. Now watch."

Without an apparent break, the Hierarch steadied after his flicker.

"By the Alembic of the Great Alchemist," he said solemnly, "I swear to you that this angel will be given every care. Look, she begins to stir—" He stood back and Lorna was seen twitching slightly.

"We will prepare her for her sojourn in this humble sphere of ours and obey her orders in all things," he went on. "You will be summoned again when she is ready to receive you. And now, my faithful people, let us chant a song of thanksgiving for this visitation from Paradise."

Dubiously the people began to sing as the horns started up again.

"That's enough of that," Coriole said, dusting his fingers and flicking off the screen. "Now I'll show you something *really* interesting. Watch this."

He got up and knelt before the screen, feeling under the ledge that held the dials. His eyes went slightly crossed with concentration. I heard metal squeak faintly on metal.

Then Coriole said, "Ah!" and lifted the whole panel of dials neatly off. Wires strung from its inner face into the intricacies of the mechanisms within. He laid the panel down on the table, keeping the connections taut, and began to fiddle delicately with bare copper wires inside. I cringed a little.

"This has to be done carefully," Coriole announced with some importance. "Invisible fires can melt your bones if you touch the wrong plates here. But Falvi showed me how to do it and it isn't hard. Now I've got to twist these threads here to those over there—like this, and the thing's done. Excellent. Now you'll see something."

Without replacing the panel, he twitched a dial again, and this time the screen lit up abruptly without the golden A, the music and the chanting. There was something very businesslike about it now.

"This," Coriole told me, "is a secret known only to the priesthood. The usual talking screens show only a selected few pictures the priests prepare. But if you know the secret you can use the same screens to look almost anywhere you like and eavesdrop on anything that happens in the Temple.

"It's a miracle," he added wryly, glancing at me. "What would you like to see now?"

"That machine," I said promptly. "The thing that opens the gate between the worlds." I expected to return by it at some very early date if possible, though there seemed no point in discussing that just now. Still, it would be useful to know a little more about this vital link in my plans.

"How does the thing really work, anyhow?" I inquired.

Coriole gave me one of his pale, oblique glances.

"I don't even know how they make the lights go on at night," he said morosely.

"Well, let's have a look at the machine anyhow. Can you show it to me in operation? From behind the scenes, I mean."

"Yes, I think so. It's on record. For some reason they put a sequence on file not long ago. I ran across it just the other day, eavesdropping. A friend of yours is in it, incidentally."

He grinned at me and worked diligently at the dials.

Without fanfare a familiar room began to take shape on the screen. The lines for a moment were fuzzy and out of focus, then they steadied and I was looking at a strictly unrehearsed scene in a room I had left a very short while ago.

There was the wall of instruments that meant nothing to me. There was the curtained corner where I'd hidden from

Falvi. The round, blank face of the machine looked emptily into the screen. But this time it was partially obscured.

The little room was full of people. The illusion was so perfect that Coriole and I seemed to be peering secretly down out of some window in the wall which had escaped my notice when I had been in the room.

Gazing down on the blue-striped heads and robed shoulders of the men around the machine, I said, "Just how does this work? I mean—"

"It's a spy system. The upper priesthood uses it to check on the junior members and the attendants. You can look into almost any room in the Temple except the Hierarch's private chambers and the secret rooms. Now and then they make recordings of something they want to study—like this. Watch."

He leaned forward a little as a stir of the crowd around the machine heralded something new. Then the heads and shoulders moved aside, leaving a lane, and apparently from directly under us a veiled figure moved. Evidently the hidden lens of the camera was located just over the door.

Coriole leaned still further forward as if he were trying to see around corners in the reflection itself. I saw the men's faces turn to the newcomer, anticipation and excitement showing under every striped headdress.

The veiled woman lifted her arms and put the silvery gauze back from her face. It was a familiar gesture. I knew the way her arms moved and the way her head and neck rose from her shoulders . . . But now there was something different. For there was a studied grace in every line of this figure, a certain theatrical self-assurance that had never existed in the original I remembered so well.

"Clia," Coriole said in a flat voice. "I think you know her?"

I craned as he had. I wanted very much to see more of this foreshortened and half-averted face. But all I could glimpse was a flicker of much longer lashes than the original Lorna ever had, a flash of beautiful nose and much improved mouth as for an instant she glanced up at the machine.

It was Lorna, all right—but not the Lorna I knew. This was the Clia of the cloud picture, with eyes like blue swimming pools.

"What makes you think I know her?" I demanded.

"Clia got a thorough questioning as soon as the priests could give it to her," Coriole assured me, still trying to catch sight of the averted, foreshortened face. He did not take his eyes from the screen, but he went on.

"They had some trouble but eventually they managed to make her understand the language. Falvi told me how. Something about abstracting the words she seemed to grasp and working out a sort of basic Malescan for her. They wanted to know how she'd happened to fall through and whether anybody else was likely to come too. That's when we got a description of you. Wait—"

He held up one hand for silence. I leaned forward again. The reflected synthetic Lorna in her upward glance had finally realized what this machine was. I think the intoxication of all those admiring glances had probably slowed down even farther her naturally slow reactions. But once she grasped what this wall full of gadgets really was she shrank back a little and said distinctly,

"Oh, no! Let me out of here!"

"What did she say?" Coriole demanded with interest.

I told him. He nodded, still watching. He had not taken his eyes from the screen since the graceful figure veiled in silvery gauze appeared on it. Now there was a small turmoil around Lorna, many voices murmured reassurance and they coaxed her forward a little farther.

"What's going on here?" I demanded.

"Wait," was all Coriole would say. So I waited. We watched the rest of the little recorded scene play itself out. There wasn't much. Lorna was objecting violently to the machine and I caught a distinct echo in her new melodious voice of the old raucousness as her temper mounted.

The priests soothed her in vain. The picture ran on for a minute or two and then Lorna whirled with a wide outswing of her veils and stalked from the room, passing directly under our observation post so that we had one brief glimpse of her transfigured face.

She had turned into the Beautiful Princess, all right, I thought morosely. Every detail was there as nearly as I could tell from glimpses. The limpid eyes, the lovely features, the melodious voice only a little marred by the old harsh tinny quality when she was angry.

So, in spite of myself I was acquiring the attributes of the hero of romance. Here I was in search of the lovely heroine. I couldn't go back without her. And the organization of rebels was ready and waiting for me to join them so I could overthrow the government, release the princess and return home in triumph.

It made me feel very uneasy.

Coriole sighed as Lorna flounced off the screen and the picture faded.

"Exactly what was happening there?" I demanded. "Why were they trying to—"

"Suppose you answer a few questions for a change," my cousin interrupted. "What do you know about Clia? What are your relations with her? She seems to have come through the Earth-Gates from your living quarters. Is she your wife by any chance?"

"God forbid," I said.

He grinned a little, not much. "Good. I see what you mean. She's a fool, of course. Nobody could mistake that. But they've made the most of her. Falvi tells me she was a very ordinary-looking woman when she came through. They gave her some of their miraculous treatments and made a beauty of her and they did a fine job.

"You saw how those priests reacted? Falvi says they studied the problem very carefully and chose exactly the features and attitudes that would be most appealing to the average man. A sort of visual semantics, Falvi says. And they called her Clia because—" He paused and chuckled.

"This shows you how clever they were. They went through the records of recent deaths in the country and located a deceased woman who'd had a facial likeness to the new angel. Then they idealized and beautified her into the sort of being you'd expect from Paradise.

"And they spread the word that the deceased Clia had led a life of such extreme virtue she'd gone straight into Paradise, bypassing various incarnations and the final incarnation of priesthood on the way. They announced that Paradise had arranged for the transfigured Clia to come back and tell her story as an inspiration to the rest of humanity."

He was smiling but it seemed to me that his gaze still lingered on the blank screen as if it searched in retrospect for the beautiful face which the priesthood's "visual semantics" had assembled so deftly. Apparently their cleverness had paid off all too well.

I had an idea that a good many Malescans were about half in love with their angelic Clia or the idealization that had been handed to them under that name. I grinned to myself. They ought to know the real Lorna. That would cure anybody of romantic ideas about Clia.

Coriole twisted a dial idly and a pale uncertain image of a hospital ward flickered before us. He twisted again and the ward dissolved into a room seething with dim translucent children, whose voices came to us in a sort of shrill whispering yammer turned down almost to silence.

It occurred to me that if the priesthood maintained hospitals and kindergartens it might not be wholly without regard for the welfare of the people, selfish though the regard probably was.

I thought in a vague way that before I threw in with Coriole's side the least I could do was try to get some unbiased slant on the opposition, too. Naturally Coriole was painting his side white and the other side black. If I'd met the priesthood first no doubt I'd have heard an entirely different story with all the values reversed.

Then I remembered it *was* the priesthood I'd met first with lamentable results. Falvi's desire to wipe me out had been purely personal, of course, to cover his own illegal tampering with the machine. Dio, on the other hand, had seemed rather interesting.

"Do you know a priest named Dio?" I asked.

"I do." Coriole sounded grim. "Why?"

Then I told him my little story about the procession through the streets. He looked thoughtful at the end of it, but he shrugged.

"Well, I hope Falvi can handle him. Dio's unpredictable. We've tried to sound him out for joining us, but what he wants is a sure thing. He never takes chances unless he's sure they'll pay off. And he isn't quite sure about us.

"Still, I think he has an idea we might just possibly get somewhere, some day. Dio's for Dio first and the winning side next. I suppose he'll keep his mouth shut, but it was clever of you to sidetrack him like that. You're just the man we need, cousin. I'm glad you're going to join us."

"Am I? You seem to have it all worked out. Just what plans have you got for me, Coriole?"

"That depends on whether you join us willingly or not." He gave me a very chilly glance. Then I saw an unexpected grin flicker across his face and the Coriole I had first met showed through for an instant—Coriole in his civilian guise, so to speak.

"As the lamb said to the curran," he added, "'How's that for High?'"

"Very funny," I told him unsympathetically. "Suppose I don't join you?"

"Then I'll turn you over to Falvi," my cousin said, reverting to his military guise with no perceptible effort. "I'm supposing you do join. Then we'll take you to the mountains and give you a course in politics and strategy. You're much too valuable to lose, my dear cousin. For instance—"

Someone rapped sharply on the door.

Coriole and I looked at each other. Neither of us moved. The knocking came again, very loud in this small room. Coriole switched off the screen. Then he got up cautiously and crossed toward the door. On the way his bare foot came down on a broken eggshell and he swore in a whisper, hopped a time or two and limped the rest of the way.

"Who is it?" he demanded.

"It's me—Falvi," an excited whisper declared through the panels. "Let me in. They're after me!"

I could see Coriole's grimace. That was Falvi, all right. Let him in so he could lead the police right to the vital spot! Coriole, standing on one foot and brushing at the injured sole, spoke softly.

"What's the matter?"

"I think I've killed Dio!"

Coriole sighed and unlocked the door, opening it just a crack. I saw Falvi's thin nose thrust eagerly through.

"Let me in, Coriole!"

"Now wait a minute," Coriole said in a patient voice. "I'm busy here. What makes you think you've killed Dio? Did you shoot him?"

"No, I hit him over the head. I tell you they're after me! Let me—"

"What did you hit him with?"

"My sandal. Coriole, will you let me—"

"Then I doubt if he's dead, you fool. You aren't that powerful. Calm down a minute, will you? Who's after you?"

"Well, the guards, I think." Falvi's excitement was beginning to subside.

"You're as safe there as you'd be here," Coriole told him unsympathetically. "Wait—I'll be with you in a second."

He shut and locked the door and turned back to me. Then his eye fell on the dismantled screen and he limped forward and began to work rapidly with the copper wiring he had just readjusted.

"I've got to calm him down," he said. "I'll give you fifteen minutes by yourself to think things over. How about it?"

"Have I got anything to say?"

"No." My cousin gave me his ready grin. "Not a word. You sit tight and don't make any fuss. When I get back we'll start in planning. I'll lock you in so you won't be bothered."

He finished the rewiring, snapped the panel into place and straightened, wrapping himself afresh in the orange towel. "Don't try to get out," he warned. "Remember, Falvi's right outside."

"Have it your own way," I said, watching him unlock the door. A drift of the fragrant fog seeped in through the opening as he looked cautiously out. He spoke to me casually over his freckled shoulder.

"Clia's our real key," he said. "You sit here and think of some way you could talk her into joining our side. We'll have to work fast, you know. Angels from Paradise can get to be a drug on the market if they hang around too long. The Hierarch's planning to send her back to New York any day now." He slipped out into the swirling fog.

"See you later," he said and shut the door. I heard the lock click.

Chapter X

I HEARD my brain click, too. So Lorna was going back to New York any day now. Well, well, I thought, in a rather dazed fashion, staring at the blank screen. And I'd had my trouble for nothing, had I? Obviously, that was what the scene with Lorna at the machine had meant. I thought back, trying to remember exactly what had been said. Lorna was objecting and the priests were coaxing her. Why?

I could understand her aversion toward the machine, once she recognized it. That transition between worlds was a very disagreeable experience. For some reason it seemed necessary to persuade her to go willingly. Probably they were planning a big public ceremony when the angel returned to Paradise. It would spoil the show if she didn't seem to want to go back.

But she *was* going back. Well, then, what was I sitting here waiting for? All I had to do was get to the Hierarch and persuade him to send me with her, and everything would be fine again. Or was it that easy?

I scratched my ear and tried to think. There was something wrong here. If this were the familiar melodrama I was reliving, I'd have dived head first into the excitement my cousin was offering. It seemed to promise unlimited chances to swing swords, gallop on fiery steeds and lead lost causes at the top of my voice. But I felt strongly that I was never cut out to be a hero.

For one thing, the hero never pauses to consider what's in it for him before he plunges into combat to overthrow the government. And how did I know the majority of the Malescans wanted their government overthrown? I had only Coriole's word for it.

Assuming that everything he'd said was perfectly accurate, even then I knew I was lacking in the stuff of heroes. It's true that when he was telling me Uncle Jim's story he seemed to be speaking to a quality in my mind that responded. I knew then what real heroes are like—and I knew I wasn't one of them.

It takes conviction, for one thing. Maybe it takes a man who's a misfit in ordinary life and I wasn't a misfit. I was an up-and-coming young actor with a future in show business. I had everything in the world to go back to if I could take Lorna with me and clear myself.

I thought of that pickpocket on the street. The average hero would have bounded to his defense without waiting to get the facts straight. Before I meddled with Malesean affairs it seemed to me I had better find out exactly what I was doing.

I told myself flatly, "Eddie, let's not get romantic about this. Uncle Jim's case was entirely different. For one thing he was a born adventurer. For another he had a wife and son in Malesco to fight for. "No," I went on, "not me. It's not my battle."

Then I poured myself a cup of the cold stuff that had once been hot tea. It had dregs in it. I sat there looking at the patterns they made in the cup, stirring them around and trying to keep my own future from taking permanent shape just yet.

The door clicked. Coriole stuck his head in, wreathed in floating fog. He looked worried.

"I've got to go and check up on this Dio business," he said. "Maybe the fool did kill him. You'll be all right for half an hour." It wasn't a question, it was a statement.

"Think so?" I asked.

"Oh, yes. I've got a man watching this door. I really have as a matter of fact. I know it sounds like a bluff, but it isn't."

"Just what do you think I can do for you as long as you keep a rope around my neck, Coriole?" I demanded.

"Oh, I have lots of plans," he assured me cheerfully. "You're going to help me get rid of the Hierarch."

"Sure, sure," I said. "That ought to be easy."

"As a matter of fact," he repeated, "it won't be too hard the way I've got it figured. Our boys couldn't do it, but you're from Paradise. You could get to him. We've got his successor all picked out too—one of us. A lot of the priests are with us, you know. Once the Hierarch's out of the way we'd have a good chance if we worked fast. Oh, you'll help us all right."

"I think you're crazy," I said. "No."

"Of course you will. Cheer up, it won't be as hard as you

think. The people are with us. You just sit tight here and watch the pretty pictures. I'll be back for you in half an hour. Remember, there's a man with a gun outside, so do as you're told." The word he used for "gun" was a Malescan word naturally and it didn't mean revolver. But the intent was obvious.

"Good-by," I said, and turned my back to him. He chuckled and the door clicked. I sat there and stared at the blank screen.

After a while I got up and squatted in front of the panel, feeling around under it the way Coriole had done. There were smooth pegs underneath, fastening it to the wall. One of them was loose. I worked at it and in a minute it fell off into my hand.

I could get the tips of my fingers under the panel and I gave it a tentative pull. It came soundlessly away from the wall and I had to grab to keep it from falling. I laid it on the table as Coriole had done and squatted there, peering into the thing's innards, wondering just why I was doing this.

"Maybe there's something to be said for the priesthood," I thought. "I'd sort of like to hear their side before I take any permanent steps either way. There's never been an argument yet where all the right was on one side. It seems to me I've been brought up on the theory that when a people has an oppressive government it's the government they really want after all.

"By and large, they keep it because they want it." I thought that over and added, "The majority anyhow." Then I said to myself, "Cut out the hedging, Burton, and see what you can make of this gadget."

Actually, it wasn't so hard, even without the secret knowledge Falvi had imparted to his boss conspirator. But being familiar with the "miracle" of electricity, I handled the Malescan version of a television set with due caution.

I'm no expert, but I've had to pick up the rudiments of hook-ups at one-night stands backstage in the days when I was working with semi-amateur groups. And I know a little about video, Earth version. Malescan-style video might be different, but I soon realized it wasn't too different to understand.

Pretty soon I discovered that Coriole hadn't known what he was doing. Obviously he'd gone through his routine by rote, without knowing the reasons. Television occupies a channel 6,000 kilocycles wide against radio's 10 kilocycles and there's

just so much space on the normal band. Back in New York—
Paradise, that is—I knew we were getting around this by shifting video to a higher band in the spectrum, and doing it with
adapters.

This set had such an adapter. It was what Coriole had re-
wired, and I went through the same motions more cautiously,
automatically changing the frequencies on which the set would
receive. I went farther than Coriole. His method had missed
a whole band of upper frequencies.

It seemed almost too easy, but when I thought about it I
saw it wasn't, given the Malescan mentality. Malesco was a
religious society—Earth's is a mechanistic society. Malescans
were conditioned to skip a link in process because they didn't
know it was an important link. They believed in the priesthood
as we believe in machines.

I'd be the last man to contend that we don't miss a few
important links in our own thinking, of course. How many
people on Earth have a real sense of process? How many can
visualize and evaluate the process that goes into the making
of a loaf of bread, for example? Or know the use of the icon-
oscope with its mosaic light cells, the real miracle of video?

I switched the screen on again and as before that businesslike fast light-up occurred, with no rigmarole of Alchemic A's
or background music. I had no idea how to get what I wanted
on the thing or even a very clear notion of what it was I wanted.

But I twirled a dial experimentally at random and found
myself apparently sailing over a range of mountains studded
here and there with shimmers of lights that were probably
villages. It was night. I could see the stars in their familiar
patterns and, far off at the edge of the sky, a glow thet looked
like a city. The one I was in? Probably—maybe there was only
one city in this world. Was Malesco the city, the country, the
world? One or all? I never knew.

I turned the dial again and the picture snapped off like a
light and instantly flickered into a focus on a mountain village.
I seemed to be looking down the main street of the little town,
lighted by overhead incandescents that filtered through the trees
lining the street.

It looked like a pleasant small-town street back home except
that the parked cars were missing, and the adolescents strolling
two by two wore strange garments and clustered around a

corner building that was not a drugstore but—perhaps—a temple. I couldn't see clearly, but I thought I caught a glimpse through the shadows of the leaves that looked like red and yellow lions and shining salamanders painted on the walls.

I tried the dial again and was at some club meeting of middle-aged Malescan women who seemed to be reading poetry to each other. I visited a theatre where a version of *Medea* was being staged and it startled me very much until I realized that Euripides belonged to a period of the past which we and the Malescans held in common.

It wasn't until much later that Rufus Agricola edged out Claudius and the two worlds split apart. I wondered briefly what had really happened at that point of cleavage. In Caligula's time there were portents in the sky, weren't there? It must have released quite a lot of energy, that cosmic schism in space-time.

There seemed to be practically nowhere in Malesco—city, state or world—which this video screen couldn't picture with the right dialing. I sat there, feeling like a spider at the center of an endless web reaching out over a world—by coaxial cable or relay towers or some version of miracle we don't use our-selves—and spying on every dweller here.

The priests were missing no bets. The wonder was that they hadn't caught Coriole already—unless they hadn't cared to. Could that be it? Was he not as important as he thought, not as dangerous? Or were the Alchemists wise enough to permit latitude for the blowing off of steam?

For ten minutes or so I swooped and soared over Malesco, my vision riding the air-waves of an alien world, moving in vast curves above the heads of unsuspecting people whom I would never see or know. I tuned in briefly on a vision of New York, and had again that disorienting feeling of being in two places at once, the surge of homesickness as I sat in an alien room on an alien world and looked right down on the familiar streets of my own neighborhood.

It was when I was trying to find in my fumbling way what kind of screen the New York scene was projected on that I ran into my fatal error.

New York without warning went suddenly blank in a blind-ing dazzle of blue-white light. The brilliance centered in the lower right-hand quarter of the screen and seemed to spread

from a minor sun which had come into unexpected being about
two feet from my face.

The light was so strong I couldn't look at it, so curiously
compelling that I couldn't look away. I sat there paralyzed for
a moment, feeling jagged lightning flashes of pain zigzag
through my head, helpless to turn my eyes away.

Then the sun blinked out and I slapped both hands to my
eyes and squeezed my forehead to keep it from splitting in
two. Bright orange after-images swam like amoebas inside my
lids. When the pain subsided a little I began to be able to hear
again and I realized that somebody had been asking me the
same question over and over, with increasingly angry intona-
tions.

"What are you doing here?" a man was demanding. "Give
me the code word before I—"

I blinked tearfully at the screen. Through streaming eyes I
saw a somewhat unshaven face between the flaps of the priestly
headdress, small squinting eyes boring into mine and, chest-
high between us, gripped in a hairy fist, a glass cylinder about
the size of a pint milk bottle, glowing and fading rather angrily
like a large irritated firefly.

I started to say, "Don't shoot!" and something told me my
voice would quaver when I did it, for I was scared and I didn't
even feel called upon to hide it, in that first moment. However
impossible it may seem that a man at the other end of a video
hookup could shoot and kill me through the relay system, I'd
just had convincing proof that he could certainly do me grave
harm. Maybe that thing would kill, at that.

I wiped my eyes on a corner of the blue towel and put on
as haughty a look as I could manage with the tears still streaming from my stinging lids. I didn't know what I was going to
say but I knew I'd better say it fast. The priest had caught me
at something I had no business to meddle with, and he'd probably feel perfectly justified in using the fullest power of his
milk bottle to punish me unless I spoke first—and fast.

It was time for Allan Quartermain or possibly John Carter
to take over. I drew a deep breath and told myself I was a
hero. In a hero's loud decisive bullying voice I said sharply,
"Drop that, you fool!"

The priest's bristly jaw fell slightly. There is this to say
about wearing nothing but a towel: manners make the man

when his clothes are missing. If I'd been wearing a peasant's outfit or a clerk's apron I wouldn't have got away with this.

But for all the priest knew I might be a visiting High Priest from the other side of the world. Certainly the fact that he'd caught me monkeying with the top-secret video band, known only to the inner circles of the priesthood, would indicate that I might be important.

He didn't drop his pint bottle, but he lowered it a little and blinked at me in a puzzled way.

"Let's have that code word," he said, somewhat more politely. "You've got no business on this band."

A rapid summary of thoughts scampered through my head. I knew now why I had been dabbling at random in the private television relay of Malesco's rulers. In a half-aware sort of way I'd been hunting an excuse for the priesthood, so I could let myself confide in them. Naturally Coriole would paint them dead black to me. He wanted my help.

I could join Coriole, overthrow the Hierarch if we were lucky, risk my neck a hundred times over and finally win the right to take Lorna back to Earth and resume my job in peace. Or I could quietly walk back to the Temple I'd recently left, report to the Hierarch and the chances were he'd be only too glad to get rid of me by sending me back where I came from, along with Lorna.

Since he'd probably not read Burroughs or Haggard he wouldn't realize that all High Priests are supposed to be wicked from preference and spend all their time persecuting the hero and heroine. Primarily the Hierarch was simply a businessman, an executive administering a very complex organization. It would be a waste motion, really, to do anything to me but send me back, especially since—unless Coriole lied—he meant to send Lorna back anyhow.

And yet there was a nagging indecision in my mind, like a mouse chewing at the foundation of all this logical construction I'd reared. Was it a moral conditioning I'd got from reading too many melodramas? Or did I really owe Coriole and the people of Malesco something?

The priest with the pint bottle settled the whole question for me.

"There's a squad on the way to pick you up," he said briskly, evidently having reached a decision while I was arguing with myself. "Be there in ten minutes. Don't try to get away or I'll burn you to a crisp."

My first feeling was relief. That was that, then. The decision had been made for me. But a few seconds of further thought told me I couldn't take this quietly. I'd got the upper hand over the priest simply by bullying, but it was a precarious hold. I'd lose it if I allowed the police to drag me off to a precinct station and work me over trying to find out my secret.

I gave the screen a brisk tap that made the priest blur.

"Fool!" I said in my best bullying manner. "I'm from New York!" I gave him the A-sign with fingers and thumbs and grinned arrogantly, trying to show I didn't believe in the sanctity of Paradise.

"Switch me to the Hierarch," I commanded while he was still staggering from the impact of my wisdom and cynicism. It had a real effect, too. His jaw dropped again and he did three double-takes in a row. He was obviously not certain whether to blast me where I stood for sacrilege or kowtow to a visitant from Hierarchical circles if not from Paradise itself.

I got away with it. This priest wasn't sure enough of himself to switch me straight to the top, but he'd had enough trying to deal with me on his own and he put me through to five or six successively higher officials, each of whom wavered between bewilderment and rage at my attitude.

Finally, unlikely as it seems, an obsequious face took shape in the screen, murmured a few warning platitudes about the great audience I was about to be vouchsafed and, with a good deal of throat-clearing and harrumphing, the Hierarch himself looked me in the eye.

Seen this closely he looked less like Santa Claus and more like a juggernaut than I'd expected from my long-view glimpse. It shows how far astray you can go when you try to judge a new world by old-world analogies. I was still a little dazed by my success in putting across such a colossal bluff on such feeble evidence. The only explanation must be the very low level of Malescan self-confidence in sub-ecclesiastical circles. The common man, in other words, must be something of a worm. Back home I'd never have got away with it. Here nobody seriously doubted that I could back up my grandiose claims.

So, looking this fat man firmly in the eye, I told him the

simple truth. And I wasn't obsequious about it. I know that in conversation with the mighty you're supposed to let them speak first and introduce all the topics, but it didn't seem to me that this man would be made easier to deal with by polite methods.

"You're the Hierarch, are you?" I said in my loud bullying voice. "I hope nobody's listening—this is private." But I didn't wait for him to cover his connections. That was his lookout, not mine. I went right on.

"I'm from New York," I said. "The girl Clia came through as Lorna Maxwell. She came from my chambers in Manhattan. I've got something important to tell you about your organization, but I'll save it until I'm with you. I understand there's a squad on the way to pick me up here now. If you're wise you'll see they act as my escort, not my captors. That's all. What do you say?"

The Hierarch was a clever man. He didn't gape or blink like the others. Neither did he puff up with outrage. He just stood there, looking at me reflectively out of his small eyes rimmed with fat. Then he blew out his cheeks and spoke in a rich rather thick voice.

"Very interesting. Very interesting, indeed. I'll give the proper orders."

Then he sank his chin into three sub-chins and looked at me stolidly. I had no idea what he was thinking. He was a remarkable character, this man. Fat, yes, but not obese—obesity changes when it's dynamic, and he was dynamic in exactly the same degree a bulldozer is.

He had the same absolute confidence. I had the impression that, like a bulldozer, if he actually found himself facing an obstacle, he'd pause, back off and roll ponderously forward again and again, until the barrier was smashed and ground under.

He wasn't going to be easy to fool. I couldn't even tell if I'd impressed him. Those small thoughtful eyes might be looking right through mine into the chaotic indecision of my brain. I wondered if they were. I wondered so much that for an instant I felt my own confidence oozing away, which showed me how dangerous the Hierarch was. I took a deep breath, reminded myself of John Carter and Allan Quartermain again and began thinking rapidly.

"Look here," I said, keeping my voice at its loud confident

level, "I've got my reasons for wanting to reach you quietly. I want to walk out of here without being noticed. Tell your men to knock quietly and then step back and let me come out without attracting attention. It's foggy here. They can do it without starting a commotion. Have you got that?"

The Hierarch nodded silently, his eyes still regarding me without expression.

"Good. I'll go to the locker and dress and then walk back to the Temple. Your men can follow me, but I want them to keep their distance. I've got good reasons for all this, but I'd rather tell you privately what they are."

The Hierarch cleared his throat carefully.

"Very well," he said. "Your orders have gone out. They'll be obeyed."

But the way he looked at me was frightening. And for the first time since I'd fallen through into Malesco, I had the sudden conviction that this was after all no game. It wasn't a melodrama whose script I was running through with wisecracking asides whenever I came across a stereotyped characterization. The Hierarch fitted no classification I knew. It wasn't a game with him. He had more confidence than I did, and he frightened me.

It was as if I'd been playing soldiers with a bunch of four-year-olds, and suddenly looked up to find myself face to face with a guy in battle dress, scowling at me and setting up a bazooka. When the Hierarch came in, abruptly it wasn't a game any more. I couldn't fool the Hierarch long. Maybe I hadn't fooled him at all.

Chapter XI

BUT HE gave me all the rope I needed. My orders were carried out to the letter. I put the video screen back in its original condition, ate a few red grapes and much sooner than I expected I heard a quick soft knock on the door.

"Who's there?" I demanded quietly through the panels.

"At your orders, sir," a voice murmured.

"Open the door then," I said. "I'm locked in."

I thought, "If it's Coriole he won't do it." But I heard a scraping and clicking outside and then the door swung inward, letting in a few wreaths of pungent fog.

"Waiting your commands, sir," the voice said softly.

"All right. Listen." I put my face into the crack and whispered to the dim unfamiliar face that looked respectfully into mine. "I think somebody may be waiting in the fog to shoot me. I've been held prisoner here. Get your men together around the door to hide me when I come out.

"Once I'm in the fog nobody will recognize me. Keep close but act as if you weren't following me and make sure nobody else does. I don't want anybody hurt, you understand—just let me get out of here without any trouble. Got it?"

"Yes, sir," the face assured me.

And that's the way I got out of the Divine Baths.

Don't ask me why I did it that way. I didn't know myself. I could have had Coriole and his whole gang rounded up and carried away in chains. But all I wanted right then was to get out without causing any trouble.

I guess I was afraid that Coriole, if he saw me being openly arrested, might try to rescue me, and I had decided I didn't want to be rescued. I doubted if he could do it anyhow, but he might try. And dubious though I felt about my cousin, I didn't want him killed or captured just then. I wanted everything to stay nice and smooth and quiet until I could get my brain started again.

And everything did—for about twenty minutes.

It took me that long to find the locker room, dress, struggle into my priestly robes and headdress and start my casual stroll back the way I had come—toward the Temple.

I felt like a very different man as I crossed the enormous rotunda of the Baths toward the front entry. The air still swam with music, voices, confetti, advertising streamers and drifts of mist. The crowd had not altered except to increase a little.

Malesco seemed to be moving toward the peak of its evening entertainment and much of it seemed to be available right under this spectacular dome. I fought my way through snowfalls of streamers that wound enticingly around my neck as they insinuated that I'd enjoy Crescence or a Nip at the Nip Bar.

I knew where I was going this time. I strode like a hero across the rotunda and out under the arch of the front door. People were streaming both ways on the broad steps. I went down without looking back. I felt confident that I was being escorted though I hadn't spotted my faithful followers in any of several backward glances. Not even Coriole was to be seen anywhere, and Falvi and Dio—if Dio were still alive—were luckily missing, too.

I turned right at the foot of the steps and retraced my path toward the Temple, which I could see towering above the roofs, a vast white building with a frieze of the usual colored symbols around its height.

I had, naturally, no idea that halfway between here and there I was going to become a hero in sober fact. I was about to perform a deed which would go ringing down the corridors of Malescan history and alter the course of empire. But I didn't know it then, nor at the time I did it, nor for some time after.

I wish I could tell you it was a real deed of heroism. I wish—now—that I could have been immortalized doing something really dramatic—fighting off fifty men with great sweeps of my trusty sword, or beheading a dragon at the corner of the Highroad of the Hierarch and Goldsmith Lane, which is where the thing happened. But it wasn't anything glorious I did.

I simply lit my cigarette lighter.

Anybody could do it. Most people do daily without going down in the annals of a world-nation as a deliverer of the highest quality. I did it absentmindedly, quite without thinking, or I wouldn't have done it at all.

I was halfway to the Temple. The streets were crowded and nobody seemed to be paying me the slightest attention. I knew if I made any false moves things would start happening fast, but I didn't mean to make any. All I wanted was to get peaceably to the Hierarch and after that back to New York as quickly and simply as possible.

The one trouble in my mind was that I'd have to work up some tale for the Hierarch when I saw him, something worthy of the build-up I'd given over the video connection. What that would be I had no idea. I'd definitely decided not to give Coriole away if I could help it.

Of course if they started limbering up the thumbscrews I'd

probably talk. Coriole had shown no signs of tender feeling for me and I wasn't obligated to undergo any third degrees for him. He had meant to use me for what I was worth to him. Since I was, in the abstract, sympathetic toward his cause, I'd protect him if I could but not at the cost of my own skin.

I was racking my brain for a plausible lie to tell the Hierarch, and realizing with a cold sensation along my backbone how hard it would be to put any lies across, when a small baldheaded man came hurrying toward me through the crowd. His bare crown was lowered as he bored along busily, not looking up.

I stepped a little aside to let him pass. He wore, I noticed without interest, a blue cloak with a flat collar of polished metal made in links. It was so shiny I could see his lowered face reflected on his chest in a rather disorienting way as if he had two heads, one of them upside down and chin to chin.

The odd thing was that he glanced up suddenly as he neared me. He kept his head down but looked up from under his brows so that I unexpectedly met two pairs of his eyes, one in the normal place and one looking up horribly from the middle of his chest, upside down. I shuddered slightly and made way for him.

He jostled me a little with his shoulder, reached out to steady me and smacked something hard, smooth and flat squarely into my palm as he did so. It was pure stupidity that saved me from lifting it openly to stare at it in the light shining down from the building along the street.

I was so startled it didn't cross my mind for a moment that this was standard melodrama straight out of Fu Manchu. I suppose I didn't think of it because the little man was so completely lacking in romance, with his bald head and his four eyes. A veiled lady would have found me with all the proper responses on tap but not a stooped little baldhead with his eyes in the middle of his chest.

He hurried on past me and melted into the crowd before I had time for any mental processes to take place. I just kept stupidly on my way, clutching the flat thing and wondering what had happened. Luckily this was exactly what I'd have done if my mind had been clicking like a Gieger counter all along, so that was okay. The trouble started when I tried to look at the thing.

Automatically, when I realized what I'd got, I thrust the

hand that held it into my pocket through a convenient side
opening in the robe I wore. All I could think of was to hide
it until I could inspect the thing in private.

My fingers told me nothing. It was smooth, square, about
the size of a soda cracker. It could be anything. (It occurs to
me at this point that most of my similes in Malesco seemed
to turn around eatables and drinkables, probably an unconscious reference to the fact that I was undernourished all during
my stay.)

These streets were all too well-lighted. You think of lights
as a sign of civilized progress. But as a matter of fact I suppose
they're really a sign of incipient lawlessness kept firmly in
check. Just as broad straight avenues when first introduced into
city planning were chiefly useful to fire volleys of musketry
and cannon down, a thing you couldn't do in crooked streets.

Malescan lighting consisted of looped and scrolled tubing
that glowed like neon and ran along both sides of the buildings.
The only break was at crossings.

It was just the opposite to our systems, in which the streets
furnish the channels of illumination late at night and the buildings are dark. I suppose this was because Malescan vehicular
traffic was quite light. Malesco is a world of pedestrians—or
was then.

I had some vague plan of trying to get a glimpse of my
mysterious object while crossing the street. With this in mind
I palmed the thing and drew it out of my pocket, as I stepped
off the low curved curbing into the lanes of lazy traffic. People
were all around me, but nobody paid me much heed except to
get respectfully out of my way when they realized what robes
I wore.

I got the thing out of my pocket. I got it up within sight in
the dim reflection from the neons. I saw only that it was white
and had several rows of gilt script on it which I couldn't read
very well. Then some clumsy fool behind me pushed past and
knocked it out of my hand.

My mind scattered its thoughts broadcast. I hadn't an idea
in my head. I just dived after the thing as it went spinning
among the feet of the passers-by, interested only in getting it
back before anybody noticed I had it. Which hope in itself
shows the low state of my mentality just then.

The white square skittered across the pavement and vanished

under the curve of the curbing on the opposite side. I wasn't thinking at all. I just groped in my pocket out of pure habit and found my cigarette lighter in its usual place down at the bottom under everything else. I pulled it out. My thumb automatically touched the wheel and spun it. Flame leaped up in my fist and I stooped above the dark overhang of the curb.

There it was, my little white and gild enigma, twinkling in the light. I reached for it—and fumbled. My finger gave it a flick and away it sailed into some dark opening under the sidewalk. I heard a distant splash. The plastic soda cracker had vanished down a sewer grating, gone on its long voyage home in the mysterious underground of Malesco.

And that, again, was that.

You may as well know now that the thing had been a message from Coriole. That fancy gilt writing on white squares is the Malescan equivalent of a scratch pad and you can use it over and over indefinitely. But just then it seemed to me that the secret of the ages had been in my hand and I'd lost it.

I squatted beside the curb, heedless of the crowd, cursing quietly and holding in my fist the newly ignited flame which, they assure me, will never go out as long as written history survives in Malesco. The first person to notice it was a middle-aged man with a stupid face. He tapped me respectfully on the shoulder and I looked up blankly.

It was then, with the sudden motion, that I felt a draft around my ears and realized I had somehow lost my headdress in my wild scramble across the street. In the same moment I realized that my hair was cut in a very unecclesiastical fashion and that, as I squatted there, my priestly robe had come apart to reveal very exotic—for Malesco—trousers and shoes and Argyle socks. I saw the man take all this in.

"Excuse me," he said. "Are you a priest?"

"No," I told him. "Why?"

Note that I'd have said I was if there seemed any chance to get away with the masquerade. But my other-worldly garments were a bad giveaway and I didn't want to get into any arguments. I wondered briefly where my escort was and if they felt this was all part of my mysterious plan. I hoped so.

"Because," the middle-aged man said, "I thought I saw you just make a fire. With a *machine!* Is that little thing a *machine?* Will you show me how it works?"

Without considering the consequences I obliged him by blowing out the flame and igniting it again with a spin of the wheel that threw out brief sparks. The man leaned closer and sniffed excitedly at the reek of lighter fluid.

"Miracle-juice !" he said. "I knew it! I've smelled the same holy smell in the air around the pumping stations. How does it work? Would you explain to me how it works?"

"The flint strikes a spark—" I began cautiously and then paused. A second man was peering over the first man's shoulder and two more had paused on both sides, looking down with incongruous excitement at the lighter as I extinguished and kindled the flame anew to illustrate my simple lecture.

That was all it took.

Nobody could have imagined the hunger for process which must have been consuming these people, unsuspected for an unguessably long time. It was function and the process of function that entranced them.

In New York a man casually working a miracle on a street corner wouldn't attract any more of a crowd than I attracted at the corner of Hierarch Highway and Goldsmith Lane in Malesco by operating a simple mechanism in sight of the public. Miracles they were used to. Machines were the real miracle to them.

"Show me how it works!" a shrill voice demanded excitedly at my elbow. "The little wheel turns—why? What happens then? What makes it turn?"

"Let me see!" another voice broke in. "Look out, I want to—"

"The little wheel turns," somebody was explaining importantly back in the crowd. "Then it makes sparks. Then the miracle-juice catches fire and the man makes a real flame jump up right out of his hand!"

"It's a machine!" I heard voices declaring several heads away in the rapidly gathering crowd. "A *machine!* The man knows how to make it work! Look here, it's like this, the little wheel turns and—"

"Sacrilege!" somebody whispered. "Treason! Let me out of here!"

But the angry mutters which greeted this reaction must have made the prudent speaker shut up, for no more was heard from him though it did seem to me that I caught murmurs of fear now and then as an undertone to the general rising babble. Most of it had to do with the little wheel turning and the miracle-juice, and everyone seemed to be explaining to everyone else exactly how the machine worked.

I stood up and flipped the lighter shut. I dropped it into my pocket.

"All right, that's enough," I said in my loud bullying hero's voice. "Stand back there and let me by. That's enough, I said!"

Rather timidly the crowd parted. These people had been conditioned to obedience for countless generations and the voice of authority made their reflexes work. But the light of excitement on their faces was not so easily quenched. I looked nervously around, trying to spot my escort. They were still obeying orders and I saw no one I knew.

Chapter XII

THERE seemed nothing to do but go on. I ordered the submissive crowd out of my way again and strode forward, the robe swirling irritatingly away from my trousered legs. The colors in my Argyle socks seemed to fascinate every eye. I was as exotically garbed as if I wore velvet and brocade on a New York street.

The crowd seemed helpless before the double charm of my socks and my astounding knowledge of mechanics. I heard awed murmurs about the little wheel sparking as I pushed through the fringe of my admirers and went hastily on toward the Temple.

It should have ended there. Probably it would have, nine times out of ten. But this was the tenth time. I went about fifteen feet, then glanced uneasily back—and they were following me. Timidly, respectfully, but determined as so many pet dogs that have no intention whatever of going home, no matter how often you shout at them.

For a moment or two I did shout. I waved them back and told them sternly to leave me alone, to go back about their business. They looked at me, scared but stubborn. What had become of my escort I had no idea. Maybe they, too, were among this irresistibly fascinated throng. Maybe they were watching from the sidelines. Anyhow, they did nothing to help.

I kept at it until I began to feel too much like a man trying to send his dog home. I had difficulty keeping my face straight. There was nothing to do but turn away and ignore them, which I did. Like a pied piper in Argyle socks I stalked down the Malescan street, hearing the rising murmur behind me as more and more curious bystanders joined my following throng. The saga of the little wheel was on every tongue. The sparks it shot out acquired fresh fame with every step I took.

Then it got worse. I heard someone say distinctly, "He's leading us to the Temple. He's going to teach us all how to make fire jump out of the little wheel."

I whirled angrily. Whoever had spoken was silent now. The eyes of my followers met mine eagerly. And what could I do? Shouts hadn't moved them. Denials wouldn't either. This was sheer determined wishful thinking. It was already bigger than I was and growing every minute. The starvation of the human mind, denied process, was a thing I couldn't cope with.

Suddenly I felt sorry for them. And I was aware of a quick, increasing respect. For all they knew the squads of the Temple guard might swoop down at any moment and arrest them all. And yet they followed, hypnotized by the glimpse they'd had of a machine openly used in the street, where every eye could see and every mind understand how it worked.

So I went on. The rumors spread. They caught up with me and began to run ahead and they were fantastic. I was going to teach all Malesco how every miracle in the city was performed. I was going to overthrow the Hierarch and administer the Alchemic Mysteries myself.

No, I was hand in glove with the Hierarch and leading them all to their doom. This latter rumor had no effect whatever. Curiosity was stronger now than fear and anyhow this crowd was getting too big to punish. Each man took courage from the number of his neighbors.

By the time I reached the great square in front of the Temple the murmuring of my followers had swelled into a low insistent roar. Nobody was shouting. Nobody was really talking loudly.

But the combined voices had their own volume, and there was irresistible excitement in it.

I saw the astonished faces of priests looking out of the gate and peering over the painted walls. There were faces at every window on this side of the Temple, and in the houses we passed women and children peered out with timid exultation, and men came from every doorway to join our throng.

I crossed the big flood-lighted square slowly, in spite of myself feeing very important. Common sense told me that I had done nothing very superlative after all but the awed admiration of the crowd was insidious. It came to me irresistibly how much more I knew than they did, how deeply they admired me for my wisdom—also, perhaps, for my socks.

I expect I strutted a little. It isn't every man who inspires thousands of people to follow him, helpless to resist as the children who followed the pied piper, hypnotized by his ability to spin a small wheel and strike sparks with it. It isn't every man who—

Suddenly it came to me what I was doing. I stopped dead still for a second. I was a hero! I was indubitably leading a vast crowd of inspired followers, obedient to my every whim. I was advancing on the stronghold of the wicked High Priest who held the beautiful heroine captive in his toils.

I was on my way to rescue Lorna and force the Hierarch to send us back to Earth and it was my own skill and knowledge that had made this possible, my own prowess with a flint and steel. Good heavens, it had happened after all!

"Quartermain, move over!" I murmured to myself and crossed the rest of the square at a rapid stride. I felt imposingly tall. I thrust my elbows out to make my cloak billow in the wind. It was a perfect setup. All I lacked was the long, glittering sword.

True, the cigarette lighter had proved more potent as a weapon, but it lacked a certain something so far as dash went. Still, you can't have everything. What I did have was far more than I had ever expected, even in my wildest dreams.

I came to the flight of steps leading up to the entrance gate. As I set my foot on the lowest step, a man in a gray tunic and cloak emerged from the crowd just behind me. Another man in the same uniform appeared suddenly on my other side. Two more followed them and two after that. Five in all—one squad,

Malescan version. Why they deemed it wise at this particular
point to take off their cloaks of invisibility I didn't know.

"Where were you?" I demanded of the nearest, remembering
his face in the fog at my door, back there in the Divine Baths.
"What happened?"

"Nothing, sir. We followed our orders. We escorted you
here."

I looked at him in silence. No reasoning processes naturally.
He might well explain in effect, "I seen my duty and I done
it," and that was that. If he'd dispersed the crowd as any rational
policeman should have done when it first showed signs of
getting out of control . . .

But by now I was very glad he hadn't. He might have
explanations to make to the Hierarch, but I was well satisfied.
I knew what I was going to say to the Hierarch. Now I had
force behind my arguments. I was going back to Earth in style
with a send-off suitable to heroes.

Unfortunately for my self-esteem, I paused at the top of the
steps to look back and bid farewell to my faithful followers.

There they seethed in their thousands. It's hard to estimate
numbers at night in such volume. They filled most of the square
in front of the Temple.

They stood solidly together, not wavering, not melting away
in the back even though the priests were eyeing them sternly
from every window. I had one final moment of egocentric pride
in which I must have looked rather like Mussolini making
chests from his balcony.

Then I caught a familiar eye in the front ranks of the crowd.
Coriole was grinning up at me cheerfully. Beside him was the
bald head of the man who had slipped the message to me and
started this whole mass movement. And then my ego deflated
suddenly and I realized what was behind this demonstration.

It hadn't been wholly spontaneous, I felt perfectly sure. It
wasn't wholly for the inspiration of my wisdom that they'd
gathered to follow me. Coriole's hand showed plainly in this—
Coriole, who had certainly had training in the handling of
mobs.

It seemed to me now that, as I glanced around the upturned
faces, I could spot here and there the sober eyes of the men
and women who had helped fan the flame I lighted. Most of
the people were still drunk with the unwonted excitement of

the mob, but there were quiet faces too and I assigned them, rightly or wrongly, to Coriole's people.

So he had outwitted me. He'd used me as a tool to rouse the rabble, taking advantage of as small an incident as the cigarette-lighter flurry to call half the city, apparently, to a mustering before the Temple. And what happened now was up to him.

Or was it up to me?

He was searching my face with sober interest, the smile gone. I met his gaze without expression. How could I tell what I was going to do? I gave him a nod and turned away. The squad of my guards closed in around me. The gate opened. I could see priests milling excitedly inside as I stepped forward.

Coriole's voice stopped me. Thin and small in the unechoing vastness of the square it soared above the low rumble of the crowd. He was shouting a single word, but it was a rabble-rouser. It was the most dangerous word a man could shout in Malescan streets.

"Jimmerton!" Coriole yelled. *"Jimmerton!"*

The sound rolled back like an echo through the crowd. You could hear it rising and taking shape on every tongue, so that at first it was a soft, dangerous babble of mingling syllables, then a coherent mutter, finally a roar.

Jimmerton, Jimmerton, Jimmerton!"

The sound filled the square and echoed from the Temple walls. The crowd rocked with it. Someone had given them a voice at last, an articulate word to speak that would express all they needed to express in a single name. They put all they had into it.

"Jimmerton, Jimmerton!"

I saw Coriole nudge the bald man, who jumped out briskly and ran up the steps a little way, then turned and waved his arms at the swaying crowd. Everybody within hearing must have known exactly what that shouted name meant, every connotation of it. But the bald man put it into explicit words.

"Don't let it happen again, men!" he cried in a shrill voice to the throng. "Remember Jimmerton! If the Hierarch gets this man too we'll never see him again!" His voice was thin and it broke on the higher notes. It didn't carry, though I could see the cords stand out on his neck as he tried. But he didn't need any mechanical amplifier to project his words.

The front ranks of the crowd caught them up and tossed them back and out until every listener in the square must have heard what he said. With embellishments and additions, if I knew that crowd—though perhaps it was done mainly by Coriole's men, who had spread some of the wilder rumors about me.

"Don't let it happen again!" my would-be benefactor shouted squeakily but valiantly. "Don't let them do it! Remember Jimmerton! Remember—"

The responding roar drowned him out. They were frighteningly agreed on the single subject of my future. The Hierarch was not to have me.

It didn't suit me at all. I was touched and impressed by this display of courage in the very face of the Temple, though I had acquired enough sense in the past few minutes to realize it was no personal tribute they were paying me. I was a symbol, not a man. I was Function. I was Process. I was all the maturity and adulthood they had been denied for nearly two thousand years.

They thought I was, that is.

But it was more of a burden than I could carry for them. This rousing moment in the night was all very well, but what could it lead to? How could I help them? I couldn't. If Coriole thought he was rescuing me from my enemies he would have to think again.

I lifted both arms dramatically at the top of the steps. The crowd milled with excitement and silence fell across it section by section, the farthest growing quiet last of all. The baldheaded man turned to look up at me, his mouth a little open in anticipation. I cleared my throat. My voice usually carries well enough in a theatre, but it sounded thin and flat in the tremendous roofless space of the square.

"Let me go in," I shouted. "I must talk to the Hierarch. I must follow my own plans. Let me go—but wait."

Coriole, who had been watching me too, with the most painful attention, suddenly jumped to the lowest step and shouted as loudly as he could, "Yes, let him go—and wait! He knows his duty. He speaks for us all. But remember Jimmerton! Be sure he comes out again! Wait until he comes! All of you! Remember Jimmerton—and wait!"

"Wait!" the crowd roared, with a volume that made the steps tremble under us. *"Wait! Remember Jimmerton!"*

I raised my arms again. "Give me an hour," I said. "I'll come back to you in an hour. Will you wait?"

The responding thunder of their voices had the volume of a summer storm. They would wait. They remembered Jimmerton once more, in a tremendous reverberant shout, and settled down into noisy milling quiet to keep their promise.

Chapter XIII

THE priests were scared. I went in through the gate with my escort, receiving awed and angry stares from every eye, hearing the sibilance of the whispers that ran before and after me all the way. Everyone was bewildered. Nobody seemed to understand exactly what had happened.

There must have been rumors about my unorthodox tampering with the top-secret video band. I'd talked to too many people on my way to contact with the Hierarch to keep that experience quiet. And then the utterly unexpected, apparently spontaneous springing up of the crowd—it looked like military genius on my part.

I wondered what would happen to the crowd. I wondered even more poignantly what would happen to me. I had a powerful weapon now, but I could so easily fumble it. I didn't know how the Hierarch usually dealt with crowds. Judging by what I'd seen and heard it should be easy for him to work a miracle and wipe out the entire mob down there in the square. I wasn't sure why he hadn't.

We crossed the big hall swarming with gaping priests, all of them looking at me but obviously stretching an ear apiece toward the dull noises of the waiting crowd. We came to the shaft down which I had so nearly dashed myself to pieces.

We stepped into empty air—the shaft stretched down indefinitely to gloomy depths underground—and rose like cher-

ubs up the shaft. I may as well say now that I never did learn
how that levitation trick worked.

None of us spoke a word. We soared the full height of the
shaft and stepped neatly out in unison on a platform on the
top floor. There was a broad hall before us painted in gold
with salamanders. At the end of it was a purple curtain looped
back over double doors. A little mob of priests, their head-
flaps agitated, hung around these doors, talking in whispers
and rolling their eyes unhappily as they saw us come.

The double doors swung open. We marched in under the
sweep of curtain. And just as we passed the agitated little group
I caught a glimpse of a calm dissipated-looking face among
them regarding me with a rather smug grin. It was Dio.

I would have said there wasn't a square inch of my brain
just then that wasn't packed with worried thoughts, but a small
pinwheel of fresh alarm went off in an unused corner and began
shooting out sparks.

How much did he know about my interview with Coriole?
Did his presence here mean Falvi's arrest for attempted murder?
Obviously Dio wasn't dead, after all. But it occurred to me
that I might be if he shot off his mouth at the wrong time and
place.

He looked overwhelmingly complacent, like a man who has
used great forethought, picked the winning side and settled
comfortably back to watch the losers put up their vain but
gallant fight.

I didn't feel gallant. I was going to pick the winning side,
too. Coriole had been just a mite too clever, I thought, in
maneuvering me into a spot where I practically had to promise
the crowd to fight for them. But he'd forgotten one minor
matter—maybe I wouldn't hang around here to see the crowd
demonstrate.

I had every intention of grabbing Lorna and making the
plunge back through the wall-between-worlds as fast as was
humanly possible. After that—well, let the two factions fight
it out between them. It wasn't my battle.

Inside the double doors was a waiting room lined with
nervous priests. Never losing a beat we marched on through.
The nearer we got to the Hierarch the higher the tension mounted
in everyone concerned.

The priests downstairs had been nervous enough. Those in

the hall had been practically biting their nails. These in the anteroom almost twanged with tense nerves. I wasn't feeling any too relaxed myself. The Hierarch had frightened me even on a video screen.

My guards flung open an inner door and stood back, deserting me. I went through alone.

The Hierarch sat at a big desk made out of solid gold. It was hideous. You couldn't have crowded one more scrolled dragon or curly lion onto its carving if your life depended on it. Queen Victoria would have loved that desk.

The Hierarch stood up. His eyes met mine. And suddenly all confidence I had been able to retain so far vanished out of me between one breath and the next. I lost all desire to make smart-aleck cracks about Malesco. I was nothing but a second-string actor from a minor Broadway play, astray in the wrong world and deserted by the phenomenal luck that had brought me this far. The Hierarch was no joking matter.

He wasn't very tall. But he was broad and solid and his purple and gold robes didn't add a thing to the immense dignity and confidence of the man. He'd have looked the same in sackcloth. His little expressionless eyes regarded me with cold dispassion from under the fat lids.

There were three jittery priests in the room with us. One of them jumped to pull the Hierarch's chair back as he rose. He rolled forward with that bulldozer gait toward me. There was a chair in the way. He didn't even glance at it. One of the priests almost dislocated an arm snatching it out of the way in time and the Hierarch surged on.

I think he would have trampled it under rather than move around the obstacle. I was reminded again of Queen Victoria, and the legend that she never looked back at her chair before she sat down. She just sat, confident that someone would shove a chair under her in time. She had been born a queen, you see.

The Hierarch paused six feet away and breathed through his nose, loudly. His voice was thick and rich. He wasted few words on me.

"Talk," he said.

I looked him in the eye. I thought of Dio hovering outside the door, undoubtedly waiting the right moment to do or say whatever would be best for Dio. I thought of the crowd seething around the Temple wall, waiting for me, and a little confidence flowed back into my mind. Not much. About a teaspoonful, perhaps. But it was more than welcome there. "You," I said in my best hero's voice, "are going to send me back to New York with Clia. *Now.*"

We important people don't waste our words. I snapped my jaw shut and glared at him with a great show of confidence.

The Hierarch's little eyes never swerved from mine, but he made a soft snapping noise with one hand. A priest hurried up beside him and lifted a familiar weapon chest-high, facing me. It was another of those glowing milk bottles and as I looked a warning flash blazed out of it, obliterating the whole room for a second.

I didn't dare hesitate. Taking careful aim, I squinted my eyes nearly shut, stepped forward a pace and with one deft smack knocked the bottle out of the priest's hands. It bounced softly in the carpet, its glow dying.

"That's enough of that," I told the Hierarch in a firm voice. "I'm no hired thug. I came here unarmed. You needn't be afraid of me if you do as you're told. But if I don't walk out of here unharmed within an hour—well, have you looked out the window lately?"

The Hierarch pulled in his topmost chin over a descending series of subsidiaries and regarded me from under his brows. He had a thin mouth set between the flat slabs of his cheeks and now the mouth curved up slightly in a grim smile. "So that's what you meant," he said. "You said you'd explain when you saw me."

I blinked stupidly at him. Then I got it. I'd promised to explain in person—and in person I'd led a mob to his door. Oh, I'd been a smart operator, all right. The world lost a military genius when I took up show business.

"Right," I said crisply. "Now let's not waste any more time. Suppose you send for Clia and start things moving. I want the two of us back in New York by the time that hour's up."

"And your—followers?" the Hierarch inquired. I hesitated briefly. I could say I'd disperse them but would they disperse? They wanted me as a leader or at least a figurehead, not as a vanishing image on a screen that showed me heading back for Manhattan.

"I'll manage them," I told the Hierarch. "Send for Clia."

He regarded me with his usual lack of expression for a painful thirty seconds. Then he snapped his fat fingers again. The priest responsible for finger-snaps hesitated uncertainly, not sure what the boss meant.

"Clia!" the Hierarch said venomously over his golden shoulder. The priest cringed and scuttled for the nearest door.

I let out a long breath unobtrusively, hoping nobody would notice. It didn't seem possible that I was going to win. I had only been certain that when you deal with a human juggernaut like this one you've got to bully louder and faster than he does or you'll be trampled under. It appeared to be working, but I didn't dare relax for a second and I had one insoluble problem still before me.

Suppose everything went fine up to the very point of my exit through the screen. The Hierarch was no fool. He would not allow himself to be left holding a bag containing a crowd that numbered some thousands. How could he explain my absence when they began to tear down the Temple wall to get at me? Did he simply mean to blast them out of existence with a miracle? If so, why wait? Why not do it now and then dispose of me by the same easy method?

If he had really given in to me, then it had to mean he was afraid of the crowd. Coriole had told me about the priesthood's very real fear of the people when they were roused. Lorna wouldn't have been allowed to survive if the voice of the people hadn't demanded her, remembering Jimmerton. Now they demanded me and I thought the Hierarch didn't dare refuse them or attack them. He could wipe out this mob, certainly, but Malesco was a big place and short of depopulating the planet it would seem he couldn't control the people when they got their temper up.

It also occurred to me as a sort of paradox, that a miracle exercised now to disperse the crowd might have exactly the opposite effect. The survivors, in their present mood of intellectual curiosity, might become violently active to find out what made the miracle work. I pictured something like a large cannon pouring out miraculous death-rays, while indefatigably curious men and women swarmed all over it poking, prying, peering into the muzzle, turning any available wheels and chattering excitedly about miracle-juice and the result of sparks.

It was at this point I experienced my first real twinge about the people of Malesco. Up to now they had been people in the abstract, a generalization that meant nothing. If Coriole told the truth, they were a downtrodden populace who had allowed a series of tyrants to dominate them for a long, long time.

I was facing the latest of the tyrants now, and I began to realize what it would be like to live as one of the common herd under a Hierarch. Maybe they did need help, at that. But, I told myself firmly, not from me. It wasn't my problem. I was no Malescan.

I had troubles enough of my own. It was true, of course, that I'd inadvertently led them into something that might turn out dangerously for everybody concerned. That depended on how the Hierarch handled things.

Chapter XIV

I HAD used a simple machine and produced a miracle on the street corner. But if the Hierarch tried to produce a miracle to disperse the crowd, I thought he would find he had presented them with a mechanism instead. And they'd want to examine the thing and see how it worked.

I didn't *think* he was a fool. It was hard to tell what he was.

At this stage I began to be aware that there was a distant, disagreeable noise coming rapidly closer, audible through one closed door and maybe two. By the look of wincing anticipation on the Hierarch's face I knew he felt about the way I did. You could always hear Lorna Maxwell a good deal further than you could see her.

"What's the idea?" her remote voice was demanding. "Stop shoving, will you? Stand aside, you—let an angel pass. Who do you think you are, anyhow? Oh, stop shoving. I'm coming. I'm coming. Just let me alone."

All this was in mingled English and bad Malescan and was as much a part of Lorna as her own skin. She didn't mean most of it. She could contrive to get shoved in the politest company and the monologue of protest was simply her artless way of being sure people were looking at her when she went by.

The door behind me opened. The Hierarch sighed audibly and Lorna Maxwell swept in, heavily disguised as Clia, the transfigured Malescan.

While she kept her mouth shut, she was a dazzling spectacle. She wore a sort of cloth-of-silver robe, heavily encrusted with the images of lions, eagles and salamanders in jewels which I had no reason to think weren't real. They had improved her figure somewhat—it hadn't needed much. Seeing her clearly for the first time now, I realized how tremendously they had improved her face. She was unmistakably still Lorna but a glorified Lorna, not the commonplace cheaply-pretty little creature I had last seen on Earth. Her face was almost funny it was so beautiful. They'd made her into a collection of cliches.

Her eyes were luminously blue, slickly soulful. Her nose was a delicate masterpiece of modeling. Her mouth—if I had a copy of *Bartlett's Quotations* handy I could tell you all about her mouth—shut. Open, it still looked and sounded just like Lorna's.

She paused at the door, looking at me sharply. It took her a few seconds to identify me. It took a few more seconds for her to get her ideas about me sorted out. What was in this for Lorna Maxwell?

You could see her doing simple sums inside her head, very fast. Then she made up her mind. She flung both arms wide, the silver sleeves flailing. She tipped her lovely head back, gave a panting breath and cried out in a truly silvery lilt, "Eddie! Eddie, *darling!*" And with a rush of glittering robes and a sweep of shining perfumed hair she was all over me.

There was a confused moment after that. Lorna is heavier than she looks and she literally flung herself into my arms. It would have been more romantic if we'd rehearsed it better.

I tripped over the silver robe trying to get my balance and we almost sprawled at the Hierarch's feet. Lorna had a tight grip around my neck and was sobbing in my ear some lines from a play I dimly remembered, something about love and reunion and bitter heartbreak.

When I got her at arms' length so I could see her face I

noticed she was keeping an eye on the Hierarch as she went through her act, just to make sure all this was being appreciated. Lorna is, of course, one of those persons who never really enjoy an emotion that isn't fully public.

"All right, Clia," the Hierarch rumbled patiently, after a moment. "I take it you know this man. He tells me he's come to take you back to New York."

Lorna eyed me without turning her head. I realized she had her better profile turned toward the Hierarch and didn't want to spoil the pose, though for all the good it did her she needn't have bothered. The Hierarch at least was not entrapped by the fatal charms his priesthood had bestowed on the visitors from Paradise.

After a certain amount of thought had passed rapidly through her mind Lorna gave a sudden squeal and swung around to give me personally the benefit of a really dazzling three-quarter view. It was wasted on me too, but I could see what an effect she might have on those who didn't know her.

"Eddie, you *didn't!*" she cried. "Really, did you come all this way just to take me home? Oh, Eddie, I've missed you terribly. I—"

I gave her a shake.

"This is Eddie Burton, remember?" I said. "I'm not a Hollywood scout. I'm just good old Eddie. Do you really want to go back?" I spoke in English and the Hierarch scowled at us.

"I certainly do," Lorna assured me, smiling a glistening smile that revealed every tooth in her head. It was clear that they'd cured her of her phobia about the machine, at any rate.

"Tired of being an angel?" I inquired curiously.

"Bored to death. Oh, it's been fun, but they never let me out of the Temple. I want to go back and show myself off. Oh, Eddie, didn't they make me beautiful?"

"They certainly did. You ought to get a Hollywood contract out of this, once you're back. How does it feel to be beautiful?"

She smiled at me with sudden unexpected humility, a sudden look of clumsiness and uncertainty, like a girl dressed up in finery she knows isn't her own. Dimly Lorna knew this face was too good for her, and she felt self-conscious about it.

Unexpectedly, I was sorry for her, seeing the old Lorna under this lovely facade, uncertain, noisy, burning with ambition, terrified of failure and starving for success. Well, this time she ought to get it.

"We're on our way back right now," I told her rather grandly, and in Malescan for the Hierarch's benefit. I hoped it was the truth. It worried me that I seemed to be getting away so easily with my bluff, but I didn't dare relax for an instant.

It was ominous in a way that no questions had been asked about how I got through into Malesco, what I'd been doing in that room at the Baths, how it happened that I spoke Malescan intelligibly if not perfectly, above all how I'd managed to call up that crowd—and why.

The Hierarch stood there, looking at me, with Lorna striking attitudes in my arms. He puffed out his slablike cheeks a couple of times, sighed and said, "You think so, do you?"

There was the soft sound of finger-snapping and right then I stopped worrying about one thing: getting away with my bluff so easily.

I stopped worrying because there was a sudden downward blur past my eyes and a tight, silky noose closed violently around my chest and arms. I felt the slam against my spine of a fist tightening the knot at my back.

At the same moment something equally tight around my ankles almost threw me off my balance. My worry about getting away with anything ceased abruptly. I wasn't getting away with a thing—not any more.

Lorna's great luminous blue eyes grew very wide. I could see the whites all round them for a moment as she stared over my shoulder. I turned my head and found myself looking upward into a face about a foot above my own. An enormous priest was holding the rope around my arms.

Slightly behind him stood another giant with a rope-end in his hands. The other end trailed downward to my ankles. A slight pull would throw me flat. I didn't see the least point in putting up a struggle. Either of these Goliaths could have pulled my head off with a flick of the wrist.

I couldn't do a thing except keep my face immobile and try not to irritate these giants into going any farther. I could only maintain dignity by being strong and silent. So I dropped my arms straight from the elbow, where the rope held them to my sides. I motioned the gaping Lorna away and regarded the Hierarch with a calm, heroic gaze.

He was permitting himself a slight smug twitch of the lips as he looked at me. "Search him," he said briefly.

A swarm of priests descended on me from some region I could not see because my back was toward the door. I felt hands slapping cautiously all over me, searching for the unfamiliar pockets of my exotic tweeds. They were thorough.

On the hideous golden desk beside the Hierarch a little heap of my belongings grew like magic. Every item was regarded with deep suspicion and handled with extreme care, particularly the cigarette lighter with which I had kindled that Promethean fire on the street corner.

Finally I stood there with all my pockets hanging wrong-side-out and no further possessions on my person anywhere. I saw the Hierarch regarding Lorna with quiet satisfaction. Suddenly, I realized why he'd waited until she came before he cracked down on me. He wanted her to observe his power. Nobody was going to bluff the Hierarch, not even a visitant from Paradise, and he wanted the other visitant to know it.

"Now," the Hierarch said comfortably, "we can talk." He moved with ponderous deliberation around the desk and sat down, stirring the pile of small change from my pocket with a forefinger. He looked at me with his impassive all-knowing stare.

"You have come here," he said to me coldly, "without invitation. You cause a great deal of trouble out of motives I'm not really interested in. I know as much about you as I need to know. Things in Malesco were going along very smoothly until you came, and I intend you to leave them just as smooth before you go."

I looked at him hopefully. So I was to go, was I? Where? I didn't ask.

"I know the method of your coming," he went on complacently. "Falvi will be properly disciplined for tampering with the Earth-Gates and for failing to report your arrival. It *was* Falvi, wasn't it?"

I maintained my look of impassive heroic calm.

"All right," the Hierarch said. "You were seen to emerge from a room you could not have entered except by the Earth-Gates a moment after Falvi had left it. You were assisted down a shaft which was obviously unfamiliar to you.

"You followed Falvi to the Baths. There you spent some

while in conference with a notorious rabble-rouser. When detected tampering with a Holy Screen you were able to impress certain of my people with your threats and I allowed you a certain latitude just to see what your plans were."

He interlaced his thick fingers and looked at them with modest pride. "The wisdom of my policy," he went on in a fat voice, "is now clear."

I doubted that. He was probably saying it to impress his audience, but there was still a crowd outside waiting for me and he couldn't argue it away. I believed I'd really succeeded in the major part of my bluff. He'd let me get away with so much because he was really baffled.

I knew more than I ought to know and he couldn't be sure where my knowledge stopped. Certainly it had been a mistake to let the crowd move on the Temple. He'd have dispersed them long ago if he dared. I was arguing myself into fresh confidence. I thought I'd better speak before it could wane again.

"The wisdom of your policy," I said with heavy irony, "will tell you to send Lorna and me back to New York before that hour the crowd gave you is over. They won't want to see any ropes on me either. An hour isn't very long for everything that's got to be done, is it? Time's getting short."

He frowned plumply at me. He hated to make any concessions. It occurred to me then that he was suffering from a form of *hubris*, something I dimly remembered defined in Plato's *Laws*. The sin against proportion had been committed here and the Hierarchs of Malesco wielded powers too big for their souls.

So they suffered congenitally, I suspected, from *hubris*, which is misbehavior through pride. This man before me would, of course, have been somewhat more than human if he hadn't developed a certain amount of that sin, since he ruled a world. The office he occupied was two thousand years old and creaking with an overload of accumulated grandeur.

Undoubtedly he was making the other classic mistake of confusing himself with his office. He arrogated to himself personally all the glory that belonged to the office of Hierarch. He was, in a word, vainglorious. Orgulous is the expressive medieval word for it.

He scowled at me blackly. It went hard with him to have to back down even by implication. But there was that crowd outside which he hadn't dealt with yet. I could almost see him remembering it. So he snapped his fingers again reluctantly.

I felt the pressure of my ropes slacken. They fell in two loose loops to my feet and I stepped out of them without even looking down.

"You'll do as you're told," he said, just to make clear he wasn't conceding anything. "It isn't that easy. You're right to rely on your mob—but don't rely too much. I can always disperse them if they push me too far. I'd prefer not to, but it's within my power to do so. I'll refrain only so long as it's more convenient to refrain. Do you understand that?"

"I see what you mean," I said.

"Very well. You and Clia will return to Paradise. A public ceremony is being organized now for that purpose. You may go on one condition." He exhaled loudly through his nose.

"On one condition," he repeated. "That is that you address the crowd before you go. A short speech is being prepared for you. The people must be instructed to disperse quietly. They must be told they have sinned in allowing the fatal treason of curiosity to overcome them. The great Alchemist is displeased with them all.

"That must be made clear. A few moral truths about obeying the priesthood and doubling their contributions to the Temple as a sign of true repentance will be incorporated in your speech. After that I believe they'll go quietly."

I looked at him thoughtfully. Maybe they would. I couldn't be sure, but I rather felt they would. It was clever of the Hierarch. Certainly it put Coriole right back in his place. He had tried to crowd me into a position of public savior which I wasn't at all ready to assume. This was the only way I could think of that would get me out of it.

But it made me feel very uncomfortable. Nobody could say I'd encouraged all those people to stick their necks out by following me to the Temple. I'd done everything I could to get rid of them. True, now that they were here they were very useful, but I hadn't asked them to follow me.

I didn't owe them anything. I'd been deftly maneuvered into this spot and, if I could be maneuvered out again, that was a matter between Coriole and the Hierarch. I was a tool and it suited me fine.

Then I remembered Uncle Jim and my discomfort deepened.

When you came right down to it this is what Uncle Jim had done, too. Pitched into Malesco unintentionally, he had accumulated a band of followers, taken on hostages to fortune— at least I'd managed to avoid that—and eventually deserted when things became more rugged than he could take. Now the pattern was repeating itself.

"You have no choice, of course," the Hierarch put in neatly at this point. "Your refusal would simply mean the deaths of the people. I'd rather not wipe out your misguided followers, but if I must I can. Remember, this is my world, not yours. I rule Malesco."

He pulled in his chins and gave me an orgulous look. I shrugged. He was perfectly right. It *was* his world. I didn't want Malesco. All I wanted was to get back to New York with Lorna. And this was the easiest way to do it.

"It's the people's problem," I assured myself. "They haven't any right to expect some magic deliverer from another world to turn up and solve everything for them. If I lay an easy solution in their laps they won't value it. You've got to work out your own problems before you get any good from them. That's one of the first lessons in life."

"If you have any notions," the Hierarch said at this point, "that you can burst into inspired speech at the last moment, please forget them."

I blinked at him. That hadn't occurred to me. He was overestimating my concern for the people of Malesco.

"Remember I control all the mechanistic resources of this world," he reminded me. "The people can't possibly overthrow me. It's no kindness to encourage them to try. Surely you can see that."

I did, all right. I glanced at Lorna, who had been unexpectedly silent. She wasn't following the conversation at all. From the moment she saw a pack of cigarettes emerge from my pocket it was clear that one devouring desire had taken control of her. But she seemed to be too afraid of the Hierarch to say anything. There was no help to be gained from her. She didn't even know what we were saying.

I sighed uncomfortably. "All right," I said. "Let's get started. I'll make your speech for you." And I began stuffing my empty pockets back into place to give myself something to do.

Chapter XV

I STOOD on the stage of the biggest theatre I'd ever played in and got ready for the largest audience. The average legitimate theatre in New York is a tiny place and it holds comparatively few people at a time.

But this vast, long chamber with the painted walls would more than contain the crowd I had left in the square before the Temple. I shuffled my feet on the golden stage and wished the ordeal were over.

Lorna was beside me, making nervous adjustments of her robes. The Hierarch sat on a hideous gold throne, even more encrusted with ornament than his desk upstairs. There were priests and priests and more priests everywhere I looked, but the people hadn't come in yet. The doors were closed.

This was the dais below the great circular screen that opened upon Earth. It was just a window now. Through it I could see over the rooftops the great watery dome of the Baths with the fountains of fire playing over it, and Lorna's pictured face painted in colored lights on the side of the building.

It was the same view I'd had from far above when I first emerged into Malesco. I never understood clearly how they switched the opening between the worlds from upstairs to the ground floor for ceremonies—but that was the way it was.

Upstairs it was privately operated and constantly attended by people like Falvi. Down here it worked only on great occasions—like this one. Of course no great mystery was involved. We use remote control and coaxial cables and such gimmicks ourselves, and in the face of such a miracle as the Earth-Gates merely technical angles were trivial enough.

I'd spent the last half hour or so cramming, studying my part with the aid of two priests who acted as prompters. It wasn't a difficult role to learn. In fact, I'd had time to ask a few tentative questions about the Earth-Gates, for I had a par-

donable curiosity as to the nature of the springboard that was
going to hurl me into a pretty frightening abyss.

To my surprise the priests had answered my questions—
not as clearly as I could have wished but I managed to piece
out some interesting details. I began to understand why it was
that Malesco had discovered the Earth-Gates whereas our own
scientists have merely theorized about such matters.

The reason was simply that alchemy accepts the idea of
transmutation in a semi-mystical way which is nevertheless
founded on solid physical science. Belief precedes practical
application in spite of Newton and the apple.

Before Newton men knew enough to get out from under,
but the theory of gravitation enabled men to go on from there
and create rather than merely to use what was already at hand.
However, not until certain alloys, methods and isotopes were
discovered was Malesco able to build the Earth-Gates.

We use energy to move ourselves from place to place. With
kinetic energy we travel far and fast. But there is another
method—potential energy. We use that when we build a bridge.
The bridge must be constructed in a special way so it won't
fall down. It must be made of special material strong enough
to endure the stresses and strains. The Romans used stone.
They couldn't have bridged San Francisco Bay. We use metal
alloys so we can do that.

Now sometimes kinetic and potential energy are joined in
one bridge—a drawbridge.

The Malescan apparatus to bridge the gap between two
worlds was similar. Cathode and anode may be solid metal;
but what jumps between is pure energy, electronic in nature.
So the Earth-Gates were part kinetic and part potential.

When you get into the theory of probability you start working with its breakdown within the atom. So far our own science
has been puzzled by this, rather as the experts of Galileo's time
were baffled when two balls, one of wood and one of iron,
were dropped from the top of a tower and behaved irrationally
in the light of the known science of that period.

Anyhow, Malescan alchemic scientists had also noticed a
breakdown of probabilities within *their* atoms. Remember, they
knew all about Earth, and the space-time cleavage back in
Roman days. They thought this might be the key. Somewhere
within the atom was the missing link. Somewhere, solidly in

Malesco—somewhere, solidly on Earth, were cathode and anode.

The trick was to find a form of energy that would bridge the widening gap.

Well, they did it. It took a long time, but they did it. They discovered atomic energy eventually and then managed to find the right type of energy to bridge the gap. Oddly enough, that wasn't the hardest part.

The really tricky work—my priests explained—came, first in building up enough sufficient potential to cross the gulf, secondly in controlling and guiding that enormous power. (Remember the atomic bomb? *We invented* it all right but as for *controlling* it—)

Moreover the powers involved were so enormous that sometimes the Earth-Gates got slightly out of control. The spark would jump the gap of its own volition and the two worlds would meet briefly—for a second or two—with only a few square feet of space involved. The gaps always closed again.

Still, this is what must have happened when I entered Malesco. There must have been a brief bridging of the gap, so that when I called Lorna's name Falvi heard a voice from the air and, sensibly connecting that phenomenon with the Earth-Gates, let his fatal curiosity get the better of him. Perhaps that explains Joan of Arc's voices too.

Legend had it that such phenomena had happened even before the Earth-Gates were built. Perhaps the two worlds were closer together then, so the gulf could be bridged more easily. A visitant from an unknown place had appeared once in Malesco—his name was something very much like Peter Rugg.

And there was the tale of the Malescan who had disappeared without trace from the middle of an open field. (Would it surprise you to know that I finally worked it out that his name, spoken phonetically, resembled Kaspar Hauser?)

I wish now I had asked more questions. I wish the priests had been clearer. For the Earth-Gates were among the great miracles of science, and I couldn't concentrate on them at all because I had stage fright.

I stood waiting, facing the far end of the enormous room, wondering where the exit door was, running over my opening lines, wishing again and again that the next half hour were over, that Lorna and I were back home again. Then the air suddenly shuddered with the hollow hooting of trumpets and the whole far end of the room shimmered before me.

I thought it was my eyes blurring. Then I saw that the entire end wall had grown translucent with a pouring flood of pale light. A vast A began to burn upon the surface of the wall, and I realized that it was no wall but a great curtain.

It shivered and began to rise. The trumpets tooted their hollow notes again and a second curtain rose, lead-gray, to reveal a third and then a fourth beyond, successively thinner and more golden. Now I could see a dim outline of the square in which I had left my faithful followers.

But the curtains distorted things. It looked as if the whole square, which had been half empty when I left, was full now of restless motion. I had thought the crowd would, if anything, thin out a little while it waited. I had even braced myself to find it entirely dispersed by the time I got to relying really heavily on the people. But Coriole had been smarter than I expected.

The last curtain rolled upward, pure golden yellow, and from the dais where I stood I could see that the entire square was one solid, seething mass of heads and faces turned toward me. And that wasn't all.

As far as the eye could reach down the streets leading into the square there were more heads, more faces, more restless pushing and surging. It looked as if all of Malesco had gathered here to send me off with appropriate ceremony. You couldn't see the pavement anywhere the crowd was packed so tight.

When the curtain rose the foremost ranks rolled forward in one solid mass and the noise of it surged into the Temple and reverberated from the walls. The people weren't shouting. They didn't make any particular noises when they saw me.

I'd rather expected some sort of demonstration, but I didn't get it. The volume of their voices rose a little, but each individual man and woman was talking in low, controlled tones and there was no shouting. It seemed to me that this crowd meant business.

It scared me. Could I handle it? Could the Hierarch? I didn't know what weapons he had, but it looked to me that nothing short of an atom blast could wipe out this entire mob at one blow. He could, at worst, destroy the foremost of the crowd.

It seemed to me those endless ranks of people disappearing

down the streets far away could and would surge forward and
find out and destroy the sources of the destruction before the
last man was anywhere near extinction. I didn't look around
at the Hierarch, but I felt a little cool breath of ... dismay? ...
move over the dais as the priesthood prepared to greet its
audience.

In less time than I'd have believed, the hall was packed
tight and solid with men and women shoulder to shoulder,
staring up at the dais and at me. And with them came a curious
atmosphere of tension and expectation, so that the enclosing
walls seemed to pack the feeling down tight under the high
roof and we all felt it pressing around us.

Down there in the front ranks I saw one familiar face—
Coriole's.

He was only about twenty feet away from me and he was
watching me like a cat, his pale blue eyes never swerving from
mine. It made me uncomfortable. I looked away—and found
I was staring at another familiar face, this time in the wings
and even closer than Coriole. This time it was Dio.

He still looked sleepy. He still had the air of a man who's
had a hard night and not enough rest. But there was a lot more
in his expression now. Sullenness, I thought, for one thing. I
had a series of quick consecutive thoughts about Dio.

There just hadn't been time until now to wonder where the
Hierarch got his detailed information about my activities since
my arrival here, but it was obvious when I thought back. Dio,
of course—he had probably been hanging around Falvi's door
hoping for a break and had got one.

Maybe he'd suspected Falvi's connection with the underground for some while and finally had caught him at it with
me. That would explain his air of avid anticipation when he
carried me down the shaft and set me adrift in the city, hoping
I'd lead him to something worthwhile.

That was Dio's policy, of course. Coriole had confirmed it
if I'd needed confirmation. Dio was on Dio's side and nobody
else's. And now he was sullen. Why? Well, he'd given the
Hierarch some valuable information, certainly. But what reward had he got? Not enough, to judge by his expression.

He hadn't even been inside the Hierarch's door when I went
to pay my formal call. He'd been hanging around in the hall,
hoping for crumbs. It wasn't enough for Dio—not nearly

enough. I wondered about promotion in the priesthood. Maybe it went by seniority. Dio was young. He wouldn't be content to wait another fifty years for recognition. He'd want it now.

Since his scheme to inform the Hierarch on Coriole had failed he'd certainly be watching for something even bigger. I didn't like having him so close to me. I meant to play right along with the Hierarch, of course—I hadn't any choice now—but if I should see any loopholes I didn't want Dio watching me with that expectant stare, waiting to jump the moment my back was turned.

There was a low rumbling along the walls. I looked up. So did everybody else. And this time a single deep breath of protest seemed to sweep the whole hall, from side to packed side. For above us, between the painted animals on the walls, were regularly spaced golden A's. There was an ominous glow dawning behind them.

I recognized it with a shudder. It was the same glow I had last seen in the bottle-shaped weapons of the priests. My eyes ached in quick retrospect as I thought of the blinding sunburst of heat and brilliance those weapons could emit.

But those had been of milk-bottle size. These were six feet across. The golden A's were simply ornamental scrollwork across the mouths of so many cannon embedded in the wall. The Hierarch was taking no chances with this dangerous crowd. One simultaneous glare from those glowing mouths above us would crisp every human in the hall to cinders.

I hoped—not at all like a hero—that the priests had some way to shut off the dais from those blasts if and when the time came to unleash them.

Still there was no demonstration from the crowd. They weren't intimidated. They weren't even angry on the surface. But they were waiting. The thousands of lifted faces I could see had a grim set look, and I could feel in the air that indefinable tension of determination and hard, controlled patience. Every eye was on me.

My speech was short. I'd learned it easily enough. The notes were on a little glass and gold table before me. I went over the opening lines in a quick mental gabble, waiting for my cue.

People of Malesco . . . gabble-gabble . . . great Alchemist in Paradise is impatient with your sinful curiosity . . . gabble-gab-

ble . . . sent me to warn you . . . gabble-gabble . . . at punish-
ment for your wilful misconduct . . . gabble-gabble . . . returning
to Paradise and taking Clia back with me out of the contam-
inating . . . gabble-gabble . . .

There it was, the deep hooting of those great curled horns.
A breathless hush fell upon the crowd. I knew I'd never have
such an audience again. They were with me to a man. They
loved me in Malesco. Well, it ought to be over in ten minutes.

"It's not your battle, Eddie," I assured myself, waiting for
the horns to stop echoing. "You're just an actor. You've played
villains before. This is a quick walk-on and then curtain. In
ten minutes you'll be home in New York and these people can
fight it out among themselves."

The echoes stopped. I took a deep breath and started talking.
My voice was a little shaky at first, but I got it under control
after the first words. The public address system here was working fine. They could hear me, I saw, even in the back rows.

I got past "Great Alchemist in Paradise" and swung into it,
putting paternal reproof into the lines, trying to sink myself in
the character I was playing so I wouldn't have to think. I hadn't
written this play. It wasn't my battle . . . it wasn't my battle . . .
it wasn't—

It wasn't going over.

There was no doubt about that. The muttering from the back
of the house began to rise before I'd got more than two lines
into my speech. I spread my arms and put more volume into
my voice, ad-libbing a little to make time for the mutter to
subside.

It worked—for a moment—and I went on with increasingly
cold feet. I didn't like it. I didn't like it at all. I didn't like my
lines or the part I was playing, and it seemed to me the Hierarch
had made a terrible mistake in his handling of the crowd.

It's simple psychology. You can't take something away from
people when they prize it very highly and not give them anything in return. These men and women had come here charged
with a tremendous potential for action and it wasn't going to
work if we just said, "Run along home now like good children."

I had misjudged the Hierarch. He knew what he was doing.

The second time the muttering from below rose to a roar
that threatened to drown out my speech. I felt a stirring at my

elbow. I stepped back a pace, drawing out a syllable long enough to give me time to glance back.

Chapter XVI

IT WAS Lorna. She came forward with a graceful, gliding step she certainly hadn't known in New York. She spread her arms and the silver sleeves caught the light and glowed like fire. She spoke in a cooing, emotional croon that filled the hall without effort.

"You are angry," she cooed at them, in the purest Malescan. "You have reason to be angry. Someone has cheated you of your rights!" Silvery indignation sounded in her voice now. I was baffled for an instant at the command she had over the language and her lines. Lorna wasn't up to ad-libbing.

Then I realized the Hierarch had been preparing for this all along. I hadn't been the only one who spent the last half hour studying my lines. Lorna had been coached too, for just this occasion.

The crowd was dead silent, waiting, puzzled. I was puzzled, too. But in the instant before Lorna went on I saw understanding light up one face below me in the crowd. Coriole's eyes met mine in a sudden blaze of anger and hatred. He knew what was coming. And then, of course, I did too.

It had been the Hierarch's plan from the start. But he hadn't told me. He must have known how far he could push me along the way he meant me to go. I'd agreed to make this fairly harmless little speech. But he suspected I wouldn't do what Lorna was now doing for me.

"A man who deserves your righteous anger!" Lorna cried throatily. "He and his men have worked like serpents underground to make trouble between you and your loving priesthood. He is jealous of your destiny. You will go on through virtuous lives to reincarnation in Paradise.

"But he will never reach New York and now he tries to trick you too out of your birthright: Paradise! People of Malesco, I give you that man, to punish as you choose!" The silver-draped arm swung dramatically and pointed straight down before her.

"Coriole!" she shrilled. *"Coriole!"*

Instantly from picked spots in the crowd a well-disciplined claque took up the shout. The Hierarch hadn't forgotten a thing. His stooges were planted all through the room and they had strong voices.

"Coriole!" they yelled with well-assumed rage. "Coriole tricked us! Grab him! Grab Coriole! Don't let him get away!"

The crowd boiled furiously, wild with indecision. Above them the golden A's glowed more and more ominously as the power stepped up behind them, waiting to be released.

"Get Coriole!" some feeble voices began to cry tentatively, as suggestibles in the crowd swung toward the people who made the most noise. "Get him—get Coriole!"

The thing hung in a perfect balance for one of those timeless moments. It needed a push one way or the other and for that instant nobody seemed capable of pushing. Time was on the side of the Hierarch.

When you have an organized group acting under strict orders it's simply a matter of time until they swing the crowd their way by pure volume of noise. And Coriole for some reason was caught flatfooted.

Either he'd relied too heavily on me or the unexpected size of the crowd had given him false confidence. But it was partly the size of the crowd that trapped him now. He was hemmed in so tightly he couldn't run even if he wanted to. I saw his mouth open and shut and the veins in his neck swell as he shouted something—perhaps the names of his friends—but the noise was too loud and nobody could hear him.

There's always a large percentage of mindless fools in any mob, ready to yell whatever the next guy is yelling. The Hierarch's boys were making headway. Probably a good many of these people had never heard of Coriole, but that didn't stop them from yapping for his blood

I stood there on the dais and dithered like my cousin in the crowd. "It isn't your fight, it isn't your fight," I kept telling myself futilely. "This is the people against their government and there isn't a thing you can do about it. Don't meddle. Keep your mouth shut and you'll come out on top. Keep your mouth shut!"

Here on the dais a separate crisis seemed in progress. The roaring mob was below us, the jammed square was in front of us—the shouting and yelling sweeping infectiously back out of the Temple and along the packed streets. But it might have been happening on the other side of the world so far as it outwardly seemed to affect the priests.

The Hierarch sat motionless on his gold-crusted throne. Lorna, having spoken her piece, had sidled up to me and was whispering urgently, "Did you keep any cigarettes, Eddie?"

I didn't answer her. I was watching the priests. They weren't as good at hiding their emotions as the Hierarch was. A lot of ambivalence seemed to be in progress in the massed priesthood in the wings. The men wound up in the curled horns each had a deep breath drawn, ready to blast away at a word from the Hierarch.

They never took their eyes from his face. I knew there were hidden priests at the controls of the sunburst weapons glowing ready in the walls, and they must be watching the boss too, each with a finger posed above the switch of whatever activated those heat-rays.

It seemed to me the priests were alarmed somewhat out of proportion to reason. I saw they were winning. All they had to do was wait. Already the roar of "Get Coriole!" could be heard clearly from several sides and it was gaining with every second.

Then I caught Dio's eye and for an instant everything else went blank and silent around me, so urgent was the look on his face. But I didn't know what the look meant. He seemed to be hanging eagerly on my next motion, my next word. He seemed to attach tremendous importance to what I did next.

There was the same avid anticipation on his face which I'd seen in our first meeting when he waited joyfully for me to give myself away. Was that what he expected now? Was he afraid I'd try to swerve the anger of the mob from Coriole to the priests? Did he think I could do it? If he did, maybe he was right. Maybe, if I could just think of the right word, Coriole might still have a chance.

But did I want to meddle that much? I'd gone through a lot to get right where I was now, on the threshold of return to New York. In a few moments Coriole would be submerged by the angry mob, all its energy diverted against the man who'd roused it. And the ceremony would go on as planned.

Dio was reaching into his robe. I saw him fumble for something, never taking his eyes from my face. Then he had it. He pulled it out, keeping his hands closed over something small.

He was smiling rather wolfishly now, the bright avid intentness stronger than ever on his face. He reminded me irresistibly of those weapons glowing in the walls. There was the same leashed blaze, the same meance held barely in check.

Still nailing me with that brilliant unswerving stare, he drew his arm back a little and snapped something shiny through the air straight at me.

It seemed to me it hung there between us for years and years. My mind ran in little circles, yelping hysterically. "Is it a bomb?" my mind demanded. "Shall I catch it? Shall I dodge it? What is it? What's eating him? What shall I do?"

But my body acted with calm independence of the frantic mind. Automatically both of my hands reached out and the object smacked neatly into them.

It was a small, flat square. The feel of it made a picture take shape in my mind before I even looked. Another of those white wafers with gold writing on it. A message from Dio?

I opened my hands slightly and looked down. It wasn't a wafer. There was no writing on it. Dio had tossed me my cigarette lighter.

You wouldn't believe what a short time all this really took. Coriole was still looking around wildly for his men. The mob was still milling indecisively. The leather-lunged stooges in the congregation were still bellowing incendiary phrases at the tops of their voices. But the tide was already on the turn.

The priests, I thought, had won. Not tangibly yet but definitely. This was one of those important moments in Malescan history when a touch would swing the balance one way or the other and the touch had been applied. It was swinging ponderously toward the Hierarch's side.

And the moment was perhaps as great a point of division as that earlier moment in Roman history when the two worlds had split apart in probability. Everything hung in the balance.

I held the cigarette lighter stupidly in my hands, blinking

at it. What did Dio mean? Was he on the side of the priests or the side of the rebels?

"Neither," I told myself rapidly. "Dio's on Dio's side and nobody else's. He's for the winners."

But he'd given me the means to swing the course of history away from his own men. What did it mean? Obviously, only one thing.

Dio thought the rebels were the likelier winners. He wanted in on the stronger side. And that meant the priests were a lot weaker than they looked. Somehow, somewhere, they were covering up with a colossal bluff. Dio knew. And he expected me to—to what?

My mind was still telling me, "Don't meddle! It isn't your battle!" but again my body calmly went its own way. Without the slightest mental processes to guide me I kicked over the gold and glass table beside me on the dais and swung both arms up over my head at full length.

The pages of my speech fluttered unnoticed from the table to the floor. But the noise of the overturned table was a quicker and higher sound than the bellowing of the mob. It caught eyes in the front ranks.

I flicked the lighter with one thumb, praying fervently that it wouldn't choose this moment to balk.

There was a strange breathless pause in the shouting down below. Then I heard the sigh that swept like a soft breeze through the room and I knew the flame had caught.

Miraculously, little by little, but marvelously fast, the uproar died away. Out in the square the crowd was still yelling, but there was a hush in the painted room. I could hear silence sweeping backward through the streets as the noise had swept a minute or two before.

I stood there like Liberty holding the torch of freedom aloft, and I didn't feel as silly as I might have. I *was* Liberty in that moment and it *was* the torch of freedom—if things went right.

I held the dramatic pose until I was sure every eye had focused on that one small flame, that one-candle-power torch that contained more power than all the Hierarch's weapons. I knew that while I held it the priests wouldn't dare touch me. But what was I going to do next? I couldn't stand forever in this melodramatic attitude.

It was my hour. I *couldn't* do the wrong thing. I snapped

the lighter shut, swung my lifted arm back, and hurled the
glittering square of metal out over the heads of the crowd.

It turned twice in the air, catching light on its shining sides,
and then dropped gently out of sight among the craning heads.
There was silence for a moment. Then the crowd seethed around
the spot where it had fallen and a shrill voice cried, "I got it.
I *got* it!"

Everybody looked. Even the Hierarch leaned forward on
his throne. We all saw the meager little half-bald man in the
mob who had caught the torch I threw.

He looked like a middle-aged clerk. He wore a shabby tunic
and his hair needed cutting, what there was of it. But he held
the lighter up in his cupped palms like a holy relic and his
insignificant little face was transfigured with rapture.

That was the point at which the Hierarch lost his head. He
was a clever man but he didn't know *everything*. And one of
the things he didn't know was how to deal with a problem like
this, with people getting so riotously out of hand so fast, with
everything depending on his decisions from minute to minute,
and no past experience to guide him.

This had never happened before. All he had to go by was
a time when something a little like it had happened—Jimmerton's coming. The priesthood had triumphed over Jimmerton by fast direct high-pressure methods. The Hierarch tried
that now. It would never do to let that dangerous cigarette
ligther float about the city, passing from hand to hand and
igniting rebellion in all who saw it.

"Bring me the sacred relic," he shouted, making majestic
gestures. "That is a relic from Paradise—too holy for human
hands! Bring it to me!"

I caught a venomous glance from his small enigmatic eyes,
but he had no time to waste on me just now. He was rising
with great pomp, surging forward across the platform. His
outspread arms brushed Lorna and me aside.

"Bring me the relic!" he shouted, making his voice so rich
and deep that even above the clamor of the crowd people heard
it and heads turned.

Especially his claque planted among the audience heard it.
When the command made itself understood I could instantly
spot the undercover agents down below. Little eddies of the

throng seethed around each as they began to surge toward the spot where the man with the lighter stood.

But they weren't the only ones who heard the orders. All within earshot caught the words, and the deep spontaneous growl of anger that rose in the wake of the command must have told the Hierarch instantly he'd made a mistake. He'd started something he couldn't finish without bringing up some heavy artillery—very heavy. Maybe nothing he had was strong enough to silence that angry growling as it grew and spread and strengthened.

The mob was like a single organism now. A word dropped into it spread in eddying rings out and out until it was lost among the vanishing throngs in the streets. An idea, a promise of success or a threat of defeat, seemed to spread in the same way. A few words spoken from the dais ran like magic through the listening crowds and eddied out there among the packed avenues almost quicker than the eye could follow the spreading tumult it made.

One or two of the Hierarch's strong-arm squad had reached the little man with the lighter by now. The others were floundering closer but against increasing opposition. The people around each of them were resisting. Knots of angry men and women came into being all about every one of the forward-surging stooges.

The mob was turning into a single organism and the organism encysted these germs of disease in its midst, isolated them, built up the anger and the strength necessary to control them exactly as a living body surrounds and overwhelms dangerous intruders within itself.

Something that was new and powerful had been born in Malesco—this crowd—this single close-knit unit of all the thousands functioning as one. It was stronger than the Hierarch, stronger than the priesthood.

It was a new being. And I had created it. It was my responsibility now. So it *was* my fight after all.

Dio was watching me with fierce expectancy. Coriole, wedged tightly in the mob twenty feet away, was watching too, his pale eyes unswervingly on mine. I felt a third intentness and glanced sidewise to find the Hierarch regarding me with that inscrutable fat stare of his. These three knew. The next

move was probably mine, and they realized it. These three—
no, it was four.

For Lorna's newly limpid eyes suddenly intercepted mine.
She edged toward me across the platform and I felt her cold
fingers clasp my hand. With unerring instinct Lorna Maxwell
had spotted the man temporarily in a key position. Whatever
there was in it for her she meant to get. She moved toward
me with all the mindless assurance of a plant turning toward
the sun.

I had no idea what to do next.

Chapter XVII

ABOUT thirty seconds had elapsed since I threw the lighter,
and already a major battle was starting in the crowd around
the little man who had caught it.

"Little Man," I thought bitterly. Not a single cliche was
being spared me. Even that nauseating phrase to denote the
masses had come into actual being right under my nose. The
representative Little Man himself was squealing and struggling
feebly for the priceless boon of a cigarette lighter, and I couldn't
do a thing to help him. I couldn't . . .

The sudden tremendous blare of the curled horns stunned
me into blankness. Some hidden amplifier must have been
turned on, for the whole hall shook with that deep-toned, vibrant blast. The Hierarch had moved while I stood there hesitating.

Down in the crowd all motion ceased for a few seconds as
every brain in the mob vibrated painfully to that fearful noise.
One vast collective headache must have throbbed through the
whole organism which was the Malescan crowd.

The Hierarch's voice amplified to godlike volume, though
I could see no mechanism to carry it, rolled majestically down
the hall as the horn blast faded. He wasted no words. He didn't
even command them to stop fighting, since obviously they had
already stopped for the moment, stunned by the noise of the

horns. He went right to the heart of his problem, which was me.

"Paradise," he roared sonorously, "awaits its children. Silence! Let the Earth-Gates open!"

For a second I think nobody quite knew what he meant. We were all too involved in our immediate problems. But then I saw a change come over the faces just below, looking up at us. Their gaze shifted to something behind me. I was aware of a slowly dawning new light on the dais and I saw my own shadow take dim shape and stretch out at my feet across the golden floor.

I turned. The great circular window that normally looked out over the city had clouded with shining opalescence. You couldn't see Malesco through it any more. But a shape was growing there. A vast luminous A, the symbol for divided worlds bridged by a crossbar between Paradise and Malesco, gleamed through the clouds.

Very rapidly the A faded, and Paradise itself replaced Malesco beyond the window. New York at night, its streets streaming with lights, appeared to lie some hundreds of feet down just beyond the great circle in the wall.

"Paradise awaits!" the Hierarch's rich bellow announced, still amplified to superhuman volume. "The two who came to us must now return to the glorious rewards of New York. Clia! Burton! The Earth-Gates open!"

Behind me in the hall a wave of silence was moving outward through the crowd, though in the distance I could still hear shouting. Now a new wave began just below me, almost at my heels. I knew it would move as the shouting and the silence had moved, out and out until it reached the limits of the streets. But the new sound was very quiet. It was a sigh, a murmur. There was nothing they could do. They waited.

Was I going to leave them to the mercies of the priesthood as Jimmerton had done? I wished I knew.

The vision of New York rocked before me like a ship and seemed to shoot upward with sickening speed as if all of us who watched were dropping toward the street. And as we dropped the clarity of the view clouded. I could see why.

If this were a real opening between the worlds, not a dressed-up version, it would never do to let the Malescans see too clearly what the real streets were like. Through a golden cloud

I saw the blur of passing traffic, their lights making rainbows in the mist. We were looking at street-level straight into the City of Paradise.

"Come," the Hierarch said. "Paradise awaits. The Gates are open. Clia, Burton—farewell!"

All we had to do was step through. It was what I'd been struggling for during all this endless eternity in Malesco. Lorna's hand was still clasping mine. I'd got what I came for. What was in it for me if I hesitated any longer? Nothing.

"Go on," the Hierarch said urgently, in his normal voice, not using the amplifier that would let the people hear. "Step through. You're all right now. Just get out of here and don't make any more trouble."

Still I hesitated. His little eyes between their rims of fat were almost closed as he looked at me. He had never seemed more of a juggernaut than now. I had a curious feeling that this wasn't all, that there was something further on his mind as he waited so impatiently for my next step. But that could all be imagination.

"Go on," he whispered again. "Get out! Or do you want some help?"

I heard the soft snapping of his fingers and a couple of burly priests put their hands together in hieratically pious gestures and came forward on each side of us. I could see perfectly well that we were going to be shoved through the Gates in a minute or two if we didn't go of our own accord.

The crowd was completely silent now. It didn't seem possible that so many people could stand so still, hardly breathing, waiting to be abandoned to the just punishment of the priesthood. Jimmerton had deserted them too, long ago.

Now I was going, and the Hierarch could hardly wait to get me out of Malesco, so he could arrest Coriole and that ridiculous Little Man and put my cigarette lighter with the other relics of Paradise. Then it would be treason again for anyone to think about how the little wheel went around and the sparks flew out.

And, I thought suddenly, maybe someday another man from New York would stumble through the Earth-Gates. Maybe somebody not yet born. What story would he hear from the descendants of these people, about how a man named Jimmerton and a man named Burton had led them into revolt and left them when the going got tough?

Don't make any mistakes about Eddie Burton. That's sentimental talk. My own skin is the most important thing in the world to me. But if I could save Lorna and myself and still have some little dividend of glory left over, that wouldn't be too bad, either.

"Farewell!" the Hierarch suddenly thundered with full volume turned on. *"Farewell!"*

I heard his fingers snap again and the two bulky priests ceased making hieratic gestures long enough to take each of us by an arm and move us at a sort of stately trot toward the Gates.

At that moment, almost too late, I knew what I could do to collect on that dividend of glory.

"Wait!" I said. "Just a second—I forgot something."

The priests paused slightly to see what the Hierarch would say to this. He looked at me very sharply and I saw no relenting on his face. He knew when he was well off. He wasn't going to give me a chance to get him into any more trouble.

And besides, there was something curious about his face and his eyes—a sort of gleam as if this weren't quite all, as if he waited for something yet to come. Coriole's arrest? Dio's punishment? Exterminating the crowd? All of those and maybe something more. I hadn't time to think about it.

"Lorna," I said rapidly and softly in English. "Have you got your amplifier turned on? I want you to say something to the crowd. Quick!"

She said in a sort of musical whine, "Oh, Eddie, I don't want to! Let's go! I—"

There was no time to waste persuading her. I got a good grip on her hand and bent her little finger painfully outward. I'd rather have twisted her arm, but that would have showed too clearly.

"Does that hurt?" I demanded in a rapid mutter. "I'll dislocate it if you don't repeat what I say after me at full volume. Understand?"

All I got in reply was a squeal of pain and anger. I paid no attention. She was trying to squirm free, but the priest on her far side had a firm hold on her and didn't understand why she was struggling so suddenly. Between us we had her where she couldn't get way.

"Say *People of Malesco*," I commanded, giving her the Malescan for it. "Go on, before I pull your finger off. *People of Malesco!*"

"People of Malesco!" she cried furiously, and the volume of the sound roaring from her throat so near me was almost deafening. I wondered where the amplifier was—in a tooth somewhere? *"People of Malesco!"*

The priests jumped slightly at the roar. The screen before us vibrated a little and the sound woke echoes in the vault of the roof over the dais. Lorna's back was to the crowd but they must have heard her speak clear out in the streets.

The Hierarch gave us both a look of pure venom. But he had to give in. He made a gesture and the grip on my arm slackened. Still holding Lorna's hand in my compelling clutch, I swung her around to face the crowd.

"I have one last message for you," I dictated.

Lorna swore at me in a whisper and then rolled the Malescan words out in the rich, sonorously sweet voice they'd given her along with the lovely face.

"Your Hierarch is a great man," I said, releasing her finger slightly. She put such emotion in the transcript when she repeated it that a very convincing half-sob broke up the words a little. It was a sound of rage and pain, but it gave the speech a touching quality.

"He has done so much for Malesco," I dictated.

"Let me go!" Lorna whispered. *"He has done so much for Malesco—"*

"That Paradise has decreed him a reward."

"Eddie, I'll kill you! Let go. Let go! *That Paradise has decreed him a reward—"*

"Listen while I tell you," I whispered. *"Listen well, for this is the greatest reward a living man ever knew. Do you hear me, people of Malesco?"*

Between the snarls of rage she got the words out. I made her pause then and in the interval the people gave us one unified roar of answer. They were with us. They knew something was up, and I thought they were ready to back almost anything I said. What did they have to lose now?

"I was a mortal among you," I dictated, ignoring her snarls.

"I lived a good life and went straight to New York when I died. But your Hierarch has lived a life so good that the Great Alchemist sent me here to claim him for Paradise—now!"

Halfway through that speech Lorna stopped struggling. Evidently she had picked up enough Malescan to realize what she was saying. She rolled her eyes at me. "I hope you know what you're doing," she whispered in the pause that followed this speech.

"Shut up," I said. "Wait a second. Let them yell. See how they like it?" I was looking straight down at Coriole as I spoke and I saw the sudden blaze of excitement on his face as he realized what I was attempting.

"Your Hierarch returns to Paradise with me—now!" Lorna parroted after me. And then, in a whisper, "Oh, Eddie, do you think he'll go? You must be crazy. What'll we do with him in New York?"

"Shut up," I said again. "Go on—make a gesture toward him. Invite him to Paradise. Go on or I'll break your arm!"

With incomparable grace she held out her hand toward the Hierarch, her silver sleeve flowing and flashing with jewels. There was a good deal of ham in her acting, but the audience wasn't critical.

The Hierarch stood there stunned at the foot of his golden throne. The entire priesthood stood stunned around him. Nobody had expected this. For an instant stillness and silence held everyone on the dais motionless.

"Say, *Come, Paradise awaits us,*" I hissed.

"Come, Paradise awaits us," Lorna cooed and the volume of her coo filled the entire hall and echoed through the city outside.

The Hierarch's eyes met mine. He shook his fat shoulders a little and said in a low growl several phrases of Malescan that Uncle Jim had never taught me. But he came. He had no choice. He couldn't repudiate Lorna before everybody. Slowly he lumbered toward us, juggernaut to the last.

The overturned table was in the way, and he rolled forward, ignoring it, knowing somebody would snatch it out of his path. Somebody did. He didn't glance down. You could see the furious thoughts racing through his mind behind his frozen face, but it was quite clear that he didn't know what to do next.

I did. It seemed perfectly simple to me. I was giving Coriole the chance he'd begged for. Coriole had friends among the priesthood and those friends were organized. I thought that if the Hierarch were suddenly snatched away Coriole would have a good chance of seizing control and putting one of his boys on that hideous golden throne. It was all I could do for him. I thought it was pretty good myself.

Chapter XVIII

WE made a little tableau before the glowing Earth-Gates. Lorna and I, with our priest escort on each side, ready to seize us again at a word from the Hierarch—and the Hierarch in all his pomp and power, entirely helpless to save himself. It was a fine moment. I felt very proud of my own cleverness.

The Hierarch shook himself again, growled deep in his throat, and spoke at about half volume, so that the crowd heard him clearly but not deafeningly.

"I am not worthy of this honor." It must have gone hard with him to say such a thing, but it was the best he could think of just now.

"Paradise thinks you more than worthy," I dictated firmly and Lorna rolled it out over the crowd.

He ground his teeth. I really heard them grind. He let his little eyes shoot angry but hopeful glances around the dais. Nobody moved. Evidently nobody could think any faster than he could. Then I saw a sudden faint hope dawn on his face.

"Come, then," he said clearly. "We will go together." And he bowed us forward toward the Gates. I didn't get it for an instant. Then I saw he meant us to go first. He was being very, very polite and urging us ahead of him through the screen. Then, no doubt, he wouldn't follow.

"Oh no!" I said. "Lorna, tell them this. *Paradise decrees your Hierarch the honor of stepping first through the Earth-Gates."*

She giggled a little and told them.

And at that a sudden, unexpected tension settled down over the dais. A murmur ran through the priesthood. They stared in new consternation at the Hierarch.

He himself froze to new rigidity. Something had happened and I didn't know what it was. But he did. All the priests did. I sought Dio's eye but he only nodded. It was okay. I waited.

It was shocking to see how the color drained slowly out of the Hierarch's ruddy face as he looked at the Earth-Gates. I couldn't understand it. Naturally he didn't want to leave Malesco, but this reaction was all out of proportion to what he was called upon to do.

I thought, "He can just face around toward the crowd and refuse to go, can't he?" and I tried to brace myself to combat that, racking my brain for something to say when he did. I was sure it was what he'd do. I think he was sure too—for a moment or two. I saw him waver just a little as if he were nerving himself to turn.

Then the crowd seemed to sense the same thing. It was still a single organism and the tremor of refusal that had started close up under the platform when the nearest people saw the Hierarch waver spread rapidly backward through the hall.

They didn't want him to stay. They weren't going to let him stay.

"Farewell!" some raucous voice bellowed just below the dais. *"Farewell!"* Other voices took it up. In a backward wave it rolled through the hall until the ceiling rocked with the efforts of the people to speed their parting leader.

He shook his thick shoulders under the golden robe. There was something bull-like about the way he swung his head around and ran a desperate glance along the ranks of the watching priests.

"Fix it!" he said inexplicably through his teeth, hardly moving his lips. "One of you fix it! Flammand, help me! Hyperion, do something! Hyperion, I'll have you burned!"

Nobody moved.

There was dense silence on the dais while the roars of determined farewell gained volume in the hall below. No one on the platform would meet the Hierarch's eye. "Flammand!" he commanded in a frighteningly fierce whisper. *"Flammand!"*

There was an almost imperceptible motion in the priestly throng near Dio. Someone took an indecisive step forward—

probably Flammand. Dio, his teeth showing in a grin, stepped
forward at the same instant and shouldered the volunteer. The
fellow could have got past him, but he didn't try. After a second
of agonizing hesitation he fell back and was lost in the ranks.

"Hyperion!" The Hierarch's whisper was almost a scream
now. And the silence on the platform had taken on a quality
of relentlessness that seemed inflexibly cruel even though I
had as yet no idea what it was about.

There was a small seething among the priests to the left. If
Hyperion were trying to respond, there seemed plenty to prevent him. Hyperion, like Flammand, subsided. And the priesthood, like the people, in that moment firmly and finally rejected
their Hierarch.

He stood there, swaying, his head down, shooting glances
of rage and helpless hatred at the ranks of the priesthood which
had been his to command until a moment ago, which by some
mysterious alchemy of their own had simultaneously decided
to defy him.

It was very curious, that moment. Before it the Hierarch
had ruled a world. After it, all in one instant, something inexplicable had happened and he was helpless.

He rolled his small, agonized eyes from face to face. He
lowered his head between the heavy golden shoulders and it
seemed to me he was about to lumber forward with his bulldozer gait to crush down opposition and force obedience again.
But the opposition was too intangible for crushing. He couldn't
crush a world. There was only one thing left which he could
trample under, if he hoped to save his face—

Looking back now, I can see that he had no real choice. It
wasn't only that the world he had ruled without question all
his life suddenly presented an unbroken front of flat rebellion
to him. There's just the barest possibility that if he'd attacked
the rebellion openly he might have breached it and lived. I
don't think he could have succeeded, but he might have.

There was much more to his surrender than that. Because
to overcome the opposition he'd have had to expose his own
trickery. He'd have had to stand self-confessed before the people and the priests as a murderer, a liar and a blasphemer against
Alchemy. And that he couldn't do. *Hubris* can be a force for
good as well as for evil in such a case as his. Unwittingly, I'd
given him a choice between death and glory, or life and dis-

grace, and once he realized what the choice was he never faltered.

For what he did then I had to concede him respect. He straightened, throwing his fat shoulders back so that the golden robes swung magnificently. There was a definite note of baiting in the farewells that roared from the crowd below now. But as he lifted his head they slackened a little to see what he would do.

He made them all a stiff, proud bow.

The little byplay on the platform had been lost upon the throng, who could neither hear nor see it. But something in the attitude of the Hierarch and the priests seemed to convey to them at least that something was about to happen which they didn't expect.

The baiting note faded from their yells, but the volume of the noise did not slacken. They meant him to go. There was a dogged quality in their voices that would not cease while he stood here in their world. He would not again hear any sound in Malesco except the roaring of the people urging him toward Paradise.

There was nothing left for him to do but accept the honor and the glory that was being thrust upon him. He turned with a regal sweep of his robes and with sudden firmness strode unhesitatingly toward the Earth-Gates. He knew what he was doing. He knew better than any of us just then. But he never faltered.

He moved like a juggernaut to the last. He'd always crushed opposition. Now, when it was his own life that stood in the way of the prestige he'd built up and lived by for so long, his *hubris* sustained him and he crushed that, too. He rolled forward with grim pride, refusing to depart from Malesco in anything less than the full dignity of his office. In his own way he was magnificent.

With majestic stride he stepped up on the brink of the Earth-Gates. The blurred sounds of New York traffic and the blurred motions of the lights flickered in his very face as he stood there. He did not hesitate or look back. He raised one arm in a gesture of farewell to the watchers and stepped forward over the threshold.

The last sound he heard must have been the roar of his people driving him out of Malesco and into Paradise.

The people couldn't see what we saw, on the dais. He'd planned it that way naturally. He hadn't wanted anybody but the priests to see the trap he'd set for Lorna and me.

He'd had no intention of letting living people return to New York and open the way for more angels from Paradise. He'd had trouble enough as it was. So the Earth-Gates were set to insure that no living person could pass between the worlds.

There was a flare of bright gold when he touched the surface of the screen. The flare was blinding. From below, in the hall, all anybody could see was the upper area of the flash. But from where I stood I saw the figure in the gleaming robes pause for an instant between two worlds, in that singing void I remembered so well myself. He was balanced on the crossbar of the Alchemic A, in effect, the bridge narrow under his feet.

Then fire sprang out all around him.

I saw the golden robes catch and go up in colored flames. I saw his hair catch and burn like a crown. But when the fire took hold on the man himself its brilliance increased suddenly a hundredfold, and the Hierarch vanished in a furnace glare which no one who watched could endure to gaze at.

I shut my eyes. Inside the lids for a moment or two the outlines of the burning man were etched clearly, an after-image incised by the brilliance of the flame that destroyed him. He stood in full outline upon my inner lids for longer than the man himself stood in his own body. I think he was consumed and destroyed before his image faded against my closed eyes.

And that's how it happened that Lorna Maxwell and I stepped through onto the corner of Fifth Avenue and Forty-Second Street at three in the morning, dressed in fantastic garments. The lumbering buses and the stone lions were a lot less real to us than the world we'd just left.

When you think about it you have to realize that a lot of clichés are self-fulfilling by definition. Given a particular setup plus a particular stimulus, the chances are strong that a particular result will follow, trite because it's more or less inevitable. It wasn't yet dawn in Malesco when we fulfilled our own cliché and rounded out the ceremony by departing with full grandeur through the Earth-Gates, back to Paradise.

Of course I could have made a speech before I left. I could have said, "There's no point in making a ceremony of this because your whole religion is based on a fraud. New York's no more a Paradise than Malesco. The theory of reincarnation is stultifying and alchemy as a religion isn't going to get you anywhere no matter how hard you try."

They would probably have mobbed me if I'd said it. You can't change the thinking patterns of a world overnight by administering a few home truths. It will be a long slow subtle process if it takes place at all. That's Coriole's problem, to be tackled sometime in the future. His immediate problem that night was to get rid of Lorna and me quickly.

I had played Prometheus and my part was over. Lorna had been too much the tool of the Hierarch to be welcome in Malesco. The sooner we were shunted back to Paradise and the Earth-Gates firmly closed behind us, the better.

So we left Malesco. And the gates were closed. I doubt if they will open again in our lifetime. The things that are going on behind them now are probably very interesting and exciting—for Malescans—but they're no business of ours. Coriole knows what he wants and traffic with Earth isn't on the list.

We left the rose-red city in the throes of its own revolution and came home to Paradise.

Epilogue

SHE calls herself Malesca now. You can see why.

And she's beautiful, all right. Probably her press agent's telling the truth when he says she's the most beautiful girl in the world—if you like that kind of beauty. It's saccharine. I know I couldn't live with it myself.

Still, the Malescan priesthood knew what it was doing. They were clever psychologists. They worked out all the features that would appeal most strongly to Malescans—who are extremely human.

Pygmalion fell in love with Galatea, didn't he? Even though he knew she was nothing but a chunk of stone. But the beauty that shaped the stone was irresistible.

Lorna says she loves me. That began a long time ago, before

the episode in Malesco. She says she hadn't changed. But she has, of course. Malesco changed her quite a lot.

She had nothing I wanted before the change and the essential Lorna, the woman behind all that beauty, is exactly the same. I know it. I wish I could forget it. The forces that drive a man or a nation or a world are inarguable. I can't fight them, myself. I wish I could.

Because blast all clichés—I love her. In my own way. After a fashion. I couldn't live with her. You know what she's like. And that's why I'd never have gone to the place that night if I'd known she was singing there.

But I sat clinking ice in my glass, listening to Malesca sing. They gave her a beautiful voice. I kept repeating axioms to myself to drown out the sweetness of the song that was hypnotizing everyone else in the room. "Beauty is only skin deep," I thought. "Handsome is as handsome does. A bird in the hand—"

Applause in a sudden storm interrupted me. I looked up to see Malesca bowing, making every motion a symphony of grace. Her luminous blue eyes were searching the dimness for me, bewildered and determined as they always were whenever she looked at me.

She wasn't going to accept refusal. She was going to come to me again as soon as the applause stopped. She was going to sit down beside me and plead again in that lovely throaty voice, soft as velvet and sweet as honey.

I finished my drink in one quick gulp, jumped up and started toward the exit. Behind me the applause died and I heard Malesca's voice calling, "Eddie, *Eddie!*"

When I reached the door I was almost running.

VALLEY
OF
THE
FLAME

I

FACE OF A GIRL

FAR OFF in the jungle an animal screamed. A river-moth flapped against the screen, nearly as large as a fruit-bat. And very far away, subsensory, almost, Brian Raft could hear the low pulsing of drums. Not unusual, drums on the Jutahy, in the great valley of Amazonas. But these were no signal messages.

Raft wasn't an imaginative man. He left all that to Dan Craddock, with his Welsh ghosts and his shadow-people of the lost centuries. Still, Raft was a doctor, and when those drums throbbed in the jungle something curious happened here in his little hospital of plastic shacks, smelling of antiseptic. Something he couldn't ignore.

When a sick man's blood beats in rhythm with the distant drums, slow or fast as the far-off echoes set the pace, a doctor has reason to wonder. . . .

The great moth beat softly against the screen. Craddock bent over a sterilizer, steam clouding up around his white head so that he looked like a necromancer stooping over a cauldron. The drums throbbed on. Raft could feel his own heart answering to their rhythm.

He glanced at Craddock again and tried not to remember what the older man had been telling him about his wild Welsh ancestors and the things they had believed. Sometimes he thought Craddock believed them too, or half believed, at least when he had been drinking.

135

He'd got to know Craddock pretty well in the months they had worked together, but he realized that even yet he knew only the surface Craddock, that another man entirely lived in abeyance behind the companionable front which the Welshman showed him, a man with memories he never spoke of, and stories he never told.

This experimental station, far up the Jutahy, was a curious contrast, with its asepsis and its plastics and its glitter of new instruments, to the jungle hemming it in. They were on assignment just now to find a specific for atypical malaria.

In the forty years since the end of World War II, nothing yet had been discovered any safer than the old quinine and atabrine treatment, and Raft was sifting the jungle lore now to make sure there might not be some truth in the old Indio knowledge, hidden behind masks of devil-worship and magic.

He had hunted down virus diseases in Tibet, Indo-China, Madagascar, and he had learned to respect much that the witch-doctors knew. Some of their treatments were based on very sound theories.

But he wished the drums would stop. He turned irritably from the window and glanced once more at Craddock, who was humming a Welsh ballad under his breath. A ballad full of wild, skirling music about ghosts and fighting.

Craddock had talked a lot lately—since the drums began—about ghosts and fighting. He said he smelled danger. In the old days in Wales men could always scent trouble in the wind, and they'd drink quarts of uisquebaugh and go out brandishing swords, ready for anything. All Raft could smell was the reek of disinfectant that filled the little hospital.

And all the wind brought to him was the sound of drums.

"In the old days," Craddock said suddenly, looking up from the sterilizer and blinking through steam, "there'd be a whisper in the air from Tralee or Cobh, and we knew the Irish were coming over the water to raid. Or maybe there'd be something from the south, and we'd get ready for the men of Cornwall. But we'd know. We'd know."

"Rot!" Raft said.

"Okay. But I felt something like this once before." Craddock sucked in his breath, a curious look of fright and incredulity on his wrinkled brown face. He turned back to the steam-cloud, and Raft watched him in puzzled wonder.

There was a mystery about Craddock. He was a biologist, and a good one, but for thirty years or more he had hung around the Jutahy country, never venturing farther away than Manaos, living precariously as a sort of jungle general practitioner.

Raft had added him to the party on impulse, since Craddock knew the country and the natives. He hadn't expected too much of the Welshman in the laboratory, for something had happened to Craddock's hands—they were badly maimed. But he was pleasantly disappointed on that score.

Raft watched the mutilated hands working with hypodermics, twisting plunger from tube, deftly pulling the hollow needles free. Craddock had three fingers on one hand, and the other was a claw, with oddly stained and textured skin. He never spoke of what had happened. His injuries didn't look like the scars of acid burns or animal teeth. Still, he was surprisingly deft, even when liquor was heavy on his breath.

It was heavy now, and Raft thought the man must be deliberately timing his motions to the rhythms of the drums. Or perhaps not. Raft himself had to pause consciously and break step with the beat. And some of the sick men in the ward were alive, he thought, solely because the drum-beats would not let their hearts stop pumping.

"A week now," Craddock said, with that rather annoying habit he had of catching another man's thought, or seeming to. "Have you noticed the charts?"

Raft ran a nervous forefinger along the lean line of his jaw. "That's my job," he grunted.

Craddock sighed.

"You haven't lived in Brazil as long as I have, Brian. It's the things you don't usually notice that count. Up to a week ago, this plague was killing off the Indians fast. The vitality level's gone up a lot in the last seven days."

"Which is crazy," Raft told him. "It's accidental—just a cycle. There's no reason. The drums have nothing to do with it."

"Did I mention drums?"

Raft glared.

Craddock put the hypos in the sterilizer and closed the lid.

"The drums aren't talking, though. It's not Western Union. It's just rhythm. And it means something."

"What?"

The Welshman hesitated. His face was in shadow, and his white hair gleamed like a fluffy halo in the overhead light. "I think, maybe, there's a visitor in the forest. I wonder now. Have you ever heard of Curupuri?"

Raft's face was a mask.

"Curupuri? What's that?"

"A name. The natives have been talking about Curupuri. Or maybe you haven't been listening."

"I seem to miss a lot around here," Raft said with heavy irony. "I haven't seen a ghost for months."

"Maybe you will." Craddock turned to stare toward the window. "Thirty years. It's a long time. I—I've heard of Curupuri before, though. I even—"

He stopped, and Raft breathed deeply. He'd heard too, but he didn't want to admit it. Superstition is apt to be psychologically dangerous in the jungle, and Raft knew that Curupuri was a widespread belief among the Indios. He'd encountered it ten years ago, when he was younger and more impressionable. And yet, he thought, it's the only possible god for the Amazon Basin.

For Curupuri was the Unknown. He was the blind, ravening, terrible life-force that the Indios think is the spirit of the jungle. A savage, primeval Pan, lairing in the darkness. But nothing so concrete as Pan.

Curupuri moved along the Amazon as vast and inchoate and yet as tangible as life itself. Here in the jungle one realizes, after a while, that a god of life can be far more terrible than a god of death. The Amazonas is too alive. Too enormous for the mind to comprehend, a great green living thing sprawled across a continent, blind, senseless, ravenously alive.

Yes, Raft could understand why the Indios had personified Curupuri. He could almost see him as they did, a monstrous shapeless creature, neither beast nor man, stirring enormously in the breathing fertility of the jungle.

"The devil with it," Raft said, and drew deeply on his cigarette. It was one of his last cigarettes. He moved to Craddock's side and stared out the window, drawing smoke gratefully into his lungs and savoring the second-hand taste of civilization.

That was all they'd had for a year—second-hand civilization. It wasn't too bad. Madagascar had been worse. But there was quite a contrast between the sleek modern architecture of the home base, the Mallard Pathological Institute overlooking the Hudson, and this plastic-walled collection of shacks, staffed by a few Institute men and some native helpers.

Three white men, Raft, Craddock, and Bill Merriday, were here. Merriday was plodding but a good research pathologist, and the three of them had worked well together.

Now the work was ready to be wound up, and presently Raft knew he'd be in New York again, rushing by air-taxi from roof night-club to club, cramming the excitement of civilization into as short a time as possible. Then a little later, he realized, he'd be feeling a familiar itch again, and would be heading for Tasmania or Ceylon or—somewhere. There were always new jobs to be tackled.

The drums were still throbbing faintly, far off in the dark. After a while Raft left Craddock in the lighted lab and wandered outside, down to the river, trying not to listen to the distant pulse of sound. . . .

A full moon rode up from the Atlantic, brightening the great pleasure-city of Rio, swinging up the Amazon to the backlands, a huge yellow disc against a starry backdrop. But across the Jutahy was the jungle, black towering walls of it, creeping and swarming with a vitality that was incredible even to a scientist. It was the fecund womb of the world.

Hot countries mean growth, but in the Amazonas is growth gone wild. Its rich alluvial soil, washed down for ages along the rivers, is literally alive; the ground beneath your feet moves and stirs with vitality. There is something unhealthy about such abnormal rioting life, unhealthy as the flaming Brazilian orchids that batten on rottenness and blaze in the green gloom like goblin corpse-lights. . . .

Raft thought of Craddock. Odd! That inexplicable mixture of incredulity and fear that Raft thought he sensed in the Welshman was puzzling. There was something else, too. He frowned, trying to analyze a vague shadow, and at length nodded, satisfied. Craddock was repelled by the drums but he was also drawn, attracted by them in some strange way. Well, Craddock had lived in this part of the forest for a long time. He was nearly Indio in many ways.

Something moving out on the surface of the river, sheet-silver under the moon, roused Raft from uncomfortable thoughts. In a moment he could see the outlines of a small boat, and two heads silhouetted against the silvery water. The men were pulling in toward shore and the hospital's lighted window.

"Luiz!" Raft called sharply. "Manoel! We've got visitors."

A feeble hail came across the water, and he saw the two outlines slump down, as if the last efforts of exhaustion had brought them to the landing. Then came excitement—the boys running with lights and shouts, everybody who could walk swarming to the doors and windows to watch. Raft helped beach the boat and superintended as the two almost unconscious men were carried up to the hospital.

One of them, he saw, wore an aviator's helmet and clothing; he was beyond speech. The other, a slender, bearded man, rather startlingly graceful even in this extremity, lurched toward the door.

"Senhor, senhor," he murmured, in a soft voice.

Craddock came out to help. He stopped dead still on the threshold, though crowding bodies hid the two arrivals from sight. Raft saw a look of absolute panic come over the Welsh-man's face. Then Craddock turned and retreated, and there was the nervous clinking of a bottle.

Bill Merriday's stolid, intent features were comfortingly normal by contrast. But as Merriday, bending over the aviator, was stripping off the man's shirt, he suddenly paused.

"I'll be hanged," he said. "I know this chap, Brian. Thomas, wait a minute. I'll have it. Da something . . . da Fonseca, that's it! I told you about that mapping expedition that flew in a couple of months ago, when you were in the jungle. Da Fonseca was piloting."

"Crack-up," Raft said. "What about the other man?"

Merriday glanced over his shoulder.

"I never saw him before."

The thermometer read eighty-six, far below normal.

"Shock and exhaustion," Raft surmised. "We'll run a stat C.B.C., just in case. Look at his eyes." He pulled back a lid. The pupils were pin-points.

"I'll take a look at the other man," Merriday said, turning. Raft scowled down at da Fonseca, a little uncomfortable, though he could not have said exactly why. Something seemed to have entered the room with the two men, and it was nothing that could be felt tangibly. But it could be sensed.

Frowning, Raft watched Luiz milk a specimen from the patient's finger. The overhead light fell yellow and unsteady on da Fonseca, upon a glitter of sudden brilliance from something that hung on a chain about his neck. Raft had thought it a religious medal, but now he saw that it was a tiny mirror, no larger than a half-dollar. He picked it up.

The glass was convex, lenticular, and made of a dark, bluish material less like glass than plastic. Raft glimpsed the cloudy, shapeless motion of shadows beneath its surface.

A little shock went through him. The mirror did not reflect his face, though he was staring directly into it. Instead he saw turbulent motion, though there was no such motion in the room. He thought of storm-clouds boiling and driving before a gale. He had the curious, inexplicable feeling of something familiar, an impression, an inchoate mental pattern.

Thomas da Fonseca. He caught the extraordinary impression, for a flashing, brilliant moment, that he was looking into da Fonseca's eyes. The—the personality of the man was there, suddenly. It was as though the two men were briefly en rapport.

Yet all Raft saw was the driving, cloudy motion in the mirror.

Then the storm-swirl rifted and was driven apart. From the tiny lens in his hand a vibration ran up the nerves of his arm, striking into his brain. He stared down.

Now that the clouds had cleared away, it was not a mirror, but a portrait. A portrait? Then a living portrait, for the face within it moved. . . .

A mirror, after all, then. But no—for that was certainly not his own face that looked back at him out of the small oval.

It was a girl's face, seen against a background of incredible richness and strangeness that vanished as he looked, because she leaned forward as if into the very mirror itself, her head blotting out the remarkable background. And it was no painted picture. She moved, she saw—Raft. He drew his breath in sharply.

* * *

There was never such a face before. He had no time to see her very clearly, for the whole unbelievable glimpse was gone in an instant. But he would have known her out of a thousand faces if they ever met again.

The look of delicate gayety and wickedness in the small, prim curve of her mouth, the enormous translucent eyes, colored like aquamarines, that looked, for a moment, into his very solemnly above the sweet, malicious, smiling mouth.

There could be no other face like it in the world.

Then the mists rolled between them as they stared. Raft remembered later that he shook the lens passionately in a childish attempt to call her back, shook it as if his own hands could part those clouds again and let him see that brilliantly alive little face, so gay and solemn, so wicked and so sweet.

But she was gone. It had all happened almost between one breath and the next, and he was left standing there staring down at the lens and remembering the tantalizing—oddness—of that face.

An oddness seen too briefly to understand except as something curiously wrong about the girl who had looked into his eyes for one fraction of a second. Her hair had been—odd.

The eyes themselves were almost round, but subtly slanted at the corners, and with a blackness ringing them that was not wholly the black of thick lashes, for a prolonged dark streak had run up from their outer corners a little way, accentuating their slant, and giving a faint Egyptian exoticism to the round, soft, dainty face with its rounded chin. So soft—he remembered that impression clearly. Incredibly soft, she had looked, and fastidious.

And wrong. Racially wrong.

The mirror was blank again, and filled with the trembling fogs. But, very briefly, it had opened upon another world.

II

DRUMBEAT OF DEATH

Luiz was staring at Raft in surprise.

"S'nhor?" Luiz said.

"What?" Raft answered.

"Did you speak?"

"No." Raft let the lens fall back on da Fonseca's bare chest.

Merriday was at his side. "The other man won't let me look at him," he said worriedly. "He's stubborn."

"I'll talk to him," Raft said. He went out, trying not to think about that lens, that lovely, impossible face. Subjective, of course, not objective. Hallucination—or self-hypnosis, with the light reflecting in the mirror as a focal point. But he didn't believe that really.

The bearded man was in Raft's office, examining a row of bottles on a shelf—fetal specimens. He turned and bowed, a faint mockery in his eyes. Raft was impressed; this was no ordinary backwoods wanderer. There was a courtliness about him, and a smooth-knit, muscular grace that gave the impression of fine breeding in both manners and lineage. He had also an air of hardly concealed excitement and a certain hauteur in his poise which Raft did not like.

"Saludades, s'nhor," he said, his too-bright eyes dazzling in the light. Fever, perhaps, behind that brilliant stare. His voice was deep, and he spoke with an odd, plaintive undertone that held a distant familiarity. "I am in your debt."

His Portuguese was faulty, but one didn't notice that. Raft had a feeling of gaucherie, entirely new to him.

"You can pay it right now," he said brusquely. "We don't want the station contaminated, and you may have caught something up-river. Take off your shirt and let's have a look at you."

"I am not ill, *doutor*."

"You recover fast, then. You were ready to pass out when you came into the hospital."

The black eyes flashed wickedly. Then the man shrugged

and slipped out of the ragged shirt. Raft was a little startled at the smooth power in his sleek body, the muscles rippling under a skin like brown satin, but rippling very smoothly, so that until he moved you hardly realized they were there.

"I am Paulo da Costa Pereira," said the man. He seemed faintly amused. "I am a garimpeiro."

"A diamond-hunter, eh?" Raft slipped a thermometer between Pereira's lips. "Didn't know they had diamonds around here. I should think you'd be in the Rio Francisco country."

There was no response. Raft used his stethoscope, shook his head and tried again. He checked his findings by Pereira's pulse, but that didn't help much. The man's heart wasn't beating, nor did he apparently have a pulse.

"What the devil!" Raft said, staring. He took out the thermometer and licked dry lips. Da Fonseca's temperature had been below normal but Pereira's was so far above normal that the mercury pushed the glass above 108°, the highest the glass tube could register.

Pereira was wiping his mouth delicately. "I am hungry, s'nhor," he said. "Could you give me some food?"

"I'll give you a glucose injection," Raft said, hesitating a little. "Or—I'm not sure. Your metabolism's haywire. At the rate you're burning up body-fuel, you'll be ill."

"I have always been this way. I am healthy enough."

"Not if your heart isn't beating," Raft said grimly. "I suppose you know that you're—you're impossible? I mean, by rights you shouldn't be alive."

Pereira smiled.

"Perhaps you don't hear my heartbeat. I assure you that it's beating."

"If it's that faint, it can't be pumping any blood down your aorta," Raft said. "Something's plenty wrong with you. Lie down on that couch. We'll need ice-packs to bring your temperature down."

Pereira shrugged and obeyed. "I am hungry."

"We'll take care of that. I'll need some of your blood, too."

"No."

Raft swore, his temper and nerves flaring, "You're sick. Or don't you know it?"

"Very well," Pereira murmured. "But be quick. I dislike being—handled."

* * *

With an effort, Raft restrained an angry retort. He drew the necessary blood into a test-tube and capped it.

"Dan!" he called. There was no answer.

Where the devil was Craddock?

He summoned Luiz and handed him the test-tube. "Give this to *Doutor* Craddock. I want a stat C.B.C." He turned back to Pereira. "What's the matter with you? Lie back."

But the diamond-hunter was sitting up, his face alive and alight with a wild, excited elation. The jet eyes were enormous. For a second Raft watched that stare. Then the glow went out of Pereira's eyes and he lay back, smiling to himself.

Raft busied himself with ice-bags. "What happened up-river?"

"I don't know," Pereira said, still smiling. "Da Fonseca blundered into my camp one night. I suppose his plane crashed. He couldn't talk much."

"Were you alone?"

"Yes, I was alone."

That was odd, but Raft let it pass. He had other things on his mind—the insane impossibility of a living man whose heart did not beat. Ice-cubes clinked.

"You a Brazilian? You don't talk the lingo too well."

The feverishly brilliant eyes narrowed.

"I have been in the jungle a long time," the man said. "Speaking other tongues. When you do not use a language, you lose it." He nodded toward the bottles on the wall. "Yours, doctor?"

"Yes. Fetal specimens. Embryonic studies. Interested?"

"I know too little to be interested. The jungle is my—my province. Though the sources of life—"

He paused.

Raft waited, but he did not go on. The strange eyes closed.

Raft found that his fingers were shaking as he screwed the tops on the ice-bags.

"That thing da Fonseca wears around his neck," he said, quite softly. "What is it?"

"I had not noticed," Pereira murmured. "I have had a difficult day. If I might rest, it would be nice."

Raft grimaced. He stared down at that cryptic, inhuman figure, remembering the odd malformation of the clavicle he had felt during his examination, remembering other things. Some impulse made him say, "One last question. What's your race? Your ancestors weren't Portuguese?"

Pereira opened his eyes and showed his teeth in an impatient smile that was near to a snarl.

"Ancestors!" he said irritably. "Forget my ancestors for to-night, doutor. I have come a long way through the jungle, if you must know it. A long, long way, past many interesting sights. Wild beasts, and ruins, and wild men, and the drums were beating all the way." His voice lowered. "I passed your ancestors chattering and scratching themselves in the trees," he said in a purring murmur. "And I passed my ancestors, too." The voice trailed off in an indescribably complacent sound. After a moment of deep silence, he said, "I would like to sleep. May I be alone?"

Raft set his teeth. Delirium, of course. That accounted for the senseless rambling. But that imperious dismissal was intrinsic in the man himself.

Now he gathered his rags about him as if they had been ermine. He seemed to fall asleep almost instantly. From his recumbent form there breathed out a tremendous vitality that set Raft's nerves jangling.

He turned away. A heartbeat so faint that it was imperceptible? Ridiculous. Some new disease, more likely, though its symptoms were contradictory. Pereira seemed in perfect health, and yet he obviously couldn't be.

There might be another answer. A mutation? One of those curious, specialized human beings that appear occasionally in the race? Raft moved his mouth impatiently. He went back to check on the aviator, conscious of a queer, rustling alertness permeating the hospital, as though the coming of the two men had roused the place from sleep to wakefulness.

There was no change in da Fonseca, and Merriday was busy with stimulants. Raft grunted approval and went in search of Craddock.

Halfway down the hall he stopped at the sound of a familiar voice. The diamond-hunter's low, smooth tones, urgent now, and commanding.

"I return this to you. I have come very far to do it, s'nhor."

And Dan Craddock replying in a stumbling whisper that held amazement and fear.

"But you weren't there! There was nothing there, except—"

"We came later," Pereira said. "By the sun and the waters we guessed. Then at last we had the answer."

Raft let out his breath. A board creaked under him. Simultaneously he heard a—a sound, a susurrus of faint wind, and felt a sense of inexplicable motion.

Startled, he hurried forward. The passage lay blankly empty before him. Nothing could have left the laboratory without his knowledge. But when he stood on the threshold he faced Craddock, and Craddock alone, staring in blank, astounded paralysis at nothing.

Quickly Raft searched the room with his eyes. It was empty. The window screens were still in place, and, moreover, were so rusted that they could not be removed without considerable noise.

"Where's Pereira?" he asked curtly.

Craddock turned to face him, jaw slack. "Who?"

"The man you were just talking to."

"I—I—there was nobody here."

"Yeah," Raft said. "So I'm crazy. That wouldn't surprise me, after what's happened already tonight." He noticed a booklet in Craddock's hand, a ring-bound notebook with its leather cover moulded and discolored by age. The Welshman hastily stuffed it into his pocket. Avoiding Raft's probing eyes, he nodded toward the microscope.

"There's the blood. I must have bungled it somehow. It's all wrong." Yet he didn't seem unduly surprised.

Raft put his eye to the lens. His lips tightened.

"So I am crazy," he said.

"It is funny, isn't it?" Craddock said, inadequately.

It was more than funny. It was appalling. The vascular system has certain types of blood cells floating free, of course; they have a definite form and purpose, and intruding organisms may affect them in various ways.

But this specimen on the slide showed something Raft had never seen before. The red cells were oval instead of disc-shaped, and in place of the whites there were ciliated organisms that moved with a writhing, erratic motion.

And moving fast—too fast!

"They've slowed down a lot since I first looked," Craddock said. "In the beginning they were spinning so quickly I couldn't even see them."

"But what sort of bug would do that? It's destroyed the phagocytes. Pereira ought to be dead, if he hasn't a white blood cell in his body. No, there's a mistake somewhere. We'd better run some reagent tests."

They did, going through the routine, but found nothing. To every test they could devise, the reaction was that of apparently normal blood. Furthermore, the writhing ciliate things seemed not to be malignant. When toxic matter was introduced the ciliates formed a barrier of their own hairy bodies, just as phagocytes should have done, but three times as effective.

A specimen slide glittered and trembled in Craddock's mutilated hand.

"It's an improvement," he said. "Those bugs are better than whites."

"But where are the whites?"

"Deus, how should I know?" Craddock's fingers slid into the pocket where he had placed that discolored notebook. "I'm not in charge here—you are. This is your problem."

"I wonder if it is," Raft said slowly. "Just what was there about the—sun and the waters?"

Craddock hesitated. Then a wry, crooked smile twisted his mouth.

"They appeared quite normal to me," he said. And, turning on his heel, was gone.

Raft stared after him. What was behind this? Craddock obviously knew Pereira. Though how that interview had been held, Raft did not know. Ventriloquism? He snorted at the thought. No, Pereira had been in the laboratory with Craddock, and then he had, seemingly, walked through solid walls.

Which meant—what?

Raft turned to the microscope again. There was no help there. In the sane, modern world of 1985 there was simply no place for such irrationalities. Incidentally, where was Pereira now?

He wasn't in the office where Raft had left him. And as Raft hesitated on the doorway, he heard a sound that brought blood pumping into his temples. He felt as though the subtle, half-sensed hints of wrongness had suddenly exploded into action.

It was merely the faint pop-popping of exhaust, but there was no reason for the motor launch to be going out at this hour.

Raft headed for the river. He paused to seize a flashlight. There were faint shouts. Others had caught the sound of the engine too. Merriday's bulky form loomed on the bank.

Raft leveled the light and sent the beam flashing out into that pit of shadows. The smooth surface of the river glinted like a stream of diamonds. He swung the beam.

There was the motor launch, ploughing a black furrow in the shining water as it melted away into the gloom where the flashlight's rays could not penetrate.

But just as it vanished the light caught one full gleam upon a face—Pereira's face, laughing back across his shoulder, white teeth glittering in the velvety beard. Triumph was arrogant in his laughter, the elation Raft had sensed before.

There was someone with him; Raft found it impossible to make out who that someone was. The Indios were running along the cleared bank, and a couple of them had put out in a canoa, but that wouldn't help. Raft drew the pistol he always carried in the jungle. The thought of sending a bullet after that arrogant, laughing face was very pleasant.

"No, Brian!" Merriday said, and pulled down his arm.

"But he's getting away with our boat!"

"Dan Craddock's with him," Merriday said. "Didn't you see?"

The pop-popping of the motor was fainter now, dying into the dim murmur of the Jutahy drums. Raft stood motionless, feeling bewildered and helpless.

"Nothing we can do till morning, anyway," he said presently. "Let's go back inside."

Then a voice he did not know jabbered something in Portuguese.

"He has gone back to his own land—and he has taken something with him."

Raft flashed the light up into the face of the aviator, da Fonseca, his flyer's cap gripped in one hand as he fumbled at his throat, groping, searching. The pupils of his eyes were no longer tiny. They were huge.

"Taken what?" Merriday said.

"My soul," da Fonseca said quite simply.

There was a moment of stillness. And in that pause da Fonseca's words fell with nightmare clarity.

"I had it in a little mirror around my neck. He put it there. It gave him the power to—to—" The thin, breathless voice faded.

"To do what?" Raft asked.

"To make men slaves," the aviator whispered. "As he did with the doutor."

Craddock! Raft had a sudden insane relief that the Welshman had not, then, gone off willingly with Pereira, in some mysterious unfathomed partnership. Then he was furious with himself for instantly accepting such a fantastic explanation from a man so obviously mad.

Yet it was an explanation. There seemed to be no other.

"Let me down," da Fonseca said, stirring against the hands that held him upright. "Without my soul I cannot stay here long."

"Carry him inside," Raft said. "Bill, get a hypo. Adrenalin."

Da Fonseca had collapsed completely by the time he was laid gently on a cot. His heart had stopped. Merriday came running with a syringe.

He had put on a long needle, guessing Raft's intention.

Raft made the injection directly into the heart muscle. Then he waited, stethoscope ready. He was conscious of something—different. Something changed.

Abruptly he knew what it was. The drums. They were louder, shouting, triumphant. Their beat was like the throbbing of a monster heart—of the jungle's heart, dark and immense.

Da Fonseca responded. Raft heard the soft pounding through the instrument, and those heart-beats were timed exactly to the rhythm of the Jutahy drums. His lids lifted slowly. His voice was hollow, chanting.

"He goes back now—and the gate of Doirada opens to his coming—He goes back—to the sleeping Flame. By the unseen road, where the devils of Paititi watch at the gate of Doirada. . . ."

Louder roared the drums. Louder beat da Fonseca's heart. His voice grew stronger.

"The sun was wrong. And the river was slow—too slow. There was a devil there, under the ice. It was—was—"

He tore again at his throat, gasping for breath. His eyes held madness.

"Curupuri!" he screamed, and the drums crashed an echo. And were still.

There was silence, blank and empty. As though at a signal, the Jutahy drums had stopped.

Da Fonseca fell back like a dead man on the cot. Raft, sweat cold on his skin, leaned forward, searching with his stethoscope at the bared chest.

He heard nothing.

Then, far out in the jungle, a drum muttered once and was still.

Da Fonseca's dead heart stirred with it.

And fell silent.

III

GATE TO PAITITI

WITH FIVE INDIOS Dr. Brian Raft went up the Jutahy after Craddock and Pereira. He went with his lips thinned grimly, and a deep doubt in his mind. Merriday he left at the base hospital, to wind up the experiment and send the records back to the Institute.

"You can't go alone," Merriday had said. "You're crazy, Brian."

Raft nodded.

"Maybe. But we worked with Dan for nearly a year, and he's a white man. As for Pereira, sometimes I'm not entirely sure that he was a—man."

Stolid Merriday blinked.

"Oh, but that's nonsense."

"I told you what happened. He had no heartbeat. His temperature was crazy. And the way he walked through the laboratory wall wasn't strictly normal, was it?"

"Da Fonseca said some queer things before he died, too. You're not starting to believe them, are you?"

"No," Raft said. "Not yet. Not without a devil of a lot of proof. Just the same, I wish I'd got a chance at that notebook of Craddock's. Pereira said he was returning it. And that stuff about the sun and the river being too slow. Two people mentioned that, you know; da Fonseca and Pereira. Moreover, Dan seemed to understand what it meant."

"More than I do," Merriday grunted. "It's dangerous for you to go up-river alone."

"I've got a hunch Craddock went up-river, a long time ago. What he found there is a mystery." Raft shook his head. "I don't know. I just don't know, Bill. Anyway, they didn't have much fuel aboard, and I think I can catch up with them."

"I wish you'd let me go with you."

But Raft wouldn't agree to that. In the end, he went out alone, the Indios paddling the big canoe untiringly up against the current. He had supplies—what he could get hastily together—and guns and ammunition. The natives helped him find Pereira's track. For, all too soon, the diamond-hunter left the river.

"Two men walking," Luiz said, eyeing the underbrush.

Walking. That meant either that Craddock was going willingly now, or else there was force being employed. Hypnosis, perhaps, Raft thought, remembering the lens-mirror. More and more often now he recalled the exotic, paradoxical face of the girl. How she tied into the mystery he could not guess, but remembrance of her made him more willing to seek out the solution.

So they went westward toward the Ecuadorian border, where a thousand little rivers rise to pour into the great Solimoes that feeds the Amazon itself. Ten days and ten nights they traveled. . . .

On the eleventh morning the Indios were gone, even the faithful Luiz. No sound, no alarm—but Raft was alone when he woke. Perhaps they had deserted. Perhaps the jaguars had got them. The beasts had been holding a devil's sabbath in the forest during the night. Raft didn't find any traces.

His lips drew down more grimly, and he went on, slower

because tracking was hard work, for another ten days. He pushed on doggedly through the green breathing walls of the silent jungle, which pulsated with invisible life—never sure that the next turn of the way might not bring him face to face with the deadly giboya, or one of the omnipresent jaguars, or Pereira himself.

He could not have done it at all except for the years of rigorous outdoor life and tropical experience. But he kept on his quarry's track.

Then, in the end, he found what the dying da Fonseca had called the unseen road.

The day before, from the height of a crest—he was getting into mountains—he had seen the great valley, an immense horizon-reaching bowl of fertile forest stretching further than his eye could follow. It was an ocean of moving green. But the track led down into it.

There was a roughly circular space down there where the shade of green was different. It must be very large, for it was far away—miles in diameter. Partly it seemed to be cupped between mountains, and Raft caught the flash of a river far off circling around the nearer curve of it. Perhaps fifty miles in diameter, the place was, but distances are deceptive in the forest. He followed the trail, and it led him directly toward that oasis of green within the green.

Raft had stood the trip well. His face was more deeply seamed, his eyes were red-rimmed, yet he felt little weakness. A sound medical knowledge helped him there. Fevers were rife in this country. Fevers, but no Indios. Animals only, and chiefly the jaguars.

Animals! The place swarmed with life, Raft thought wearily. Everything around him was movement, the bright flutter of insects and brilliant birds, the watery gliding of a snake rippling to cover, the smooth, furtive motion of the big cats, the erratic hysteria of tapir or peccary. All about him was the jungle itself, like a vast composite animal, terribly alive.

Then, in a clearing, he saw plainly the tracks he had been following. Craddock's, and the diamond-hunter's. Pereira had been leading. A rare blaze of sunlight glanced down from overhead, picking out the colors of leaf and flower.

At one spot in the green wall Raft saw something curious—

an oval tunnel curving away into the matted jungle as if some gigantic serpent had passed this way, pressing the vines and trees aside, flattening the floor, leaving its own shape carved out of the living vegetation. The footprints led across the clearing toward that green tunnel of gloom.

The footprints stopped halfway across the open space.

Instinctively Raft looked up. But there were no trees close enough. With a long sigh he let the pack slide from his shoulder, but he didn't let go of the rifle.

There was a path, he saw now, beginning where the footprints stopped, six feet wide, depressed a little below the surface of the ground.

Odd!

He went forward—and jerked back, startled. Something had touched him. An invisible, cool tangibility that stood unseen here in the quiet air of the glade.

Raft put his hand out cautiously. It was halted in midair. A smooth, glassy, invisible surface. He explored the surface by touch, since sight could not help him. The thing seemed to be a hollow tube, nine or ten feet high—he threw pebbles to test that—and it was made of some perfectly transparent substance, on which not even dust could settle.

As Raft glanced along its unseeable winding length into the jungle he could observe how it pressed the trees aside to make way for it, supporting hanging orchids in midair, stopping the flight of a humming-bird that dashed itself in bewilderment against the solid air.

As he stood there, wondering, the first deep roar of the jaguar echoed through the clearing. Raft whirled, lifting his rifle. He could see the leaves vibrate to that deep-throated sound, but of the jaguar itself he could see nothing.

Yet it must be very near—it must be very large—and it must be on the verge of a charge, Raft decided, listening to the coughing breathing of the great cat.

He was in the open here. Coming to a quick decision, he bent, seized his rucksack, and tossed it behind him into the invisible tunnel. Rifle at the ready, he backed after it, and under his feet the yielding earth gave place to something hard and smooth. The great, echoing yell came once more, reverberating strangely from the tunnel walls.

Then something soughed past him. A whispering—dim,

distant, fainter than a breath. Before him, like heat-waves in the air, a shimmer swept across the tunnel-mouth.

Instantly all sound ceased. Raft's ears rang with the dead, intense silence. He reached out into empty air, and it was not empty.

Across the mouth of the tube stretched the same glass-smooth barrier that were walls and roof and floor to him. The doorway was closed. The gate—the Gate to Paititi?

A trap? Had Pereira set this snare?

Raft patted the stock of his rifle. All right, a trap, then. But he wasn't exactly unarmed. He'd go ahead, since that had been his intention anyway. Only he would not go it blind. He would be ready.

There was no sign of the jaguar. He put the pack on his shoulders and started walking. The footing was smooth, but not slippery. Something seemed to hold his feet down. This wasn't glass. It was, perhaps, a force-field, an invisible screen of pure energy. Da Fonseca had spoken of the unseen road.

Check.

He hiked on, across the clearing, into the forest, not letting himself wonder too much yet. There was plenty to think about. Raft had long ago learned the trick of shutting his mind to thoughts which he was not yet ready to entertain.

He had closed his mind time after time in these twenty days to one recurring vision—the gay, solemn, radiant face of the girl in the mirror, seen impossibly in one glance, and never to be forgotten.

It was not exactly a path. Had Raft not known that he walked in a tunnel, and had it not been for the utter, dead stillness, there would have seemed no reason for alarm. The jungle still rose solid and shadowy about him.

Butterflies fluttered brilliantly past. Birds trailed their fantastic plumage through the leaves. Now and then a cloud of tiny stinging puims blew past outside the stuff that was not glass.

Magellan, very long ago, had written of Brazilian trees that gave soap and glass, distorted versions of the hevea that flows rich latex. There was often truth in legends. The Seven Cities of Cibola—they were real, even though they had never been paved with gold.

Vespucci, Raft recalled from some dark cranny of memory, had mentioned a Lake Doirada, somewhere in the sertão, with shining cities on its banks. And the kingdom of Paititi, that da Fonseca had spoken of. In the old days bands of mamelucos had gone out on more than one expedition to find Paititi.

He could recall only fragmentary scraps. Paititi, where some of the natives were dwarfs and some were giants, some had their feet turned backwards, and others had legs like birds. The usual legendary yarns.

Nobody had ever found Paititi.

Raft got the torch out of his pack. The path had been sinking deeper and deeper below ground level. Now, a few yards ahead, the black depths of a tunnel loomed. The tube was plunging underground. It was impossible to keep one's footing on that breakneck slant, and Raft advanced very cautiously, wondering how Pereira and Craddock had managed it.

The light stabbed out. There was nothing to see but the compressed earth walling him in. The tunnel angled down steeply. Too steeply. Raft realized abruptly that he had gone too far. Something had tricked him, a shifting of balance, a— a warping of gravity, it seemed. For, he realized unmistakably, an unknown force was keeping him upright as a fly keeps its footing on perpendicular walls.

For an instant giddiness made his head swim. This ramp was not perpendicular, of course, but he had no suction cups on his feet. Nevertheless he maintained his balance on a slope of at least forty-five degrees.

Pure energy, he thought. Walls of force!

He went on down, though now he had no way of telling whether he was climbing or descending. Only logic showed that, since it was dark, he was probably going deep into the earth.

Then, after a long time, came a sudden change. Light glowed curiously from around a curve ahead. Dim light, more like a darkness alive with twisting, coiling refractions. Raft went on warily.

It was water.

It went over and around the tunnel in a smooth, swift, glassy current, foam-marbled, perfectly silent, gleaming in the beam of the torch.

Raft thought, The Children of Israel went upon dry land in the midst of the sea, and the waters were a wall unto them.

Still another miracle occurred on a journey beginning to be laden with miracles. Raft's jaw set a bit harder. He went ahead, vaguely hoping that what had happened to the Egyptians wouldn't happen to him. If that wall should break, it would be unfortunate.

The wall did not break. He went forward into a long period of blackness, broken only by the light beam. He was, he realized, very far down now. For all he knew he might be descending a completely perpendicular path, the warped gravity of the tunnel making such a fantastic descent possible.

A faint glow warned him to switch off the light. Darkness closed in, but it did not last for long. His eyes adjusted themsevles to a dim violet glow that seemed to come from all sides, above, below, everywhere. Vertigo made Raft's head spin sickeningly.

Far, far below him, but at an impossible angle, seen slantingly through the transparent floor, was the jagged curve of an immense cavern.

In a moment more logic asserted itself and the vertigo grew even worse, for Raft saw now that it was he himself who stood at that incredible angle, not the apparently tilted cave. It was bathed in faint violet light. The walls were crags, the roof, high above, dripped with stalactites that glittered wanly in the dimness.

The cave was narrow and curved right and left out of sight. The tunnel swept down in a dizzying arc and vanished into a spot of darkness in a distant wall. Raft knew that he should be totally unable to keep his footing on that tremendous slide. But as he advanced gingerly on the invisible flooring, it seemed the cavern and not himself was defying gravity.

Far down in the violet darkness something moved. Something alive. Raft could not see it clearly. Beyond it was another motion, and up among the crags of the walls, still more motion. The high, narrow, violently tilted cavern was coming alive all around him with those moving shadows which converged upon him as he stood frozen there in midair.

Devils of Paititi!

Biologically they were impossible. He could see only their

outlines, but there were shadows that looked like wings—and
great talons—and—and other things. No two of them were
alike. The logic of anatomy had gone wrong, somehow, and
Raft's mouth felt dry and sour.

They had seen him, obviously. They were moving sluggishly
toward him, with a slowness more disturbing than any speed—
as if they knew they could afford to take their time.

A shudder shook Raft. Though he knew that Pereira and
Craddock had come this way, suddenly his footing did not
seem so secure on that airy bridge. He had the sensation of
toppling on the brink of a pit thronging with monsters from
pure nightmare. If there were a break in this tunnel of glass,
disaster would overwhelm him.

Biological sports, he told himself, and went on.

Ten minutes further along the dark tunnel he came to a fork
of the way, the first one he had encountered. There was no
clue as to which way he should turn. At random Raft took the
right-hand branch, and this time luck was with him.

The ending of the tunnel was an anti-climax. He saw the
circle of light long before he reached it. It was a deep, clear
radiance which seemed to block the passage. Another force-
wall, Raft thought, like the substance of the tube itself. But it
was different in that it reflected light, or glowed with a cool
brilliance of its own.

He touched the smooth glossy surface of it. Nothing. Simply
light made tangible. Light that was, he saw, growing paler as
he watched.

Shadows and shapes appeared in the cloudy whiteness,
ghostly and strange. A wavering outline darkened and altered.
It was man-shaped, and Raft's gun slipped easily into his hand.
Beyond the figure were other dim traceries, tall columns, and
what seemed to be a stream.

The light faded and was gone. With a whispering murmur
the barrier dissolved.

The stream became a staircase, dropping steeply away from
Raft's feet to the floor of an immense hall empty save for the
columns, huger than the Karnak pillars, that marched in diminishing rows into the distance. Empty, save for these, and
for the girl who stood facing him, ten feet down the stairway,
very lovely, and—with something subtly wrong about her round,
soft face.

She moved her hands quickly. Behind Raft a whisper sang softly. He looked back, in time to see the barrier of the light spring into being across the tunnel's mouth.

The road back was closed.

IV

JANISSA

SHE WAS as he remembered her from that brief glimpse in da Fonseca's lens. There was a prim, gay touch of wickedness about her small mouth. The shadowed eyes were aquamarine, given a subtle slant by the darkness about them. Her hair was—was tiger-striped.

Honey-yellow and dim gold, it was a cloud about her head, so fine that it seemed to fade off into invisibility.

Her garments, blue and gold, clung so closely to her slim body that they seemed like a second skin. At her waist was a wide belt, and now she thrust something into a pocket of it as she smiled at Raft.

With that smile her face changed. It was infinitely appealing, completley tender and welcoming. Her voice, when Raft heard it, was as he expected. A rippling murmur, with that same familiar haunting undertone he had caught in Pereira's voice.

The language was unknown to him, though. Seeing this, the girl switched to stumbling Portuguese, and then, shrugging her slim shoulders, tried an Indio dialect that Raft knew, though he had never heard it spoken in quite this way.

"Don't be frightened," she said. "If I guided you this far, do you think I'll let anything harm you now? Though once I was afraid, when you hesitated at the fork of the road. But you took the right turning."

Raft had holstered his gun, but his hand still lingered on its cool, reassuring metal. In the same dialect he answered her.

"You guided me here?"

"Of course. Parror does not know; he was too busy getting enough to eat outside." She chuckled. "He hated that. He's a

good hunter, but burning meat over open flames—ugh! Parror
is not as complacent as you may have thought."

"Parror?" Raft said. "Would that be Pereira?"

"Yes. Now come with me, Brian Raft. You see that I know
your name. But there's much that I do not know, and you must
tell me those things."

"No," Raft said. He hadn't moved from his position at the
top of the staircase. "If you know so much, you know why I
came here. Where's Dan Craddock?"

"Oh, he's awake now." She took a tiny lens from her belt
and swung it idly. "Parror gave me back my mirror when he
returned, since it was no longer needed to keep Craddock
controlled. So I was able to see you coming through the jungle.
You had looked into my mirror, and after that I could see you.
Which was lucky for you, or you'd never have been able to
open the gateway to Paititi."

"Take me to Craddock," Raft commanded, feeling very
unsure of himself, and therefore acting very sure. "Now."

"All right." The girl's hand touched Raft's arm, urging him
down the steps. As they descended the enormous columns
seemed to rise above them, the vastness of the huge hall becoming more and more apparent.

"You haven't asked me my name," the low voice said.

"What is it?"

"Janissa," she told him. "And this is Paititi. But you must
have known that."

Raft shook his head.

"You may know a lot about the outside world, but it's a
one-way circuit. The only place I'd ever heard of Paititi was
in a legend."

"We have our legends too."

They were at the foot of the stairs. Janissa guided him across
the hall and through an arched opening into a mosaic-walled
passage.

There were symbols on those walls, but they struck a note
entirely strange to Raft. Once or twice he noticed pictures, but
the figures in them seemed to have no resemblance to either
Janissa or Pereira—Parror. He had no time to observe closely.

The girl led him into a smaller hall, up a stairway, and at
last into a round room whose walls were softly padded with
velvet, cushioned and quilted in patterns like flowers. The floor

was padded, too. The whole room was like a great pillowed sofa.

He had a moment to take it all in—the cushiony room, its strangeness and luxury, and the rich, deep colors of the velvet. He saw at one end of the room an oval door of some semi-translucent substance opening upon dim light, and in another wall was an archway, broad and low, which looked out upon moving trees.

There was something rather startling about the trees, but he had no time to look closely. He caught the fragrance of a breeze, though, smelling of flowers and damp jungle lushness where the sun seldom shines, and realized that he had come out at last upon the surface of the earth somewhere, after the long journey underground.

"Sit down and rest," Janissa said. "You've come far."

Raft shook his head.

"You said you were taking me to Craddock. Well?"

"I cannot do that yet. Parror is with him."

"Good." Raft touched his gun. Janissa merely smiled.

"In Parror's castle—in this land where he has power—you think that will help you?"

"I think so. If it won't, there are other ways." He unslung the rifle from his shoulder and leaned it against a cushioned wall. "I don't know what kind of superman Parror may be, but I'll bet he can't dodge a bullet."

"A bullet? Oh, I see. You are both right and wrong. Your weapon would have been useless against Parror outside, but in Paititi he is more vulnerable."

Raft stared at the strange, lovely, disturbingly different face upturned to him.

"Meaning what?"

"Parror does not know that you are here. So—"

"But Parror does know," said a very soft, smooth voice. Raft whirled, surprise heightening his pulse and making his breath catch. Parror!

He had come soundlessly through the oval door, and Raft realized, with some distantly logical corner of his mind, that Parror must have been much farther ahead than he had thought, for the man had had time to bathe and change from his ragged garments. The black beard was trimmed to no more than a velvety shadow outlining the heavy, but curiously delicate chin.

The garments he wore were thick, soft, gleaming like dull satin, and fitting so perfectly they might have been literally painted upon his body. He was fingering an odd weapon like a silver whip that hung from the broad jeweled belt he wore.

Raft felt suddenly very unsure of himself. This was too different a meeting from the one he had been anticipating. For this was not the jungle. There was, very definitely, something about Parror that made Raft's skin crawl. Wrong—wrong— a racial wrongness he could not define. He had felt it about Janissa, but not with the violence he felt now.

Arrogance clothed Parror like a garment. He was in his own environment. He was regally confident. Raft had an uncomfortable realization of his own awkwardness and crudity and, from the mockery in the velvety black eyes, he knew that Parror shared the thought.

Parror lifted his lip in a fastidious smile.

"You were not needed here," he said, in the Indio dialect. "But perhaps, after all, I can find a use for you. Yes, I think I can."

"We may, Parror," Janissa murmured, and for an instant unsheathed swords seemed to flash between the two.

"Listen, Pereira or whatever you call yourself, we're going to have a talk," Raft said angrily. "Now. It'll be fast talking, too."

"It will?" Parror murmured, and moved the silver whip jingling in his hand.

"Where's Craddock? What did you do to him?"

"I did nothing. I showed him a certain mirror. Through it he saw—well, I do not know what he saw. But he was tranced."

"Wake him up. Take me to him."

"He is awake now."

"He'd better be," Raft said coldly, his eye on Parror's whip and his fingers touching a cool gun-butt. "You killed da Fonseca with this same funny business, didn't you?"

"Killed him? The mirror is mine. I lent it to him and took it back."

"Yours?" Janissa breathed.

* * *

Parror ignored her. "What happened after that is no concern of mine. I had no further use for da Fonseca. And his tongue might have been a danger."

Sudden rage flooded Raft. The bearded man's arrogance, his indifference, even the subtle wrongness he could not put a name to made all the tension of the past three weeks crystallize into a hot fury. A bullet was not enough. Raft wanted to use his hands.

"You bicho!" he snarled. "If Craddock dies I'll break your filthy neck. Take me to him!"

He lunged forward and seized Parror's shoulder, feeling a savage delight in coming to grips with the man at last.

He knew judo. He was well-muscled and agile. But he did not expect Parror to—explode.

It was as if the handsome bearded face vanished and a demon glared out through the flesh and bone of the features. In that instant of utter, inhuman rage Raft saw the lips flatten away from Parror's teeth in a tigerish snarl, and he hissed shockingly as he struggled to tear free. Raft felt the smooth surge of muscles, and the power in them was shocking too, out of all proportion to that sleek, long-limbed slenderness. There was a moment of straining conflict.

Behind him, above the roaring in his ears, Raft heard Janissa's voice.

"Brian! Let him go—quick!"

The desperate urgency of her tone made Raft respond.

Shaken, a little dazed by his own anger and by the sudden, explosive violence it had roused, he released Parror. He felt oddly dazzled. He had never seen any human being, sane or mad, in the grip of a fury as sudden or as demoniac as Parror's.

There was another thing, too. The closeness of the grip had revealed a new, totally unexpected feature. Under the muscular arch of Parror's chest Raft had felt a steady throbbing that was unmistakable.

And yet—back in the base hospital—the man had had no heartbeat!

Parror drew back, shook himself, relaxed into an imperturbable dignity. Miraculously, the insane fury was gone as suddenly as it had been roused.

"You must not touch those of our race in such a way, Brian," Janissa said softly. "If you must kill, then kill. But not maul."

Raft's own voice sounded strange to him.

"What is your race?" he asked, and his questioning gaze
moved from the girl's demure face to the man's enigmatic dark
eyes.

Parror said nothing. He only smiled, a long, slow, infinitely
proud smile. And Raft read the answer. He had been seeing it
more and more clearly every moment that passed, in every
smooth, flowing motion of his body, even in his insane, inhuman fury at being touched. Inhuman indeed. Raft remembered what Parror had said in the hospital.

"I passed your ancestors, chattering and scratching themselves in the trees. And I passed my ancestors, too."

Yes, Raft knew now that he had passed them in the jungle
unseeing, many times. They had gone silently by in the underbrush, on great padding feet, the shadows of the forest
gliding across the shadowy markings of their bodies. He had
heard their roaring in the dark, and seen their lambent eyes in
the firelight.

He thought he knew, now, what race Parror's was. And
Janissa's.

Not human. They came from a different stock. As a phy-
sician who had done biological and anthropological work, Raft
knew that the incredible thing was not theoretically impossible.
Evolution is not rigid. It was an accident that had made man
the dominant, intelligent race. Accident, and the specialization
of opposing thumbs.

Our ancestors were simian, arboreal, using those flexible
hands to build the foundations of civilization. But in a different
setup, the ruling race might have descended from dogs or
reptiles or cats.

Cats.

It struck Raft suddenly, and he was shocked by the realization, that of all animals there is, except for the rodents who
do not use it, only one which shows signs of developing an
opposing thumb. The domestic cat does occasionally have an
extra toe on each forefoot. An opposing toe.

The owner names it Mittens or Boxer and thinks no more
about the matter. But given a little flexibility in that extra
member, and given time and a favorable environment, such as
this secret world of Paititi he did not yet know, what miracles
might now develop!

* * *

Feline stock. That, perhaps, explained a great deal, but it did not clear up the entire mystery by any means. Raft still had no idea of the connection between Parror and Dan Craddock, nor exactly what was the lens-mirror that had killed da Fonseca. There were many other problems as well. Too many.

He noticed a tenseness ripple through Janissa, as though she had bristled. The word sprang unbidden into his mind. Almost simultaneously, he caught a distant noise, the tramp of feet, the ringing of metal upon metal.

Parror did not seem surprised. He turned toward the translucent door, and shadows loomed against the pale panel. There was a knock.

"Parror?" Janissa said. Her voice held a question.

He spoke to her briefly in the tongue Raft did not understand. She looked quickly toward Raft. Her eyes grew blank. A veil of demure withdrawal dropped down upon her. Suddenly, with a smooth, lithe motion, she was on her feet and vanishing among the trees beyond the arched portal.

Parror called a command. The oval swept up and vanished. Across that threshold, silhouettes against faint light, came men. Men?

They wore close-fitting chain-mail, very finely meshed. Glittering caps of tiny metal links, interwoven into designs, protected their heads. There were ten of them, and each had at his belt a thin, bare blade like a rapier.

They had the same mingled strength and delicacy of features that marked Parror, the same lithe, flowing agility. The taint of the tiger was in the way they moved, and the way their slanted eyes glowed intently on Raft.

Parror had stepped back, with a little shrug, and the ten men, without pausing, closed in on Raft. He realized his danger, though none of them had drawn a sword. He sprang toward the wall where his rifle leaned, saw that he would be intercepted, and snatched out his revolver.

Thin, wiry metal burned like a hot brand about his wrist. Parror had lashed out with his whip. The gun spun from Raft's grip. He felt the onrush of charging bodies, but, curiously, none of the soldiers touched him.

The shining rapiers were out, flickering, gleaming, weaving a deadly mesh all around him. Up and down, feinting, dancing, the steel sang, and Raft drew back, respecting the menace of those glittering swords. He swung toward Parror, but the bearded man had retreated and stood by the open archway, watching alertly.

"He speaks the Indio?" a deep voice asked.

Parror nodded. A soldier with a bronzed, scarred face gestured toward Raft.

"Will you come with us peacefully?"

"Where?" Raft countered.

"To the Great Lord."

"So you're not the big shot around here," Raft said to Parror. "Okay, I'll play it that way. Maybe it won't turn out exactly as you expect."

Parror smiled. "I said I thought I could find a use for you," he murmured in Portuguese. Then he relapsed into the cryptic tongue of the cat-people, and the scarred soldier asked a quick question. Parror's answer seemed to be satisfactory, for the man lowered his rapier.

"Well, Craddock, will you come?" The guard looked at Raft and spoke in Indio.

Craddock? Raft started to answer but Parror cut him off. There was another quick, enigmatic exchange.

Raft interrupted.

"My name's not Craddock. I'm Brian Raft, and I came here after Craddock. That man—" He pointed at Parror "—kidnapped him."

"I'm sorry," Parror said. "Such a trick won't work, and I cannot help you now. The Great Lord rules here. You must talk to him. Best to go with Vann."

Vann, the scarred soldier, grunted.

"He's right. Lies will not save you. Come! As for you, Parror..."

He spat out a few words Raft could not understand. Parror's eyes narrowed, but he made no reply.

A point pricked Raft's back. With a longing glance toward his fallen gun, now, with rifle and rucksack, in the hands of the soldiers, he moved unwillingly forward. Over his shoulder he looked hard at Parror.

"I'll be back," he said, a world of promise in his tone.

Then he stepped through the oval portal and was in Paititi.

V

VALLEY OF WONDERS

AGAIN, AND EVER after that, he was conscious of the indefinable strangeness about the lost land that set it apart from any other of which he had heard. Raft had read tales of hidden civilizations, of Atlantis, Lemuria, and fantastic survivals from the past.

But in Paititi he found nothing of such arabesques—no jewel-city set down on an uncharted sea, no isolated world cut off from the earth outside. Nevertheless Paititi was as secret, as isolated, as if it had been on another planet.

It was too alive to be regarded as anything but a vivid, vital reality. Mixed with that tremendous vitality which pulsed through Paititi was the strangeness that hung like an intangible veil between earth and sky, the thing that had made this secret valley a place blessed and cursed as no spot on earth ever had before been.

Something had leaned down and touched the soil of Paititi, the trees of Paititi, the very air that breathed through alien leaves, and there had come a change. It was as though the touch of that unearthly thing had altered all that dwelt here, changing and transmuting until what remained was different.

It was a valley, probably a meteoric one, Raft thought, remembering that fifty-mile-wide circle of jungle he had seen from above. But it was well camouflaged. No earthly trees could have fulfilled that task, and no earthly trees grew here. Looking out across that dim twilit land, he was reminded of the columnar pillars that had marched across the hall where the invisible tube ended. Pillars of Karnak—but dwarfed by comparison with these trees that might have upheld the sky itself.

Yggdrasil is the tree of life which Norsemen say supports the world.

Only the largest California redwoods could have approached their sheer magnitude. For each one, in diameter, was as thick as a city block is long. They grew at irregular intervals, a half-mile or more apart, and they towered up to a luminous green ceiling which was incredibly far above. A tree five miles high!

Up they plunged into that green sky, and down into the depths those vast columns fell, like arrows of titan gods deeply embedded in the earth.

Their roots, Raft thought, might tap the very roof of Hell. Without branches, smooth and straight, they grew until, at their tops, they burst into a rank lushness of green.

Yet that green vault was translucent. At one point, almost directly overhead, an emerald brilliance told of the noonday tropic sun. But in the valley itself hung a clear, cool dawnlight that hid nothing.

Transparent as the air was, the trees themselves made a barrier. Raft could see a curving arch winding down from where he stood, fifty yards or more to a path that disappeared into that mighty forest. From far away came a very low, scarcely audible rumble, almost below the threshold of hearing.

That was all. Except that Vann tilted back his head and stared up questioningly. Raft followed his example.

Behind him were smooth walls and towers, the bulk of Parror's palace that jutted out from the base of a rock cliff, an escarpment which swept up and up till it vanished amid the ceiling of green. And dropping toward them with nightmare slowness was a cloud of rubble and stone.

"It's only a landslide," Vann said casually. He pushed Raft forward. "There's no danger."

"No danger!"

"Of course not." The soldier was surprised. "Surely you know why."

Again Raft looked up. The avalanche was perceptibly nearer, but by no means as close as it should normally have been. A great boulder struck a ledge, bounded out, and Raft fixed his gaze upon it.

It fell slowly—slowly!

It drifted down, revolving gently as it fell, floating out in an arc that ended briefly at one of the castle's turrets. It rebounded, doing no harm to the structure that Raft could see. It dropped past him, so sluggishly that he could make out every detail of its craggy surface, and embedded itself in the ground below.

* * *

That boulder had not been featherlight. Yet it had floated down as slowly as any feather.

"Move, Craddock," Vann said, and pushed Raft away from a watermelon-sized rock that struck the ramp and bounded away gently. The other soldiers, looking up, shifted casually to avoid the falling stones. Raft, utterly dumbfounded, stared up.

"I thought it would wreck the castle," he said.

"No. The ones who built here built for an eternity," Vann told him. "Not our race, but they were very great once."

"What the devil made those rocks fall so slowly?"

The soldier shrugged.

"They fell faster now than in the days of our fathers. But they are still not dangerous. Only living things can harm one of us. Now we've talked enough. Come."

He took Raft's arm firmly and led him down the aerial pathway. The soldiers followed, their arms clinking softly, mesh-armor murmuring metallically against steel blades.

Yes, Raft thought, they had talked enough. Or else not nearly enough. Mystery after mystery was piling up here, and no sooner did he seem to solve one puzzle than another appeared.

The fact that this race sprang from feline stock explained much but it certainly did not begin to explain boulders that dropped from the sky as lightly as air-inflated, toy balloons.

Nor did it solve the mystery that surrounded Parror's actions, or Janissa's. At first the girl had seemed friendly. Then she had given up to Parror without an argument. Moreover, the soldiers thought he was Dan Craddock.

Parror had taken advantage of that twist very neatly, and Raft knew there was no use trying to prove his identity to Vann. But when he was taken to the Great Lord, presumably the ruler of Paititi, there would be a chance then. Unless, of course, the Great Lord was a hairy savage who wore human skulls at his belt.

Raft grinned wryly. Savagery there was in this land, he knew already, but it was not barbarous. There was a high culture here, an intelligent civilization, though it was alien. A feline world would be strikingly different from a human one, yet the same basics would apply. An isosceles triangle was the same on Earth or Mars.

Unfortunately, he probably would not be dealing in geometry. The subtler pitfalls of psychology loomed before him, and in that feline and anthropoid might be very dissimilar. A cat people, in fact, would not be builders.

They would be artisans. Vann had already said that some other race had built Parror's castle. A race that had been very great once. When? A thousand years ago? Or a million? It had taken man eons to evolve into rational beings, and evolution moved at a predetermined rate. Not even mutations could create an intelligent cat-race from feline stock in a few generations.

There was no use even in wondering about such things now. He stepped from the smooth footing of the ramp on to an ordinary dirt pathway that led off among the colossal trees. Now, with his feet actually touching the ground of Paititi, he felt the strangeness of his surroundings more strongly than ever. Those incredible columns seemed to be moving toward him, a giant Birnam Wood malignantly alive. Trees!

For they were trees, not Jurassic cycads, not tree-ferns. He could tell that. They were true trees, but they should have grown on a planet as large as Jupiter, not on Earth.

They were sanctuaries as well, retreats for living organisms, he saw as the trail passed near the towering wall of one. From a distance he had thought the bark smooth. Instead, it was literally covered with irregular bumps and swellings.

Vines slid across the trunk like snakes, creeping with a slowness that belied the sudden flash of tendrils as—tongues?—snapped out to capture the insects and birds that fluttered past.

Rainbow flowers glowed on the leafless vines, and a heavy, sweet scent drifted into Raft's nostrils. From something like a shallow shell that jutted from the trunk a lizard darted out, seized a vine, and carried it back, writhing, to its water-brimming den. There it proceeded to drown the snaky thing and devour it at leisure.

But the reptile was no lizard. It was, Raft decided, a saurian. Only three feet long, it nevertheless reminded him of the great caymans that teem in Brazilian rivers. Except, of course, that crocs are meat eaters.

The saurian was no freak, for there were others just like it.

Swelling pale excrescences bulged on the tree, like wasps' nests thirty feet tall, with myriad window-openings from which bright eyes glittered at Raft. Furry brown bodies moved rapidly across these nests, little mammals with tapir-snouts, but adapted to tree-life.

There were other parasites on that enormous tree, like the great crimson leech that clung to the bark and sucked sap out to nourish its hideous length, and the inch-long, hairless, white creatures like monkeys that lived like lice upon the sloth things that clambered with extraordinary agility in pursuit of insect prey.

It would have been symbiosis, except that the parasites had nothing to give the trees upon which they lived as on a world. Trees and living vines and the rubbery pale moss that bordered the path, there was no other vegetation here.

But of the fantastic there was much. Before Raft's amazement had died they crossed a brook, a half mile further on, by a narrow bridge that might have been made of glowing plastics. No fish were visible through that glassy translucence, and as Raft looked down, he felt that nothing remotely normal could ever exist in those enchanted waters. For the stream, too, was wrong.

It was silent. It did not purl and ripple softly over the rocky bed. Small cascades and waterfalls dropped, with hypnotic, quiet slowness, into the pools beneath. Ripples spread out very gently, very slowly, to die against the mossy banks.

It was not water. Water it could not be. It seemed half congealed.

Yet when Raft, with a questioning glance at Vann, knelt beside the brook and lifted cupped hands to his mouth, it was water. Droplets escaped from between his fingers and floated down gently to fall upon the thirsty moss.

Slowly as the boulders that had dropped upon Parror's castle the waters glided on—silently. It was Oberon's glade, where sorcery lay heavy. The sweeet fragrance of the living vine-flowers hung on the clear air.

What spell holds this land, Raft thought? What magic stooped and touched it once, long ago? Surely a god walked here once. But what god? One of Earth, or one from beyond even the stars?

Silently, he let Vann urge him along the path. The sooner

he reached his destination, the sooner his questions might be answered.

But the monotony of the journey grew tiring at last. Once a castle, a small structure compared to Parror's fortress, was visible under the shelter of the forest, but the soldiers by-passed it without a glance. Raft eyed the scar-faced Vann.

"How much further have we to go?"

"It is still a long way."

He was right. The hours dragged past, and Raft's occasional glances at his wristwatch made him conscious of a puzzling new factor. They must have covered more than fifteen miles, but his watch said that only fifteen minutes had passed. Overhead that brightness in the green vault had not moved. The sun, apparently, stood still over Paititi.

Nor had it moved when, a long while later, they came out of the forest at the edge of a mile-wide clearing—or what seemed to be a clearing.

Directly ahead, blocking the way, stood a turreted palace that would have seemed huge except for the trees that dwarfed it. Even so, it was an enormous structure.

What lay beyond it Raft could not see, but he could make out a shapeless pale cloud that hung in the sky beyond those thrusting pinnacles, a formless whiteness that seethed and curled slowly into new suggestions of luminous hugeness.

A broad river ran toward the castle, and under it. The torrent plunged into a high-arched opening beneath that architectural colossus, and was lost.

Raft was stumbling and exhausted. The two long journeys, first through the underground tube that led to Paititi, and then this fast hike, had turned his muscles to water. He was so utterly tired by now that he saw his destination through a sort of mist; and Vann's voice came from a long distance away. He let himself be urged forward, mechanically moving his legs to keep up with the soldiers.

There was a courtyard. Figures moved about it. A throng of brightly clad figures, with the half-Egyptian faces of the cat-people, all intent on the spectacle in their midst. A high-pitched singing came from a man crouching atop a high stone block.

Exultant wildness shrilled out as he chanted a song in the

language Raft did not understand. The crouching man played some complicated string instrument that sounded vaguely like the bagpipes.

In the center of the courtyard two men were fighting. One was a giant, tall, smoothly-muscled, with a strong face already masked by blood. The other man was more remarkable. Raft's eyes were drawn to him.

He was like Parror, and yet unlike. In place of the sleek, powerful look of the puma, this man was as lithe and swift as the hunting cheetahs of the old Hindu rajahs.

Supple and light, his hair a fine mist about that strong, delicate face, the man sprang out of his opponent's way, laughing, and slashed down with claws.

He wore a glove, a gauntlet, that was tipped with three curved metal blades like talons. Needle-sharp they were, for three long cuts opened like mouths across the larger man's bare chest, and blood spouted.

The minstrel's song rose to a thin shrilling in which there was something drunken and almost mad. The music sang and sang. It cried of love and death, and in it was the choking, musty smell of fresh blood.

Turn and dodge and slay.

Metal grated as the two taloned gloves clawed together. The men bounded apart as though on springs instead of muscles of flesh. The giant shook his head, wiping crimson from his eyes. The other paused, with a careless gesture, to glance at Raft. His irises were blazing yellow. He had slit-like pupils.

His blond hair, almost orange, was oddly marked by shadowy patterns of cloudy black. As he smiled, Raft almost expected to see the sharp teeth of a predatory leopard. Red droplets fell from those murderous gauntlets to a brown thigh. He called a question.

Vann answered, and the yellow-haired man lifted one shoulder impatiently. He spoke a few casual syllables, and turned back to the giant, lifting a taloned glove.

For answer his opponent leaped in, and the two agile figures were again lost in that deadly, graceful dance. Vann, his eyes glowing, touched Raft's arm.

"Come. You must sleep now."

Raft's brief excitement had died. The dull stupor of exhaustion made a protective barrier around Raft. Without another glance at the duel, he went with Vann through a portal, along halls and up spiraling ramps, lost in a foggy dimness of sheer physical tiredness. He felt Vann's hand halt him at last.

"Sleep, now. Darum will see you after you've rested."

"Darum?" Raft saw cushions at his feet, and dropped heavily upon them. "Who's Darum?"

"You just saw him fighting. He is the Great Lord. He rules. But now he fights, and after that—"

Vann's voice died away, merging with the faint, drowsy humming of—of what?

A purring, sub-sonic vibration thrilled through Raft. Deep, comforting it throbbed through the very structure of the castle. As though the castle lived. As though the hidden pulse of life stirred in the stone.

That alien whisper lulled Raft to sleep.

VI

MAD KING

MANY HOURS LATER, Raft awoke, refreshed but stiff and aching. Colored light came through tall windows, pastel patterns that shifted and glowed on the pallor of the thick carpet.

He was in what seemed to be a sleeping-chamber. There were mirrors on the walls, many of them, and the room, he noticed, had no corners. It was a silken, padded nest, strewn carelessly with silks and pillows, and with low, round couches here and there.

There was an oval door in the wall, but no shadow loomed against it. That did not, however, mean that there was no guard. Raft yawned, stretched, and felt his muscles and joints crackle with stiffness. But, aside from various dull aches, he felt alert and ravenously hungry.

The dim humming still vibrated through him. He turned to the window, pushed open a pane, and stepped out onto the balustraded porch beyond. There he paused, staring.

Overhead the sun had moved a fraction—that was all. He

saw it vaguely, for a towering pillar of mist dimmed his vision.
Looking down, he understood the reason. ~

Beneath him a gulf opened. The porch overhung a broad
platform lower down which jutted out over an abyss clouded
with white fog. A silver torrent of ice shot out in an arc and
fell away into that incredible depth.

Not ice, no, for it moved slowly. It was the river that flowed
beneath the castle, to drop into the gulf that lay directly under
Raft. He tried to probe the depths, but the boiling maelstrom
of mist baffled him. The cataract fell and was lost.

Fell—slowly. Mist rose slowly too, a gelid ghost towering
high above the castle. The deep humming was louder now, and
the stone beneath Raft's feet vibrated to its murmuring. Sub-
sonic. The crashing roar of a waterfall, resolved by some physical warp or distortion into that dim throbbing he felt rather
than heard.

Frowning, Raft left the balcony. He was beginning to understand a little now. His mind, refreshed by deep sleep, was
clearer. Slow water, stones that fell like feathers, a sun that
dragged itself wearily across that green sky. Time, it seemed,
was different here. Was this lost land actually on Earth? The
same Earth that held the Amazon Basin, and Rio, and New
York? Perhaps not.

He tried to fathom the mystery of the oval door. He could
not, but it slipped upward and vanished suddenly, and Vann
stood on the threshold, his scarred face alert.

"So you're awake," Vann said in the Indio. "Good. Darum
wants to see you, but he's resting now. You'll want a bath."

"And food," Raft said. "Does Darum wear those gloves all
the time?"

Vann called a command over his shoulders. Then he stepped
forward into the room, smiling.

"Only for tourneys. He's less dangerous when he wears the
gloves. I'll show you the bath, Craddock."

"I'm not Craddock. I told you before I'm not Craddock."

But Vann paid no attention. He moved levers on the wall,
and part of the floor slid aside, revealing a shallow, wide basin
filled with a liquid the color of creme de menthe. Gratefully
Raft slipped out of his ragged clothes and lowered himself into
the bath. Vann watched with a grimace of distaste.

"It'll take several washings to get you clean," he remarked.

"Here." He found a jar and sprinkled blue powder into the water. An astringent, tingling sensation ran across Raft's skin.

There were brushes, many of them, instruments like Roman strigils, and other gadgets Raft experimented with under Vann's guidance. The water was awkward to handle because of its sluggishness.

Once Raft dropped a brush. He watched it float gently down till it dug a hole in the water, a hole that gradually refilled, while ripples crept out to the rim.

But a bath was luxury, and the aches began to leave Raft's muscles. Vann watched unblinkingly, commenting once on the coarseness of his prisoner's hair, and providing a gleaming unguent which Raft's skin absorbed leaving him stimulated. Finally a page appeared, pushing a wheeled table laden with unfamiliar food, and stood motionless, struck with amazement as he eyed the figure in the bath.

Vann gestured, and the loose-limbed, dapper youngster, with his daintily malicious triangular face, bowed and fled, without removing his startled gaze from Raft.

"No wonder he's surprised," Vann remarked. "Your musculature is so different from ours that you looked deformed to him. But I'd like to fight you some time, if opportunity arises."

"Thanks," Raft said. "You'd have a fine time cutting my throat with one of those gloves."

"Not at all." Vann smiled savagely. "Killing is a different thing entirely. The point in murder is not to be found out. But a fight, a duel—they're very seldom fatal." He found tight garments like his own and helped Raft don them. "I'd have too much of an advantage if I wore the gloves. What weapons do you use usually?"

"Rifles," Raft said. He explained about duels.

"Strange," the soldier said. "I should think there'd be little satisfaction in propelling a missile. You wouldn't be able to feel your blade go in. There'd be no physical pleasure."

"All right. We'll box, fight with our fists."

"Depending on impact alone? That doesn't seem interesting. Don't you use swords at all?"

"Some of us do," Raft said. "But I'm no swordsman myself. What was that you said about murder? Is homicide legal here?"

"No," Vann said. "We're not barbarians. A murderer has to pay restitution, if he's found out. But only the stupid are caught."

"Oh," Raft said blankly, tackling a pulpy, acrid fruit like an orange. "There's a police force, then?"

He had to explain, but finally Vann understood.

"We have specialists in detection. If a murderer can escape their skill, he's safe enough. The trick is—I think—to conceal the motive. Killers are caught because they haven't disguised their motives." He shook his head deprecatingly.

"Just what is the set-up here?" Raft asked. "Does Darum rule all Paititi?"

Vann nodded.

"Yes. The set-up is—well, that of any civilized land."

"Sure. Homicide for fun. How is it you can talk the Indio tongue?"

"You aren't the first outsider to enter Paititi. We have had brown-skinned men here in our fathers' time, though it has always been difficult for us to leave our valley. Parror's ancestors had captive Indios sometimes, and most of us know the language."

Raft thought that logical. Linguist ability was a mark of the cosmopolitan, even if it never left this hidden valley.

"And Portuguese?"

"What?"

"Falam português?"

"That is strange to me," Vann admitted.

"Then Parror picked it up? And Janissa, too." Raft nodded thoughtfully.

Then he remembered the aviator. "Was there a man of my race here, a man named da Fonseca, who had a machine which flew through the air? About—about fifty sleeps ago?"

Vann's face lighted up. "The machine that flies fell into Paititi about four hundred sleeps ago, killing all but one man, whom Parror took to his castle. Yes, that was da Fonseca, for with his aid Parror read the notebook you left in the Cavern of the Flame."

Raft put down a morsel untasted.

"Four hundred sleeps?" he said, a queer hesitation in his voice. "Over a year ago. How long have I been in Paititi, Vann?"

"I captured you yesterday," the soldier said. "And that was

directly after your arrival. I was watching for Parror's return from the outer world. So I knew when to strike."

"I see," Raft said, though he didn't. "What about this notebook, and the Cavern of the Flame? What's that?"

"You did not see the Cavern?"

"I saw a cavern, with some unpleasant creatures in it. Is that what you mean?"

A shudder shook Vann. Briefly a touch of fear showed in his eyes. "No—no. That is not what I mean." He changed the subject abruptly. "You must see Darum now. Are you ready?"

"As ready as I ever will be, I suppose."

"Very well." Vann stood up, turning toward the door. Raft accompanied his guard into a dimly-lighted hall and along it. After a while Vann broke silence.

"The Great Lord has fought and had his pleasure afterward, and slept. He will be strange now. A word of advice, Craddock."

"I'm—well, what is it?"

"Something hangs in the balance now," Vann said thoughtfully, his gaze on the floor as they walked. "For myself, I am not sure. I am on neither side as yet. Darum, too, hesitates.

"He had you taken from Parror before the—the final step could be taken, but he may yet side with Parror. If he does, that will be well for you. Or perhaps evil, in the end. I cannot see that far ahead. But I will say this, since you are of an alien race, you would do well to heed it. Darum—is mad."

A little shock went through Raft. He stared at the soldier. "Mad? Your king?"

"Yes."

"And he rules?"

"Of course," Vann said. "Why not? For often he is not mad, and when he is, that does not matter much. But with you it may mean the difference between life and death. Perhaps," he went on musingly, "life and death for Paititi. Remember that Darum is not your kind."

"I hope not," Raft said candidly.

"He is of our kind," Vann murmured, and his eyes were luminous. "Now—I hope you live. For I'd enjoy a duel with you, Craddock. And here is your way." He held aside a heavy tapestry, revealing a dim corridor. "Go in."

"Thanks," Raft said.

He stepped forward. Behind him, Vann let the curtain fall. There was silence, except for the never-ceasing vibration that shook the castle. Even here its steady humming could be felt.

Raft walked toward another drapery that barred the way ahead.

A different race, he thought, and a different species. They murder for intellectual pleasure and duel for physical excitement. They see nothing amiss in a mad king.

He hesitated before the curtain. Then he pushed it aside and stepped through, into a ruddy darknenss.

The dim, faint glow came from all around. How large the room might be Raft had no way of guessing. He saw shrouded shapes looming before him, and, in heavier shadow, something stirred and looked at him with eyes that were glowing disks. A cool, sharp perfume was in his nostrils. That infernal humming seemed to shake the dark air.

There was no sound. Raft, after a moment, moved forward. The eyes watched him steadily. At last he could make out a slim figure reclining on a bulkier, shapeless mass—the smooth outline of a jaw, and the cloudy mist of hair fading into invisibility.

Raft stood there, waiting.

He sensed that this was not the same man he had seen fighting and laughing in the courtyard. There was a difference, even physically. In the gloom a change had come upon Darum, a strangeness that was indefinable and yet unmistakable.

"Sit down," the king said, in the Indio tongue. Even his voice had altered. It was passionless, like music heard from very far away.

Raft fumbled, found a couch, and dropped upon it. The eyes had a touch of green in them as they watched.

"Listen," Darum said.

At the king's feet a shadow stirred. Its soft curves were those of a woman, but from that vague figure a subtle breath of terror breathed out, chilling Raft. There was a sound, almost a voice. Woodwind and sighing strings—plaintive, questioning.

Again the king spoke.

"Yrann wonders. She wonders why you come to Paititi,

Craddock. Music is her voice, for she will not speak. But she asks who are you? What is your world?"

The soft strings sang again. Sang a question.

Raft leaned forward, as though to break the spell. But the king's eyes held him.

"He is a god, Yrann. Craddock was in the beginning, and now he comes again, very near the end. Since his eyes first saw Paititi, a race has been born and draws close to the shadow. The shadow that the Flame casts over all living things."

The sighing oboe-flute spoke of a gathering darkness, of a cloud that stooped above the land.

"And yet there are other shadows," the king whispered. "There was a woman once, Yrann, whose loveliness burned like magic fires. Fires that could make men drunken. A fire that could make men mad, as I know. As I know."

Stealthy fear circled Raft's heart. Poignant, eerie, the music sang, and the dim gloom showed the half-seen, half-veiled curves of soft skin and rounded shoulders. At Darum's feet Yrann swept slim fingers across sobbing strings.

"And the fire burned," the king went on softly. "In all Paititi there was none so beautiful as this woman. When she danced, the tall trees inclined in homage. When she smiled, the stones bowed down."

A note of pride crept into the wordless song. The sun-drenched spring of green forests came into the dark chamber; the sound of laughter, and flaunting bright cloaks, and clashing steel. The music pirouetted into a gay, lilting dance.

Heavily the king's voice broke in. The music sank to a whisper.

"There was a man who loved this woman. He took her for his own. And she laughed. Laughed—knowing power as well as beauty, growing drunken at the thought of ruling Paititi. Of ruling the man who was the king."

Proud, triumphant, the song rose. Ivory arms gleamed.

"And her eyes fell upon a man who was not a king. But she knew that in her arms, any man might be the emperor of the universe, and the equal of the gods. Nor was she wrong. If her embrace meant death, death would be sweet poison."

Tinkling, mocking laughter, and an undertone of sadness in the music now.

"She was faithless," the king said, his words falling heavily as stones into the still air. "Those lips were faithless. And the arms of Yrann sought another, and the white body of Yrann yearned too."

The song hushed almost to silence.

"Long ago. Very long ago. Now she is no longer faithless. Nor is the king sorrowful. Maidens dance before him. They ask his love, but he has none to give. His love is for Yrann, most beautiful of all womankind, and she—she loves him now."

Tender, obedient, the oboe murmured softly.

"But the king is mad," the quiet, cool voice said, and the music died into stillness. "There was a red hour long ago when the madness entered into him. That hour will not pass, Yrann, and love and madness dwell forever side by side."

For a long time, there was no sound but the faint vibration of the cataract making the castle tremble in its iron grip.

"We speak together, Yrann and I, of things forgotten and things that are not forgotten," the king said at last. "But music is her tongue now." His voice changed. "Yrann must not die, though Paititi does. I think that you hold a certain answer in your hand, Craddock, and whether I let you open your grip upon that great secret is something I cannot tell yet. We must talk first. There are many questions."

For the first time Raft spoke. He moistened his lips.

"One question has to be settled first," he said.

"And that is?"

"I'm not Craddock."

The eyes watched him. Raft plunged on.

"I tried to tell your soldier, Vann, but he didn't believe me. I don't know what story Parror had. It must have been a good one. For Craddock's in Parror's castle now, his captive. I came here to rescue Dan Craddock, and my name is Brian Raft."

"I cannot believe that."

"Why should I lie?" Raft asked. "What could I gain?"

"You might have many reasons. And yet Parror is clever too. If he had wanted to gain time, he might use deception."

"Janissa knows who I am. The girl in Parror's castle."

"But will Janissa speak the truth?" Darum asked. "Her mind is like a wind, changing and changing. Tell me your story, then. It may be a lie, or it may not. But I will listen."

Raft talked. He marshaled his thoughts as clearly as he could, though the ruddy dimness of the room played strange tricks on his nerves. When he had finished, the glowing eyes of King Darum were half-closed.

"Go," Darum said.

Raft hesitated. The deep voice sounded again, more commandingly.

"Go, I said. We will speak again later. Now I must test your story."

Raft stood up. From the half-glimpsed figure at Darum's feet that exotic, haunting music breathed out again. Caressing, gentle, and indefinably sad.

The king's eyes watched him.

Stumbling, Raft moved across the chamber. He felt the velvet folds of the curtain against his face. He lifted it, stepped under its soft drape. Behind him light flared. The music rose shrilly. Raft half-turned.

On a dais strewn with cushions Darum was standing, his face hidden as he looked down at the figure at his feet. Nor had Raft's guess been wrong as to the loveliness of those ivory limbs, that half-veiled beautiful body. But Yrann's face was not veiled.

And her face was—horror.

Into Raft's mind flashed unbidden memory of the cruel-taloned gauntlet he had seen on the king's hand. Something terrible and savage and mad had destroyed the beauty of Yrann's face, leaving her goddess body untouched.

The king looked up. His eyes met Raft's.

Raft stepped backward into the corridor and let the shielding curtain fall into place.

VII

DREAD FLAME

HIS WATCH SAID minutes had passed, but Raft knew that it had been hours since his interview with the lord of Paititi. Impatiently he waited in his apartment, left alone with his puzzled thoughts. He could not fathom the trick of the door, and Vann, after escorting him back here, had not reappeared. From the balustraded porch nothing could be seen but the torrent pouring lazily into the abyss below.

The room was sterile. It was beautiful, luxurious, but it held nothing that aroused Raft's interest. Inaction was twanging his nerves into tense irritability. He seemed the only thing not frozen into semi-stasis in this strange land.

A long time had passed when from beyond the window he heard his name called softly. He knew the voice. A stir of excitement quickened him as he hastily stepped out on the balcony. But there was nothing.

Only falling water. Lazy falling water.

"Brian!" The low call came again. "Brian Raft!"

He leaned over the rail, and found himself looking down into the soft, familiar face of Janissa. The aquamarine eyes were darker now, almost purple. She was clinging to grips and footholds on the castle's wall, crannies where it seemed not even a squirrel could find lodgment.

Catching his breath, Raft leaned down, extending his arm. But Janissa murmured a quick warning.

"Get a cushion, Brian. Bring it. No, I'm safe enough here. Do as I say."

He hesitated, turned, and hurried back into the room, where he snatched up the nearest cushion and carried it out with him. Janissa had not moved. Her slim body was flattened against the stone.

"Hold it by a corner. Yes, that's it. And lower it toward me, very carefully. Don't lose your grip on it."

Raft obeyed. There was a sudden whir and a flash of steel,

and the cushion was almost torn from his hand. From the
smooth wall beneath the railing a fan of sharp blades had leaped
out, one of them impaling the pillow as Janissa's flesh would
have been pierced had she continued her climb.

Her teeth showed in a smile.

"Now it's safe, I think. Give me your hand." With feline
agility she clambered up, writhing between the swords so that
no blade or edge touched her. On the balcony she shook herself,
patted her hair, and took the cushion from Raft.

"You're alone? I thought you would be. I asked questions
before trying this climb."

"You might have been killed," Raft said, looking down into
dizzying emptiness where the slow cataract poured into bottomless deeps and the slower mist wreathed up in a swaying
tower. Then he turned to the girl and, as he met her smile, he
felt a little dizziness that did not come from vertigo.

This was the face that had drawn him over miles of river
and jungle almost as unerringly as Craddock's trail had drawn
him. No one, he thought, could have looked once upon this
delicate, soft, malicious little creature and not wanted to look
again.

In their first meeting he had been tired and bewildered.
Today he could gaze more clearly into the aquamarine eyes
and the gay, yet prim face of this contradictory girl. He stared
frankly, trying to make the clear gaze waver.

Janissa laughed.

"We've met before, remember?" she jibed.

Raft grinned.

"Sorry. It was just— Do your people here know how beautiful you are?"

"Men of all races must be very much alike," Janissa parried
demurely. "We must think about you just now, Brian Raft.
You're in trouble."

"Trouble you walked out on, I remember." He did not mean
to let her attractiveness blind him to that memory.

She shrugged lithely.

"What could I do then? Now I've walked in again, and you
must forgive me."

He glanced over the balcony rail and shuddered. "You certainly did take a long chance. Lucky you weren't killed."

"Not by a fall. Not my race! Though if you hadn't been

here to spring the trap, I might have had some trouble. Let's go in. We may be seen from another balcony."

She stepped through the window, stared around, and tossed the slashed cushion away. "Now we can talk."

Raft followed her, seeing how supple was the movement of her round, smooth limbs as they glided beneath velvety garments. She tilted him a sweetly wicked smile over one shoulder and shook the cloudy tiger-striped hair. There was a mound of silken cushions against the nearer wall. She laid a hand on Raft's arm and drew him down beside her to a cross-legged seat among them.

"We have much to tell each other," she said. "And perhaps not a very long time to do it in."

"You'll have to start, then. Remember, I don't know anything at all."

"I suppose not," Janissa murmured. There was a soft roughness to her voice when she lowered it, a luxuriant roughness, like a purr. "Not even Craddock knew, really, though he—created—our race. And now he does not remember certain things. So Parror will have to build a device that—"

"Suppose you start at the beginning," Raft interrupted her. "First, where is Paititi? On my own planet?"

"Yes. We know that, for some of us have gone through the unseen road to the jungle land outside. Not many, and only guardians, like Parror and myself. I went once and only once. It was horrible. Your world is frozen. Nothing moves.

"When we meet others outside, you know, we have to force ourselves to do everything as slowly as people in a nightmare. Otherwise we'd be only a blur when they looked at us. But we cannot live long outside Paititi, unless we carry something of the Flame with us."

"The Flame?" Raft echoed. "The Flame?"

"The Flame is the source of all life," Janissa said soberly. "In our whole land there are only two amulets that hold a little fiery seed of the Flame itself. We do not know how to make them. These two are very old, our heritage from the ancient race that lived here before us." Her eyes narrowed. "Parror has one. I should have the other. It's my right as Guardian. But the king claims it, and—well, never mind. I have my plans. The time is coming when—"

"Please," Raft broke in. "First tell me about this business of speed, and your people moving faster than ours. Why?"

"The Flame is sinking," Janissa said in a somber voice. "That is why Parror sought out Craddock. You see, Paititi was not always as it is now. In the old days, generations lived and died during the day, and other generations in a night. And before that, hundreds of generations in a day. The cycle slows now. Water moves faster than in the days of our fathers. Our memories go back a long way. We have written records, but certain things we had to guess. Before we were human, long, long ago, another race dwelt in Paititi.

"That race built these castles. Men and women not of our species but akin to yours, strong and wise and happy, dwelt in this land and lived beneath the Flame. Then the Flame sank and slept."

Raft scowled.

"That race died?"

"It did not die."

"What happened to it?"

She looked away.

"As you came through the unseen road, you must have seen a cavern there—a dark place where things crept and flew in shadow. You saw the monsters that dwelt in it. Those things—their ancestors—built this castle, and Parror's castle, and a hundred others. But as the Flame sank, they sank below the level of beasts. We know that now. But we did not always know."

Raft tried to marshal the facts. "The first race degenerated, eh? As your own evolved?"

"They degenerated long before we had the first glimmers of intelligence. I said that the Flame slept. Craddock wakened it, millions and millions of cycles ago. We know that, because our ancestors penetrated to the cave of the Flame, and found certain things there—a cloth sack, metal containers, a notebook with symbols we could not read.

"Not until da Fonseca came here, in his machine that flew, did we have any knowledge of the real truth, though we had often theorized. Parror and I took da Fonseca and through him learned the contents of that notebook."

"Millions of cycles? Craddock isn't that old!"

"The tides of time are altered in Paititi," Janissa said. "Craddock awakened the Flame, and our race was given birth. Now the Flame sinks, and that means great evil."

Dan Craddock! How much did he really know about the man, Raft wondered. For thirty years the Welshman had wandered the Amazon Basin. Why? Because of some secret he had stumbled on, long ago?

"What is this Flame?" he asked.

Janissa made a curious symbolic gesture. "It is the giver of life and the taker-away of life. It is Curupuri."

Raft stared at her. "All right, leave that, then. What do you want?"

The eyes shaded to purple again. "I am of royal blood. In the old days there were once three kings, enemies. They fought, and two were conquered. But the two vanquished kings were not shamed. They were given the hereditary honor of guardians of the Flame. They dwelt, after that, in the castle Parror holds now, while the conqueror dwelt in this place, by Doirada Gulf. It was so for generations. Until now!"

She seemed to bristle.

"Parror uses me—uses me! And I am of blood no less royal than his own. I held the secret of the lens, which he needed, but now that he has Craddock, he can waken the Flame, and I will be stripped of my birthright." Her eyes glowed. "Holding the castle of the Flame is a trust. We guard. Parror intends to break the trust, and act on his own, without waiting for the king's decision. That will be a shameful thing. It will bring shame on me, one of the guardians."

"Yet you helped him murder da Fonseca," Raft said. "You helped him kidnap Craddock."

"As for the murder, I did not know he intended that. The spell of the mirror can be broken, but it must be done slowly, carefully, or the victim will die. I had no love for da Fonseca, yet I did not want his death, and I would have stopped Parror could I have done so.

"Craddock—well, Parror lied to me. He told me he would do no more than bring Craddock here. I would not have trusted his word alone, but he gave me logic I could not deny. False logic, I know now. For he will get the knowledge he needs from Craddock's brain, and waken the Flame. That—

that—" She hesitated. "It may be a very great sin. I am no longer sure what is the right way, Brian."

"Well, one way is for me to get out of here and see Craddock," Raft said practically.

"I cannot get you out—yet," she told him. "But the rest is easy. I have the mirror. See?" She drew the little lens from her bosom and held it out. Raft, remembering da Fonseca, found himself instinctively glancing away.

Janissa laughed softly.

"There's no harm in it, unless the psychic cleavage is violent. Look into my mirror."

"Not so fast," Raft said. "How does it work?"

"We know much of the mind," Janissa said. "The device is—is a mental bridge. Once it has caught the matrix of a man's mind, it can be put en rapport with that man. Each brain has a different basic vibration. You could not use the mirror alone, Brian, for it needs a trained mind to direct. But with my aid, you can. Look."

He obeyed. In the tiny lens the gray storm-clouds misted and swirled. They were driven aside. Tiny and alive, Raft saw the face of Dan Craddock.

He had a stubbly white beard. His eyes were bloodshot, and he looked utterly exhausted. Beyond him Raft could make out vague outlines. Silks, he thought, of many colors.

"He is alone, and resting," Janissa whispered. "So you may speak with him freely."

"Speak?"

"In the mind. Look closer now, while I summon him."

Raft stared down at the lens. He saw Craddock's gaze lift, and sudden awareness spring into them.

Raft heard his name!

He did not hear it. He sensed the impact of Craddock's thought. Abruptly he was conscious of nothing but his friend's presence. The room about him darkened and vanished. There was present only the odd feeling that Janissa was here, somewhere, alive and guiding.

"Dan. Are you all right?" His thought formed words.

"All right, Brian. Yes. You?"

"So far I'm alive, anyway," Raft thought grimly. "Janissa's here."

"Good. She managed to tell me a little. And Parror's told me more."

"Is he—has he tried any tricks?"

Craddock grinned wanly.

"More or less. He's the most dangerous altruist I've ever met. You shouldn't have come after me, Brian."

"You should have told me the set-up back in the hospital, when Parror first showed up," Raft pointed out. "But that's water under the bridge. What we've got to figure on now—"

"I didn't know," Craddock interrupted. "When Parror brought da Fonseca to the hospital, I hadn't the least idea what was going on. When he showed me my notebook, I was—well, as flabbergasted as I looked."

"You were here before, though."

"Yes. I was here. Thirty years ago by our time, a hundred million, maybe, by Paititi's time. For it's variable. There's the Flame . . ."

"Tell him," Janissa's thought urged.

Craddock nodded.

"Yes, I—I'd better, I suppose. Though thirty years ago I hadn't much idea what I was getting into. I was pretty young. I was on the trail of the secret medicines the Indio witch-doctors were supposed to have around here, and that's how I stumbled on the unseen road. It wasn't closed then. It lay wide open. A trap, as it proved."

"A trap?"

"One set by fate," Craddock thought grimly. "I went on, though, past the cavern of the monsters, and to the place where the road forks. One branch leads to Paititi. The other leads to the thing the Indios call Curupuri."

"The Flame," Raft supplemented. "What is it?"

"I don't know. Radiant energy of some kind. It may be alive. It may not. But certainly it's nothing that ever was spawned on this earth. Paititi's a meteoric crater, Brian, and I think Curupuri came to this planet in a meteor. Perhaps it was the meteor. It's—life."

"The creator and the destroyer," Janissa put in quietly.

"Destroyer? Yes. There are forms of energy we know nothing about. Sometimes we see them through telescopes, in the giant nebulae light-years away. The stuff of primal energy, spawned in interstellar space, where that tremendous force can safely exist. It can't exist—safely—on a planet. Not unless the planet is still gaseous, still molten. Curupuri, the thing that fell on Brazil in a meteor ages ago, is a source of life, Brian."

"A living thing?"

"Too colossal for us to conceive of or measure. You know the Arrhennius theory, that life reached Earth in the form of spores, drifting through space on light-pressure tides. Well, that's fair enough, but what gave life to those spores?

"It's the old chicken or the egg problem, with a difference. The spores may have been the dust, the waste-products of things like the nebulae. Or that vast force raging in space may have had power to create life in dust, a galaxy away. I don't know. I'm theorizing, that's all. But radiant energy, vibration, power—they're tied up with it, somehow."

Craddock's tired face brightened.

"And the merest fraction of that energy fell on Earth once, in a meteor. It must have been a microscopic amount, for anything more would have devastated the planet. Growth, unchecked. I guessed some of that, and learned a little more, from records I found in Paititi."

"Records? Left by whom?"

"I didn't know then. There was no one in the valley, no life except birds and insects, peccary, tapir, and the jaguars. Remember the jaguars, Brian. They're important. Meanwhile, I found those records in what is now Parror's castle.

"They weren't unlike the written Indio language. I suppose that's where the Indios get their lingo in the first place. Anyway, I found out the truth. Curupuri had given life to Paititi. The merest touch of that energy has made the Amazon Basin the most fertile and prolific place on Earth."

Raft nodded.

"Keep going. How does this trick work?"

"In cycles. There are cycles in suns, giants and dwarfs, and in nebulae too, though our lives are too short to comprehend them. When the Flame is at full tide, a certain type of energy pours forth from it. The result is peculiar."

"Time is speeded up?"

* * *

Slowly Craddock shook his head. "No. Not objectively. What happens is a metabolic change. The rate of growth is tremendously increased. Not only in men, in mammals, but in all living things. When the Flame is at the top of its cycle, a man may be born, live a complete life, and die in one second. Yet it will be a lifetime to him.

"Inanimate things are not affected, of course. The radiation won't make stone crumble faster. It influences living cells only. The animal world, and plants. That is what happened."

"The Flame wakened," Janissa supplemented. "And in its light all things sprang to life."

"Yes. Long ago. But that cycle was more normal. The First Race, the one that built these castles, lived here, evolved, and—and then the Flame sank. They did not die. But apparently the radiation is a false stimulus.

"When the Flame's power falls below a certain level, its rays are actively malignant. Cellular tissue may be stimulated, but it can also become cancerous. When the Flame sinks, there is a retrogression. It's freakish. It's—horrible."

"I saw what was left of the First Race," Raft mentioned. "Those monsters in the cavern."

"Yes. They saw their fate coming, and made plans. They were skilled scientists. They found a way to rekindle the Flame before its cycle had been run, but they failed to do it. Because it was dangerous. If they were not accurate to a hair's breadth, if they failed to control the Flame exactly, it would mean total destruction. The radiation would rage out unchecked. The Flame would devour itself instantly, but in that instant Paititi would be seared lifeless."

"They didn't do it, then."

"No. They waited. Each generation thought it could live out its own span. Each generation let the problem go on to its children. And the children thought the same. In the end, the beast-minds were too dull to comprehend.

"The creatures that had been the First Race remembered only the Flame, and they found their way to the cavern where you saw them. Their nearness to the radiation keeps them alive, and they've lived and bred there in the dark for a long time."

Raft frowned.

"But the cat-people. How did they come into being?"

Craddock's eyes held a touch of deep horror.

"I created them. I—wakened the Flame."

VIII

KHARN, THE TERRIBLE

VISUALIZING THAT SCENE of thirty years ago, Raft could picture a younger Craddock lost in wonder before the secrets he had uncovered, feeling a dangerous exaltation burning in his mind, and, of all the world, the only man who knew of that tremendous, intergalactic Force that blazed hidden in the jungles. Yes, he could understand why Craddock might have been tempted to meddle with forbidden forces.

"I wakened the Flame. The records I had found, they told the way. I couldn't understand all of it, but I understood enough. Too much. That was when—" Craddock held up his maimed hands—

"I succeeded and I failed," Craddock continued. "For the Flame wakened raging with power, too much power, though it was far beneath its—maximum. I was lucky to escape as I did."

The worn face held horror again.

"Against that flaming terror I watched my hands change. I saw the living flesh alter. I saw human tissues writhe and blacken into something that was—was a blasphemy, Brian. Even as I ran, I could feel those—things—where my fingers had been. I could feel them—writhing!"

He drew a deep breath, went on more steadily.

"I escaped into the jungle, and there I amputated—those horrors. I had my surgical kit. There wasn't sulfa in those days, but I managed. I thought then I'd never go back to Paititi. My career was ruined, of course; my hands were—not hands.

"Yet something kept me in the Amazon Basin. I was too close to the Flame once; part of it touched me, and I could never leave Brazil after that. Sometimes I thought I could hear Curupuri in the Jutahy drums."

He nodded.

"Then I did hear it, after thirty years. Parror brought something of the Flame with him when he came down the river, and the Indios sensed it. That incredible vitality sent its message through the jungle. When I saw Parror for the first time, in the hospital, I felt that same life-energy I had found in Paititi. It was faint, but I couldn't mistake it. I was afraid.

"Parror came to me in the laboratory and gave me my notebook. He'd traced me through that. There's the woods-telegraph, and he knew my name. He'd left Paititi on a crazy chance, hoping I was still alive, hoping to find me.

"And he succeeded. He told me I must come back to Paititi with him, and of course I said no. Then you came along the hospital hall."

"I remember." Raft nodded. "But you were alone in the lab."

"Remember Parror's faster metabolism. He could move at tremendous speed when he wanted to, in our slower world. He had to restrict himself and do everything in slow motion when we were watching. He simply ran out so fast you couldn't see him. Later, he hypnotized me with his mirror. Though I knew what I was doing, I couldn't help myself. Not till I woke here in his castle. Now I know the truth, but I'm helpless."

"What is the truth? You mean the cat-people evolved in thirty years from primitives?"

"From the jaguars of the valley," Craddock supplemented. "But it was not merely thirty years. Thirty million or billion, with the radiations pouring out from the Flame. Remember I told you a man could have a lifetime in a second? What took place in our world over a period of eons, happened in Paititi in three decades. The metabolism, the life-rate, was speeded up so enormously that the jaguars evolved in hours or days to savages. And thence to reasoning beings. Their paws became hands.

"They learned to walk upright. If we could have looked down on Paititi from above, in those times, we could have seen the shapes actually flowing, living flesh melting and changing." He paused, glancing at his hands.

"Yes," he went on, after a time. "The cat-people evolved and became intelligent. They created a culture of their own based on the older culture that had preceded them. The other life-forms in the valley reached dead ends. Only one species becomes dominant in any milieu. Here it was the cat.

"Only lately, the Flame has begun to sink again. When I wakened it, I gave it an artificial stimulus, and its flare-up will die as swiftly. In another generation or two, it will sink beneath the danger-level, and then the malignant radiations that destroyed the First Race will come pouring out."

Quickly Raft sucked in his breath. "I see. I'm getting it now, finally."

"Yes. That's why Parror abducted me. Because the records of the First Race that held the secret of the Flame no longer exist. I left them in the cavern then, and they were destroyed by that horror. As I would have been destroyed if I'd stayed longer. Parror thought I knew how to waken the Flame."

"Don't you?"

"I could not understand all the records," Craddock admitted. "I told you that. I can waken the Flame, but I can't control it. That's the danger."

"Not even Parror will risk that," Janissa suggested. "Until he finds the knowledge he seeks, he won't take chances."

Craddock gestured urgently. "Someone is coming. Parror, I think."

Janissa touched the mirror. "We can speak no more, then, until he is gone. But tell him nothing, Craddock."

"How can I? the man asked. Then gray clouds blotted out his face.

Raft leaned back, realizing that he was sweating and exhausted. Janissa watched him sympathetically.

"It is not an easy road unless you know the way," she told him. "But it is a road we must take again."

"Yeah. I'd like to get my hands on Parror personally. Or see him in my rifle-sights."

"Perhaps you will, later." The cat-face was somber. "You see, there is still danger. Craddock did not understand all the old records, but he read them."

"So?"

"The memory is in his mind. It is forgotten now, hidden away, but it is not lost. Such memories can be recovered. And if they are, Parror will know how to use the wisdom of the First Race."

"He can dig up Craddock's memories, eh? Mnemonics—hypnosis, I suppose."

"Not easily." The girl looked troubled. "He is working on a device that will aid him."

Raft's lips tightened. "But if he succeeds, he'll try to waken the Flame?"

"He will, and there is the peril," Janissa said. "The First Race supposedly learned how to control Curupuri, but their experiment was never performed. How do we know they found the answer?"

"We don't."

Janissa moved uneasily.

"It may mean destruction. The Flame unchecked, raging through Paititi. Many of us think as the First Race did, that we can live our lives safely, and let our children make the test. But the Flame sinks fast. The waters run more swiftly than the old days. We do not know when the danger-level will be reached. And—and the king has not yet decided."

"Which side does he favor?"

"Who knows?" she asked, shrugging. "We cannot read Darum's mind. Many in Paititi want freedom to live as they always have. They are willing to procrastinate rather than risk extinction. But there are others who think differently.

"I, for one, do not know, Brian. I know only this: I have my trust. I am of royal blood, and must guard the Flame. Against Parror if need be! When the king decides, I'll obey him. Meanwhile, Craddock has the answer locked in his brain. An answer that may mean death or life."

Raft stared toward the open window and the cloudy veil that hung above the great deep beyond. His voice was low.

"There's one thing, Janissa. I'm in this game now. I don't know quite where I'll fit, but I'm not just a spectator any more." His eyes hardened. "I don't like being pushed around. Darum—Parror—even you—have been treating Craddock and me like chessmen. And there wasn't much we could do about it, because we didn't know the answers."

She watched him unblinkingly. He went on.

"We were dragged into this. What we want most is to get out, back to our own world. If you'll help us, we'll help you. So let me tell you this straight. You don't mind if Parror gets the secret of controlling the Flame, but you don't want him to use it. Not without the king's permission. Right?"

"That's correct."

"Fine. Then it's simply a matter of convincing Darum that I'm Brian Raft. He had me captured because he thought I was Craddock."

Her green eyes flashed. "Darum has left the castle, with a band of soldiers. I've learned that."

"Then he believed me! He went to get Craddock himself." Raft hesitated. No, he realized, the king had not taken his word for the substitution. Instead, Darum was investigating the possibility, cutting the Gordian knot of uncertainty by going directly to the source—Parror.

"Parror is resourceful," Janissa said. "I don't know . . ." She shook her head, the soft curls stirring with her movement.

"Well, what am I supposed to do? Sit here waiting till Darum gets back?"

The girl pondered.

"Let me use the mirror again," she said at last. She took out the tiny lens, bending her head to stare intently into those cloudy depths. Raft saw her start.

"What's wrong?"

"Wait." She held up a warning hand. "It is difficult to get through. There's a barrier . . ."

She straightened, thrusting the mirror back into her dress.

"Craddock is tranced," she said. "Not the spell of the mirror, but a kind of hypnosis. Parror is taking him somewhere—I can't see where. But they have left the castle."

Raft bit at his lower lip. "Can't you communicate with Craddock at all?"

"I can catch only a few stray thoughts. Not much."

"Can you find out where they're going? Try again, Janissa. If we could discover that, it might help."

She took out the lens, bent above it in an agony of concentration. Raft saw diamonds of perspiration glittering on her forehead.

"It's hard. His mind is veiled."

"Try!"

She let the mirror drop, amazement in her eyes. "No. Kharn—no! He'd never go there!"

Raft gripped the girl's slim arms. "Kharn? Is that where the Flame is?"

Janissa drew away, shivering.

"Oh no. I thought he might take the unseen road, but to go to Kharn. He must have some method of protection I know nothing about. Or else it's suicide."

"What is Kharn? Where is it?"

"At the source of the great river," she said. "The river that flows here, under Doirada Castle. That is Kharn. But no man goes there."

"Why not?"

Janissa seemed to draw inward into herself.

"The Garden of Kharn has life which isn't like ours. There are beings in Kharn who are—I don't know what. I've never been in the Garden. But I've been near it, though. I've felt something reaching out to touch my mind, something cold and crawling and deadly."

Raft uttered a harsh laugh.

"I'd be willing face any ghost if I had my rifle back."

"Kharn is unhealthy," the girl said quietly. "If Parror has found a way to protect himself against the Garden, he's wiser than I thought. But I fear for Craddock."

"Why? Parror will take mighty good care of Dan Craddock, till he get the information he wants. Apparently this Kharn is taboo. Which is fine for Parror. He can take his time getting the information he wants."

A change had come over Janissa.

"This alters things, Brian. When Darum reached Parror's castle, he'll find Parror gone. But if he knew his quarry goes to Kharn, he might intercept him, if he goes fast." She rose to her feet in a lithe, smooth motion. "Yes, this changes the face of our plans. I must get to Darum and warn him."

"I'll go with you," Raft said.

"No, you cannot. You couldn't leave by my path." She waved toward the window. "And there are guards outside the door."

"I can take care of them."

"You are not that strong. I must move fast, and alone."

Raft caught her arm as she moved away. "At least tell me how to open that door!"

*   *   *

The elfin face smiled up at him maliciously.

"Lay your hand on the brightest spot of light. But you'd better wait here for my return, Brian. A door sometimes has more than one lock."

They were on the balcony now, and Janissa swung a slim leg over the railing.

"You'll be back?" Raft said.

"I promise."

"Her mind is like the wind," Darum had said. How much could Raft trust this cat-girl of an alien species?

He gripped her arms hard. He drew her toward him. That slim, strong body tensed in revolt, but Raft's mouth came down hard and covered hers.

After a moment he let her go. There was a touch of mockery in his eyes now.

"At least, you may not find it so easy to forget now," he said.

Janissa touched her lips with questioning fingers. She stared at him.

"No," she said enigmatically. "I shall not forget—that."

She slipped over the balustrade and was gone, writhing to avoid the keen blades, clinging precariously to the face of the stone. Raft watched her descent till her figure vanished around a turret. Then, still undecided, he returned to his luxurious prison.

He had solved nothing.

He had learned a great deal, but nothing that could be of immediate use. Except—he nodded—the key to the door. That might be of very real help. Unless he wanted to sit here quietly until Janissa or the king returned.

He found a heavy metal statuette, wrapped it in a silken scarf, and went to the door. He stared at the translucent panel, seeing now that glowing flecks of light moved slowly within the oval, like pallid moon-flames caught in a lazy current.

The brightest spot of light.

He found it and laid his palm over its glow. But nothing happened. The fleck slid from under his hand. He tried again, with no result.

A door has more than one lock. That was what she had meant, then. Smiling sourly, Raft tossed his weapon away and returned to the balcony.

Janissa had descended, but he could not follow her. He had no illusions on that score. Nor would any rope he might improvise reach to firm footing. He bent and tried to break off one of the swords. All he accomplished was the wounding of a finger.

Raft swore softly and savagely. After that he felt a little better. He dropped on a pile of cushions and tried to plan. It was difficult. What he wanted, obviously, was to get out of Paititi and take Craddock with him. The way to do that—what was the method?

He knew the road out. Once back in the Amazon jungle, he'd take his chance, even without a rifle. But escaping wouldn't solve Raft's problems now.

The amulets, Parror's, and the one taken by the king. They, apparently, gave the possessor power to live outside Paititi, to slow down the metabolism to a speed normal to life beyond the valley's cliffs. But the effects were variable. Back in the hospital, Parror had once moved too fast for human eyes to observe.

Suppose, then, Raft thought, he and Craddock managed to escape. They might reach the Jutahy. They might get a week's start, or a month's. But in a day pursuers from Paititi could overtake them. With the aid of the amulets, Parror or the king could flash through the jungle in pursuit, and kill or hypnotize with Janissa's trick mirror. And back he and Craddock would go to Paititi.

So he was up against a dead end there.

It was difficult to judge time. The sun didn't move appreciably, and the second-hand on his watch went so slowly he couldn't see its progress. He was living at an abnormally increased rate of speed here, which meant that in Paititi he was on more nearly equal terms with the cat-people. Once outside, that slight advantage would be instantly lost, as his metabolism slowed to its former rate.

The psychology of a feline race—that might be the answer. . . .

Raft was lost in thought for a long time. He roused when the panel opened to admit not Vann, but a guard and a page, with a food-cart. After the meal he again fell into his reverie. It should be night now, but the days in this land would be as long as the nights, abnormally long.

Basically the people of Paititi were feline, as he was of simian stock. Monkeys are curious. The instinct of curiosity is strong in the human race. But cats lose interest quickly. They are not builders. They had taken possession of these castles, reared long ago by the mysterious First Race, and renovated. Cats were essentially hedonists. But the factor of intelligence was a strong influence, and one whose strength Raft could not estimate.

Could he base any plans on rules of logic, in a land where the human factor was so alien to his own experience? A race of cats might have unpredictable reaction. . . .

Low, urgent, warning, a wordless murmur whispered softly from across the room.

IX

ASSASSIN'S PLOT

RAFT WAS on his feet facing the doorway before those last echoes had died. The translucent oval was open now, the way of escape clear. But barring his path was a figure, veiled in soft grays, her face hidden, and both loveliness and horror breathed out from beneath the shrouding veils.

Her hands, slim, pale, were bare, and held an instrument unfamiliar to Raft, though he had heard it before. Again the white fingers moved across intricate strings and keys. Once more the music breathed out. More urgent now, summoning him.

"Yrann?" Raft said questioningly. The shrouded head bowed once. He stepped forward.

"The guard?"

Yrann beckoned. She turned toward that inviting portal, and Raft was at her heels, but warily. The corridor outside held no menace.

The guard was standing motionless. He did not turn his head. By the door, he stood frozen, his eyes wide, staring at a milky, glittering little sphere on the floor at his feet.

Raft's eyes were drawn to that globe. Colors were moving and coiling slowly beneath its surface. It was growing larger. . . .

The soft, urgent strings roused him. Yrann moved forward, bending to lift the sphere and hide it in her veils. The spell snapped. But the guard, Raft saw, still was motionless.

He pointed to the man and raised his brows questioningly. The music sounded reassuring, somehow.

"The guard will not wake. Not for a while. *The spell holds him.*"

Raft noticed that the oval door had closed behind him. Yrann was beckoning again. Which meant exactly what? Treachery? Perhaps. The cat people were unpredictable. But, at least, it was better than sitting in his prison waiting, and Raft felt quite able to protect himself against a woman.

He followed her along the corridor.

She took a circuitous route, Raft thought. They met no one, with the exception of a page who came hurrying toward them from the distance. Instantly Yrann pressed Raft aside, into a shelter behind a velvet tapestry. The page passed unsuspiciously, bowing to Yrann as he went. Then, after a moment, the journey was resumed.

It ended before another hanging that Yrann thrust aside, urging Raft through and letting the drape fall again. Now that familiar dim light—or, rather, absence of it—made Raft close his eyes briefly. There was utter silence.

Through the stillness Yrann's music sang. Her fingers dwelt on his arm.

She guided him forward, making no misstep even in this vague gloom. Swiftly they approached the silk-heaped dais where the king had sat.

The shrouded form beside him began sending out emanations which were curiously ominous.

"What is it, Yrann?" Raft said. "What do you want?"

The oboe murmured, the strings twanged, and there was something evil in the minor notes that sounded.

The music held malignance.

Yrann touched the cushions of the dais reflectively. Her hand lingered on the softness where Darum's body had lain. Then again that cool, wordless song whispered evilly, with a conspiratoral secrecy about it. It was heavy with suggestion.

Yrann turned toward the back of the dais. Curtains hung

there. She held one aside, beckoning till Raft came to her side. Gently she guided him to a little alcove in the wall.

She pressed something into his hand. And stepped back, letting the curtain drop.

Wait, the music said. Wait now.

He was in utter darkness. But he knew what it was that he held. His free hand investigated cautiously. And recoiled from vicious, razor-sharp metal.

He pulled at the curtain. Yrann's harp-oboe shrilled sharp warning. The velvet fell back.

Then soft footsteps fading into stillness. A rustle. He sensed that Yrann had gone.

But he knew unmistakably now why she had brought him here.

Working his lips as though he tasted something unpleasant, Raft leaned back against the wall. Yrann had helped him, if only for her own purposes. Now the idea was to get out of the castle, somehow.

On the curtain before him a ghostly, pale movement was visible. His eyes had adjusted now, and he could make out a shadow, man-shaped, cast on the fabric—the shadow of a man whose hand held a long-bladed dagger.

His own shadow. He turned. Behind him was no wall, but one of the familiar oval doors. But its glow was dimmed, and the crawling flecks of light were very faint.

He located the brightest one and laid his hand upon it.

The oval panel lifted and was gone. Instantly a blaze of light dazzled him.

His weapon ready, Raft waited, blinking. But there was nothing alive in the room before him. Only a fantastic glitter of brightness and shining metals, a richness of flamboyant color that contrasted strangely with the gloom of the chamber behind him.

Struck by a new thought, he stepped back, through the curtain, and swung it into place. The material was opaque. No hint of light filtered through. If Yrann, or anyone else, entered, his hiding-place would not be betrayed by an oval glow on the dark hanging.

Satisfied on that scorn, Raft again entered what he saw to be Darum's treasure-vault.

If he expected a hoard of gold and diamonds, he was disappointed. There were diamonds, highly polished and many-faceted, but they seemed to hold equal place with quartz crystals that were used for the same purpose of jewelry and decoration. There was metal here, curious alloys in which hints of rainbow colors rippled, like oil on water. And weapons, many weapons.

The blades were of good quality, which was to be expected, for manganese, beryllium, and chromium were found in Brazil. There must be deposits of the elements here in Paititi. Certainly there was silver, for delicately shaped and engraved vases of it, burnished and shining, were set in a row around the walls.

It was the loot of a strangely alien civilization. Some of the objects the cat people found beautiful were ugly to Raft's eyes. One set of very plain, sleek metals reminded him of Brancusis. His gaze followed arcs and curves that were curiously satisfying and oddly suggestive, though he realized he could probably never completely understand the principles that underlay the art-forms of this race.

There were more utilitarian objects. Many of them were dueling-gloves, with their razor-keen triple talons curving out viciously from the fingers. Raft picked up one of these, jeweled and ornate, and drew it on his hand. The claws ran the full length of his fingers, he found, and instinctively his hand tensed and curved.

Encrusted as it was with gems, the glove could be used as a handy substitute for brass knuckles. Which would probably shock the cat people, Raft thought sardonically, as he slipped the gauntlet into a capacious pocket he had discovered in his garments.

There were a number of maps, engraved in metal, and jewel-framed, too heavy to be portable, but interesting. One seemed to show Paititi. Raft could make nothing of the symbols, but he located Parror's castle, and the great gulf into which the torrent poured.

Thoughtfully he traced the river back to its source, where a tiny ring of zircons surrounded a few cryptic markings. The Garden of Kharn, eh? Where Parror was heading, with his captive Craddock.

Another map showed the castle itself, and was made with a dozen thin metal sheets that lifted on hinges. Raft studied this closely. What he wanted was a way out. Unfortunately, he found orientation difficult, until he managed to identify his own prison apartment. After that, it was easier.

Finally he drew back, nodding. Yes, he thought he could find his way now.

Yrann's music came urgently to his ears.

Raft whirled toward the door. Nothing. But the song kept on, warning, shrill.

He moved forward. The shape of a familiar object on a shelf caught his glance.

It was a revolver, a small, ornate weapon of mother-of-pearl and silver filigree. Beside it lay a heap of cartridges. Raft swept the cartridges into his pocket and lifted the gun, staring at the initials on the butt. TDF—Thomaz da Fonséca, the aviator who had crashed in Paititi. His revolver, then.

It was not Raft's own heavy, powerful Colt, but it was far better than a dagger. He slipped his finger through the guard, saw that it was unloaded, and deftly thrust shells into the chamber. Then he stepped across the threshold and waited, his hand on the curtain before him.

Yrann's music had changed. It was softer now, welcoming. But under it ran a counterpoint of menace, a soft susurrus of treachery and evil.

"Parror had escaped me, Yrann," the king's low voice said. "There was another man from outside in his castle, I found traces. But they are gone. We could find no tracks."

The wordless song was questioning.

"They are still in Paititi. I had guards at the gate to the unseen road. Parror will not get at the Flame till I am willing. Nevertheless, I do not know where he is, now."

Tenderness breathed across the strings—and hidden hatred.

Darum sighed.

"I was ready. I was ready for anything I might find. I even thought Parror might take the unseen road to outside, and I was ready to pursue him even there. But how can I find him when he has vanished with this other man?"

Raft rubbed his jaw reflectively. He knew where Parror had gone. If he told the king, would that help?

Yrann played lightly, and now slumber breathed out from the hollow crying of the pipes.

"Yes," the king said. "Yes, there is always this, Yrann. The world does not come into our chamber here." He sighed. "There is nothing here but our love."

Sleep, the music said. Sleep, my lover and my king. Only sleep—and wake no more.

But Darum sensed no menace. His breathing grew quieter. Drowsiness crept through the curtain, taking Raft in a warm embrace. Yrann's music was magic.

Dark magic, Raft thought angrily. He shook his head savagely:

After a time Yrann's arm crept through the soft barrier, touching Raft, pulling him forward. The glare of light from behind him struck full on Yrann's face—or what should have been a face. With a wordless sound she pulled her veil in place. Raft felt her gaze go from him to the treasure chamber. But the harp was silent. It asked no question.

The curtain remained looped back, and the light struck out to the dais, where Darum lay asleep, his face relaxed and peaceful. He stirred uneasily. Yrann's fingers rippled across the strings, and the king was silent once more.

Yrann touched the little revolver hesitantly. Then she pulled the dagger from Raft's bent, where he had placed it, and thrust it into his hand. She pushed him forward, pointing to the dais.

Raft halted. The veiled face was lifted to his. He shook his head slowly and emphatically.

"No," he said under his breath. "Even if that would save my life, I don't think I could do it."

Yrann's hand poised over the harp-strings, somehow threateningly. The tableau held for a moment. Then she must have seen that he meant what he said. She made a dreadful snarling sound deep in her throat and snatched the dagger from Raft's grip, whirling toward the sleeping king. Her draperies swirled as she bent and plucked at Darum's shirt, tearing the thin silk open. Darum murmured and stirred in his music-drugged sleep. Yrann swung the dagger high, poised it.

Raft's reaction was instinctive. He had begun his leap forward before he saw what gleamed upon the king's bared chest, something square and shining, on a silver chain. Something that seemed to give out light that quivered like the pulse of life itself.

The amulet!

There was no time to examine it. There was no time to ask questions and be sure.

But Raft had an inner certainty which needed no confirmation. A man could not look upon that shaking gleam and not recognize it.

With one hand Raft snatched at the amulet. The chain snapped under his violent pull. With the other he seized Yrann's as her knife began to plunge downward. She snarled again and bent like a bow against him, fighting hard for the weapon.

They swayed together beside the couch, battling in desperate silence. The harp crashed to the floor. A string broke with a ringing snap. On the couch Darum sat up dizzily, peering at the dimly seen figures reeling before him.

Then with a suddenness that made Raft stagger, Yrann released the knife. She sprang back, stooping to snatch up the harp. Her fingers swept across it, dragging a wild discord of alarm from the strings.

Waken! Beware!

Loud with ringing urgency, the music crashed against the walls. The king struggled up, shaking his head, crying out confused questions. But he was caught in the shaft of light from the treasure room, and could see Raft as no more than a shadow—a shadow, and a glint of threatening steel.

The music screamed and wailed. There was a distant sound of running feet.

Cursing under his breath, Raft whirled and raced for the door by which he had entered, praying that it was open. He swept the drapery aside, saw an open passage before him, and plunged into it. Now he was tagged as an assassin. That meant he had to escape, and fast. The king might listen to explanations, but the probability was that he wouldn't, especially since they involved Yrann.

The map he had seen burned in Raft's mind. If he got off the track once, he knew he was lost. There should be another branching corridor here, at about this point.

He dodged into it, but did not slacken his pace. The sound of distant, aroused voices gave him warning. He gripped the revolver tighter. It would be more useful than the dagger. As for Yrann, he knew now what she had intended. If necessary, she would have killed Darum herself, and put the blame on Raft. Which was thoroughly human as well as feline.

Twice he hid behind curtains while guards raced past. Once he stopped, not breathing, before an oval door, wondering what lay beyond. It led to escape, he knew, but there might be soldiers behind it.

There were. Shadows showed against the panel. Raft turned silently and raced back, knowing he was lost now. Unless another way opened up before him, which wasn't likely.

He turned into another passage, where windows stood open in one wall. Glancing out, he found himself staring, not into the Gulf of Doirada, but at the river, where it curved in and finally poured over the edge of an arched opening, beneath the castle.

Beyond the mossy plain loomed the enormous pillars of the forest, sanctuary if he could reach it. But the river lay far below, and was flowing too fast. It would sweep him into the abyss, if its rush gripped him.

Too fast?

Not in Paititi, where the metabolism of all living things was speeded up so enormously. For all its power, the waters below glided past so smoothly, so gently, he might have been watching the gentle boiling of a cloud-river.

Raft thrust the revolver into his pocket, closing over it a fastening. The contrivance sealed it tightly, which indicated the pocket might be waterproof. That would help. Raft gave a quick glance to left and right. He saw no one, though the sounds of pursuit were louder.

Then he climbed into the window-frame, two hundred feet above that molten silver cataract—and dived.

X

NIGHTMARE GARDEN

ONE THING RAFT had forgotten, and the fantastic thing was that he had time to remember it as he fell. The rate of speed of a freely falling body does not vary. Friction of air has some effect, but very little when an object weighing a hundred and sixty pounds, in the form of a man, drops free.

Raft's metabolism had been tremendously accelerated by the radiation that pervaded Paititi. He was living far faster than in his own world. And he had seen immense boulders float down lightly as feathers from the towering cliffs.

To his own mind, he did not fall. He dropped gently as in an elevator, utterly stunned with surprise, so astonished was he that the truth did not strike him immediately. When it did, there was nothing he could do about it.

Gently he revolved as he drifted down. Beside him the wall of the castle slipped past. At any moment someone might come out on a balcony and see him. A thrown spear would be dangerous. It could be thrown sufficiently fast to impale him, since the wielder could easily gauge the rate of Raft's fall.

He had never felt so helpless and naked in his life. It was like hanging free and unsupported in interplanetary space. He had time for a hundred questions and fears to pass through his mind before, finally, with agonizing slowness, his body struck the waters of the torrent.

His mass was the same, and he sank, angling slowly in the direction of the current. But he was breathing perhaps a hundred times faster than normal, so there was a new danger. Under ordinary conditions he could have held his breath until he reached the surface. As it was he might not emerge above the water for five minutes!

Now the accelerated metabolism was helpful. Raft managed to turn and swim up, though it was like moving in glue, against that slow, inexorable thrust of driving waters. He was a fly drowning in syrup. But the fly reached the surface at last.

Under ordinary conditions he would have been swept over the brink into Doirada Gulf, but his stimulated time-sense fought the slow pressure of the water. He fought his way upstream. He dragged himself to a shallow pool and collapsed, gasping.

There was no time to rest yet, though. He was not yet out of range of pursuit. Nor did he think he could cross the clearing to where the forest began without being spotted.

Wildly he stared about him, searching for a hiding place.

Reeds grew thickly about the margin of the pool. The water itself was roiled with thick mud, and opaque. Raft found a hollow reed, tested it, and made use of an old trick. He simply lay down in the water, anchoring himself by gripping embedded rocks, and breathed through the improvised lifeline.

He could not see, but he could not be seen, either. The cat people might discover his hiding-place, of course. Yet the chance was worth taking, Raft thought, remembering the difference between feline and simian psychology.

The pursuers would expect him—as a descendant of simians—to depend on flight, and probably to head for the forest. They would themselves be too fastidious to hide in dirty water if any other way of escape opened, and automatically might expect Raft to think in the same manner. If so, they would be mistaken.

His eyes shut, Raft concentrated on breathing. It was not too easy.

The amulet—could that help him now? It contained a spark from the Flame, from the tremendous energy-source called Curupuri. And it had the property of lowering the metabolic rate, somehow.

If, instead, it accelerated metabolism, Raft would have been more satisfied. It might actually do that, but that seemed improbable.

The sparks, probably, were keyed to the original Flame, kept powered by induction, unless they were each complete in themselves, like a speck of radium. To decelerate would mean that Raft would become the equivalent of a living statue among enemies moving like flashes of lightning.

Anyhow, the amulet was in his sealed pocket, and could not be secured without ruining da Fonseca's revolver. It was something to be investigated later. There was nothing to do now but play possum, and wait.

So Raft waited, while the chill of the river crept stealthily into his flesh, numbing nerves and muscles. He forced himself to wait, unhitching his mind till he seemed to float in a vacuum where neither light nor sound existed, nothing save the slow, jellied motion of the current in the pool. He couldn't afford to wait for nightfall. It might be several weeks, to his time-sense, before the sun dropped out of sight.

There were, Raft thought wryly, certain handicaps to a land where metabolism had gone so fantastically haywire.

Anyway, Darum had not caught Parror. That arrogant individual had taken Craddock, to Kharn, which lay at the source of this very river. What lay in the Garden of Kharn, Raft hadn't the slightest idea. Janissa had feared it. And she wasn't easily frightened, Raft surmised. His thoughts drifted toward the girl, with her strange, dark-circled eyes and her tiger-striped hair.

For no apparent reason, he thought of Balzac, and the French writer's story, "A Passion in the Desert." Then he had the connection: a man's love for a—had it been a lioness? Or a leopard. Not a jaguar, anyway. There were no jaguars in the Sahara.

Janissa?

Feline she was, but she was human too. Though child of an alien species, she was no beast, no stalking beast of prey.

Raft caught himself.

"Good grief!" he thought. "Am I imagining I'm in love with the girl? I've seen her just twice, in the flesh. It's novelty. I'm attracted by her exotic strangeness. When I get out of here, in five years or so, maybe, I'll meet a girl from Peoria and marry her." The very term marriage made him realize the fantasy of the situation. He grinned inwardly.

"Biologically I rather imagine it's impossible. Besides, such things don't happen. I certainly wouldn't want my wife going out at night to sit on the back fence and howl."

Nevertheless the thought did not entirely leave him. The union of two races, two species, rather, had never occurred in the history of biology. He broke the problem down into basic equations of genes and chromosomes, and that passed time, but finally made him feel foolish. Eventually he was glad to raise his head warily above water and prepare to emerge.

A long time had passed, and the alarm must long since have died down. No one was visible on any of the castle's many balconies, nor could the courtyard be seen from here. But if Raft attempted to cross that open plain, he would inevitably be spotted.

He could keep to the river—though its slow, powerful current was a danger. So he set off upstream, hugging as closely to the bank as he could, crawling mostly, swimming at times, and keeping the reed always ready. Once, at a suspicious flash of movement, he lay hidden, but he was overly cautious then. By the time he reached the forest, he was freezing cold and bleeding from scraped elbows and wrists.

He hoped the cat people did not trail by scent. It was unlikely. They were a civilized race, and the dulling of certain senses is the price evolution exacts. The lower species, depending on scent and sound, have those faculties highly developed. On the other hand, man's vision is far more powerful and more easily adjustable than the vision of most beasts.

Darum would not know his destination. The closer he got to Kharn, the safer he would be from pursuit.

A cyclopean tree shut out the turrets of the castle. Raft went on cautiously for perhaps half a mile. Then he opened the sealed pocket, made sure his revolver was dry, and put the dagger into his belt. The amulet he took out for a closer inspection.

It told him nothing. A spark of fire glittered in the depths of a cloudy crystal chip that was in turn set in a thick metallic lozenge, square with rounded corners. The flat gem could, he found on experiment, be revolved like the dial of a safe. He turned it cautiously.

There was no change, except, perhaps, for a freshening of the breeze. How could he test the device?

His watch, of course.

Luckily the watch was waterproof. He stared at the dial, noticing that the second hand was moving very slowly. He turned the crystal on the amulet again and the pointer moved faster. Another turn, and it raced.

Which meant that his metabolism was correspondingly slower.

Would the amulet also increase the rate of life? If so, that would solve many problems. He could get to Kharn, perhaps, even before Parror arrived there. But he was doomed to disappointment on that score. The amulet could retard metabolism, but it could not increase it beyond the rate prevalent in Paititi.

That meant the spark, undoubtedly, was attuned to the Flame itself, radiating at the same energy-rate and moving in the same cycle. Well, Raft didn't want to be handicapped by moving more slowly than the rest of his temporary world, and he adjusted the device till it was as he had found it.

He now put it in the pocket that held the revolver, and went on. He was estimating, as well as he could remember, the velocity of a bullet, and wondering if, under the current conditions, any target he fired at might be able to dodge lead.

He must remember to use the gun at close range, the closer the better!

The use of artillery would be handicapped in Paititi. If a bomb were dropped on Doirada Castle, the cat people would almost have time to dismantle the structure and move it elsewhere before the egg landed. No wonder the species fought with steel, instead of propellents. Only an energy-ray could be truly efficient here.

Which explained, Raft decided, why mental powers were so highly developed—Janissa's mirror, Yrann's hypnotic sphere. Timelag would be minimized with such devices.

The whole inanimate part of the valley was indeed under a spell, such a one as had protected the Norse god Baldur. There could be few fatalities through accident. Not when stones floated, rivers ran like treacle, and a man fell as slowly as Alice descending the rabbit-hole!

As he went on, he paid more attention to the life around him, the curious creatures that used the gigantic trees as hiding places. In the cool, clear light he could make out new details.

The flower-bright vines, with their dangerous tentacles, slithered swiftly across the bark. There were many of the three-foot alligators, lurking in the pools they themselves seemed to have constructed on the trunks, shells that resembled the cups rubber-workers fasten to the hevea bark as they drain their milky latex.

The 'gators had surprisingly flexible claws. Raft noticed a couple of them constructing their pools, scraping resinous wood from the tree and making it into a kind of cement with a fluid they secreted from salivary glands.

Only the sloths were truly familiar, and they were all the stranger because of the rapidity with which they moved. The true sloth hangs motionless by its claws, as its tongue flashes out to reap a nutritious harvest of insects. Its metabolism is abnormally slow.

But it was not slow here.

As for the inch-long parasites that crept through the sloths' hair, Raft found those creatures too unpleasantly familiar to be truly interesting. Only their ape-like tails kept them from resembling too closely the species that was not dominant in Paititi, though it might be elsewhere.

Most intriguing were the brown furry mammals in the apartment-house nests. They had sucking-disks on their paws, which were none too efficient, but their elongated snouts ended in tabs of flesh like the extremity of an elephant's trunk, a finger and thumb, which they used as man might use his hands. Its prehensile delicacy was amazing.

Raft wondered what the interior of the nests was like. He felt that what lay inside might be surprising.

Underfoot was only the moss. There was no underbrush. Those incredible trees seemed to have sucked all the nutriment out of the ground, leaving so little that only moss could flourish. That gave a logical explanation for the tree-parasites.

Where else could they live, except in a closely integrated society, where hunger made an automatic check-and-balance? Even the trees were part of that inexorable system, for they had drained the earth of life. And in return, they were hosts to other species.

Species had reached dead end in this land. They would never evolve to dominance, as the cat people had evolved, Raft surmised. They had found their balance.

And, meanwhile, he had to find Craddock.

Keeping a wary eye out for possible pursuit, he followed the river. Never at any time could he see more than a half-mile ahead. The trees made a maze. But the river itself was a guide. Raft plunged on doggedly, until at last exhaustion forced him to rest.

There might be shelter on one of the encrusted tree-trunks, but life was too teeming there. None of the things seemed to venture to the ground, however, and Raft finally lay down on the river bank, in lieu of better shelter. He might be attacked while he slept, but there was no way of guarding against that. He laid the revolver ready and slept, hoping for the best.

When he awoke, he went on again. Nor had he far to travel now. An hour's walk, as he estimated time, brought him to a wall which blocked further progress. It was only twenty feet high, dwarfed by the trees, but it was of some age-resistant plastic or alloy, and had eroded scarcely at all.

To left and to right it stretched away and was lost amid the trees. But it was broken at one spot by an archway, through which the river poured. Sediment had built up a narrow ledge bordering the water, a precarious path that led beneath the arch.

Unhesitatingly Raft stepped out on that muddy trail. He could see faint outlines that might have been footprints, and, further along, his suspicion was confirmed when he observed a track that was unmistakably that of Craddock's heavy boots. He was very nearly at the end of the trail.

Ahead he could make out irregular vegetation darkening that hemispherical opening, blocking his vision. He went on, more carefully now. There were bushes, he noted with surprise.

He began to push through their tangled mass, and abruptly drew back, contact with the things startling him. Their texture had been unlike the rough, bristly texture of plants. They were warm.

They were not plants.

Lacy filigrees, arabesque nets of interwoven mesh, made a curtain on each side of the river. They were grayish-pink, reminding Raft unmistakably of the neutral structure of a living body, networks of nerves, raw and unpleasant. Nor were they rooted like plants.

They quivered, vibrated. They drew back to let him pass.

As he stepped forward, they drew into themselves like contracting anemones touched by an intrusive finger. A dozen grayish, irregular little balls hugged the ground, blending with it in protective camouflage.

Beyond them lay the Garden of Kharn, a sickly, yellowish tangle of vegetation blocking Raft's view. He could see the guarding wall marching to left and right, curving in to form what must be an enclosure. There were none of the giant trees within the wall, though their columns loomed above and beyond it.

Raft moved on, keeping to the river bank. The bushes were strange to him, though he was no botanist. They seemed a rather impossible hybrid of fungus and true plant. They were fern and mushroom in one.

Oddly he thought of them as vampires, draining life from the very ground.

That forest was not normal—no. The cyclopean trees outside were friendly by comparison. They, at least, were as immense and aloof as gods.

But these plants, these sickly hybrids, grew with a rank

luxuriance that was in itself unhealthy. Movement crawled through the yellow jungle, not the wave-motion of wind, but secretive, stealthy movements which made Raft's scalp prickle.

Very faintly, scarcely noticeable, he felt a presence in the Garden. And he knew, then, why Janissa had not wanted to speak of Kharn.

For that intangibly sensed presence was not malignant. It was worse. It was cold and distant and alien.

And, intrinsically, it was very evil.

Raft moved even more cautiously now. There was menace here, the more ominous because he could not define it. It was a brooding, enigmatic presence which was sensed by the cat-people as well as by himself. This added up to significance.

Felines and simians react in different ways to the same stimulus. Cats are notorious for their acceptance of the super-natural, which meant simply the supernormal, vibrations and radiations too subtle to be sensed fully by mankind. Psychic menaces that would give a man cold chills would rouse a cat to purring ecstasy.

Similarly, cats react violently to a canine menace—a wolf— whereas a man simply reaches for the nearest weapon.

This malignancy, therefore, was a presence alien to both feline and simian.

Perhaps, it was alien chiefly because of the altered evolutionary standard in this hothouse valley of forced growth. There was an old sort of familiarity about that unseen presence. Raft felt certain that he had encountered something of the sort before, and often. Yet never had his living flesh shrunk from the mere nearness of any creature as it did now. Whatever dwelt in the Garden of Kharn, it was nothing remotely normal or healthy.

He stepped beneath the broad leaves and mushroom-caps of the forest. A sulphurous yellow light filtered through from above, lacking in the cool clarity of the atmosphere outside the Garden.

The ground underfoot was spongy, a moist, slippery muck into which his sandals sank mushily, with an unpleasant sucking sound. It was not silent here. There were furtive, quick movements all about him, hidden in that yellow jungle.

He was an intruder and felt it. A fleshy stem bent slowly

toward him, sticky juice exuding from its surface. The sweetish odor of the liquor was sickening. Raft stepped away, and the branch rose slowly toward the perpendicular, as though it was dragging itself painfully upright against the fetters of gravity.

Yes, the forest was conscious of him. But there were no cannibal trees here, no gigantic Venus fly-traps that could swallow him whole. There was something horrible about the straining, awkward motion of those heavy leaves and stems.

The place was alive with insects. The forest crawled with them, flies, moths, butterflies, a myriad varieties crept and buzzed and fed on the ichor the trees sweated.

Some of the fungi had hollow caps like huge bowls, and the stench that rose from those liquid-filled basins was overpowering. Yet it was not entirely unpleasant.

Attar of roses is sickening in quantity, but the merest suggestion of attar has the opposite effect. Had the forest not sweated their perfume till the very air was saturated with it, Raft might not have objected. As it was, his clothes were moist and stinking with the stuff before he had traveled more than a few yards.

The trail of Parror and Craddock was well marked. There were other tracks in the soil, ambiguous prints Raft did not recognize. But he ignored these to follow his quarry. Parror had headed directly toward the center of the Garden.

One of the pink webwork creatures crept slowly into view. A filament of raw nerves, it crawled up the stem of a fungus and pulled itself into the liquid-filled cap. It immersed itself, floating motionless, its tendrils spreading out like the hair of a drowned woman.

A little creature, plated like an armadillo, rolled into view. Raft watched it warily. All over the armored body sharp spines struck out.

It rolled toward Raft, but he avoided it easily. The spines looked dangerous. They might be toxic. Luckily the creature could not move fast.

It rolled into the jungle and was gone.

Raft went on. He saw another of the armored animals, but it was licking the stem of a fern-mushroom, and did not notice him. Then a clearing opened ahead, and it was—carpeted.

That was Raft's first impression. Patterns of flowers, arabesque and exotic, blazed with a riot of color within a circular expanse twenty feet in diameter. But they were not flowers. A queer, smooth glaze seemed to overlie that expanse—and it was a carpet, after all. The meaningless, twisting pattern was the first touch of vivid color he had seen in the saffron forest.

Raft stood scowling, sensing more strongly now that dim pulse of a living presence in the Garden.

Slowly there crept into his mind the thought of a voice—whispering.

XI

CREEPING MENACE

IT CAME so slowly, so imperceptibly, that eerie voice, that Raft could not tell when it took form and shape in his brain. Yet it was not exactly a voice nor a thought. Rather, it was something akin to each, but with a difference. Communication is aimed at what psychologists call empathy—the transference of the senses from one mind to another, so that perfect understanding may be approached. It is rapport, never complete, always groping—

Till now.

Because the Intruder understood Raft. With its ancient wisdom it knew the very structure of his soul. Like ivy sliding through crevices in a wall, the thing permeated Raft, as though he stood bathed in a light that flowed into his body. As though he were a living sponge through which tidewater stole.

The slow tide mounted.

The heavy scent of the forest was not so unpleasant now. Raft could sort out the component elements which made up the perfume, the sharp, pungent fluid that the armadillo-creatures liked, the warm, oily, sweet ichor that fed the nerve-things. Other juices, musk-heavy, eucalyptus-keen, salty and sour and pungent were present. It was oddly fascinating, this business of analyzing the odors and recognizing each one.

For they were, in essence, food-odors. Not human food.

But nevertheless those smells stimulated the purely physical part of Raft and, through that, struck deep into his mind.

Feeding was an integral part of the life-cycle, the purpose for which all things were created. Dulled senses could not appreciate the pure ecstasy of absorbing nourishment. Only specialized beings could understand the delight which went through every cell of the body.

The nerve-things. They lay immersed in their warm, steaming liquor, tingling with electric pleasure as they absorbed the fluid that was food and drink to them. The armadillo-beasts. The feeling of taste on the taste-buds of a tongue. Cool liquid slipping down a dry throat, sharp and refreshing. The pleasure of taste, and taste alone.

You have always known hunger, Brian Raft.

He was standing in the center of that patterned carpet, he noticed. It did not matter. He was trying to concentrate on that message, that inviting whisper which spoke to him of delights so purely physical that they transcended anything else.

Not only animal-beings, but plants as well, knew hunger and satiation. For plants fed through their root-sytems, set deep into the breathing earth that is the primal source of all life. Something utterly unimaginable crawled through Raft, the physical sensation of having roots, of feeling himself absorb nourishment through vegetable tissue. Plant-cells. He was part of the earth itself, and it fed him.

He sank to his knees on that smooth, vivid carpet.

Now he was looking up at a shimmering dance of faint light. He was on his back, arms flung wide, and a tingling, delightful warmth was saturating him. He was on quicksand which very slowly, very gently, settled beneath him.

Or it was not settling. It was he who was dissolving, being absorbed into that alien substance on which he lay. He was becoming part of the composite, hungry life that beat distantly all around him, murmuring in the slow motions of the trees, shuddering through the very earth.

You have always known hunger, Brian Raft. You are one. I am many.

Therefore feed and be content, the silent voice said. Sip the sharp, tingling essence that nourishes the armored beasts. Steep yourself in the warm smoothness of the liquor in the fungus-cups. Thrust roots into the soil, and know the subtle delight of a feeding which permeates all of you, body and mind.

Brighter grew the swirling mists. They blotted out vision. But there was no need for eyes. The trees were blind, yet they thrilled with ecstasy as their roots sucked up food.

The trees?

No, they could not feel. And yet they could. Something bound them to all other life here, by an unbreakable cord.

The Garden of Kharn hungered and was fed.

Memories flashed through Raft's mind. The Intruder was questioning, seeking, probing for what? He remembered the sharp catnip taste of beer, the peppery spiciness of curry, the fresh hot taste of newly-baked bread. The sweet juice of tangerines was in his mouth, and the heavy richness of cocoa. The aromatic tickling of old brandy.

Eagerness touched Raft. The probing grew more violent. He half roused himself from his trance.

Still the memories were dragged into the forefront of his consciousness. The tastes of things he had known once, elsewhere.

Where, then?

In a world where brandy was sipped from sleek glass inhalers, where bread was baked in ovens, where cocoa was served in cups, on tables upon which white linen was spread. Association clicked in Raft's brain. He remembered more than food now.

He remembered civilization. And with that thought came realization of himself, of Brian Raft. He was not a sensuous machine for sucking up nourishment.

The bright mists swept down like a shrouding blanket. The Garden of Kharn sent its heavy perfume like a tide over Raft. But he remembered, very suddenly and chillingly, another Garden, and a Tree which had borne strange fruit. A command that said, "Ye shall not eat of it."

You have always known hunger, Brian Raft. Feed as I feed. Know ecstasy as I know it.

A still, cool, distant voice, infinitely alluring, impossible to resist, although it, too, aroused memory. That indefinable familiarity was stronger now. The presence that infiltrated the Garden was one that Raft had known before, in different form.

Then he remembered.

And the serpent said unto the woman, Ye shall not surely die.

The blind shock of realization stabbed through Raft with abysmal violence. His muscles jerked into tenseness. He attempted to spring up, and found that he could not.

That gelid carpet had flowed upon him, over him, as he had lain motionless.

Yet it was possible to move. With infinite effort he dragged his arm down till his hand closed over the hilt of the dagger. He could feel the treacherously pleasant embrace of the thing all around him. A winding sheet that would have absorbed him, he thought, as he lay helpless.

He stabbed up, claustrophobia bringing dry panic to his throat. He slashed in a blind frenzy of panic till the living carpet was ribboned. The worst part was that the entity did not try to flee. It let itself be cut to rags, till all that flowery beauty was torn and spoiled. Raft stumbled away into the dubious shelter of the saffron forest, choking for a breath of clean air. He felt filthy and contaminated.

It revolted him that any one of his senses, the purely animal one of taste, could be so treacherous!

What monstrous dead-end evolution had developed such a devil's Garden as this?

It was more than symbiosis. It was an attunement of all life within these walls. Outside, on the cyclopean trees, various species killed each other, ate, propagated, and died. But in Kharn there had been a gradual absorption, a bond growing into existence between plant and animal life.

One species—dominant!

Raft presently saw that species.

Deeper in the forest, the shapeless mound of flesh lay under a transparent hemisphere that seemed to be unbreakable. Raft yielded to impulse and smashed a rock down upon it, without result. He did not wish to fire his revolver, for fear of forewarning Parror, but he had an idea that a bullet would not harm that protective barrier either. Immersed in a watery liquid the gray mass floated. Small conduits like arteries led down into the ground.

A brain? Only partially. Sections of it were abnormally developed, others vestigial. There were other additions which

Raft could not understand. But he felt more strongly than ever the intangible evil that throbbed out from the thing.

For it was reptilian. Here in Kharn the reptilian species had become dominant, subjugating all other life into a fantastic rapport that made the Garden itself a single entity. There was no really recognizable intelligence in the being. Reptilian instincts are not mammalian, and a tremendously evolved reptile might have nothing at all in common with other creatures.

The thing lived only for the specialized pleasure of taste. It had developed the necessity of feeding into a sensory ecstasy that was exclusive of all other faculties. Intelligence there might be, or a sort, but it was applied only to purposes that would aid the monster's dominant instinct.

Through the Garden, through living trees and and living flesh, that horrible, ravening hunger-urge had swept. Trees and flesh ate as their—brain—commanded. In return, they transmitted their sensory reactions to the reptilian thing that had gone beyond the touch of any sense but one.

Impregnable, alien, living only for blind delight, the horror floated within the transparent dome.

Shuddering, Raft turned away. Once more he turned to the easily-discernible trail of Parror and Craddock. The sooner he caught up with them, the sooner he could get out of the Garden. Unless they themselves had fallen victim to Kharn's menace.

They had not. The white gleam of pillars showed ahead. A figure was visible there, working at something, and Raft recognized Parror's sleek hair and the velvet beard that shadowed the jaw. The Flame's guardian sensed Raft's presence instantly. He whirled, eyes narrow, and then, relaxing, laughed.

The familiar anger began to rise in Raft. As always, he was conscious of Parror's calm arrogance, his complete self-assurance. He tried to fight down the feeling.

"So you got away from Darum," Parror said, smiling with some secret amusement. "You're shrewder than I'd thought. How did you know where to find me?"

Raft ignored the question. "Where's Craddock?" he asked.

Parror's head moved slightly. Beyond a pale column lay a motionless figure, eyes closed.

"There he is. Don't bother to take out your knife. He's unharmed." Parror finished winding up a thin coil. He dropped the silvery wire into a pocket and fumbled there for a moment. When his hand emerged, it wore one of the taloned gauntlets.

"You touched me once in anger," Parror said silkily. "I haven't forgotten that. I've no further use for you or Craddock." He was almost purring. "I've an extra glove. Here."

Raft said, "Thanks. I can take care of myself." He had an idea that might remove the careless smile from Parror's face. It would be a pleasure to do just that.

He took out the jeweled glove he had stolen from Darum's treasure-chamber and slipped it on his right hand. Parror nodded.

"You learn fast," he said, flexing his fingers so that the dull claws spread and closed menacingly. Raft poised himself and waited silently.

Dull claws.

They were bright metal where they joined the gloves, but their three-inch blades were stained dark. Raft suddenly guessed the significance of that. He had an idea that if those razor-sharp talons penetrated his skin, he would die, no matter how slight the wound.

Treachery, to a feline, was not dishonorable, it seemed.

Too late now to call a halt. Parror was stalking forward, his eyes shining. Moveover, Raft still had an ace in the hole. But he dared not fail.

Then Parror sprang. He was laughing, his velvet motion almost careless, as he came in with the agility of a jaguar. With rippling, nimble speed he charged, swerving at the last moment, while the talons raked straight at Raft's face.

Raft ducked under the slash. His hand came up, clenched into a fist. That short, deadly blow cracked solidly against Parror's chin. Raft felt flesh grind against his knuckles as hard gems ripped through skin and grated on bone.

Whatever Parror had expected, it was not this. He was flung back, dazed and reeling, and for a few seconds was actually unconscious as he wavered there. Then the blinding berserk rage dropped upon him like a scarlet cloak. His lips flattened. His eyes flamed green. His face was that of a devil—or a beast.

Raft had torn off his glove. He held da Fonseca's revolver now, and he was smiling coldly.

"Come on," he whispered. "Come on, Parror. It's just what I want. Close quarters. So I won't be able to miss."

Parror's gaze flashed to the weapon. Briefly mad fury and caution battled within him. He strained forward with tigerish blood-hunger in his contorted face.

He—hissed!

Raft started to walk toward his opponent. Parror snarled something that sounded like an oath. He made a furious, baffled gesture and whirled away. Raft's finger tightened on the trigger, and, on impulse, he sent a snap shot after Parror.

Either he missed completely, or the bullet was too slow in this accelerated world. For the cat-man was gone in the saffron jungle. The tangled underbrush swallowed him.

Raft shrugged and turned to the motionless Craddock. He worked on the man for a short time. Respiration was slow, and the skin was moist and clammy. Shock, probably. And with good cause, Raft thought, his mouth twisting into an ugly shape.

At last Craddock's eyes fluttered open. There was intelligence behind them, not the hypnotic stupor Raft had feared. He managed a crooked, weak smile.

"Brian. How—how's tricks?"

"Okay, for the moment," Raft said. "How do you feel?"

"Nearly normal," Craddock murmured, his voice growing stronger. "It's just reaction from hypnosis, I think. It'll pass."

"Don't try to get up. Just take it easy."

"Where's Parror?"

Raft explained. Craddock nodded slowly.

"He won't be back. He got what he wanted."

"You mean—what?"

"Information. He had a machine, a little gadget that probed my mind. It dug up memories I didn't even know I had. That was why he brought me here. He needed time to adjust the thing to my brain. I'm of a different species, so there were difficulties. But he solved them."

Raft frowned.

"Too bad he's such a devil. He's smart."

"He's no devil, except by human standards," Craddock said oddly. The maimed hands lifted. Craddock rubbed his eyes and shook his head as though to clear it. "A different psychology. To them, the end always justifies the means. Parror's end is to stimulate the Flame. Curupuri."

"And he can do it now?"

"When he gets the equipment he needs. That'll take time."

"Yeah," Raft said thoughtfully. "And Darum's got the unseen road guarded by his soldiers."

"Darum?"

"The king of Paititi. Listen, Dan. Do you feel strong enough to tell me what happened?"

"There isn't much," Craddock said. "I was in a trance, but I could see what was going on. Parror brought me here. He had a claw-tipped glove he'd poisoned, and he fought off some creatures with it, pretty nasty specimens."

"In here? In the Garden?"

"The yellow forest," Craddock said doubtfully. "Yes, it was here. When we got to this place, he rigged up a barrier of some sort, with wire. I don't know what it was. But it worked. It must have. We weren't bothered after that.

"Parror put his gadget on my head and kept adjusting it, dragging out all the memories I'd ever had. Eventually he got the secret of the Flame. The part I'd read, from the old records of the First Race, but that I hadn't understood."

Craddock hesitated.

"Funny. The symbols were stored up in my brain, though I never knew what they meant. You never really forget anything, you know, Brian. It's all there, in your subconscious, layer after layer of submerged memories that go back to the time your brain first became capable of storing up thoughts and impressions.

"Eventually I remembered. But I had to write it out. It had been written, not spoken. The Indio language is a degraded version of it. Just the same Parror figured it out. And he's going to waken the Flame, when he gets the equipment ready."

"That's dangerous," Raft said.

"I suppose it is. Still—" Craddock looked at his deformed hands. "—I risked it once. Blindly, of course. Parror knows what he's doing."

Raft thought of that tremendous power unleashed and raging unchecked through Paititi.

"I wonder."

Craddock shivered a little. "I hope so, Brian! If the Flame ever gets out of control, the game is over."

"We'd better get out of here. This isn't a safe spot. Are you able to walk yet?"

"Sure, if you can help me a little." But Craddock was still weak, and he needed more than a little assistance as they retraced their steps through the saffron jungle. Raft supported him over the rougher spots, and he leaned heavily on the younger man's arm.

They kept a sharp eye out for Parror, though Raft felt certain that the Flame's guardian had left the Garden by now, intent upon gathering the equipment he would need for the ultimate experiment.

Nevertheless, there was still danger. Kharn—watched. Raft could sense the hidden, reptilian menace lurking in the yellow shadows under the trees.

They were almost at the river-gap when Raft touched Craddock's arm and they halted. There was something ahead, blocking their path. Not the nerve-bushes, but a sickly, saffron thing which lay like half-solid dough along the bank for twenty feet or more. Raft's brows contracted.

"It wasn't here before," he said slowly. "I don't like it."

Craddock straightened and drew a deep breath. "Guess I'll have to stand on my own feet for awhile. You may need both hands. See those pseudopods sliding this way? The thing's alive."

"An amoeba?"

"It isn't that. It's—there's no sharp line of demarcation between animal and vegetable here. It may be protoplasm but, I think, it's allied to those fern-mushrooms. If it caught us we'd probably get digested. However, it's slow."

"Yeah. But it's big. You feel up to running?"

Craddock drew himself together. "Okay. Where?"

"Let's move along the shallows here and then run like blazes for the tunnel."

Craddock nodded. They stepped into a cold, slow current and waded forward, feeling the water slide leisurely around their legs as they watched the jellied, saffron entity on the bank. They came abreast of it, and the tunnel-mouth lay only a little way ahead.

Raft began to think, as he splashed on, that they would

make the tunnel without trouble after all. The monster of Kharn, he told himself, was not a creature of action. Its danger lay in the mind. It used purely mental power to attract and overpower its prey. Nor was it accustomed to highly developed minds, able to resist. Perhaps it had never needed to develop physical offense.

The water suddenly boiled just before them, sliding with nightmare slowness from a round saffron arm. A pseudopod, stretching after them from the bank, broke the surface. Another lifted out of the water close behind it.

They tried to circle farther out to avoid them, but the footing shelved off steeply into dangerous depths. The pseudopod reached inexorably out—farther—farther—and touched Raft.

It was filled with a living, hothouse warmth that made his flesh crawl. It wound about his waist, its moist heat striking inward against his skin as if digestion were already at work upon him.

He felt its strong pull toward the bank. He tried to get out his knife, but another coil came up from somewhere and laid a warm, wet embrace about his arms, fastening them to his sides. He felt himself being pulled shoreward, and struggled hard to keep his footing in the slow water.

"Hold firm, Brian!"

Craddock stumbled forward, lips set, fighting his own weakness.

He got the knife from Raft's belt with a violent surge of effort, and slashed at the tentacle. That yellowish, half-fungoid flesh gave like cheese. It had surface tension, apparently, but it was not more than half solid. Craddock slashed, and the pseudopods fell away and were washed slowly, slowly off down the current. The incident was like a nightmare in its gentle, deliberate, inexorable sluggishness.

The whole mass of the thing was sliding into the stream now.

"Come on," Raft said. "Can you make it?"

He seized Craddock's arm as they ran for the archway, the water sucking like glue around their feet.

On their right the entire bank seemed to be giving way and dropping toward them in a hungry, malignant pile that could afford to take its time.

Craddock's weakness hampered them. The water parted reluctantly under their splashing feet. It was like running through semi-liquid rubber, with the great, slow, yellow thing rolling its bulk forward to intercept their way.

The mouth of the tunnel opened before them, and the nerve-networks that acted as sentries made a quick, concerted, abortive motion to stop them, as if the whole valley answered a single brain, as perhaps it did. But Craddock slashed weakly at them with the knife, and when the blade had severed two or three the rest shrank and folded down out of harm's way as the two men plunged through.

"They've—stopped," Craddock panted, glancing back. "They won't—follow outside, I guess."

"Keep going," Raft urged him grimly. "No use taking chances now."

They stumbled on, out of the gloom at last into the cool green light from the leafy vault, far overhead, that roofed Paititi. It was like finding sanctuary.

But not quite. A quarter of a mile away, rounding one of the giant trees, a little column was moving steadily toward them. Raft groaned.

"Darum's soldiers. That looks like—yeah, it's Vann, all right. Come on, Craddock. Maybe we can make it."

"I—I can't." The older man staggered as he tried to keep up with Raft's quick strides. "Go on ahead. Don't mind about me."

Raft halted and shrugged. "They'd have caught us anyway. We'll wait, I guess. And fight it out." He touched the butt of the revolver, and watched that glittering column draw nearer.

Finally, the column deployed, showing two score of soldiers, wary, armed men who spread out to surround their prisoners. Vann's scarred, hard face was impassive.

"You're captives," he said. "There'll be time for a duel later, if you want, but the king needs you both now. So you are Brian Raft, after all, eh? And this man is Craddock?" He stared curiously.

"What does Darum intend to do?" Raft asked. "Cut my throat?"

"No," Vann said. "Not yet, at least. Where is Parror?"

"Gone. I don't know where."

"We'll find him." Vann issued swift orders. Half of the group broke up, spreading out into the forest.

"Now we'll go back to Doirada Castle. Meanwhile, you can tell me, Raft, what lies in the Garden of Kharn. I'd have entered it to carry out my orders, but not with any pleasure. What devils lair in Kharn?"

"I'll tell you later," Raft said wearily. He let the revolver drop back into his pocket. "Right now, I'm too tired to care. Let's go back to Doirada."

XII

POWER OF SCIENCE

QUIETLY THEY STOOD before the king, waiting, in the dim-lit room where Yrann's harp had sung. But it was brighter now. The veiled woman was not around. In her place Janissa sat on a cushioned couch near the dais. She had looked at Raft once, given him a cryptic smile, and turned back to watch Darum, who squatted cross-legged amid his silks.

Darum watched Raft out of hooded eyes.

"You think I am going to kill you," he said. "Why? Don't trouble to answer. I can read that much in your face. Because you tried to kill me, with that knife Vann took from you. Also because you stole my amulet."

Raft attempted to speak, but the king lifted his hand.

"Wait. Your race is not as mine. I see no great evil in your attempt at murder. You'd have succeeded had you deserved to succeed. Since you didn't—" He nodded "—it is over and done with. What is past is past. Tomorrow you may try again, or I may, and succeed. And I will take back the amulet too. Meanwhile, Janissa has told me a great deal."

"When I found you'd escaped, Brian—I told Darum," the girl said. "I knew you'd gone after Parror."

"Yes," the king said silkily. "And I wanted Parror. He goes too far, I think. After all, I rule in Paititi, not Parror."

"For a while," Raft said quietly. "If he starts the Flame, and it gets out of control, you won't rule anything."

"So he learned Craddock's secret." Darum sighed. "He is outlawed now. Every man's hand is against him. And I have guarded the unseen road so he cannot enter it. I do not think he will reach the Flame."

"Parror is clever," Janissa said.

Craddock broke in.

"He'll need instruments. I know that much. It'll take time."

Darum shrugged.

I am no scientist. I know only that there is danger both ways. If the Flame fades below a danger level—well, Janissa? What then?"

"We will become as the cavern-beasts," she told him. "We will degenerate as the First Race did."

"But when that day will come none can say. In our lifetime, or our children's, or perhaps not even then. And if Parror tries to rouse the Flame, and fails to check it, that will mean immediate destruction."

"He doesn't think so," Craddock said. "He's sure he can control the Flame."

"But can he?" Darum leaned forward. "That is what I seek to know. Can he—surely?"

"I wish I knew," Craddock said. "Parror got certain memories out of my mind, but they were mere superficial memories, not knowledge. I don't even know what most of the symbols I wrote down for him meant. I didn't know thirty years ago, when I translated part of the record."

"The record that was destroyed when the Flame wakened," Darum said. "A secret only Parror and you know now?"

"I don't know," Craddock said. "It was dragged out of my mind by hypnosis. I wasn't conscious most of the time. I've only the vaguest idea what Parror intends to do."

"Well, the first step is to capture Parror, so he won't rouse the Flame," Darum said practically. "I hope my guards will find him soon. Meanwhile, how am I to deal with you two?"

"Why not just let us go?" Raft said slowly.

"Simians are too curious. Your race would try to enter Paititi. Two species, both dominant, cannot live together successfully."

"Why not?" Raft asked. "There's the possibility of mutual benefit."

"Our minds are too unlike."

"I think you underestimate Parror, Darum," Janissa said. "He's clever, and he has more knowledge than I. There are— powers connected with the Flame that not even I understand. But Parror understands them. Also, I have heard legends of a secret way to reach the cave where Curupuri burns."

"He must not reach the Flame!" Darum said.

Raft glanced at Janissa, and drew courage from her steady gaze. "Suppose he does though. In spite of everything. That means that he'll waken the Flame. If he makes a mistake, nothing can save Paititi. Right?"

The king nodded.

"True."

"All right," Raft said. "Here's an answer. Forestall him."

Darum jerked his head up to stare.

"Waken the Flame ourselves?"

"Why not?" Raft asked. "We've got the science of two cultures here in this room, which gives us an edge on Parror. Janissa knows the Flame. She's its hereditary guardian. I know biochemistry, and Craddock isn't a layman. And you must have technicians here."

"We do."

"Well, then, what's to prevent us from making the device ourselves?"

"The question of possible failure," Darum said. "The First Race never tested their machine. They waited too long. There is absolutely no way of fortelling whether it would actually control the Flame. Trial and error is the only way, and one error means destruction."

"There is a way," Raft said.

Janissa breathed a question.

Raft took out the amulet. Seeing it, the king's eyes narrowed.

"You know what this is, Darum. It holds a spark of Flame. It is the Flame, but too tiny to be very dangerous. Why not use this as the control? If this spark from the Flame itself can be stimulated, and leashed, you'd know the machine was successful.

Darum shrugged.

"Parror may have the same idea," Raft continued. "I hope so. But in case he doesn't, we'll have the jump on him, and know definitely whether the device the First Ones planned is safe."

Darum hesitated.

"Perhaps that is true."

Raft talked fast. "If this works, it'll remove the menace of the Flame forever. It'll mean complete control of that source of energy. The threat of degeneration will be removed from Paititi completely. Suppose we do fail—we'll simply be right back here where we stand now, won't we?"

"He's right," Janissa said breathlessly. "It's a chance, Darum. The only one, if Parror outwits us. And it may mean safety for Paititi forever."

Darum did not speak for a long moment. Then he nodded slowly.

"I agree, then. Janissa, this is in your hands. And now leave me. We will talk later."

The girl led them out. Behind them the lights dimmed, and, as Raft moved along the passage that led from the king's chamber, he heard a murmuring of faint music.

Yrann. Should he have warned the king against her? Perhaps. But he doubted whether Darum would have believed him. He shelved the thought for future reference.

Meanwhile Craddock was pulling at his arm.

"Brian."

"Well?"

"I didn't want to queer the pitch, but—" His voice lowered "—you forgot one thing. I can't remember what Parror dragged out of my mind. He forced it out with his gadget, but I was in a trance. I don't remember now."

Janissa had overheard even Craddock's soft whisper.

"It is well you didn't mention that to Darum," she said. "But I think the problem can be solved. I don't know what device Parror used. Nevertheless, when a gate has been opened once, it opens more easily the next time. I have some knowledge of the mind, Craddock, and possibly we can succeed."

"We'll get it out of you," Raft said. "If it means a course in psychonamics!"

It did, almost. Raft had used medical hypnosis himself, and could help Janissa, who otherwise might have been hindered by the alienage of minds, the more than racial difference between Craddock's thought-patterns and her own. But with Raft as mentor, the secret wisdom was slowly, painfully pulled into the light.

They did not sleep. Some drug like benzedrine, Raft guessed, kept them alert and stimulated for their long sessions. There was technical equipment in the castle, and there were scientists as well, though their knowledge lay chiefly in the realm of the psychic. Many allied sciences were represented among the cat-people. Surgery was highly developed, as was biology.

It was Craddock's subconscious they were probing, and it was like fishing in a teeming pool. Too often they caught the wrong fish, till they learned the right sort of bait to use. But finally symbols began to take form on the pad that was always ready to Craddock's hand. He scribbled a line—hesitated, corrected himself—and, step by step, pieced out the record he had read only once, thirty years before, but which his sub-conscious mind had never forgotten.

"If Parror hadn't opened the way, we'd never be able to do this," Janissa said later as she was standing on a balcony with Raft, taking a well-earned breathing-space after a particularly arduous session. Before them the slow cloud of mist hung like an enormous tower.

Raft looked at her. He remembered his half-mocking question of long ago, whether two species could mingle. But logic did not seem so important now. The warm, living presence of Janissa was more vital.

Till lately he had not known her, really. She had been a paradoxical, fascinating girl who had revealed few of the traits that make humanity human. But now, since they had been working together, he had come to understand her more, and to know that he would never be able to understand her fully.

That sweetly curved, softly malicious little face, with its hint of diablerie, its lovely, feline strangeness, was more at-tractive than he dared admit to himself. The aquamarine, shad-owed eyes were turned up to his . . . Eyes of Bast, whose velvet aloofness guards the night of Egypt. Yet she could be playful too, gay as a kitten might be, and with the same endearing charm.

Now as he stood there, something hidden and secret flashed between them. There was no need for a physical embrace. It was subtler than that. But, briefly, it seemed as though a veil had been lifted, a veil that hung between two beings who had been alien.

His hand stole out and touched hers. They looked out across Doirada Gulf, to the colossal columns of giant trees that supported the sky of Paititi.

He thought, Only here in this lost land beyond space and time, could I have found Janissa.

They were silent. Speech was not necessary. Hand in hand they stood, lost in the warm, comforting awareness of each other's presence, until Craddock's voice called them back to the work of harnessing the Flame.

What could harness such a tremendous force, a power which burned in the heart of the spiral nebulae and kindled giant suns? The chain that bound Fenris-wolf? What was the Flame?

They did not know. But men do not know what electricity is, either. Yet they can tame it with insulated wires. What was needed here was insulation, but not only that. There must also be a means of stimulating the Flame. A safe way.

That was not easy to find. First the last fragments of the lost record had to be taken from Craddock's mind. Time after time hypnosis probed into his memories, and gradually the cryptic symbols made longer lines on the recording pad. Janissa could read those symbols for her own language was founded upon it, as her own civilization was built on the earlier culture of the vanished First Race. Also technicians were helpful.

For there were semantic difficulties. Raft knew the Indio dialect thoroughly, but he did not know the intricacies of Janissa's more highly developed language. There were symbols she could not explain to him. Then a chemist, perhaps, would sketch charts, electro-chemical hookups, or atomic patterns, until the answer clicked in Raft's mind.

He was no technician, though, and could not have built the device alone. Nor could Janissa. But his different background of human science was invaluable in casting light from another angle on the problem. There was the matter of the amulet, for example.

"When you turn the stone, it slows down metabolism," Raft pointed out. "That means the radiation is blocked at a variable rate. What blocks it? Something opaque to the vibration, eh?"

"The metal?" a physicist hazarded. "It's an alloy of chromite. Vanadium, perhaps. We'll have it tested."

For, though the last secrets of the records in Craddock's memory had been discovered by now, there were still gaps. In the days of the First Race, different elements had existed in the valley, elements which were now exhausted.

They found that the truth lay not only in the material of the amulet's setting, but in the intricate interlocking of alloys, a very tiny machine powered by the induced radiation of the energy-source itself, the spark in the crystal. That crystal was simply quartz, but how the radiant atom had been put into it Raft couldn't guess.

The secret, then, lay in a complicated arrangement of various alloys that seemed to block the energy-output of the spark. Part of this knowledge they gleaned from Craddock's hypnotically-stimulated memories; the rest they found by simple analysis. There was, finally, a dead end.

For they knew what elements they needed, and some of them no longer existed in Paititi.

Then the practical value of an alien culture was demonstrated. Raft thought of the possibility first. He had brought considerable equipment to Paititi in his rucksack, medical supplies, concentrated food in little tins, and there were his personal belongings, as well as Craddock's.

His watch yielded platinum, which was vital. There was tin to be found in the rucksack, and the firearms were taken apart to provide a treasure of necessary metals.

The laboratories of the technicians swiftly analyzed the loot, broke it down, and formed new alloys. Given the raw material, they could, at last, work out the equation.

The machine, when finished, was not large. Specifications had clearly indicated its proportions. It stood on a tripod, coming approximately to Raft's chest, a surprisingly simple device of crystal, metal, and hollow tubes.

The integral part of it was the fuse, which floated free in a mercury bath atop the gadget. This was the safety, the innocuous-seeming footlong tube that had the power to control the tremendous radiations the rest of the machine was built to stimulate.

"Parror's bound to fail," Raft said. "Those special alloys—

they don't exist in Paititi. He can't possibly make the safety control, and without it he'd know the experiment would be too dangerous."

Janissa was less certain.

"Parror has a blind confidence in himself. He might try to substitute other materials. The sooner we test this, Brian, the better I'll feel.

But the test was not spectacular. The thing was handled by remote control, to minimize the danger. Even with the tiny spark of energy in the amulet, there was peril.

Raft used a scanning glass to examine the amulet, five hundred feet away on the mossy plain. He looked briefly around the crowd that surrounded him—Craddock, Janissa, the technician and, with a silent prayer, turned on the power. Nothing happened. Machine and amulet remained as they had been.

"Doesn't it power the spark?" Janissa breathed.

"It ought to stimulate it," Raft said, and moved the needle on his rheostat device. He moved it too far. From the amulet a spear of light shot straight up, and simultaneously the moss for a hundred feet around sprang into—life! It writhed and crawled visibly, the ordinary progress of growth accelerated incredibly by the radiation of the stimulated spark.

Hastily Raft adjusted the rheostat. But he was smiling. He knew, without the need for further experiment, that the machine was a success. It remained now only to discover whether its power could control the Flame itself. Raft thought it could, since it would, via induction, have all the Flame's power.

But the danger struck too soon.

XIII

FLYING DEMONS

BRIAN RAFT wakened to see Janissa's face above him. The light she carried glowed through the darkened room.

"Brian!"

He blinked at her.

"Janissa—what's wrong?"

"It's Parror," she said. "I've touched his mind. He's on his way to the Flame."

That brought Raft bolt upright. "Good god! You're sure?"

She nodded, her eyes shadowed with fear.

"His barrier slipped for an instant. I had been watching my mirror and, suddenly, I felt his thought. He goes by a secret way to waken the Flame."

"Where is he now?"

"In the forest somewhere. I could not tell. I could see only what he intended, and the secret way he will take. Brian, we must stop him somehow."

"We will," Raft said. "Wake up Craddock. Then we'll rouse the king."

Janissa slipped away, and Raft hastily donned his garments. His mind was working at top speed. He could not have guarded against this contingency, yet he felt at fault. Parror must have a duplicate machine, but it could not possibly be successful, without the special alloys that did not exist in Paititi. If Parror aroused the Flame, disaster would result.

The three of them went to Darum's suite. Vann was guarding the entrance, since it was the hour for sleep. He stared at them curiously, his scarred soldier's face hard. But when he heard the nature of their errand, he let them pass.

"Nevertheless, I'd better go with you," he said, falling in at their heels. "Assassinations have been cleverly managed before this."

Lights softly illuminated Darum's chamber. The king himself was there, relaxed on the cushions of his dais. He sprang awake instantly as they approached. His hand dropped toward the silks and came up with a long-bladed dagger. But he said nothing.

"There's no need for weapons" Raft growled. "Parror's got his own and he's ready to use it."

"Parror?" Darum let the knife fall. "You mean—the Flame?"

"Tell him, Janissa."

She explained swiftly. The king frowned in indecision.

"You say his machine will not work?"

"Oh, it'll work all right, but it will wreck things without the safety device," Raft pointed out. "Our only chance now is to get there before him, if we can. And if we can't, we'll take our own instrument. We may be able to check the Flame before it's too late."

"I was dreaming a strange dream," Darum said slowly. "I lay dead, I thought, here in my own chamber, and a shadow hung over Paititi. A shadow of light. Of life. But it could not bring life back to me, and it had power only to destroy. I wonder, now, if the vision will come true."

His voice was remote and strange, as if the memory of the dream had carried him back into the dream itself.

"It was a true dream, so far as the shadow goes," Janissa said. "There will be death for all of us, unless Parror is stopped."

"Death!" the king murmured as if he had heard only that one word out of all she said.

"Death."

Raft thought he recognized something in the timber of the soft, deep voice. He had heard Darum speak that way before. If the madness was coming back upon the king, at this moment of all moments when action and clear thinking were needed, ghastly things might happen.

"Parror will reach the Flame before you," Darum said in a soft monotone. "That much I—see." He dropped his head suddenly and hid his face in his hands. "I see no further yet." His voice came muffled. "Death—death in my dream. This room is full of death!"

The voice was wild now, but his face was still hidden. Madness wailed in the deep resonance of Darum's words, and yet there was conviction too, as if even in his madness he knew he spoke the truth.

"There is death here," he shrieked. "Too much death for one man. I shall not die alone. I think you must fail with the Flame, Janissa, Craddock, Raft! I think you must fail and doom us all, for this room reeks with death."

Raft felt a thrill of horror. Utter conviction rang true in the king's voice. Conviction and madness.

"Death over all Paititi!" said Darum, lifting his face suddenly and showing them a wild and shining glare that saw nothing before it.

And suddenly "Death!" wailed a shiver of resounding strings from the curtains behind him. If ever music spoke a word, that music spoke and threatened. The promise was as clear as the

sudden flash of a bared blade. It needed no articulation to speak
its single syllable of prophecy.

The curtain swept aside, and Yrann's veiled figure stood
there, fingers poised above the still-quivering strings. Faceless
and veiled, like the Norn Atropos, ready to cut the thread that
held Darum's life.

For a moment nobody moved. The room was too full of
that certainty of doom which Darum's mad voice had made
them all believe whether they would or no. For that instant,
against all hope and reason, even Craddock, even Raft, knew
certainly that there was no chance for life. In the single moment, they were all as mad as the king.

But only Raft understood what happened next. Only he knew
what must have passed through Yrann's clouded mind. Death
hung over Doirada Castle and the whole world she knew. The
king had spoken, and in this moment there was no doubting
the king. And she had waited so long for vengeance. The Flame
would rob her of it now, unless—unless—she acted.

One last wild shrilling cry came shivering from the harp-
strings. With the same motion that swept music across the
instrument she flung the harp aside, letting it crash to the floor
with a last jangling discord of its own.

She moved forward with a swift, stooping rush toward the
couch. Her white hand, darting from the veils, was like a flung
weapon in itself as she snatched up the long dagger he had
dropped. Headlong, she hurled herself against him, swinging
the blade like a scythe.

He was off guard. He tried to rise, to leap away from the
blade's glittering descent, but the tangling silks caught and
betrayed him. He managed only to writhe aside, so that the
first blow only raked his ribs in a glancing wound. Yrann, still
silent, brought up the knife again with deadly singleness of
purpose.

Then Raft had her.

He felt her arch against his restraining arm with the desperate
strength he remembered from their other struggle in this room,
and a shock of unreasonable horror went through him as that
veiled face turned to his.

She flung herself against his grip with a cat's sudden, explosive fury, and with one last frantic surge broke free. Spring-

ing back, still gripping the dagger, she turned her faceless gaze toward the king.

He was on his feet now, facing her, ready. Her chance was gone. She knew it. They could see the knowledge slacken the tautness of the lovely body beneath her veils. They heard her sigh once, deeply, in the tense silence of the room.

Then she moved suddenly; her draperies swirling like slow smoke, and sank the knife hilt-deep in her own heart!

Motionless, speechless, they watched her sink to the floor. Red came slowly out through the gray veils pinned by the knife against her.

Darum brushed past Raft. He knelt beside Yrann. His hand went out, poising over the veiled face. But he did not touch the gauzy webs that hid her.

"Yrann?" he said. "Yrann?"

But she did not stir. The red stain widened upon the gray.

Darum's fingers closed upon the hilt that stood up from her chest. He knelt there for a heartbeat, his hand caressing the weapon as if it were Yrann herself. Then his grip tightened.

He tore the knife free, dripping scarlet drops, and rose in a lithe, inhuman motion, facing Raft. His lips had flattened back, and the light in his eyes was the dark blaze of pure madness. He lifted the blade, and the red drops spattered in an arch across the carpet.

Raft stood motionless, his mind racing. He was too close to the king, and he was unarmed. There was no way of escaping that blow, unless he came to grips with the man, and he had no illusions about which of the two was stronger. Power flowed tremendously through the feline's rippling body, and madness lent it double strength.

"You saved my life," he said in a hissing snarl. "You came between us! You turned the knife against her as surely as if you held the blade. What use do you think life is to me now?" His features convulsed in the mad inhumanity of feline rage. "You—ape!"

Darum sprang.

From behind Raft a thin, shining flash of light darted, to quench itself in the king's throat. Darum's body arched. He strained to take one step more forward—to keep the dagger raised for its blow—

Then with shocking suddenness, all the strength went out

of him and he dropped to the silks with the lithe, silken limpness of the silks themselves. His fingers released the dagger, and he pulled the rapier from his throat, blood gushing from wound and mouth as it came free.

"Vann," he said, and coughed. "Vann. We have dueled before—but never thus!"

Vann's deep voice answered heavily.

"I served you, Darum, but I serve Paititi first. Yrann was not worth any man's love."

"She was so beautiful," the king whispered. "She could not bear to die—with Paititi—without slaying me. She hated me always. And—and—" He tried to choke back blood.

He lifted himself on suddenly strong arms and dragged himself forward a few feet. He ran gentle fingers down the dead woman's arm. Her harp lay where it had fallen, almost beneath her fingers. He touched the strings, and their sad music hung forlornly in the quiet air.

"I would have crushed Paititi," Darum said. "I would have—crushed the world—for her. Rather than have her harmed. She was so beautiful."

The king's head fell upon the soft body of Yrann. The tiger eyes closed. One hand sought for and found Yrann's.

His blood mingled with hers.

The red stream flowed slower and slower—

And flowed no more.

Vann stood motionless, his heavy shoulders sagging.

"Go now, while there's time," he said. "I did this to save Paititi, and now I find myself wondering whether I have struck steel into the wrong throat."

"Vann," Janissa said.

"Take them away, Janissa. Take these men from another world out of the king's presence. Let them stop Parror if they can."

"Parror?" Craddock whispered. He touched Raft's arm. "We'll have to move fast."

"Yes," Raft said tonelessly.

He turned and led the way out of the chamber. His face was gray, and sweat stood out in fine droplets on his cheeks.

Once outside, he did not mention the king.

"We'll need the machine," he said. "It's a portable, so we can manage the weight. But I'll want some straps."

They found silken scarves that would do as well, and the machine was adjusted on Raft's back. The light alloys made its weight less than its bulk would have indicated. That would help, since fast travel would be necessary if they hoped to forestall Parror.

Silently they left the castle, darkened now for the sleep-period. Outside the cool, clear daylight of Paititi was dazzling.

"We should have remembered weapons," Craddock said.

"It's too late now," Raft told him. "Janissa, you'll guide. Do you know the secret way to the Flame?"

"I think I can find it, yes. The thought in Parror's mind was clear enough. But it is a long way."

Yet it was shorter than they expected. They did not head for Parror's castle. They angled off toward the base of the rock barrier that guarded Paititi. Four hours of fast travel brought them to it. There, however, time was lost as Janissa searched for the secret entrance.

"There are ruins here," she said. "Ruins of the Old Race. There should be a double column. Parror was thinking of it when I read his mind."

Silently Raft pointed. With a little cry Janissa ran to the spot he indicated. She felt the smooth surface of the rock-face, searching for a key.

Silently, smoothly, an oval opened in the bare stone.

Raft turned to stare back the way they had come.

"No sign of Parror," he said. "He may be ahead of us. Or he may not. We'll soon know." He followed Janissa and Craddock into the opening. Behind him the hidden door closed.

But they were not in darkness. A pale, cool glow came from the walls and roof and the smooth floor on which they stood. The tunnel wound upward at a steep slant, and the silence made Raft feel the blood beating in his ears.

"Come on," he said, shouldering the machine.

It was not long, that passage in the cliff. It made a short-cut through the rock to the cavern of the Flame. But, before them there was another cavern.

An oval door barred their path. Janissa opened it easily, but she did not pass through the portal. Raft saw her slender figure poise, hesitate, and shrink back. He brushed past Craddock.

"What is it?" he asked.

Janissa did not answer.

"The First Race," Craddock said, in a breathless voice. "The First Race."

It was the cavern Raft had seen when he had first entered Paititi. Leprous violet light bathed the dripping stalactites and crept over the thrusting stalagmites that made an upthrust forest. High overhead, slanting down at a dizzy angle, was the gravity-defying, nearly transparent tube of the unseen road, made visible now only because of the hordes of creatures that crawled upon it, as though striving to break through the glassy barrier.

The monsters!

Raft had seen them before, but only dimly. Now he felt his throat go dry and close with loathing.

Bat-winged and beast-snouted, degenerate and horrible, the things swarmed in the violet light there in the great cave. They were the descendants of what had once been the First Race, the mighty civilization that had reared the proud castles of Paititi.

And fallen now—fallen into the primal pit of horror.

The baleful radiations that had once raged through Paititi when the Flame waned long ago and had changed them to demons. Few were alike. Some had immense bat-wings, while others flopped and dragged their fat, shining bulks among the stalagmites. And some were dwarfed. Some were giants. Some had the clawed feet of giant birds.

Straight as a lance across that arena of terror ran the path they had been following, a faint white glow that ended at the farther wall, before an oval panel that was obviously a door.

"Through—there?" Craddock said.

Raft looked at Janissa. She was white-faced, but she caught her breath and stepped out of the tunnel's protection, into the violet light of the cavern.

"We'll run for it," Raft said. "If we can reach that other door, we'll be all right."

They ran, panic spurring their heels. The sight of the nightmare horde flapping and crawling and leaping all about them was horrible. And the thought of those black talons actually touching them—it was not a good thought.

A stir went through the monsters, a ripple of interest. As Raft ran, he saw from the corners of his eyes that shapes were converging upon them. But the three were more than halfway across the cavern now, and there was more than an even chance that they could reach their goal before the monsters rallied to investigate.

Raft reckoned without the winged beings. Something struck him heavily from behind, sending him to his knees. He struggled to regain his feet. Janissa, glancing back, saw what had happened, and with a little cry, ran back to help him.

A nightmare shape, scaled and horned like a medieval demon, sprang at her—caught her in its grip.

Cursing, Raft plunged forward, heedless of the creature on his back. His fist smashed out into the face of the monster. It was driven back, screaming in a thin, high-pitched wail of agony.

That was the signal. From all around the devils of Paititi swooped and lumbered and dragged themselves toward the intruders. Raft went down under the weight of foul-smelling bodies. He was blind with nausea and hatred and revulsion. His fists hammered a pulpy flesh, and the shrieking grew to a shrill crescendo.

That sickening odor almost choked him. The touch of the monsters against his skin was loathsome. They felt like fungoid things, like dead creatures raised to a ghastly similitude of life. And the faces were ghoulish demons.

Craddock came back to use as a spear a fallen stalactite he had picked up. Raft was relieved of his burden for a moment. He staggered up, looking for Janissa.

He saw her, in the midst of a group of monsters.

He had enough reasoning power left to find another fallen spike of stone before going to her rescue. The creatures, interbred and degenerate, were physically weak, but they had the advantage of numbers, and Raft realized that the sheer weight of those deformed bodies could press him down and smother him. His lips lifted in a snarl, he charged forward, stabbing with his improvised spear.

He felt flesh tear. He heard the squealing redouble in volume. The monsters came at him like a wave. They had the feeble malevolence of rats. As he went down on his back he tried desperately to turn, to shield the precious burden he carried—and failed.

He heard the machine's crash as it was crushed against the rock beneath him.

There was only hopelessness then, and blind hatred, and a feeling that he was drowning in floods of evil, living flesh. But he fought on. The remnants of the machine were ripped from his back. He lashed about him savagely with the sharp stalactite, till at last he had cleared a little space free of the monsters.

As he stood there, panting and half-naked, he saw that they had fought their way almost to the door. But at his feet coils and broken crystal and twisted metal told of the wreck of the machine that could save Paititi.

One thing remained whole—a foot-long cylinder of burnished alloy. It was the safety fuse that controlled the device's stimulating power. Raft snatched it up and thrust the tube into his belt.

"Brian," Craddock called. "Here!"

Raft lifted his spear and rushed. The monsters had learned the menace of that sharp spike of stone by now, and there was a little flurry as they gave back. Janissa was with Craddock, the two of them back to back, though the girl was unarmed. But she was bristling with fury, her hands clawed, like a cat roused to anger.

"The door," Raft said. "Open it, Janissa."

He cut a red path for her. The worst danger was the flying monsters. More than once Raft swung up his weapon in time to rip the flesh of a swooping demon that came rushing down at him from the violet depths above. He fought on, grimly silent, conscious only of those devil-masks, distorted and horrible, glaring at him, spouting crimson as he struck, screaming in thin, wailing agony.

"Brian!" Janissa shrilled. "The door!"

He saw with surprise that it lay open. Craddock, white hair flying, broke through with a stumbling rush. Together the two charged that waiting portal.

They reeled through it. Raft whirled, thrust out at a pressing horde of monsters, as Janissa's hand swept out.

The oval door closed—barring the cavern.

The high screaming gave place to silence.

"They smashed the machine," Raft said hopelessly.

XIV

RAFT CHOOSES

CRADDOCK WAS PANTING with excitement. His eyes were tired looking and weary.

"You saved the safety fuse," he said. "Maybe that's enough. If Parror's machine is a duplicate of the one we built, maybe we have a chance, even yet."

"It has to be, unless the man's a complete fool," Raft said. "But if we can stop him before he wakens the Flame, that'd be even better." He caught himself and laughed. "Parror's probably behind us, not ahead of us. If he passed through that cavern, they'd have broken his gadget too."

"Unless he knew another route," Janissa put in somberly. She tried to adjust her tattered garments, with fastidious, feline delicacy. Raft thought, watching her, even now she's half cat.

Then something quivered through the air about them, a burning shaking vibration that raced through their bodies, quickening the living flesh and was gone. A low thunder faded into silence.

White-faced, Janissa turned to Raft. Her hands went out helplessly.

"The Flame!" she said. "It—wakes!"

With a curse, Raft sprinted forward, the others at his heels. To fail now, so close to success, would be intolerable. The tunnel was miles long, it seemed.

It ended at last, though not before that warning vibration had rushed in deep thunder through them twice more. Each time the effect was stronger. Each time the force grew more vital, more alive.

Janissa fumbled at the door, searching for the key. At last, the panel slipped away and was gone.

They stepped out on a small balcony of rock, from which a curving ramp twisted down to—to what?"

It was dark, too dark to make out details clearly. Emptiness, it seemed, stretched far out above and below them.

Yet there was light. It was too faint to be more than a hint, or else it was too far away below him. Raft leaned on that dizzy railing and stared down, down, down almost to the bottom of the world, an immeasurable gulf in which one flicker of brilliance gleamed.

But it was not vertigo that struck Raft then. It was fear.

Fear plain and simple, and reasonless. He knew that feeling.

Once, in Madagascar, he had had to go through a guard-hut where sentries were sleeping. A noise, a false move, would have meant spears through his body. He had known then that they were going to waken. He had felt it, with every bit of his mind and every inch of his skin.

Like that. Something down below, where the light was, so vitally alive that he felt himself standing on its palm.

And something more as well. It was the jungle. Or the life that makes up the jungle. Steaming, fertile Amazon forests, roaring rivers, all that teeming, tremendous life that stirs in the green moist heat of the tropics. Blind and terrible and hungry—there in the abyss burned the energy that rages in the heart of the great nebulae, the destroyer and the awakener—Curupuri!

"The Flame sleeps," Janissa breathed.

But in the depths was a distant brightening. A low sound, below the threshold of hearing almost, deepened and grew louder. It became an intolerable thunder, crashing out like the roaring birth-pains of a god.

From that gulf that dropped toward the heart of the world— far down—very far below—rose the Flame.

It expanded and lifted, a spear, a tower, a mountain of purest brilliance burning with intolerable fires. It was the essence of life. Raft felt himself, his whole body, swinging toward that kindling torch.

His mind swept toward it. His soul swung out across the abyss.

The thunder crashed deafeningly against the walls. The Flame brightened, blazed and towered—pulsing with eagerness— mad with delight—with ecstasy of living.

Beneath him, Raft saw, was a darker shape. Two shapes. The silhouette of a man, standing beside a machine that was curiously familiar.

Parror! And the device he had built from the First Race's records!

As the Flame brightened, Raft sprang toward the descending ramp. He raced down it, praying that he would be in time. That unchecked violence—Parror might not recognize the symptoms, blinded as he was with egotism—but Raft knew that the Flame was wakening uncontrolled.

The spark in the amulet had not reacted in this manner.

The galactic force of a nebula—raging unchecked in Paititi. Perhaps loosed on the whole world!

Down he raced, toward his quarry, while the fires brightened. They blazed with supernal brilliance and began to fade. The column of light slowly sank unwillingly. The thunders subsided.

Now Raft stood on the glassy, transparent floor of the cave. He looked down once, and reeled dizzily. He was standing unsupported above a gulf that dropped down to earth's burning center.

He dashed toward Parror. And Parror ran to meet him.

The light came from below, casting curious shadows on the man's face. Raft saw he was wearing one of the talon-gauntlets, snarling silently as he charged. Raft had no objection to killing Parror, but quelling the Flame was more important. He slowed, pulling the safety fuse from his belt.

"Parror!" he shouted, in the stillness as the thunders died. "Your machine's out of control! This will restrain it."

Parror did not even hear. He was lost in a berserk bloodthirst, blind and nearly insane with the demon's rage that Raft had seen before. His clawed fingers, tipped with sharp steel, slashed at Raft's face.

Raft did not duck quickly enough. His cheek was laid open, agonizing pain darting through him. The fuse spun from his grasp.

He closed with Parror or tried to. That agile body leaped out of reach. Again the claw ripped down, and again. A blaze of pain stung Raft's chest and side. Raft struck out savagely, but Parror eluded his driving fists.

Thunder crashed. The light from below brightened.

The Flame leaped from its bondage, bellowing with delight!

The fires surged up—poured up—sprang high as though trying to return to their interstellar cradle.

Again the claw reached out.

Raft felt a razor drawn across one eye, and sight was suddenly altered. Half-blinded, his cheek torn to the bone, his nose almost ripped away, he sent blow after blow at his elusive enemy.

Janissa ran in, threw herself between them.

Parror balled his fist and struck her hard and clean upon the jaw. The girl was flung back, to crumple motionless on that glassy floor.

"You taught me that, Raft," Parror purred.

Raft mouthed frenzied curses. If he could only get his hands on that smiling devil, sink his fingers into that bearded neck.

Intolerably bright blazed the Flame. The thunders raved and crashed within the cavern. This time the star-kindled fires did not sink.

Higher they rose, and higher—questing—eager. Wakening from slumber to a life beyond the conception of earthly minds!

Suddenly, amazingly, Raft could see from both eyes again. The agony in face and body was gone. The dripping of blood had stopped. He saw a look of amazement cross Parror's face.

The radiations from the Flame healed. They rejuvenated living tissue with miraculous speed. They hastened life.

Craddock's voice cried something. Raft could make out only a word or two through the thunder, but he saw Craddock, thirty feet away, running toward the distant machine. In Craddock's hand was a foot-long cylinder Raft recognized.

Raft never knew what Parror thought was happening. He saw the cat-man whirl, cry out in a thick, furious voice, and take one step after Craddock.

One step. No more. For then Raft had him.

But it was not easy. Raft had never battled a jaguar, but he was battling one now. The mad, raging fury that filled Parror had turned him into a wild beast. The eyes were all green now, blazing with hatred and blood-thirst. Writhing, struggling, gasping, the two crashed down together.

The Flame rose ever higher. The thunders were an intolerable ache drumming against Raft's skull. That shadowless, inter-galactic light burned into his brain.

The claw tore at his face, and instantly the wounds healed.

Snarling, as helpless in the grip of murder-lust as Parror himself, Raft surged to his knees, with an effort not even his enemy's strength could resist. Nothing existed, for a flashing, crimson second, but that red-stained claw.

He caught Parror's arm in a judo grip, and broke it with savage fury.

For a moment he held the man motionless. That was enough. The power of the Flame healed bone and tissue, but Parror's wrist and lower arm jutted out at an impossible angle.

But he fought on, with teeth and nails and feet, though Raft's fingers were clawed deep into his throat. Inexorably, with the blind savagery of his kind, he fought on until not even the Flame could bring life back to his strangled body.

Then Raft looked up.

Far across the cavern stood the machine on its tripod, perilously close to the Flame itself. And moving painfully toward it, like a man breasting a strong wind, was Craddock.

Craddock?

Something about that shape made Raft catch his breath. The outline was altering even as he watched. Raft remembered Craddock's maimed hands, and the power that had destroyed them, the same star-born energy that now thundered through the cavern in burning ecstasy of awareness.

The figure still gripped the fuse-cylinder.

Raft got to his feet. He began to run after Craddock, but the distance was too great. Nearly at the machine now, the figure was fantastic.

It was not Craddock. It was not even human any more.

The living flesh boiled and altered and flowed under the monstrous force that could create whole universes. Something utterly inhuman, at last, stumbled and dragged itself forward into the full blaze of the radiation.

And yet there was a human purpose.

It reached the machine. For an instant it crouched there, adjusting the fuse. Beyond it, Curupuri shouted in cataclysmic fury as the fires poured torrentially up from the abyss. One instant of utter madness, while the power of universes, of galaxies, stooped and touched that cavern—

One instant—and then the thunders died.

The Flame pulsed once, twice, and sank. With a sigh almost

human, the fires of life dwindled and dropped into the great gulf.

There remained, far below, a point of light, burning with unquenchable fires!

Harnessed!

The fire that had come from beyond the stars was harnessed.

Tamed—chained—by the flesh to which it had once, long ago, given life. . . .

Janissa stirred.

Fear came into her eyes. She raised herself against Raft's supporting arm to look around questioningly. Then her gaze came back to Raft's.

"It's over, Janissa," he said. "The Flame sleeps."

"The machine is working?"

"Yes. Parror had made a duplicate of ours, after all. But he didn't have the safety fuse. Once Craddock inserted that, it worked."

"But, Craddock?"

"He's dead," Raft said quietly. "He died, I suppose, because he had to. The man who once wakened the Flame died to quell it again. This time, I think, the danger is over forever."

She watched him.

"I tested the machine," he said. "It's exactly what's needed. The First Race were right, after all. They waited too long to build their own machine, or they'd never have become monsters. Anyway, the Flame will burn, will send out its radiations, at this normal rate forever."

"Normal?"

Raft nodded. "I altered the adjustment. Not to the danger-point, but so that metabolism in Paititi will be same as metabolism in my own world. There's no barrier now. The talismans aren't necessary."

"I can live in your world? It won't be—slow?"

"Your world or mine, Janissa," he said. "You can choose."

But she had chosen already. And so had Raft. He had made his decision long ago, he thought, the first time he had seen Janissa's face in the little mirror. She had drawn him across the miles into the lost land where the Flame from infinity had burned and, after all, there was no choice. What problems the future might hold could be solved, somehow.

"We need not go back through the cavern of the monsters," she said. "There is a way to reach the unseen road from here."

Raft's lips found hers.

But he was thinking: My world will be strange to you, Janissa. I will make you happy, if I can. And I think I can, for I love you.

But will you turn back, sometimes, and remember? Will you remember Paititi, and the great trees that hold up the sky? Will you remember the castle above Doirada Gulf, where the white cloud from the cataract hangs forever in the sky?

Will the heritage of the jaguar stir in your blood, Janissa, to memories I cannot share? Or will you find contentment in my world?

Silently Raft let Janissa guide him toward the way that led to freedom, and to a destiny he could not foretell. But the girl's hand lay warm in his, and that, for the while, was enough of an answer for them both.

THE
DARK
WORLD

I

Fire in the Night

TO THE north thin smoke made a column against the darkening sky. Again I felt the unreasoning fear, the impulse toward nightmare flight that had been with me for a long time now. I knew it was without reason. There was only smoke, rising from the swamps of the tangled Limberlost country, not fifty miles from Chicago, where man has outlawed superstition with strong bonds of steel and concrete.

I knew it was only a camper's fire, yet *I knew it was not*. Something, far back in my mind, knew what the smoke rose from, and who stood about the fire, peering my way through the trees.

I looked away, my glance slipping around the crowded walls—shelves bearing the random fruit of my uncle's magpie collector's instinct. Opium pipes of inlaid work and silver, golden chessmen from India, a sword...

Deep memories stirred within me—deep panic. I was beneath the sword in two strides, tearing it from the wall, my fingers cramping hard around the hilt. Not fully aware of what I did, I found myself facing the window and the distant smoke again. The sword was in my fist, but feeling wrong, not reassuring, not as *the* sword ought to feel.

"Easy, Ed," my uncle's deep voice said behind me. "What's the matter? You look—sort of wild."

"It's the wrong sword," I heard myself saying helplessly.

Then something like a mist cleared from my brain. I blinked at him stupidly, wondering what was happening to me. My voice answered.

"It isn't the sword. It should have come from Cambodia. It should have been one of the three talismans of the Fire King and the Water King. Three very great talismans—the fruit of *cui*, gathered at the time of the deluge, but still fresh—the rattan with flowers that never fade, and the sword of Yan, the guarding spirit."

My uncle squinted at me through pipe-smoke. He shook his head.

"You've changed, Ed," he said in his deep, gentle voice. "You've changed a lot. I suppose because of the war—it's to be expected. And you've been sick. But you never used to be interested in things like that before. I think you spend too much time at the libraries. I'd hoped this vacation would help. The rest—"

"I don't want rest!" I said violently. "I spent a year and a half resting in Sumatra. Doing nothing but rest in that smelly little jungle village, waiting and waiting and waiting."

I could see and smell it now. I could feel again the fever that had raged so long through me as I lay in the tabooed hut.

My mind went back eighteen months to the last hour when things were normal for me. It was in the closing phases of World War II, and I was flying over the Sumatran jungle. War, of course, is never good or normal, but until that one blinding moment in the air I had been an ordinary man, sure of myself, sure of my place in the world, with no nagging fragments of memory too elusive to catch.

Then everything blanked out, suddenly and completely. I never knew what it was. There was nothing it could have been. My only injuries came when the plane struck, and they were miraculously light. But I had been whole and unhurt when the blindness and blankness came over me.

The friendly Bataks found me as I lay in the ruined plane. They brought me through a fever and a raging illness with their strange, crude, effective ways of healing, but I sometimes thought they had done me no service when they saved me. And their witch-doctor had his doubts, too.

He knew something. He worked his curious, futile charms

with knotted string and rice, sweating with effort I did not understand—then. I remembered the scarred, ugly mask looming out of the shadow, the hands moving in gestures of strange power.

"Come back, O soul, where thou are lingering in the wood, or in the hills, or by the river. See, I call thee with a *toemba bras*, with an egg of the fowl Rajah *moelija*, with the eleven healing leaves. . . ."

"Yes, they were sorry for me at first, all of them. The witch-doctor was the first to sense something wrong and the awareness spread. I could feel it spreading, as their attitude changed. They were afraid. Not of me, I thought, but of—what?

Before the helicopter came to take me back to civilization, the witch-doctor had told me a little. As much, perhaps, as he dared.

"You must hide, my son. All your life you must hide. Something is searching for you—" He used a word I did not understand. "—and it has come from the Other World, the ghostlands, to hunt you down. Remember this: all magic things must be taboo to you. And if that too fails, perhaps you may find a weapon in magic. But we cannot help you. Our powers are not strong enough for that."

He was glad to see me go. They were all glad.

And after that, unrest. For something had changed me utterly. The fever? Perhaps. At any rate, I didn't feel like the same man. There were dreams, memories—haunting urgencies as if I had somehow, somewhere left some vital job unfinished. . . .

I found myself talking more freely to my uncle.

"It was like a curtain lifting. A curtain of gauze. I saw some things more clearly—they seemed to have a different significance. Things happen to me now that would have seemed incredible—before. Now they don't.

"I've traveled a lot, you know. It doesn't help. There's always something to remind me. An amulet in a pawnshop window, a knotted string, a cat's-eye opal and two figures. I see them in my dreams, over and over. And once—"

I stopped.

"Yes?" my uncle prompted softly.

"It was in New Orleans. I woke up one night and there was something in my room, very close to me. I had a gun—a

special sort of gun—under my pillow. When I reached for it
the—call it a dog—sprang from the window. Only it wasn't
shaped quite like a dog." I hesitated. "There were silver bullets
in the revolver," I said.

My uncle was silent for a long moment. I knew what he
was thinking.

"The other figure?" he said, finally.

"I don't know. It wears a hood. I think it's very old. And
beyond these two—"

"Yes?"

"A voice. A very sweet voice, haunting. A fire. And beyond
the fire, a face I have never seen clearly."

My uncle nodded. The darkness had drawn in; I could
scarcely see him, and the smoke outside had lost itself against
the shadow of night. But a faint glow still lingered beyond the
trees . . . Or did I only imagine that?

I nodded toward the window.

"I've seen that fire before," I told him.

"What's wrong with it? Campers make fires."

"No. It's a Need-fire."

"What the devil is that?"

"It's a ritual," I said. "Like the Midsummer fires, or the
Beltane fire the Scots used to kindle. But the Need-fire is
lighted only in time of calamity. It's a very old custom."

My uncle laid down his pipe and leaned forward.

"What is it, Ed? Do you have any inkling at all?"

"Psychologically I suppose you could call it a persecution
complex," I said slowly. "I believe, in things I never used to.
I think someone is trying to find me—*has* found me. And is
calling. Who it is I don't know. What they want I don't know.
But a little while ago I found out one more thing—this sword."

I picked the sword up from the table.

"It isn't what I want," I went on, "But sometimes, when
my mind is—abstract, something from outside floats into it.
Like the need for a sword. And not any sword—just one. I
don't know what the sword looks like, but I'd know if I held
it in my hand." I laughed a little. "And if I drew it a few inches
from the sheath, I could put out that fire up there as if I'd
blown on it like a candleflame. And if I drew the sword all
the way out—the world would come to an end!"

My uncle nodded. After a moment, he spoke.

"The doctors," he asked. "What do they say?"

"I know what they *would* say, if I told them," I said grimly. "Pure insanity. If I could be sure of that, I'd feel happier. One of the dogs was killed last night, you know."

"Of course. Old Duke. Another dog from some farm, eh?"

"Or a wolf. The same wolf that got into my room last night, and stood over me like a man, and clipped off a lock of my hair."

Something flamed up far away, beyond the window, and was gone in the dark. The Need-fire.

My uncle rose and stood looking down at me in the dimness. He laid a big hand on my shoulder.

"I think you're sick, Ed."

"You think I'm crazy. Well, I may be. But I've got a hunch I'm going to know soon, one way or the other."

I picked up the sheathed sword and laid it across my knees. We sat in silence for what seemed like a long time.

In the forest to the north, the Need-fire burned steadily. I could not see it. But its flames stirred in my blood—dangerously—darkly.

II

Call of the Red Witch

I COULD not sleep. The suffocating breathlessness of late summer lay like a woollen blanket over me. Presently I went into the big room and restlessly searched for cigarettes. My uncle's voice came through an open doorway.

"All right, Ed?"

"Yeah. I can't sleep yet. Maybe I'll read."

I chose a book at random, sank into a relaxer chair and switched on a lamp. It was utterly silent. I could not even hear the faint splashing of little waves on the lakeshore.

There was something I wanted—

A trained rifleman's hand, at need, will itch for the feeling of smooth wood and metal. Similarly, my hand was hungry for the feel of something—neither gun nor sword, I thought.

A weapon that I had used before. I could not remember what it was. Once I glanced at the poker leaning against the fireplace, and thought that was it; but the flash of recognition was gone instantly.

The book was a popular novel. I skimmed through it rapidly. The dim, faint, pulsing in my blood did not wane. It grew stronger, rising from sub-sensory levels. A distant excitement seemed to be growing deep in my mind.

Grimacing, I rose to return the book to its shelf. I stood there for a moment, my glance skimming over the titles. On impulse I drew out a volume I had not looked at for many years, the Book of Common Prayer.

It fell open in my hands. A sentence blazed out from the page.

I am become as it were a monster unto many.

I put back the book and returned to my chair. I was in no mood for reading. The lamp overhead bothered me, and I pressed for the switch. Instantly moonlight flooded the room— and instantly the curious sense of expectancy was heightened, as though I had lowered a—a barrier.

The sheathed sword still lay on the window-seat. I looked past it, to the clouded sky where a golden moon shone. Faint, far away, a glimmer showed—the Need-fire, blazing in the swampy wilderness of the Limberlost.

And it called.

The golden square of window was hypnotic. I lay back in my chair, half-closing my eyes, while the sense of danger moved coldly within my brain. Sometimes before I had felt this call, summoning me. And always before I had been able to resist.

This time I wavered.

The lock of hair clipped from my head—had that given the enemy power? Superstition. My logic called it that, but a deep, inner well of conviction told me that the ancient hair-magic was not merely mummery. Since that time in Sumatra, I had been far less skeptical. And since then I had studied.

The studies were strange enough, ranging from the principles of sympathetic magic to the wild fables of lycanthropy and demonology. Yet I was amazingly quick at learning.

It was as though I took a refresher course, to remind myself of knowledge I had once known by heart. Only one subject really troubled me, and I continually stumbled across it, by roundabout references.

And that was the Force, the entity, disguised in folklore under such familiar names as the Black Man, Satan, Lucifer, and such unfamiliar names as Kutchie, of the Australian Dieris, Tuña, of the Esquimaux, the African Abonsam, and the Swiss Strätteli.

I did no research on the Black Man—but I did not need to. There was a recurrent dream that I could not help identifying with the dark force that represented evil. I would be standing before a golden square of light, very much afraid, and yet straining toward some consummation that I desired. And deep down within that glowing square that would be the beginning of motion. I knew there were certain ritual gestures to be made before the ceremony could be begun, but it was difficult to break the paralysis that held me.

A square like the moon-drenched window before me—yet not the same.

For no chill essence of fear thrust itself out at me now. Rather, the low humming I heard was soothing, gentle as a woman's crooning voice.

The golden square wavered—shook—and little tendrils of crepuscular light fingered out toward me. Ever the low humming came, alluring and disarming.

Golden fingers—tentacles—they darted here and there as if puzzled. They touched lamp, table, carpet, and drew back. They—touched me.

Swiftly they leaped forward now—avid! I had time for a momentary pulse of alarm before they wrapped me in an embrace like golden sands of sleep. The humming grew louder. And I responded to it.

As the skin of the flayed satyr Marsyas thrilled at the sound of his native Phrygian melodies! I knew this music. I knew this—chant!

Stole through the golden glow a crouching shadow—not human—with amber eyes and a bristling mane—the shadow of a wolf.

It hesitated, glanced over its shoulder questioningly. And

now another shape swam into view, cowled and gowned so
that nothing of its face or body showed. But it was small—
small as a child.

Wolf and cowled figure hung in the golden mists, watching
and waiting. The sighing murmur altered. Formed itself into
syllables and words. Words in no human tongue, but—I knew
them.

"Ganelon! I call you, Ganelon! By the seal in your blood—
hear me!"

Ganelon! Surely that was my name. I knew it so well.

Yet who called me thus?

"I have called you before, but the way was not open. Now
the bridge is made. Come to me, Ganelon!"

A sigh.

The wolf glanced over a bristling shoulder, snarling. The
cowled figure bent toward me. I sensed keen eyes searching
me from the darkness of the hood, and an icy breath touched
me.

"He has forgotten, Medea," said a sweet, high-pitched voice,
like the tone of a child.

Again the sigh. "Has he forgotten me? Ganelon, Ganelon!
Have you forgotten the arms of Medea, the lips of Medea?"

I swung, cradled in the golden mists, half asleep.

"He has forgotten," the cowled figure said.

"Then let him come to me nevertheless. Ganelon! The Need-
fire burns. The gateway lies open to the Dark World. By fire
and earth, and darkness, I summon you! Ganelon!"

"He has forgotten."

"Bring him. We have the power, now."

The golden sands thickened. Flame-eyed wolf and robed
shadow swam toward me. I felt myself lifted—moving forward, not of my own volition.

The window swung wide. I saw the sword, sheathed and
ready. I snatched up the weapon, but I could not resist that
relentless tide that carried me forward. Wolf and whispering
shadow drifted with me.

"To the Fire. Bring him to the Fire."

"He has forgotten, Medea."

"To the Fire, Edeyrn. To the Fire."

Twisted tree-limbs floated past me. Far ahead I saw a flicker.
It grew larger, nearer. It was the Need-fire.

Faster the tide bore me. Toward the fire itself—

Not to Caer Llyr!

From the depths of my mind the cryptic words spewed.
Amber-eyed wolf whirled to glare at me; cowled shadow swept
in closer on the golden stream. I felt a chill of deadly cold
drive through the curling mists.

"Caer Llyr," the cloaked Edeyrn whispered in the child's
sweet voice. "He remembers Caer Llyr—but does he remember Llyr?"

"He will remember! He has been sealed to Llyr. And, in
Caer Llyr, the Place of Llyr, he will remember."

The Need-fire was a towering pillar a few yards away. I
fought against the dragging tide.

I lifted my sword—threw the sheath away. I cut at the
golden mists that fettered me.

Under the ancient steel the shining fog-wraiths shuddered
and were torn apart—and drew back. There was a break in
the humming harmony; for an instant, utter silence.

Then—

"Matholch!" the invisible whisperer cried. "Lord Matholch!"

The wolf crouched, fangs bared. I aimed a cut at its snarling
mask. It avoided the blow easily and sprang.

It caught the blade between its teeth and wrenched the hilt
from my grip.

The golden fogs surged back, folding me in their warm
embrace.

"Caer Llyr," they murmured.

The Need-fire roared up in a scarlet fountain.

"Caer Llyr!" the flames shouted.

And out of those fires rose—a woman!

Hair dark as midnight fell softly to her knees. Under level
brows she flashed one glance at me, a glance that held question
and a fierce determination. She was loveliness incarnate. Dark
loveliness.

Lilith. Medea, witch of Colchis!

And—

"The gateway closes," the child-voice of Edeyrn said.

The wolf, still mouthing my sword, crouched uneasily. But the woman of the fire said no word.

She held out her arms to me.

The golden clouds thrust me forward, into those white arms.

Wolf and cowled shadow sprang to flank us. The humming rose to a deep-pitched roar—a thunder as of crashing worlds.

"It is difficult, difficult," Medea said. "Help me, Edeyrn. Lord Matholch."

The fires died. Around us was not the moonlit wilderness of the Limberlost, but empty grayness, a featureless grayness that stretched to infinity. Not even stars showed against that blank.

And now there was fear in the voice of Edeyrn.

"Medea. I have not the—power. I stayed too long in the Earth-world."

"Open the gate!" Medea cried. "Thrust it open but a little way, or we stay here between the worlds forever!"

The wolf crouched, snarling. I felt energy pouring out of his beast-body. His brain that was not the brain of a beast.

Around us the golden clouds were dissipating.

The grayness stole in.

"Ganelon," Medea said. "Ganelon! Help me!"

A door in my mind opened. A formless darkness stole in.

I felt that deadly, evil shadow creep through me, and submerge my mind under ebon waves.

"He has the power," Edeyrn murmured. "He was sealed to Llyr. Let him call on—Llyr."

"No. No. I dare not. Llyr?" But Medea's face was turned to me questioningly.

At my feet the wolf snarled and strained, as though by sheer brute strength it might wrench open a gateway between locked worlds.

Now the black sea submerged me utterly. My thought reached out and was repulsed by the dark horror of sheer infinity, stretched forth again and—

Touched—something!

Llyr . . . *Llyr!*

"The gateway opens," Edeyrn said.

The gray emptiness was gone. Golden clouds thinned and vanished. Around me, white pillars rose to a vault far, far above. We stood on a raised dais upon which curious designs were emblazoned.

The tide of evil which had flowed through me had vanished.

But, sick with horror and self-loathing, I dropped to my knees, one arm shielding my eyes.

I had called on—*Llyr!*

III

Locked Worlds

ACHING in every muscle, I woke and lay motionless, staring at the low ceiling. Memory flooded back. I turned my head, realizing that I lay on a soft couch padded with silks and pillows. Across the bare, simply furnished room was a recessed window, translucent, for it admitted light, but I could see only vague blurs through it.

Seated beside me, on a three-legged stool, was the dwarfed, robed figure I knew was Edeyrn.

Not even now could I see the face; the shadows within the cowl were too deep. I felt the keen glint of a watchful gaze, though, and a breath of something unfamiliar—cold and deadly. The robes were saffron, an ugly hue that held nothing of life in the harsh folds. Staring, I saw that the creature was less than four feet tall, or would have been had it stood upright.

Again I heard that sweet, childish, sexless voice.

"Will you drink, Lord Ganelon? Or eat?"

I threw back the gossamer robe covering me and sat up. I was wearing a thin tunic of silvery softness, and trunks of the same material. Edeyrn apparently had not moved, but a drapery swung apart in the wall, and a man came silently in, bearing a covered tray.

Sight of him was reassuring. He was a big man, sturdily muscled, and under a plumed Etruscan-styled helmet his face was tanned and strong. I thought so till I met his eyes. They were blue pools in which horror had drowned. And ancient fear, so familiar that it was almost submerged, lay deep in his gaze.

Silently he served me and in silence withdrew.

Edeyrn nodded toward the tray.

"Eat and drink. You will be stronger, Lord Ganelon."

There were meats and bread, of a sort, and a glass of colorless liquid that was not water, as I found on sampling it. I took a sip, set down the chalice, and scowled at Edeyrn.

"I gather that I'm not insane," I said.

"You are not. Your soul has been elsewhere—*you* have been in exile—but you are home again now."

"In Caer Llyr?" I asked, without quite knowing why.

Edeyrn shook the saffron robes.

"No. But you must remember?"

"I remember nothing. Who are you? What's happened to me?"

"You know that you are Ganelon?"

"My name's Edward Bond."

"Yet you almost remembered—at the Need-fire," Edeyrn said. "This will take time. And there is danger always. Who am I? I am Edeyrn—who serves the Coven."

"Are you—"

"A woman," she said, in that childish, sweet voice, laughing a little. "A very *old* woman, the oldest of the Coven, it has shrunk from its original thirteen. There is Medea, of course, Lord Matholch—" I remembered the wolf—"Ghast Rhymi, who has more power than any of us, but is too old to use it. And you, Lord Ganelon, or Edward Bond, as you name yourself. Five of us in all now. Once there were hundreds, but even I cannot remember that time, though Ghast Rhymi can, if he would."

I put my head in my hands.

"Good heavens, I don't know! Your words mean nothing to me. I don't even know where I am!"

"Listen," she said, and I felt a soft touch on my shoulder. "You must understand this. You have lost your memories."

"That's not true."

"It *is* true, Lord Ganelon. Your true memories were erased, and you were given artificial ones. All you think you recall now, of your life on the Earth-world—all that is false. It did not happen. At least, not to you."

"The Earth-world? I'm not on Earth?"

"This is a different world," she said. "But it is your own

world. You came from here originally. The Rebels, our enemies, exiled you and changed your memories."

"That's impossible."

"Come here," Edeyrn said, and went to the window. She touched something, and the pane grew transparent. I looked over her shrouded head at a landscape I have never seen before.

Or had I?

Under a dull, crimson sun the rolling forest below lay bathed in bloody light. I was looking down from a considerable height, and could not make out details, but it seemed to me that the trees were oddly shaped and that they were moving. A river ran toward distant hills. A few white towers rose from the forest. That was all. Yet the scarlet, huge sun had told me enough. This was not the Earth I knew.

"Another planet?"

"More than that," she said. "Few in the Dark World know this. But *I* know—and there are some others who have learned, unluckily for you. There are worlds of probability, divergent in the stream of time, but identical almost, until the branches diverge too far."

"I don't understand that."

"Worlds coexistent in time and space—but separated by another dimension, the variant of probability. This is the world that might have been yours had *something* not happened, long ago. Originally the Dark World and the Earth-world were one, in space and time. Then a decision was made—a very vital decision, though I am not sure what it was. From that point the time-stream branched, and two variant worlds existed where there had been only one before.

"They were utterly identical at first, except that in one of them the key decision had *not* been made. The results were very different. It happened hundreds of years ago, but the two variant worlds are still close together in the time stream. Eventually they will drift farther apart, and grow less like each other. Meanwhile, they *are* similar, so much so that a man on the Earth-world may have his twin in the Dark World."

"His twin?"

"The man he might have been, had the key decision not been made ages ago in his world. Yes, twins, Ganelon—Edward Bond. Do you understand now?"

I returned to the couch and sat there, frowning.

"Two worlds, coexistent. I can understand that, yes. But I think you mean more—that a double for me exists somewhere."

"You were born in the Dark World. Your double, the true Edward Bond, was born on Earth. But we have enemies here, woods-runners, rebels, and they have stolen enough knowledge to bridge the gulf between time-variants. We ourselves learned the method only lately, though once it was well-known here, among the Coven.

"The rebels reached out across the gulf and sent you—sent Ganelon—into the Earth-world so that Edward Bond could come here, among them. They—"

"But why?" I interrupted. "What reason could they have for that?"

Edeyrn turned her hooded head toward me, and I felt, not for the first time, remote chill as she fixed her unseen gaze upon my face.

"What reason?" she echoed in her sweet, cool voice. "Think, Ganelon. See if you remember."

I thought, I closed my eyes and tried to submerge my conscious mind, to let the memories of Ganelon rise up to the surface if they were there at all. I could not yet accept this preposterous thought in its entirety, but certainly it would explain a great deal if it were true. It would even explain—I realized suddenly—that strange blanking out in the plane over the Sumatra jungle, that moment from which everything had seemed so wrong.

Perhaps that was the moment when Edward Bond left Earth, and Ganelon took his place—both twins too stunned and helpless at the change to know what had happened, or to understand.

But this was impossible!

"I don't remember!" I said harshly. "It can't have happened. I *know* who I am! I know everything that ever happened to Edward Bond. You can't tell me that all this is only illusion. It's too clear, too real!"

"Ganelon, Ganelon," Edeyrn crooned to me, a smile in her voice. "Think of the rebel tribes. Try, Ganelon. Try to remember why they did what they did to you. The woods-runners,

Ganelon—the disobedient little men in green. The hateful men who threatened us. Ganelon, surely you remember!"

It may have been a form of hypnotism. I thought of that later. But at that moment, a picture did swim into my mind. I could see the green-clad swarms moving through the woods, and the sight of them made me hot with sudden anger. For that instant I was Ganelon, and a great and powerful lord, defied by these underlings not fit to tie my shoe.

"Of course you hated them," murmured Edeyrn. She may have seen the look on my face. I felt the stiffness of an unfamiliar twist of feature as she spoke. I had straightened where I sat, and my shoulders had gone back arrogantly, my lip curling a feeling of scorn. So perhaps she did not read my mind at all. What I thought was plain in my face and bearing.

"Of course you punished them when you could," she went on. "It was your right and duty. But they duped you, Ganelon. They were cleverer than you. They found a door that would turn on a temporal axis and thrust you into another world. On the far side of the door was Edward Bond who did not hate them. So they opened the door."

Edeyrn's voice rose slightly and in it I detected a note of mockery.

"False memories, false memories, Ganelon. You put on Edward Bond's past when you put on his identity. But he came into our world as he was, free of any knowledge of Ganelon. He has given us much trouble, my friend, and much bewilderment. At first we did not guess what had gone wrong. It seemed to us that as Ganelon vanished from our Coven, a strange new Ganelon appeared among the rebels, organizing them to fight against his own people." She laughed softly. "We had to rouse Ghast Rhymi from his sleep to aid us. But in the end, learning the method of door-opening, we came to Earth and searched for you, and found you. And brought you back. This is your world, Lord Ganelon! Will you accept it?"

I shook my head dizzily.

"It isn't real. I'm still Edward Bond."

"We can bring back your true memories. And we will. They came to the surface for a moment, I think, just now. But it will take time. Meanwhile, you are one of the Coven, and Edward Bond is back upon Earth in his old place. Remem-

bering—" She laughed softly. "Remembering, I am sure, all
he left undone here. But helpless to return, or meddle again
in what does not concern him. But we have needed you, Ganelon. How badly we have needed you!"

"What can I do? I'm Edward Bond."

"Ganelon can do much—when he remembers. The Coven
has fallen upon evil days. Once we were thirteen. Once there
were other Covens to join us in our Sabbats. Once we ruled
this whole world, under Great Llyr. But Llyr is falling asleep
now. He draws farther and farther away from his worshippers.
By degrees the Dark World has fallen into savagery. And, of
all the Covens, only we remain, a broken circle, dwelling close
to Caer Llyr where the Great One sleeps beyond his Golden
Window."

She fell silent for a moment.

"Sometimes I think that Llyr does not sleep at all," she said.
"I think he is withdrawing, little by little, into some farther
world, losing his interest in us whom he created. But he returns!" She laughed. "Yes, he returns when the sacrifices stand
before his Window. And so long as he comes back, the Coven
has power to force its will upon the Dark World.

"But day by day the forest rebels grow stronger, Ganelon.
With our help, you were gathering power to oppose them—
when you vanished. We needed you then, and we need you
more than ever now. You are one of the Coven, perhaps the
greatest of us all. With Matholch you were—"

"Wait a minute," I said. "I'm still confused. Matholch? Was
he the wolf I saw?"

"He was."

"You spoke of him as though he were a man."

"He *is* a man—at times. He is lycanthropic. A shape-changer."

"A werewolf? That's impossible. It's a myth, a bit of crazy
folklore."

"What started the myth?" Edeyrn asked. "Long ago, there
were many gateways opened between the Dark World and
Earth. On Earth, memories of those days survive as superstitious tales. Folklore. But with roots in reality."

"It's superstition, nothing else," I said flatly. "You actually
mean that werewolves, vampires and all that, exist."

"Ghast Rhymi could tell you more of this than I can. But

we cannot wake him for such a matter. Perhaps I—well, listen. The body is composed of cells. These are adaptable to some extent. When they are made even more adaptable, when metabolism is accelerated sporadically, werewolves come into being."

The sweet, sexless child's voice spoke on from the shadow of the hood. I began to understand a little. On Earth, college biology had showed me instances of cells run wild—malignant tumors and the like. And there were many cases of "wolf-men," with thick hair growing like a pelt over them. If the cells could adapt themselves *quickly*, strange things might occur.

But the bones? Specialized osseous tissue, not the rigidly brittle bones of the normal man. A physiological structure that could, theoretically, so alter itself that it would be wolf instead of man, was an astounding theory!

"Part of it is illusion, of course," Edeyrn said. "Matholch is not as bestial in form as he seems. Yet he *is* a shape-changer, and his form does alter."

"But how?" I asked. "How did he get this power?"

For the first time Edeyrn seemed to hesitate. "He is—a mutation. There are many mutations among us, here in the Dark World. Some are in the Coven, but others are elsewhere."

"Are you a mutation?" I asked her.

"Yes."

"A—shape-changer?"

"No," Edeyrn said, and the thin body under the robe seemed to shake a little. "No, I cannot change my shape, Lord Ganelon. You do not remember my—my powers?"

"I do not."

"Yet you may find them useful when the Rebels strike again," she said slowly. "Yes, there are mutations among us, and perhaps that is the chief reason why the probability-rift came ages ago. There are no mutants on Earth—at least not our type. Matholch is not the only one."

"Am I a mutant?" I asked very softly.

The cowled head shook.

"No. For no mutant may be sealed to Llyr. As you have been sealed. One of the Coven must know the key to Caer Llyr."

The cold breath of fear touched me again. No, not fear. Horror, the deadly, monstrous breathlessness that always took me when the name of Llyr was mentioned.

I forced myself to say, "Who is Llyr?"

There was a long silence.

"Who speaks of Llyr?" a deep voice behind me asked. Better not to lift *that* veil, Edeyrn!"

"Yet it may be necessary," Edeyrn said.

I turned, and saw, framed against the dark portiere, the rangy, whipcord figure of a man, clad as I was in tunic and trunks. His red, pointed beard jutted; the half-snarling curve of his full lips reminded me of something. Agile grace was in every line of his wiry body.

Yellow eyes watched me with wry amusement.

"Pray it may not be necessary," the man said. "Well, Lord Ganelon? Have you forgotten me, too?"

"He has forgotten you, Matholch," Edeyrn said. "At least in this form!"

Matholch—the wolf! The shape-changer!

He grinned.

"It is Sabbat tonight," he said. "The Lord Ganelon must be prepared for it. Also, I think there will be trouble. However, that is Medea's business, and she asks if Ganelon is awake. Since he is, let us see her now."

"Will you go with Matholch?" Edeyrn asked me.

"I suppose so," I said. The red-beard grinned again.

"Ai, you *have* forgotten, Ganelon! In the old days you'd never have trusted me behind your back with a dagger."

"You always knew better than to strike," Edeyrn said. "If Ganelon ever called on Llyr, it would be unfortunate for you!"

"Well, I joked," Matholch said carelessly. "My enemies must be strong enough to give me a fight so I'll wait till your memory comes back, Lord Ganelon. Meanwhile the Coven has its back to the wall, and I need you as badly as you need me. Will you come?"

"Go with him," Edeyrn said. "You are in no danger—wolf's bark is worse than wolf's bite—even though this is not Caer Llyr."

I thought I sensed a hidden threat in her words. Matholch shrugged and held the curtain aside to let me pass.

"Few dare to threaten a shape-changer," he said over his shoulder.

"I dare," Edeyrn said, from the enigmatic shadows of her saffron cowl. And I remembered that she was a mutant too—though not a lycanthrope, like a red-bearded werewolf striding beside me along the vaulted passage.

What was—Edeyrn?

IV

Matholch—and Medea

UP TO now the true wonder of the situation had not really touched me yet. The anaesthesia of shock had dulled me. As a soldier—caught in the white light of a flare dropped from an overhead plane—freezes into immobility, so my mind still remained passive. Only superficial thoughts were moving there, as though, by concentration on immediate needs, I could eliminate the incredible fact that I was not on the familiar, solid ground of Earth.

But it was more than this. There was a curious, indefinable familiarity about these groined, pale-walled halls through which I strode beside Matholch, as there had been a queer familiarity about the twilit landscape stretching to forested distance beneath the window of my room.

Edeyrn—Medea—the Coven.

The names had significance, like words in a language I had once known well, but had forgotten.

The half-loping, swift walk of Matholch, the easy swing of his muscular shoulders, the snarling smile on his red-bearded lips—these were not new to me.

He watched me furtively out of his yellow eyes. Once we paused before a red-figured drapery, and Matholch, hesitating, thrust the curtain aside and gestured me forward.

I took one step—and stopped. I looked at him.

He nodded as though satisfied. Yet there was still a question in his face.

"So you remember a little, eh? Enough to know that this

isn't the way to Medea. However, come along, for a moment. I want to talk to you."

As I followed him up a winding stair, I suddenly realized that he had not spoken in English. But I had understood him, as I had understood Edeyrn and Medea.

Ganelon?

We were in a tower room, walled with transparent panes. There was a smoky, sour odor in the air, and gray tendrils coiled up from a brazier set in a tripod in the middle of the chamber. Matholch gestured me to one of the couches by the windows. He dropped carelessly beside me.

"I wonder how much you remember," he said.

I shook my head.

"Not much. Enough not to be too—trusting."

"The artificial Earth-memories are still strong, then. Ghast Rhymi said you would remember eventually, but that it would take time. The false writing on the slate of your mind will fade, and the old, true memories will come back. After a while."

Like a palimpsest, I thought—manuscript with two writings upon its parchment. But Ganelon was still a stranger; I was still Edward Bond.

"I wonder," Matholch said slowly, staring at me. "You spent much time exiled. I wonder if you have changed, basically. Always before—you hated me, Ganelon. Do you hate me now?"

"No," I said. "At least, I don't know. I think I distrust you."

"You have reason. If you remember at all. We have always been enemies, Ganelon, though bound together by the needs and laws of the Coven. I wonder if we need be enemies any longer?"

"It depends. I'm not anxious to make enemies—especially here."

Matholch's red brows drew together.

"Ai, that is not Ganelon speaking! In the old days, you cared nothing about how many enemies you made. If you have changed so much, danger to us all may result."

"My memory is gone," I said. "I don't understand much of this. It seems dream-like."

Now he sprang up and restlessly paced the room. "That's well. If you become the old Ganelon again, we'll be enemies

again. That I know. But if Earth-exile has changed you—
altered you—we may be friends. It would be better to be
friends. Medea would not like it; I do not think Edeyrn would.
As for Ghast Rhymi—" He shrugged. "Ghast Rhymi is old—
old. In all the Dark World, Ganelon, you have the most power.
Or can have. But it would mean going to Caer Llyr."

Matholch stooped to look into my eyes.

"In the old days, you knew what that meant. You were
afraid, but you wanted the power. Once you went to Caer
Llyr—to be sealed. So there is a bond between you and Llyr—
not consummated yet. But it can be, if you wish it."

"What is Llyr?" I asked.

"Pray that you will not remember that," Matholch said."When
Medea talks to you—beware when she speaks of Llyr. I may
be friend of yours or enemy, Ganelon, but for my own sake,
for the sake of the Dark World—even for the sake of the
rebels—I warn you: do not go to Caer Llyr. No matter what
Medea asks. Or promises. At least be wary till you have your
memories back."

"What is Llyr?" I said again.

Matholch swung around, his back to me. "Ghast Rhymi
knows, I think. I do not. Nor do I want to. Llyr is—is evil—
and is hungry, always. But what feeds his appetite is—is—"
He stopped.

"You have forgotten," he went on after a while. "One thing
I wonder. Have you forgotten how to summon Llyr?"

I did not answer. There was a darkness in my mind, an ebon
gate against which my questioning thoughts probed vainly.

Llyr—Llyr?

Matholch cast a handful of powdery substance into the glowing brazier.

"Can you summon Llyr?" he asked again his voice soft.
"Answer, Ganelon. Can you?"

The sour smoke-stench grew stronger. The darkness in my
head sprang apart, riven, as though a gateway had opened in
the shadow. I—recognized that deadly perfume.

I stood up, glaring at Matholch. I took two steps, thrust out
my sandaled foot, and overturned the brazier. Embers scattered
on the stone floor. The red-beard turned a startled face to me.

I reached out, gripped Matholch's tunic, and shook him till

his teeth rattled together. Hot fury filled me—and something more.

That Matholch should try his tricks on me!

A stranger had my tongue. I heard myself speaking.

"Save your spells for the slaves and helots," I snarled. "I tell you what I wish to tell you—no more than that! Burn your filthy herbs elsewhere, not in my presence!"

Red-bearded jaw jutted. Yellow eyes flamed. Matholch's face altered, flesh flowing like water, dimly seen in the smoke-clouds that poured up from the scattered embers.

Yellow tusks threatened me through the gray mists.

The shape-changer made a wordless noise in his throat—the guttural sound a beast might make. Wolf-cry! A wolf mask glared into mine!

The smoke swam away. The illusion—illusion?—was gone. Matholch, his face relaxing from its snarling lines, pulled gently free from my grip.

"You—startled me, Lord Ganelon," he said smoothly. "But I think that I have had a question answered, whether or not these herbs—" He nodded toward the overturned brazier. "—had anything to do with it."

I turned toward the doorway.

"Wait," Matholch said. "I took something from you, a while ago."

I stopped.

The red-beard came toward me, holding out a weapon—a bared sword.

"I took this from you when we passed through the Need-fire," he said. "It is yours."

I accepted the blade.

Again I moved toward the curtained archway.

Behind me Matholch spoke.

"We are not enemies yet, Ganelon," he said gently. "And if you are wise, you will not forget my warning. Do not go to Caer Llyr."

I went out. Holding the sword, I hurried down the winding stairway. My feet found their path without conscious guidance. The—intruder—in my brain was still strong. A palimpsest. And the blurred, erased writing was becoming visible, as though treated with some strong chemical.

The writing that was my lost memory.

The castle—how did I know it was a castle?—was a labyrinth. Twice I passed silent soldiers standing guard, with a familiar shadow of fear in their eyes—a shadow that, I thought, deepened as they saw me.

I went on, hurrying along a pale-amber hallway. I brushed aside a golden curtain and stepped into an oval room, dome-ceilinged, walled with pale, silken draperies. A fountain spurted, its spray cool on my cheek. Across the chamber, an archway showed the outlines of leafy branches beyond.

I went on through the arch. I stepped out into a walled garden. A garden of exotic flowers and bizarre trees.

The blooms were a riot of patternless color, like glowing jewels against the dark earth. Ruby and amethyst, crystal-clear and milky white, silver and gold and emerald, the flowers made a motionless carpet. But the trees were not motionless.

Twisted and gnarled as oaks, their black boles and branches were veiled by a luxuriant cloud of leafage, virulent green.

A stir of movement rippled through that green curtain. The trees roused to awareness.

I saw the black branches twist and writhe slowly—

Satisfied, their vigilance relaxed. They were motionless again. They—knew me.

Beyond that evil orchard the dark sky made the glowing ember of the sun more brilliant by contrast.

The trees stirred again.

Ripples of unrest shook the green. A serpentine limb, training a veil of leaves, lashed out—struck—whipped back into place.

Where it had been a darting shape ran forward, ducking and twisting as the guardian trees struck savagely at it.

A man, in a tight-fitting suit of earth-brown and forest-green, came running toward me, his feet trampling the jewel-flowers. His hard, reckless face was alight with excitement and a kind of triumph. He was empty-handed, but a pistol-like weapon of some sort swung at his belt.

"Edward!" he said urgently, yet keeping his voice low. "Edward Bond!"

I knew him. Or I knew him for what he was. I had seen dodging, furtive, green-clad figures like his before, and an anger already familiar surged over me at the very sight of him.

Enemy, upstart! One of the many who had dared work their magic upon the great Lord Ganelon.

I felt the heat of rage suffuse my face, and the blood rang in my ears with this unfamiliar, yet well-known fury. My body stiffened in the posture of Ganelon—shoulders back, lip curled, chin high. I heard myself curse the fellow in a voice that was choked and a language I scarcely remembered. And I saw him draw back, disbelief vivid upon his face. His hand dropped to his belt.

"Ganelon?" he faltered, his eyes narrow as they searched mine. "Edward, are you with us or are you Ganelon again?"

V

Scarlet Witch

GRIPPED in my right hand I still held the sword. I cut at him savagely by way of answer. He sprang back, glanced once over his shoulder, and drew his weapon. I followed his glance and saw another green figure dodging forward among the trees. It was smaller and slenderer—a girl, in a tunic the color of earth and forest. Her black hair swung upon her shoulders. She was tugging at her belt as she ran, and the face she turned to me was ugly with hate, her teeth showing in a snarl.

The man before me was saying something.

"Edward, listen to me!" he was crying. "Even if you're Ganelon, you remember Edward Bond! He was with us—he believed in us. Give us a hearing before it's too late! Arles could convince you, Edward! Come to Arles. Even if you're Ganelon, let me take you to Arles!"

"It's no use, Ertu," the voice of the girl cried thinly. She was struggling with the last of the trees, whose flexible bough-tips still clutched to stop her. Neither of them tried now to keep their voices down. They were shouting, and I knew they must rouse the guards at any moment, and I wanted to kill them both myself before anyone came to forestall me by accident. I was hungry and thirsty for the blood of these enemies, and in that moment the name of Edward Bond was not even a memory.

"Kill him, Ertu!" cried the girl. "Kill him or stand out of the way! I know Ganelon!"

I looked at her and took a fresh grip on my sword. Yes, she spoke the truth. She knew Ganelon. And Ganelon knew her, and remembered dimly that she had reason for her hate. I had seen that face before, contorted with fury and despair. I could not recall when or where or why, but she looked familiar.

The man Ertu drew his weapon reluctantly. To him I was still at least the image of a friend. I laughed exultantly and swung at him again with the sword, hearing it hiss viciously through the air. This time I drew blood. He stepped back again, lifting his weapon so that I looked down its black barrel.

"Don't make me do it," he said between his teeth. "This will pass. You have been Edward Bond—you will be again. Don't make me kill you, Ganelon!"

I lifted the sword, seeing him only dimly through a ruddy haze of anger. There was a great exultation in me. I could already see the fountain of blood that would leap from his severed arteries when my blade completed its swing.

I braced my body for the great full-armed blow!

And the sword came alive in my hand. It leaped and shuddered against my fist.

Impossibly—in a way I cannot describe—that blow reversed itself. All the energy I was braced to expend upon my enemy recoiled up the sword, up my arm, crashed against my own body. A violent explosion of pain and shock sent the garden reeling. The earth stuck hard against my knees.

Mist cleared from my eyes. I was still Ganelon, but a Ganelon dizzy from something more powerful than a blow.

I was kneeling on the grass, braced with one hand, shaking the throbbing fingers of my sword-hand and staring at the sword that lay a dozen feet away, still faintly glowing.

It was Matholch's doing—I knew that! I should have remembered how little I could trust that shifting, unstable wolfling. I had laid hands upon him in his tower-room—I should have known he would have his revenge for that. Even Edward Bond—soft fool that he was—would have been wise enough not to accept a gift from the shape-changer.

There was no time now for anger at Matholch, though. I

was looking up into Ertu's eyes, and into the muzzle of his weapon, and a look of decision grew slowly in his face as he scanned mine.

"Ganelon!" he said, almost whispering. "Warlock!"

He tilted the weapon down at me, his finger moving on the trigger.

"Wait, Ertu!" cried a thin voice behind him. "Wait—let me!"

I looked up, still dazed. It had all happened so quickly that the girl was still struggling in the edge of the trees, though she cleared them as I looked and lifted her own weapon. Behind it her face was white and blazing with relentless hate. "Let me!" she cried again. "He owes me this!"

I was helpless. I knew that even at this distance she would not miss. I saw the glare of fury in her eyes and I saw the muzzle waver a little as her hand shook with rage, but I knew she would not miss me. I thought of a great many things in that instant—confused memories of Ganelon's and of Edward Bond's surged together through my mind.

Then a great hissing like a wind swept up among the trees behind the girl. They all swayed toward her more swiftly than trees have any right to move, stooping and straining and hissing with a dreadful vicious avidity. Ertu shouted something inarticulate. But I think the girl was too angry to hear or see.

She never knew what happened. She could only have felt the great bone-cracking sweep of the nearest branch, reaching out for her from the leaning tree. She fired as the blow struck her, and a white-hot bolt ploughed up the turf at my knee. I could smell the charring grass.

The girl screamed thinly once as the avid boughs writhed together over her. The limbs threshed about her in a furious welter, and I heard one clear and distinct snap—a sound I had heard before, I knew, in this garden. The human spine is no more than a twig in the grip of those mighty boughs.

Ertu was stunned for one brief instant. Then he whirled to me, and this time I knew his finger would not hesitate on the trigger.

But time had run out for the two woods-people. He was not fully turned when there came a laugh, cool and amused, from behind me. I saw loathing and hatred flash across Ertu's bronzed face, and the weapon whirled away from me and pointed toward someone at my back. But before he could press the trigger something like an arrow of white light sprang over my shoulder and struck him above the heart.

He dropped instantly, his mouth frozen in a snarling square, his eyes staring.

I turned, getting slowly to my feet. Medea stood there smiling, very slim and lovely in a close-fitting scarlet gown. In her hand was a small black rod, still raised. Her purple eyes met mine.

"Ganelon," she murmured in an infinitely caressing voice. "Ganelon." And still holding my gaze with hers, she clapped her hands softly.

Silent, swift-moving guardsmen came and lifted the motionless body of Ertu. They carried him away. The trees stirred, whispered—and fell silent.

"You have remembered," Medea said. "Ganelon is ours again. Do you remember me—Lord Ganelon?"

Medea, witch of Colchis! Black and white and crimson, she stood there smiling at me, her strange loveliness stirring old, forgotten memories in my blood. No man who had known Medea could ever forget her wholly. Not till time ended.

But wait! There was something more about Medea that I must remember. Something that made even Ganelon a little doubtful, a little cautious. Ganelon? Was I Ganelon again? I had been wholly my old self when the woods-people stood before me, but now I was uncertain.

The memories ebbed. While the lovely witch stood smiling at me, not guessing, all that had made me so briefly Ganelon dropped from my mind and body like a discarded cloak. Edward Bond stood there in my clothing, staring about the clearing and remembering with dismay and sick revulsion what had just been happening here.

For a moment I turned away to hide from Medea what my face must betray if she saw it. I felt dizzy with more than memory. The knowledge that two identities shared my body was a thought even more disturbing than the memory of what I had just done in the grip of Ganelon's strong, evil will.

This was Ganelon's body. There could be no doubt of it now. Somewhere on Earth Edward Bond was back in his old place, but the patterns of his memory still overlaid my mind,

so that he and I shared a common soul, and there was no
Ganelon except briefly, in snatches, as the memories that were
rightfully mine—mine?—returned to crowd out Edward Bond.

I hated Ganelon. I rejected all he thought and was. My false
memories, the heritage from Edward Bond, were stronger in
me than Ganelon. I *was* Edward Bond—now!

Medea's caressing voice broke in upon my conflict, echoing
her question.

"Do you remember me, Lord Ganelon?"

I turned to her, feeling the bewilderment on my own face,
so that my very thoughts were blurred.

"My name is Bond," I told her stubbornly.

She sighed.

"You will come back," she said. "It will take time, but
Ganelon will return to us. As you see familiar things again,
the life of the Dark World, the life of the Coven, the doors of
your mind will open once more. You will remember a little
more tonight, I think, at the Sabbat." Her red smile was suddenly almost frightening.

"Not since I went into the Earth-world has a Sabbat been
held, and it is long past time," she went on. "For in Caer Llyr
there is one who stirs and grows hungry for his sacrifice."

She looked at me piercingly, the purple eyes narrowing.

"Do you remember Caer Llyr, Ganelon?"

The old sickness and horror came over me as she repeated
that cryptic name.

Llyr—Llyr! Darkness, and something stirring beyond a
golden window. Something too alien to touch the soil that
human feet touched, something that should never share the
same life humans lived. Touching that soil, sharing that life,
it defiled them so that they were no longer fit for humans to
share. And yet, despite my revulsion, Llyr was terribly inti-
mate, too!

I knew, I remembered—

"I remember nothing," I told her shortly. For in that particular moment, caution was born in me. I could not trust
anyone, not even myself. Least of all Ganelon—myself. I *did*
remember, but I must not let them know. Until I was clearer
as to what they wanted, what they threatened, I must keep this
one secret which was all the weapon I had.

Llyr! The thought of him—of it—crystallized that decision in my mind. For somewhere in the murk of Ganelon's past there was a frightening link with Llyr. I knew they were trying to push me into that abyss of oneness with Llyr, and I sensed that even Ganelon feared that. I must pretend to be more ignorant than I really was until the thing grew clearer in my memory.

I shook my head again. "I remembered nothing."

"Not even Medea?" she whispered, and swayed toward me. There was sorcery about her. My arms received that red and white softness as if they were Ganelon's arms, not mine. But it was Edward Bond's lips which responded to the fierce pressure of her lips.

Not even Medea?

Edward Bond or Ganelon, what was it to me then? The moment was enough.

But the touch of the red witch wrought a change in Edward Bond. It brought a sense of strangeness, of utter strangeness, to him—to me. I held her lovely, yielding body in my arms, but something alien and unknown stooped and hovered above me as we touched. I surmised that she was holding herself in check—restraining a—a demon that possessed her—a demon that fought to free itself.

"Ganelon!"

Trembling, she pressed her palms against my chest and thrust free. Tiny droplets stood on her pale forehead.

"Enough!" she whispered. "You know!"

"What, Medea?"

And now stark horror stood in those purple eyes.

"You have forgotten!" she said. "You have forgotten me, forgotten who I am, *what* I am!"

VI

The Ride to Caer Sécaire

LATER, in the apartments that had been Ganelon's, I waited
for the hour of Sabbat. And as I waited, I paced the floor
restlessly. Ganelon's feet, pacing Ganelon's floor. But the man
who walked here was Edward Bond. Amazing, I thought, how
the false memory-patterns of another person, impressed upon
Ganelon's clean-sponged brain, had changed him from himself
to—me.

I wondered if I would ever be sure again which personality
was myself. I hated and distrusted Ganelon, now. But I knew
how easily the old self slipped back, in which I would despise
Edward Bond.

And yet to save myself, I must call back Ganelon's memories. I must know more than those around me guessed I knew,
or I thought Ganelon and Bond together might be lost. Medea
would tell me nothing. Edeyrn would tell me nothing. Matholch
might tell me much, but he would be lying.

I scarcely dared go with them to this Sabbat, which I thought
would be the Sabbat of Llyr, because of that strange and terrible
link between Llyr and myself. There would be sacrifices.

How could I be sure I, myself, was not destined for the
altar before that—that golden window?

Then, for a brief but timeless moment Ganelon came back,
remembering fragmentary things that flitted through my mind
too swiftly to take shape. I caught only terror—terror and
revulsion and a hideous, hopeless longing....

Dared I attend the Sabbat?

But I dared not fail to attend, for if I refused I must admit
I knew more about what threatened Ganelon than Edward Bond
should know. And my only frail weapon against them now was
what little I recalled that was secret from them. I must go.
Even if the altar waited me, I must go.

There were the woodspeople. They were outlaws, hunted
through the forests by Coven soldiers. Capture meant enslave-

ment—I remembered the look of still horror in the eyes of those living dead men who were Medea's servants. As Edward Bond, I pitied them, wondered if I could do anything to save them from the Coven. The real Edward Bond had been living among them for a year and a half, organizing resistance, fighting the Coven. On Earth, I knew, he must be raging helplessly now, haunted by the knowledge of work unfinished and friends abandoned to the mercies of dark magic.

Perhaps I should seek the woodspeople out. Among them, at least, I would be safe while my memories returned. But when they returned—why, then Ganelon would rage, running amuck among them, mad with his own fury and arrogance. Dared I subject the woodspeople to the danger that would be the Lord Ganelon when Ganelon's memories came back? Dared I subject myself to their vengeance, for they would be many against one?

I could not go and I could not stay. There was safety nowhere for the Edward Bond who might become Ganelon at any moment. There was danger everywhere. From the rebel woodspeople, from every member of this Coven.

It might come through the wild and mocking Matholch.

Or through Edeyrn, who had watched me unseen with her chilling gaze in the shadows of her cowl.

Through Ghast Rhymi, whoever *he* was. Through Arles, or through the red witch!

Yes, most of all, I thought, through Medea—Medea, whom I loved!

At dusk, two maidens—helot-servants—came, bringing food and a change of garments. I ate hurriedly, dressed in the plain, fine-textured tunic and shorts, and drew about me the royal blue cloak they had carried. A mask of golden cloth I dangled undecidedly, until one of the maidens spoke:

"We are to guide you when you are ready, Lord," she reminded me.

"I'm ready now," I said, and followed the pair.

A pale, concealed lighting system of some sort made the hallways bright. I was taken to Medea's apartment, with its singing fountain under the high dome. The red witch was there breathtakingly lovely in a clinging robe of pure white. Above the robe her naked shoulders gleamed smoothly. She wore a scarlet cloak. I wore a blue one.

The helots slipped away. Medea smiled at me, but I noticed a wire-taut tenseness about her, betrayingly visible at the corners of her lips and in her eyes. A pulse of expectation seemed to beat out from her.

"Are you ready, Ganelon?"

"I don't know," I said. "It depends, I suppose. Don't forget that my memory's gone."

"It may return tonight, some of it anyway," she said.

"But you will take no part in the ritual, at least until after the sacrifice. It will be better if you merely watch. Since you do not remember the rites, you'd best leave those to the rest of the Coven."

"Matholch?"

"And Edeyrn," Medea said. "Ghast Rhymi will not come. He never leaves this castle, nor will he unless the need is very great. He is old, too old."

I frowned at the red witch. "Where are we going?" I asked.

"To Caer Sécaire. I told you there had been no sacrifice since I went to Earth-world to search for you. It is past time."

"What am I supposed to do?"

She put out a slender hand and touched mine.

"Nothing, till the moment comes. You will know then. But meantime you must watch—no more than that. Put on your mask now."

She slipped on a small black mask that left the lower half of her face visible.

I donned the golden mask. I followed Medea to a curtained archway, and through it.

We were in a courtyard. Two horses stood waiting, held by grooms. Medea mounted one and I the other.

Overhead the sky had darkened. A huge door lifted in the wall. Beyond, a roadway stretched toward the distant forest.

The somber, angry disc of the red sun, swollen and burning with a dull fire, touched the crest of the mountain barrier.

Swiftly it sank. Darkness came across the sky with a swooping rush. A million points of white light became visible. In the faint starshine Medea's face was ghost-pale.

Through the near-darkness her eyes glowed.

Faintly, and from far away, I heard a thin, trumpeting call. It was repeated.

Then silence—and a whispering that rose to a rhythmic thudding of shod hoofs.

Past us moved a figure, a helot guardsman, unmasked, unspeaking, his gaze turned to the waiting gateway.

Then another—and another. Until three score of soldiers had gone past, and after them nearly three score of maidens—the slave-girls.

On a light, swift-looking roan stallion Matholch came by, stealing a glance at me from his yellow eyes. A cloak of forest green swirled from his shoulders.

Behind him, the tiny form of Edeyrn, on a pony suited to her smallness. She was still cowled, her face hidden, but she now wore a cloak of purest yellow.

Medea nodded at me. We touched our heels to the horses' flanks and took our places in the column. Behind us other figures rode, but I could not see them clearly. It was too dark.

Through the gateway in the wall we went, still in silence save for the clopping of hoofs. We rode across the plain. The edges of the forest reached out toward us and swallowed us.

I glanced behind. An enormous bulk against the sky showed the castle I had left.

We rode under heavy, drooping branches. These were not the black trees of Medea's garden, but they were not normal either. I could not tell why an indefinable sense of strangeness reached out at me from the dim shadows above and around us.

After a long time the ground dipped at our feet, and we saw below us the road's end. The moon had risen belatedly. By its yellow glare there materialized from the deep valley below us a sort of tower, a dark, windowless structure almost Gothic in plan, as though it had thrust itself from the black earth, from the dark grove of ancient and alien trees.

Caer Sécaire!

I had been here before. Ganelon of the Dark World knew this spot well. But I did not know it; I sensed only that unpleasant familiarity, the *déjà vu* phenomenon, known to all psychologists, coupled with a curious depersonalization, as though my own body, my mind, my very soul, felt altered and strange.

Caer Sécaire. Sécaire? Somewhere, in my studies, I had encountered that name. An ancient rite, in—in Gascony, that was it!

The Mass of Saint Sécaire!

And the man for whom that Black Mass is said—dies. That, too, I remembered. Was the Mass to be said for Ganelon tonight?

This was not the Place of Llyr. Somehow I knew that. Caer Llyr was elsewhere and otherwise, not a temple, not a place visited by worshipers. But here in Caer Sécaire, as in other temples throughout the Dark Land, Llyr might be summoned to his feasting, and, summoned, would come.

Would Ganelon be his feast tonight? I clenched the reins with nervous hands. There was some tension in the air that I could not quite understand. Medea was calm beside me. Edeyrn was always calm. Matholch, I could swear, had nothing to take the place of nerves. Yet in the night there was tension, as if it breathed upon us from the dark trees along the roadside.

Before us, in a silent, submissive flock, the soldiers and the slave-girls went. Some of the soldiers were armed. They seemed to be herding the rest, their movements mechanical, as if whatever had once made them free-willed humans was now asleep. I knew without being told the purpose for which those men and maidens were being driven toward Caer Sécaire. But not even these voiceless mindless victims were tense. They went blindly to their doom. No, the tension came from the dark around us.

Someone, something, waiting in the night!

VII

Men of the Forest

FROM out of the dark woods, suddenly, startlingly, a trumpet-note rang upon the air. In the same instant there was a wild crashing in the underbrush, an outburst of shouts and cries, and the night was laced by the thin lightnings of unfamiliar gunfire. The road was suddenly thronging with green-clad figures who swarmed about the column of slaves ahead of us, grappling with the guards, closing in between us and the mindless victims at our forefront.

My horse reared wildly. I fought him hard, forcing him down again, while stirrings of the old red rage I had felt before mounted in my brain. Ganelon, at sight of the forest people, struggled to take control. Him too I fought. Even in my surprise and bewilderment, I saw in this interruption the possibility of succor. I cracked my rearing horse between the ears with clubbed rein-loops and struggled to keep my balance.

Beside me Medea had risen in her stirrups and was sending bolt after arrowy bolt into the green melee ahead of us, the dark rod that was her weapon leaping in her hand with every shot. Edeyrn had drawn aside, taking no part in the fight. Her small cowled figure sat crouching in the saddle, but her very stillness was alarming. I had the feeling she could end the combat in a moment if she chose.

As for Matholch, his saddle was empty. His horse was already crashing away through the woods, and Matholch had hurled himself headlong into the fight, snarling joyously. The sound sent cold shudders down my spine. I could see that his green cloak covered a shape that was not wholly manlike, and the green people veered away from him as he plunged through their throngs toward the head of the column.

The woodsfolk were trying a desperate rescue. I realized that immediately. I saw too that they dared not attack the Coven itself. All their efforts were aimed at overpowering the robot-like guards so that the equally robotlike victims might be saved from Llyr. And I could see that they were failing.

For the victims were too apathetic to scatter. All will had long ago been drained away from them. They obeyed orders—that was all. And the forest people were leaderless. In a moment or two I realized that, and knew why. It was my fault. Edward Bond may have planned this daring raid, but through my doing, he was not here to guide them. And already the abortive fight was nearly over.

Medea's flying fiery arrows struck down man after man. The mindless guards fired stolidly into the swarms that surged about them, and Matholch's deep-throated, exultant, snarling yells as he fought his way toward his soldiers were more potent than weapons. The raiders shrank back from the sound as they did not shrink from gunfire. In a moment, I knew, Matholch would reach his men, and organized resistance would break the back of this unguided mutiny.

For an instant my own mind was a fierce battleground. Ganelon struggled to take control, and Edward Bond resisted him savagely.

As Ganelon I knew my place was beside the wolfling; every instinct urged me forward to his side. But Edward Bond knew better. Edward Bond too knew where his rightful place should be.

I shoved up my golden mask so that my face was visible. I drove my heels into my horse's sides and urged him headlong down the road behind Matholch. The sheer weight of the horse gave me an advantage Matholch, afoot, did not have. The sound of drumming hoofs and the lunging shoulders of my mount opened a way for me. I rose in the stirrups and shouted with Ganelon's deep, carrying roar:

"Bond! Bond! Edward Bond!"

The rebels heard me. For an instant the battle around the column wavered as every green-clad man paused to look back. Then they saw their lost leader, and a great echoing hail swept their ranks.

"Bond! Edward Bond!"

The forest rang with it, and there was new courage in the sound. Matholch's wild snarl of rage was drowned in the roar of the forest men as they surged forward again to the attack.

Out of Ganelon's memories I knew what I must do. The foresters were dragging down guard after guard, careless of the gunfire that mowed their disordered ranks. But only I could save the prisoners. Only Ganelon's voice could pierce the daze that held them.

I kicked my frantic horse forward, knocking guards left and right, and gained the head of the column.

"In the forest!" I shouted. "Waken and run! Run hard!"

There was an instant forward surge as the slaves, still tranced in their dreadful dream, but obedient to the voice of a Coven member, lurched through the thin rank of their guard. The whole shape of the struggle changed as the core of it streamed irresistibly forward across the road and into the darkness of the woods.

The green-clad attackers fell back to let the slaves through. It was a strange, voiceless flight they made. Not even the guards shouted, though they fired and fired again upon the retreating column, their faces as blank as if they slept without dreams.

My flesh crawled as I watched that sight—the men and women fleeing for their lives, the armed soldiers shooting them down, and the faces of them all utterly without expression. Voiceless they ran and voiceless they died when the gun-bolts found them.

I wrenched my horse around and kicked him in the wake of the fleeing column. My golden mask slipped sidewise and I tore it off, waving to the scattering foresters, the moonlight catching brightly on its gold.

"Save yourselves!" I shouted, "Scatter and follow me!"

Behind me I heard Matholch's deep snarl, very near. I glanced over one shoulder as my horse plunged across the road. The shape-changer's tall figure faced me across the heads of several of his soldiers. His face was a wolflike snarling mask, and as I looked he lifted a dark rod like the one Medea had been using. I saw the arrow of white fire leap from it, and ducked in the saddle.

The movement saved me. I felt a strong tug at my shoulders where the blue cape swirled out, and heard the tear of fabric as the bolt ripped through it and plunged hissing into the dark beyond. My horse lunged on into the woods.

Then the trees were rustling all about me, and my bewildered horse stumbled and tossed up his head, whinnying in terror. Beside me in the dark a soft voice spoke softly.

"This way," it said, and a hand seized the bridle.

I let the woodsman lead me into the darkness.

It was just dawn when our weary column came at last to the end of the journey, to the valley between cliffs where the woodsmen had established their stronghold. All of us were tired, though the blank-faced slaves we had rescued trudged on in an irregular column behind me, unaware that their feet were torn and their bodies drooping with exhaustion.

The forest men slipped through the trees around us, alert for followers. We had no wounded with us. The bolts the Coven shot never wounded. Whoever was struck fell dead in his tracks.

In the pale dawn I would not have known the valley before me for the headquarters of a populous clan. It looked quite empty except for scattered boulders, mossy slopes, and a small

stream that trickled down the middle, pink in the light of
sunrise.

One of the men took my horse then, and we went on foot
up the valley, the robot slaves crowding behind. We seemed
to be advancing up an empty valley. But when we had gone
half its length, suddenly the woodsman at my right laid his
hand upon my arm, and we paused, the rabble behind us jos-
tling together without a murmur. Around me the woodsmen
laughed softly. I looked up.

She stood high upon a boulder that overhung the stream.
She was dressed like a man in a tunic of soft, velvety green,
crossbelted with a weapon swinging at each hip, but her hair
was a fabulous mantle streaming down over her shoulders and
hanging almost to her knees in a cascade of pale gold that
rippled like water. A crown of pale gold leaves the color of
the hair held it away from her face, and under the shining
chaplet she looked down and smiled at us. Especially she
smiled at me—at Edward Bond.

And her face was very lovely. It had the strength and in-
nocence and calm serenity of a saint's face, but there was
warmth and humor in the red lips. Her eyes were the same
color as her tunic, deep green, a color I had never seen before
in my own world.

"Welcome back, Edward Bond," she said in a clear, sweet
gently hushed voice, as if she had spoken softly for so many
years that even now she did not dare speak aloud.

She jumped down from the boulder, very lightly, moving
with the sureness of a wild creature that had lived all its lifetime
in the woods, as indeed I suppose she had. Her hair floated
about her as lightly as a web, settling only slowly about her
shoulders as she came forward, so that she seemed to walk in
a halo of her own pale gold.

I remembered what the woodsman Ertu had said to me in
Medea's garden before her arrow struck him down.

"Arles could convince you, Edward! Even if you're Ganelon, let me take you to Arles!"

I stood before Arles now. Of that I was sure. And if I had
needed any conviction before that the woodsmen's cause was
mine, this haloed girl would have convinced me with her first
words. But as for Ganelon—

How could I know what Ganelon would do?

That question was answered for me. Before my lips could frame words, before I could plan my next reaction, Arles came toward me, utterly without pretense or consciousness of the watching eyes. She put her hands on my shoulders and kissed me on the mouth.

And that was not like Medea's kiss—no! Arles' lips were cool and sweet, not warm with the dangerous, alluring honey-musk of the red witch. That intoxication of strange passion I remembered when I had held Medea in my arms did not sweep me now. There was a—a purity about Arles, an honesty that made me suddenly, horribly homesick for Earth.

She drew back. Her moss-green eyes met mine with quiet understanding. She seemed to be waiting.

"Arles," I said, after a moment.

And that seemed to satisfy her. The vague question that had begun to show on her face was gone.

"I wondered," she said. "They didn't hurt you, Edward?"

Instinctively I knew what I had to say.

"No. We hadn't reached Caer Sécaire. If the woodsmen hadn't attacked—well, there'd have been a sacrifice."

Arles reached out and lifted a corner of my torn cloak, her slim fingers light on the silken fabric.

"The blue robe," she said. "Yes, that is the color the sacrifice wears. The gods cast their dice on our side tonight, Edward. Now as for this foul thing, we must get rid of it."

Her green eyes blazed. She ripped the cloak from me, tore it across and dropped it to the ground.

"You will not go hunting again alone," she added. "I told you it was dangerous. But you laughed at me. I'll wager you didn't laugh when the Coven slaves caught you! Or was that the way of it?"

I nodded. A slow, deep fury was rising within me. So blue was the color of sacrifice, was it? My fears hadn't been ground-less. At Caer Sécaire I would have been the offering, going blindly to my doom. Matholch had known, of course. Trust his wolf-mind to appreciate the joke. Edeyrn, thinking her cool, inhuman thoughts in the shadow of her hood, she had known too. And Medea?

Medea!

She had dared betray me! Me, *Ganelon!*

The Opener of the Gate, the Chose of Llyr, the great Lord
Ganelon! They dared! Black thunder roared through my brain.
I thought: By Llyr, but they'll suffer for this! They'll crawl to
my feet like dogs. Begging my mercy!

Rage had opened the floodgates, and Edward Bond was no
more than a set of thin memories that had slipped from me as
the blue cloak had slipped from my shoulders—the blue cloak
of the chosen sacrifice, on the shoulders of the Lord Ganelon!

I blinked blindly around the green-clad circle. How had I
come here? How dared these woodsrunners stand in defiance
before me? Blood roared in my ears and the woodland swam
around me. When it steadied I would draw my weapon and
reap these upstarts as a mower reaps his wheat.

But wait!

First, the Coven, my sworn comrades, had betrayed me.
Why, *why*? They had been glad enough to see me when they
brought me back from the other world, the alien land of Earth.
The woodsmen I could slay whenever I wished it—the other
problem came first. And Ganelon was a wise man. I might
need these woods-people to help me in my vengeance. Afterward—ah, afterward!

I strove hard with memory. What could have happened to
turn the Coven against me? I could have sworn this had not
been Medea's original intention—she had welcomed me back
too sincerely for that. Matholch could have influenced her, but
again, why, why? Or perhaps it was Edeyrn, or the Old One
himself, Ghast Rhymi. In any case, by the Golden Window
that opens on the Abyss, they'd learn their error!

"Edward!" a woman's voice, sweet and frightened, came
to me as if from a great distance. I fought my way up through
a whirlpool of fury and hatred. I saw a pale face haloed in
floating hair, the green eyes troubled. I remembered.

Beside Arles stood a stranger, a man whose cold gray eyes
upon mine provided the shock I needed to bring me back to
sanity. He looked at me as if he knew me—knew Ganelon. I
had never seen the man before.

He was short and sturdy, young-looking in spite of the gray
flecks in his close-cropped beard. His face was tanned so deeply
it had almost the color of the brown earth. In his close-fitting
green suit he was the perfect personification of a woodsrunner,

a glider through the forest, unseen and dangerous. Watching the powerful flex of his muscles when he moved, I knew he would be a bad antagonist. And there was deep antagonism in the way he looked at me.

A white, jagged scar had knotted his right cheek, quirking up his thin mouth so that he wore a perpetual crooked, sardonic half-grin. There was no laughter in those gelid gray eyes, though.

And I saw that the circle of woodsmen had drawn back, ringing us, watching.

The bearded man put out his arm and swept Arles behind him. Unarmed, he stepped forward, toward me.

"No, Lorryn," Arles cried. "Don't hurt him."

Lorryn thrust his face into mine.

"Ganelon!" he said.

And at the name a whisper of fear, of hatred, murmured around the circle of woodsfolk. I saw furtive movements, hands slipping quietly toward the hilts of weapons. I saw Arles' face change.

The old-time cunning of Ganelon came to my aid.

"No," I said, rubbing my forehead. "I'm Bond, all right. It was the drug the Coven gave me. It's still working."

"What drug?"

"I don't know," I told Lorryn. "It was in Medea's wine that I drank. And the long journey tonight has tired me."

I took a few unsteady paces aside and leaned against the boulder, shaking my head as though to clear it. But my ears were alert. The low murmur of suspicion was dying.

Cool fingers touched mine.

"Oh, my dear," Arles said, and whirled on Lorryn. "Do you think I don't know Edward Bond from Ganelon? Lorryn, you're a fool!"

"If the two weren't identical, we'd never have switched them in the first place," Lorryn said roughly. "Be sure, Arles. Very sure!"

Now the whispering grew again. "Better to be sure," the woodsmen murmured. "No risks, Arles! If this is Ganelon, he must die."

The doubt came back into Arles' green eyes. She thrust my hands away and stared at me. And the doubt did not fade.

I gave her glance for glance.

"Well, Arles?" I said.

Her lips quivered.

"It can't be. I know, but Lorryn is right. You know that; we can take no risks. To have the devil Ganelon back, after all that's happened, would be disastrous."

Devil, I thought. The devil Ganelon. Ganelon had hated the woodsfolk, yes. But now he had another, greater hatred. In his hour of weakness, the Coven had betrayed him. The woodsfolk could wait. Vengeance could not. It would be the devil Ganelon who would bring Caer Sécaire and the Castle crashing down about the ears of the Coven!

Which would mean playing a careful game!

"Yes, Lorryn is right," I said. "You've no way of knowing I'm not Ganelon. Perhaps you know it, Arles—" I smiled at her "—but there must be no chances taken. Let Lorryn test me."

"Well?" Lorryn said, looking at Arles.

Doubtfully she glanced from me to the bearded man.

"I—very well, I suppose."

Lorryn barked laughter.

"My tests might fail. But there is one who can see the truth. Freydis."

"Let Freydis test me," I said quickly, and was rewarded by seeing Lorryn hesitate.

"Very well," he said at last. "If I'm wrong, I'll apologize now. But if I'm right, I'll kill you, or try to. There's only one other life I'd enjoy taking the more, and the shape-changer isn't in my reach—yet."

Again Lorryn touched his scarred cheek. At the thought of Lord Matholch, warmth came into his gray eyes; a distant ember burned for an instant there. I had seen hatred before. But not often had I seen such hatred as Lorryn held for—the wolfing?

Well, let him kill Matholch, if he could! There was another, softer throat in which I wanted to sink my fingers. Nor could all her magic protect the red witch when Ganelon came back to Caer Sécaire, and broke the Coven like rotten twigs in his hands!

Again the black rage thundered up like a deluging tide. That fury had wiped out Edward Bond—but it had not wiped out Ganelon's cunning.

"As you like, Lorryn," I said quietly. "Let's go to Freydis now."

He nodded shortly. Lorryn on one side of me, Arles, puzzled and troubled, on the other, we moved up the valley, surrounded by the woodsfolk. The dazed slaves surged ahead.

The canyon walls closed in. A cave-mouth showed in the granite ahead.

We drew up in a rough semi-circle facing that cavern. Silence fell, broken by the whispering of leaves in the wind. The red sun was rising over the mountain wall.

Out of the darkness came a voice, deep, resonant, powerful.

"I am awake," it said. "What is your need?"

"Mother Freydis, we have helots captured from the Coven," Arles said quickly. "The sleep is on them."

"Send them in to me."

Lorryn gave Arles an angry look. He pushed forward.

"Mother Freydis!" he called.

"I hear."

"We need your sight. This man, Edward Bond—I think he is Ganelon, came back from the Earth-world where you sent him."

There was a long pause.

"Send him into me," the deep voice finally said. "But first the helots."

At a signal from Lorryn the woodsfolk began herding the slaves toward the cavemouth. They made no resistance. Empty-eyed, they trooped toward that cryptic darkness, and one by one, vanished.

Lorryn looked at me and jerked his head toward the cavern. I smiled.

"When I come out, we shall be friends again as before." I said.

His eyes did not soften.

"Freydis must decide that."

I turned to Arles.

"Freydis shall decide," I said. "But there is nothing to fear, Arles. Remember that. I am not Ganelon."

She watched me, afraid, unsure, as I stepped back a pace or two.

The silent throng of woodsfolk stared, waiting warily. They had their weapons ready.

I laughed softly and turned.

I walked toward the cave-mouth.

The blackness swallowed me.

VIII

Freydis

STRANGE to relate, I felt sure of myself as I walked up the sloping ramp in the darkness. Ahead of me, around a bend, I could see the glimmer of firelight, and I smiled. It had been difficult to speak with these upstart woodsrunners as if they were my equals, as if I were still Edward Bond. It would be difficult to talk to their witchwoman as if she had as much knowledge as a Lord of the Coven. Some she must have, or she could never have managed the transfer which had sent me into the Earth-world and brought out Edward Bond. But I thought I could deceive her or anyone these rebels had to offer me.

The small cave at the turn of the corridor was empty except for Freydis. Her back was to me. She crouched on her knees before a small fire that burned, apparently without fuel, in a dish of crystal. She wore a white robe, and her white hair lay in two heavy braids along her back. I stopped, trying to feel like Edward Bond again, to determine what he would have said in this moment. Then Freydis turned and rose.

She rose tremendously. Few in the Dark World can look me in the eye, but Freydis' clear blue gaze was level with my own. Her great shoulders and great, smooth arms were as powerful as a man's, and if age was upon her, it did not show in her easy motions or in the timeless face she turned to me. Only in the eyes was knowledge mirrored, and I knew as I met them that she was old indeed.

"Good morning, Ganelon," she said in her deep, serene voice.

I gaped. She knew me as surely as if she read my mind.

Yet I was sure, or nearly sure, that no one in the Dark World could do that. For a moment I almost stammered. Then pride came to my rescue.

"Good day, old woman," I said. "I come to offer you a chance for your life, if you obey me. We have a score to settle, you and I."

She smiled.

"Sit down, Covenanter," she said. "The last time we matched strength, you traded worlds. Would you like to visit Earth again, Lord Ganelon?"

It was my turn to laugh.

"You could not. And if you could, you wouldn't, after you hear me."

Her blue eyes searched mine.

"You want something desperately," she said in a slow voice. "Your very presence here, offering me terms, proves that. I never thought to see the Lord Ganelon face to face unless he was in chains or in a berserker battle-mood. Your need of me, Lord Ganelon, serves as chains for you now. You are fettered by your need, and helpless."

She turned back to the fire and sat down with graceful smoothness, her huge body under perfect control. Across the flame in its crystal bowl she faced me.

"Sit down, Ganelon," she said again, "and we will bargain, you and I. One thing first—do not waste my time with lies. I shall know if you tell the truth, Covenanter. Remember it."

I shrugged.

"Why should I bother with lies for such as you?" I said. "I have nothing to hide from you. The more of truth you know, the stronger you'll see my case is. First, though—those slaves who came in before me?

She nodded toward the back of the cave.

"I sent them into the inner mountain. They sleep. You know the heavy sleep that comes upon those loosed from the Spell, Lord Ganelon."

I sat down, shaking my head.

"No—no, that I can not quite remember. I—you asked for the truth, old woman. Listen to it, then. I am Ganelon, but the false memories of Edward Bond still blur my mind. As Edward Bond I came here—but Arles told me one thing that brought Ganelon back. She told me that the Coven, in my hour

of weakness, had dressed me in the blue cloak of the sacrifice
and I was riding for Caer Sécaire when the woodsmen attacked
us. Must I tell you now what my first wish in life is, witch-
woman?"

"Revenge on the Coven." She said it hollowly, her eyes
burning into mine through the fire. "This is the truth you speak,
Covenanter. You want my help in getting your vengeance.
What can you offer the woodsfolk in return, save fire and
sword? Why should we trust you, Ganelon?"

Her ageless eyes burned into mine.

"Because of what you want. My desire is vengeance. Yours
is—what?"

"The end of Llyr—the ruin of the Coven!" Her voice was
resonant and her whole ageless face lighted as she spoke.

"So. I too desire the ruin of the Coven and the end—the
end of Llyr." My tongue stumbled a little when I said that. I
was not sure why. True, I had been sealed to Llyr in a great
and terrible ceremony once—I could recall that much. But
Llyr and I were not one. We might have been, had events run
differently. I shuddered now at the thought of it.

Yes, it was Llyr's end I desired now—must desire, if I
hoped to live.

Freydis looked at me keenly. She nodded.

"Yes—perhaps you do. Perhaps you do. What do you want
of us then, Ganelon?"

I spoke hastily:

"I want you to swear to your people that I am Edward Bond.
No—wait! I can do more for them now than Edward Bond
could do. Give thanks that I am Ganelon again, old woman!
For only he can help you. Listen to me. Your foresters could
not kill me. I know that. Ganelon is deathless, except on Llyr's
altar. But they could fetter me and keep me prisoner here until
you could work your spells again and bring Edward Bond back.
And that would be foolish for your sake and for mine.

"Edward Bond has done all he knows for you. Now it's
Ganelon's turn. Who else could tell you how Llyr is vulnerable,
or where Matholch keeps his secret weapons, or how one can
vanquish Edeyrn? These things I know—or I once knew. You
must help me win my memories back, Freydis. After that—"
I grinned fiercely.

She nodded. Then she sat quiet for awhile.

"What do you want me to do, then, Ganelon?" she asked, at last.

"Tell me first about the bridging of the worlds," I said eagerly. "How did you change Edward Bond and me?"

Freydis smiled grimly.

"Not so fast, Covenanter!" she answered. "I have my secrets too! I will answer only a part of that question. We wrought the change, as you must guess, simply to rid ourselves of you. You must remember how fiercely you were pressing us in your raids for slaves, in your hatred of our freedom. We are a proud people, Ganelon, and we would not be oppressed forever. But we knew there was no death for you except in a way we could not use.

"I knew of the twin world of Earth. I searched, and found Edward Bond. And after much striving, much effort, I wrought a certain transition that put you in the other world, with memories of Edward Bond blotting out your own.

"We were rid of you. True, we had Edward Bond with us, and we did not trust him either. He was too like you. But him we could kill if we must. We did not. He is a strong man, Covenanter. We came to trust him and rely upon him. He brought us new ideas of warfare. He was a good leader. It was he who planned the attack upon the next Coven sacrifice—"

"An attack that failed," I said. "Or would have failed, had I not swung my weight into the balance. Edward Bond had Earth-knowledge, yes. But his weapons and defenses could only have breached the outer walls of the Coven. You know there are powers, seldom used, but powers that do not fail!"

"I know," she said. "Yes, I know, Ganelon. Yet we had to try, at least. And the Coven had been weakened by losing you. Without you, none of the others would have dared call on Llyr, except perhaps Ghast Rhymi." She stared deeply into the fire. "I know you Ganelon. I know the pride that burns in your soul. And I know, too, that vengeance, now, would be very dear to your heart. Yet you were sealed to Llyr, once, and you have been Covenanter since your birth. How do I know you can be trusted?"

I did not answer that. And, after a moment, Freydis turned toward the smoke-blackened wall. She twitched aside a curtain I had not seen. There, in an alcove, was a Symbol, a very ancient Sign, older than civilization, older than human speech.

Yes, Freydis would be one of the few who knew what that Symbol meant. As I knew.

"Now will you swear that you speak with a straight tongue?" she said.

I moved my hand in the ritual gesture that bound me irrevocably. This was an oath I could not break without being damned and doubly damned, in this world and the next. But I had no hesitation. I spoke truth!

"I will destroy the Coven!" I said.

"And Llyr?"

"I will bring an end to Llyr!"

But sweat stood out on my forehead as I said that. It was not easy.

Freydis twitched the curtain back into place. She seemed satisfied.

"I have less doubt now," she said. "Well, Ganelon, the Norns weave strange threads together to make warp and woof of destiny. Yet there is a pattern, though sometimes we cannot see it. I did not ask you to swear fealty to the forest-folk."

"I realize that."

"You would not have sworn it," she said. "Nor is it necessary. After the Coven is broken, after an end is made to Llyr, I can guard the people of the woods against even you, Ganelon. And we may meet in battle then. But until then we are allies. I will name you—Edward Bond."

"I'll need more than that," I told her. "If the masquerade is to pass unchallenged."

"No one will doubt my word," Freydis said. Firelight flickered on her great frame, her smooth, ageless face.

"I cannot fight the Coven till I get back my memories. The memories of Ganelon. *All* of them."

She shook her head.

"Well," she said slowly, "I cannot do too much on that score. Something, yes. But writing on the mind is touchy work, and memories, once erased, are not easily brought back. You still have Edward Bond's memories?"

I nodded.

"But my own, no. They're fragmentary. I know, for example, that I was sealed to Llyr, but the details I don't remember."

"It would be as well, perhaps, to let that memory stay lost,"

Freydis said somberly. "But you are right. A dulled tool is no use. So listen."

Rock-still, boulder-huge, she stood across the fire from me. Her voice deepened.

"I sent you into the Earth-World. I brought your double, Edward Bond, here. He helped us, and—Arles loved him, after a while. Even Lorryn, who does not trust many, grew to trust Edward Bond."

Who is Lorryn?"

"One of us now. Not always. Years ago he had his cottage in the forest; he hunted, and few were as cunning as Lorryn in the chase. His wife was very young. Well, she died. Lorryn came back to this cottage one night and found death there, and blood, and a wolf that snarled at him from a bloody muzzle. He fought the wolf; he did not kill it. You saw Lorryn's cheek. His whole body is like that, scarred and wealed from wolf-fangs."

"A wolf?" I said. "Not—"

"A wolfling," Freydis said. "Lycanthrope, shape-changer. Matholch. Some day Lorryn will kill Matholch. He lives only for that."

"Let him have the red dog," I said contemptuously. "If he likes, I'll give him Matholch flayed!"

"Arles and Lorryn and Edward Bond have planned their campaign," Freydis said. "They swore that the last Sabbat had been celebrated in the Dark World. Edward Bond showed them new weapons he remembered from Earth. Such weapons have been built and are in the arsenal, ready. No Sabbats have been held since Medea and her followers went searching to Earth; the woodsfolk held their hands. There was nothing to strike at except old Ghast Rhymi. Now Medea and the rest of the Coven are back, they're ready. If you lead against them Ganelon, the Coven can be smashed, I think."

"The Coven has its own weapons," I muttered. "My memory fails—but I think Edeyrn has a power that—that—" I shook my head. "No, it's gone."

"How can Llyr be destroyed?" Freydis asked.

"I—I may have known once. Not now."

"Look at me," she said. And leaned forward, so that it seemed as though her ageless face was bathed in the fires.

Through the flames her gaze caught mine. Some ancient

power kindled her clear blue eyes. Like pools of cool water under a bright sky—pools deep and unstirring, where one could sink into an azure silence forever and ever. . . .

As I looked the blue waters clouded, grew dark. I saw a great black dome against a black sky. I saw the thing that dwells deepest and most strongly in the mind of Ganelon—Caer Llyr!

The dome swam closer. It loomed above me. Its walls parted like dark water, and I moved in memory down the great smooth, shining corridor that leads to Llyr Himself.

IX

Realm of the Superconscious

ONWARD I moved. Faces flickered before me—Matholch's fierce grin, Edeyrn's cowled head with its glance that chilled, Medea's savage beauty that no man could ever forget, even in his hatred. They looked at me, mistrustfully. Their lips moved in soundless question. Curiously, I knew these were real faces I saw.

In the magic of Freydis' spell I was drifting through some dimensionless place where only the mind ventures, and I was meeting here the thoughts of the questing Coven, meeting the eyes of their minds. They knew me. They asked me fiercely a question I could not hear.

Death was in the face Matholch's mind turned to mine. All his hatred of me boiled furiously in his yellow wolf-eyes. His lips moved—almost I could hear him. Medea's features swam up before me, blotting out the shape-changer. Her red mouth framed a question—over and over.

"Ganelon, where are you? Ganelon, my lover, where are you? You must come back to us. Ganelon!"

Edeyrn's faceless head moved between Medea and me, and very distantly I heard her cool, small voice echoing the same thought,

"You must return to us, Ganelon. Return to us and die!"

Anger drew a red curtain between those faces and myself.

Traitors, betrayers, false to the Coven oath! How dared they threaten Ganelon, the strongest of them all? How dared they—and why?

Why?

My brain reeled with the query. And then I realized there was one face missing from the Coven. These three had been searching the thought-planes for me, but what of Ghast Rhymi?

Deliberately I groped for the contact of his mind.

I could not touch him. But I remembered. I remembered Ghast Rhymi, whose face Edward Bond had never seen. Old, old, old, beyond good and evil, beyond fear and hatred, this was Ghast Rhymi, the wisest of the Coven. If he willed, he would answer my groping thought. If he willed not, nothing could force him. Nothing could harm the Eldest, for he lived on only by force of his own will.

He could end himself instantly, by the power of a thought. And he is like a candle flame, flickering away as one grasps at him. Life holds nothing more for him. He does not cling to it. If I had tried to seize him he could slip like fire or water from my grasp. He would as soon be dead as alive. But unless he must, he would not break his deep calm to think the thought that would change him into clay.

His mind and the image of his face remained hidden from my quest. He would not answer. The rest of the Coven still kept calling to me with a strange desperation in their minds—return and die, Lord Ganelon! But Ghast Rhymi did not care.

So I knew that it was at his command the death-sentence had been passed. And I knew I must seek him out and somehow force an answer from him—from Ghast Rhymi, upon whom all force was strengthless. Yet force him I must!

All this while my mind had been drifting effortlessly down the great hallway of Caer Llyr, borne upon that tide that flows deepest in the mind of Ganelon, the Chosen of Llyr—Ganelon, who must one day return to Him Who Waits. . . . As I was returning now.

A golden window glowed before me. I knew it for the window through which great Llyr looks out upon his world, the window through which he reaches for his sacrifices. And Llyr was hungry. I felt his hunger. Llyr was roaming the thought-planes too, and in the moment that I realized again where my mind was drifting, I felt suddenly the stir of a great reaching, a tentacular groping through the golden window.

Llyr had sensed my presence in the planes of his mind. He knew his Chosen. He stretched out his godlike grasp to fold me into that embrace from which there is no returning.

I heard the soundless cry of Medea, vanishing like a puff of smoke out of the thought-plane as she blanked her mind defensively from the terror. I heard Matholch's voiceless howl of pure fear as he closed his own mind. There was no sound from Edeyrn, but she was gone as utterly as if she had never thought a thought. I knew the three of them sat somewhere in their castle, eyes and minds closed tightly, willing themselves to blankness as Llyr roamed the thought-lanes seeking the food he had been denied so long.

A part of me shared the terror of the Coven. But a part of me remembered Llyr. For an instant, almost I recaptured the dark ecstasy of that moment when Llyr and I were one, and the memory of horror and of dreadful joy came back, the memory of a power transcending all earthly things.

This was mine for the taking, if I opened my mind to Llyr. Only one man in a generation is sealed to Llyr, sharing in his godhead, exulting with him in the ecstasy of human sacrifice— and I was that one man if I chose to complete the ceremony that would make me Llyr's. If I chose, if I dared—ah!

The memory of anger came back. I must not release myself into that promised joy. I had sworn to put an end to Llyr. I had sworn by the Sign to finish the Coven and Llyr. Slowly, reluctantly, my mind pulled itself back from the fringing contact of those tentacles.

The moment that tentative contact was broken, a full tide of horror washed over me. Almost I had touched—*him*. Almost I had let myself be defiled beyond all human understanding by the terrible touch of—of— There is no word in any language for the thing that was Llyr. But I understood what had been in my mind as Edward Bond when I realized that to dwell on the same soil as Llyr, share the same life, was a defilement that made earth and life too terrible to endure—if one knew Llyr.

I must put an end to *him*. In that moment, I knew I must stand up and face the being we knew as Llyr and fight him to his end. No human creature had ever fully faced him—not even his sacrifices, not even his Chosen. But his slayer would have to face him, and I had sworn to be his slayer.

Shuddering, I drew back from the black depths of Caer Llyr, struggled to the surface of that still blue pool of thought which had been Freydis' eyes. The darkness ebbed around me and by degrees the walls of the cave came back, the fuelless flame, the great smooth-limbed sorceress who held my mind in the motionless deeps of her spell.

As I returned to awareness, slowly, slowly, knowledge darted through my mind in lightning-flashes, too swiftly to shape into words.

I knew, I remembered.

Ganelon's life came back in pictures that went vividly by and were printed forever on my brain. I knew his powers; I knew his secret strengths, his hidden weaknesses. I knew his sins. I exulted in his power and pride. I returned to my own identity and was fully Ganelon again. Or almost fully.

But there were still hidden things. Too much had been erased from my memory to come back in one full tide. There were gaps, and important gaps, in what I could recall.

The blue darkness cleared. I looked in Freydis' clear gaze across the fire. I smiled, feeling a cold and arrogant confidence welling up in me.

"You have done well, witch-woman," I told her.

"You remember?"

"Enough. Yes, enough." I laughed. "There are two trials before me, and the first is the easier of the two, and it is impossible. But I shall accomplish it."

"Ghast Rhymi?" she asked in a quiet voice.

"How do you know that?"

"I know the Coven. And I think, but I am not sure, that in Ghast Rhymi's hands lie the secrets of the Coven and of Llyr. But no man can force Ghast Rhymi to do his bidding."

"I'll find the way. Yes, I will even tell you what my next task is. You shall have the truth as I just learned it, witch. Do you know of the Mask and the Wand?"

Her eyes on mine, she shook her head. "Tell me. Perhaps I can help."

I laughed again. It was so fantastically implausible that she and I should stand here, sworn enemies of enemy clans, plan-

ning a single purpose together! Yet there was only a little I hid
from her that day, and I think not very much that Freydis hid
from me.

"In the palace of Medea, is a crystal mask and the silver
Wand of Power," I told her. "What that Wand is I do not quite
remember—yet. But when I find it, my hands will know. And
with it I can overcome Medea and Matholch and all their
powers. As for Edeyrn—well, this much I know. The Mask
will save me from her."

I hesitated.

Medea I knew now. I knew the strange hungers and the
stranger thirsts that drove the beautiful red and white witch to
her trystings. I knew now, and shuddered a little to think of
it, why she took her captives with those arrows of fire that did
not kill at all, but only stunned them.

In the Dark World, my world, mutation has played strange
changes upon flesh that began as human. Medea was one of
the strangest of all. There is no word in Earth-tongues for it,
because no creature such as Medea ever walked Earth. But
there is an approximation. In reality perhaps, and certainly in
legend, beings a little like her have been known on Earth. The
name they give them is Vampire.

But Edeyrn, no. I could not remember. It may be that not
even Ganelon had ever known. I only knew that in time of
need, Edeyrn would uncover her face.

"Freydis," I said, and hesitated again. "What is Edeyrn?"

She shook her massive head, the white braids stirring on
her shoulders.

"I have never known. I have only probed at her mind now
and then, when we met as you met her today, on the thought-
lanes. I have much power, Ganelon, but I have always drawn
back from the chill I sensed beneath Edeyrn's hood. No, I
cannot tell you what she is."

I laughed again. Recklessness was upon me now.

"Forget Edeyrn," I said. "When I have forced Ghast Rhymi
to my bidding, and faced Llyr with the weapon that will end
him, what shall I fear of Edeyrn? The Crystal Mask is a talisman
against her. That much I know. Let her be whatever monstrous
thing she wills—Ganelon has no fear of her.

"There is a weapon, then against Llyr too?"

"There is a sword," I said. "A sword that is—is not quite

a sword as we think of weapons. My mind is cloudy there still. But I know that Ghast Rhymi can tell me where it is. A weapon, yet not a weapon. The Sword Called Llyr."

For an instant, as I spoke that name, it seemed to me that the fire between us flickered as if a shadow had passed across its brightness. I should not have called the name aloud. An echo of it had gone ringing across the realms of thought, and in Caer Llyr perhaps Llyr Himself had stirred behind the golden window—stirred, and looked out.

Even here, I felt a faint flicker of hunger from that far-away domed place. And suddenly, I knew what I had done. *Llyr was awake!*

I stared at Freydis with widened eyes, meeting her blue gaze that was widening too. She must have felt the stir as it ran formlessly all through the Dark World. In the Castle of the Coven I knew they had felt it too, perhaps that they looked at one another with the same instant dread which flashed between Freydis and me here.

Llyr was awake!

And I had wakened him. I had gone drifting in thought down that shining corridor and stood in thought before the very window itself, Llyr's Chosen, facing Llyr's living window. No wonder he had stirred at last to full awakening.

Exultation bubbled up in my mind.

"Now they must move!" I told Freydis joyfully. "You wrought better than you knew when you set my mind free to rove its old track. Llyr wakens and is hungrier than the Coven ever dared let him grow before. For overlong there has been no Sabbat, and Llyr ravens for his sacrifice. Have you spies watching the Castle now, witch-woman?"

She nodded.

"Good. Then we will know when the slaves are gathered again for a Sabbat meeting. It will be soon. It must be soon! And Edward Bond will lead an assault upon the Castle while the Coven are at Sabbat in Caer Sécaire. There will be the Mask and the Wand, old woman!" My voice deepened to a chant of triumph. "The Mask and the Wand for Ganelon, and Ghast Rhymi alone in the Castle to answer me if he can! The Norns fight on our side, Freydis!"

She looked at me long and without speaking.

Then a grim smile broke across her face and stooping, she spread her bare hand, palm down, upon the fuelless flame. I saw the fire lick up around her fingers. Deliberately she crushed it out beneath her hand, not flinching at all.

The fire flared and died away. The crystal dish stood empty upon its pedestal, and dimness closed around us. In that twilight the woman was a great figure of marble, towering beside me.

I heard her deep voice.

"The Norns are with us, Ganelon," she echoed. "See that you fight upon our side too, as far as your oath will take you. Or you must answer to the gods and to me. And by the gods—" she laughed harshly "—by the gods, if you betray me, I swear I'll smash you with no other power than this!"

In the dimness I saw her lift her great arms. We looked one another in the eye, this mighty sorceress and I, and I was not sure but that she could overcome me in single combat if the need arose. By magic and by sheer muscle, I recognized an equal. I bent my head.

"So be it, Sorceress," I said, and we clasped hands there in the darkness. And almost I hoped I need not have to betray her.

Side by side, we went down the corridor to the cave mouth.

The half-circle of foresters still awaited us. Arles and the scarred Lorryn stood a little forward, lifting their heads eagerly as we emerged. I paused, catching the quiver of motion as calloused hands slipped stealthily toward hilt and bowstring. Panic, subdued and breathless, swept around the arc of woods-folk.

I stood there savoring the moment of terror among them, knowing myself Ganelon and the nemesis that would bring harsh justice upon them all, in my own time. In my own good time.

But first I needed their help.

At my shoulder the deep voice of Freydis boomed through the glade.

"I have looked upon this man," she said. "I name him— Edward Bond."

Distrust of me fell away from them; Freydis' words reassured them.

X

Swords for the Coven

Now the sap that runs through Ygdrasill-root stirred from its wintry sluggishness, and the inhuman guardians of the fate-tree roused to serve me. The three Norns—the Destiny-weavers—I prayed to them!

Urdur who rules the past!

She whispered of the Covenanters, and their powers and their weaknesses; of Matholch, the wolfling, whose berserk rages were his great flaw, the gap in his armor through which I could strike, when fury had drowned his wary cunning; of the red witch and of Edeyrn—and of old Ghast Rhymi. My enemies. Enemies whom I could destroy, with the aid of certain talismans that I had remembered now. Whom I would destroy!

Verdandi who rules the present!

Edward Bond had done his best. In the caves the rebels had showed me were weapons, crude rifles and grenades, gas-bombs and even a few makeshift flame-throwers. They would be useful against the Coven's slaves. How useless they would be against the Covenanters I alone knew. Though Freydis may have known too.

Yet Arles and Lorryn and their reckless followers were ready to use those Earth-weapons, very strange to them, in a desperate attack on the Castle. And I would give them that chance, as soon as our spies brought word of Sabbat-preparations. It would be soon. It would have to be soon. For Llyr was awake now—hungry, thirsting—beyond the Golden Window that is his door into the worlds of mankind.

Skuld who rules the future!

To Skuld I prayed most of all. I thought that the Coven would ride again to Caer Sécaire before another dawn came. By then I wanted the rebels ready.

Edward Bond had trained them well. There was military discipline, after a fashion. Each man knew his equipment thoroughly, and all were expert woodsmen. We laid our plans,

Arles and Lorryn and I—though I did not tell them everything I intended—and group by group, the rebels slipped away into the forest, bound for the Castle.

They would not attack. They would not reveal themselves until the signal was given. Meantime, they would wait, concealed in the gulleys and scrub-woods around the Castle. But they would be ready. When the time came, they would ride down to the great gates. Their grenades would be helpful there.

Nor did it seem fantastic that we should battle magic with grenades and rifle. For I was beginning to realize more and more, as my memory slowly returned, that the Dark World was not ruled by laws of pure sorcery. To an Earth-mind such creatures as Matholch and Medea would have seemed supernatural, but I had a double mind, for as Ganelon I could use the memories of Edward Bond as a workman uses tools.

I had forgotten nothing I had ever known about Earth. And by applying logic to the Dark World, I understood things I had always before taken for granted.

The mutations gave the key. There are depths in the human mind forever unplumbed, potentialities for power as there are lost, atrophied senses—the ancient third eye that is the pineal gland. And the human organism is the most specialized thing of flesh that exists.

Any beast of prey is better armed with fang and claw. Man has only his brain. But as carnivores grew longer, more deadly talons, so man's mind developed correspondingly. Even in Earth-world there are mediums, mind-readers, psychomantic experts, ESP specialists. In the Dark World the mutations had run wild, producing cosmic abortions for which there might be no real need for another million years.

And such minds, with their new powers, would develop tools for those powers. The wands. Though no technician, I could understand their principle. Science tends toward simpler mechanisms; the klystron and the magnetron are little more than metal bars. Yet, under the right conditions, given energy and direction, they are powerful machines.

Well, the wands tapped the tremendous electromagnetic energy of the planet, which is, after all, simply a gargantuan magnet. As for the directive impulse, trained minds could easily supply that.

Whether or not Matholch actually changed to wolf-form I

did not know, though I did not think he did. Hypnosis was part of the answer. An angry cat will fluff out its fur and seem double its size. A cobra will, in effect, hypnotize its prey. Why? In order to break down the enemy's defenses, to disarm him, to weaken the single-purposiveness that is so vital in combat. No, perhaps Matholch did not turn into a wolf, but those under the spell of his hypnosis thought he did, which came to the same thing in the end.

Medea? There was a parallel. There are diseases in which blood transfusions are periodically necessary. Not that Medea drank blood; she had other thirsts. But vital nervous energy is as real a thing as a leucocyte, and witch though she was, she did not need magic to serve her needs.

Of Edeyrn I was not so sure. Some stray remembrances hung like mists in my mind. Once I had known what she was, what chilling power lay hidden in the darkness of her cowl. And that was not magic either. The Crystal Mask would protect me against Edeyrn, but I knew no more than that.

Even Llyr—*even Llyr!* He was no god. That I knew well. Yet what he might be was something I could not even guess at as yet. Eventually I meant to find out, and the Sword Called Llyr, which was not a true sword, would aid me then.

Meanwhile, I had my part to play. Even with Freydis as my sponsor, I could not afford to rouse suspicion among the rebels. I had explained that Medea's drug had left me weak and shaken. That helped to explain any minor lapses I might make. Curiously, Lorryn seemed to have accepted me fully at Freydis' word, while in Arles' behavior I detected a faint, almost imperceptible reserve. I do not think that she suspected the truth. Or, if she did she was trying not to admit it, even in her own mind.

And I could not afford to let that suspicion grow.

The valley was very active now.

Much had happened since I came there in the dawn. I had been through enough exertion both physical and emotional to last an ordinary man for a week, but Ganelon had only begun his battle. It was thanks to Edward Bond that our plans for attack would be formulated so readily, and in a way I was glad I had been too busy for anything but the most impersonal planning with Arles and Lorryn.

It helped to cover the great gaps of my ignorance about things Edward Bond should know. Many times I angled craftily for information, many times I had to call upon the excuse of the mythical drug and upon the exhaustion of my ordeal at the Castle. But by the time our plans were laid, it seemed to me that even Arles' suspicions were partly lulled.

I knew I must lull them utterly.

We rose from the great map-table in the council-cavern. All of us were tired. I met Lorryn's scar-twisted grin, warmth in it now as he smiled at the man he thought his sworn friend, and I made Edward Bond's face smile back at him.

"We'll do it this time," I told him confidently. "This time we'll win!"

His smile twisted suddenly into a grimace, and the light like embers glowed in his deep eyes.

"Remember," he growled. "Matholch—for me!"

I looked down at the relief-map of the table, very skillfully made under Edward Bond's directions.

The dark green hills rolling with their strange forests of semi-animate trees, every brook traced in white plaster, every roadway marked. I laid my hand on the little mound of towers that was a miniature Castle of the Coven. From it stretched the highway I had ridden last night, beside Medea, in my blue sacrificial robe. There was the valley and the windowless tower of Caer Sécaire which had been our destination.

For a moment I rode that highway again, in the darkness and the starshine, seeing Medea beside me in her scarlet cloak, her face a pale oval in the dusk, her mouth black-red, her eyes shining at me. I remembered the feel of that fiercely yielding body in my arms as I had held her last night, as I had held her so many times before. In my mind whirled a question.

Medea, Medea, red witch of Colchis, why did you betray me?

I ground my palm down on the tiny plaster towers of the Castle, feeling them powder away beneath my hand. I grinned fiercely at the ruin I had made of Edward Bond's model.

"We'll have no need for *this* again!" I said through my teeth.

Lorryn laughed.

"No need to repair it. Tomorrow the Coven Castle will be wreckage too."

I dusted the powdered plaster from my hand and looked

across the table at the silent Arles. She looked at me gravely, waiting. I smiled.

"We haven't had a moment alone together," I said, making my voice tender. "I'll need sleep before I leave tonight, but there's time for a walk, if you'll come with me."

The grave green gaze dwelt upon mine. Then she nodded, without smiling, and came around the table, stretching out her hand to me. I took it and we went down the steps to the cave-mouth and out into the glen, neither of us speaking. I let her lead the way, and we walked in silence toward the upper end of the valley, the little stream tinkling away beside us.

Arles walked very lightly, her gossamer hair floating behind her in a pale misty veil. I wondered if it was by intent that she kept her free hand resting upon the holstered weapon at her side.

It was hard for me to keep my mind upon her, or to care whether or not she knew me for myself. Medea's face in all its beauty and its evil floated before me up the glen, a face no man who looked upon it could ever forget. For a moment I was angry at the recollection that Edward Bond, in my flesh, had taken last night the kisses she meant for Ganelon.

Well, I would see her again tonight, before she died by my hand!

In my mind I saw the tiny roadway of the map-table, winding down from Coven Castle to the sacrificial temple. Along the real road, sometime in the night to come, I knew the cavalcade would ride again as it had ridden with me last night. And again there would be forest men hiding along the road, and again I would lead them against the Coven. But this time the outcome would be very different from anything either the rebels or the Coven could expect.

What a strange web the Norns had woven! Last night as Edward Bond, tonight as Ganelon, I would lead the same men in the same combat against the same foe, but with a purpose as different as night from day.

The two of us, deadly enemies though we shared the same body in a strange, inverted way—enemies though we had never met and never could meet, for all our common flesh. It was an enigma too curious to unravel.

"Edward," a voice said at my shoulder. I looked down.

Arles was facing me with the same enigmatic gaze I had met so often today. "Edward, is she very beautiful?"

I stared at her.

"Who?"

"The witch. The Coven witch. Medea."

I almost laughed aloud. Was this the answer to all her aloofness of the day? Did she think my own withdrawal, all the changes she sensed in me, were due to the charms of a rival beauty? Well, I must set her mind at rest about that, at any rate. I called upon Llyr to forgive me the lie, and I took her shoulders in my hands and said:

"There is no woman on this world or on Earth half so beautiful as you, my darling."

Still she looked up at me gravely.

"When you mean that, Edward, I'll be glad," she said. "You don't mean it now. I can tell. No." She put her fingers across my mouth as I began to protest. "Let's not talk about her now. She's a sorceress. She has powers neither of us can fight. It isn't your fault or mine that she's too beautiful to forget all in a moment. Never mind now. Look! Do you remember this place?"

She twisted deftly from my grasp and swept out a hand toward the panorama spread below us. We stood in a grove of tall, quivering trees high on the crest of the low mountain. The leaves and branches made a bower around us with their showers of shaking tendrils, but through an opening here and there we could see the rolling country far below us, glowing in the light of the red westering sun.

"This will be ours some day," said Arles softly. "After the Coven is gone, after Llyr has vanished. We'll be free to live above ground, clear the forests, build our cities—live like men again. Think of it, Edward! A whole world freed from savagery. And all because there were a few of us at the start who did not fear the Coven, and who found you. If we win the fight, Edward, it will be because of you and Freydis. We would all have been lost without you."

She turned suddenly, her pale gold hair flying out around her face like a halo of floating gauze, and she smiled at me with a sudden, bewitching charm I had never seen upon her face before.

Until now she had always turned a grave reserve to my

advances. Now suddenly I saw her as Edward Bond had, and it came to me in a flash of surprise that Bond was a very fortunate man, after all. Medea's sultry scarlet beauty would never wholly vanish from my mind, I knew, but this Arles had her own delicate and delightful charm.

She was very near me, her lips parted as she smiled up into my face. For an instant I envied Edward Bond. Then I remembered. I *was* Edward Bond! But it was Ganelon who stooped suddenly and seized the forest girl in a fiercely ardent embrace that amazed her, for I felt her gasp of surprise against my breast and her stir of protest in the moment before my lips touched hers.

Then she protested no longer.

She was a strange, wild, shy little creature, very pleasant in my arms, very sweet to kiss. I knew by the way she responded to me that Edward Bond had never held her like this. But then Edward Bond was a weakling and a fool. And before the kiss had ended I knew where I would turn first for solace when Medea had paid for treachery with her life. I would not forget Medea, but I would not soon forget this kiss of Arles', either.

She clung to me in silence for a moment, her gossamer hair floating like thistledown about us both, and above her head I looked out over the valley which she had seen in her mind's eyes peopled with free forest folk, dotted with their cities. I knew that dream would never come true.

But I had a dream of my own!

I saw the forest people toiling to raise my mighty castle here perhaps on this very mountaintop, a castle to dominate the whole countryside and the lands beyond it. I saw them laboring under my overseers to conquer still further lands. I saw my armies marching, my slaves in my fields and mines, my navies on the dark oceans of a world that might well be mine.

Arles should share it with me—for awhile. For a little while.

"I will always love you!" I said at her ear in the voice of Edward Bond. But it was Ganelon's lips that found her lips in the one last ardent kiss I had time for then.

Curiously, it seemed to me that it took Ganelon's kisses at last to convince her I was Edward Bond....

After that, for a few hours I slept, snug in Edward Bond's cavern rooms, in his comfortable bed, his guards watching beside the door. I slept with the memory of his sweet forest girl in my arms, and the prospect of his kingdom and his bride before me when I woke. I think in the Earth-world, Edward Bond must have dreamed jealous dreams.

But my own dreams were bad. Llyr in his castle was awake and hungry, and the great, cold, writhing tendrils of his hunger coiled lazily through my mind as I slept. I knew they stirred through every mind in the Dark World that had senses to perceive them. I knew I must wake soon, or never. But first I must sleep and grow strong for the night's ordeal. Resolutely I shut Llyr from my thoughts, resolutely I shut away Arles.

It was Medea's red smile and sidelong sultry glance that went down with me into the caverns of slumber.

XI

In Ghast Rhymi's Tower

QUIETLY Lorryn and I crouched among the trees and looked out at the Castle of the Coven, aglitter with lights against the starry sky. This was the night! We both knew it, and we were both tense and sweating with a nervous exultation that made this waiting hard indeed.

All around us in the woods, unseen, we heard the tiny sounds that meant an army of forest people waited our signal. And this time they were here in force. I caught a glint of starlight now and then on rifle-barrels, and I knew that the rebels were armed to put up a good fight against the soldiers of the Coven.

Not, perhaps, too good a fight.

I did not care. They thought they were going to storm the Castle and the Coven by sheer force of arms. I knew their only purpose was to divert attention while I made my way into the Castle and found the secret weapons that would give me power over the Covenanters. While they were striking, I would make my way to Ghast Rhymi and learn what was essential for me to learn.

After that, I did not care. Many foresters would die. Let them. There would still be slaves aplenty for me when my hour came. And nothing could stop me now. The Norns fought with me; I could not fail. . . .

There was much activity within the Castle. Voices floated out to us in the still night air. Figures moved to and fro against the lights. Then great gates were flung open upon a burst of golden radiance and the outlines of many riders crowded against it. A procession was coming out.

I heard chains clash musically, and I understood. This time the sacrifices rode chained to their mounts, so that no siren voices from the wood could lure them away. I shrugged. Let them go to their death, then. Llyr must be fed while he lasted. Better these than Ganelon, offered at the Golden Window. We saw them go off down the dark road, their chains ringing.

That was Matholch—there on the tall horse. I knew his vulpine outlines, the lift of the cloak upon his shoulders. And I would have known him too because of the great start, quickly checked, that Lorryn made beside me. I heard the breath whistle through his nostrils, and his voice grated in my ear.

"Remember! That is mine!"

Edeyrn went by, tiny on her small mount, and a breath of chill seemed to me to sweep the darkness as she passed.

Medea came!

When I could no longer make out her outlines in the distance, when her white robe was no more than a shimmer and her scarlet cloak had melted into the dark, I turned to Lorryn, my mind spinning, my plans already chaotic with change. For a new compulsion had come upon me, and I was not even trying to resist it.

I had not seen a sacrifice in Caer Sécaire. This was one of the blank places in my memory, and a dangerous blank. Until Ganelon remembered the Sabbat, until he watched Llyr accept the offerings through the Golden Window, he could not wholly trust himself to fight the Coven and Llyr. This was a gap that must be filled. And curiosity was suddenly very strong upon me. Curiosity—and could it be—the pull of Llyr?

"Lorryn, wait for me here," I whispered in the darkness. "We've got to make sure they enter Caer Sécaire, start the Sabbat. I don't want to attack until I'm sure. Wait for me." He stirred protestingly, but I was away before he could speak.

I was out upon the road and running softly and silently after that processional winding toward the valley and the Mass of St. Sécaire, which is the Black Mass. It seemed to me as I ran that the fragrance of Medea's perfume hung upon the air I breathed, and my throat choked with the passion of my hatred for her, and of my love.

"She shall be the first to die," I promised myself in the dark. . . .

I watched the great iron doors of Caer Sécaire swing shut upon the last of the procession. The Caer was dark inside. They went quietly in, one by one, and vanished into the deeper night within. The doors clanged resonantly after them.

Some memory of Ganelon's, buried beneath the surface of conscious thought, urged me to the left, around the curve of the great wall. I followed the impulse obediently, moving almost like a sleep-walker toward a goal I did not know. Memory took me close under the looming rampart, made me lay my hands on its surface. There were heavy scrollings of pattern there, writhing like tendrils over the dark walls. My remembering fingers traced the curves, though my mind still wondered.

Then the wall moved beneath my hands. The scroll-work had been a key of sorts, and a door sank open in the blackness before me. I went confidently forward, out of black night, through a black door into deeper blackness within. But my feet knew the way.

A stairway rose beneath me in the dark. My feet had expected it and I did not stumble. It was very curious to move so blindly through this strange and dangerous place, not knowing where or why I moved, yet trusting my body to find the way. The stairs wound up and up.

Llyr was here. I could feel his hungry presence like a pressure on the mind, but many times intensified because of the narrow spaces within these walls, as if he were a sound of thunder reverberating again and again from the enclosed spaces of the Caer. Something within me reverberated soundlessly in answer, a roar of exultation that I suppressed in quick revolt.

Llyr and I were no longer linked by that ceremony of long ago. I repudiated it. I was not Llyr's Chosen now. But within me a sense I could not control quivered with ecstasy at the thought of those sacrifices who had fled blindly through the great doors of Caer Sécaire. And I wondered if the Coven—if Medea—thought of me now, who had so nearly stood with the sacrifices last night.

My feet paused upon the stairs. I could see nothing, but I knew that before me was a wall carved with scroll-patterns. My hands found it, traced the raised designs. A section of darkness slid sidewise and I was leaning upon a wide ledge, looking down, very far down.

Caer Sécaire was like a mighty grove of columns whose capitals soared up and up into infinite darkness. Somewhere above, too high for me to see its source, a light was beginning to glow. My heart paused when I saw it, for I knew that light—that golden radiance from a Golden Window.

Memory came fitfully back to me. The Window of Llyr. The Window of Sacrifice. I could not see it, but my mind's eye remembered its glow. In Caer Llyr that Window's substance shone eternally, and Llyr Himself lolled behind it—far behind it—forever. But in Caer Sécaire and in the other temples of sacrifice that had once dotted the Dark World, there were replicas of the Window which glowed only when Llyr came bodilessly through the dark to take his due.

Above us, hovering and hungry, Llyr was dawning now in that golden radiance, like a sun in the night time of the temple. Where the Window of Sécaire was located, how it was shaped, I still could not remember. But something in me knew that golden light and shivered in response as I watched its brilliance strengthen through the columns of the temple.

Far below me I saw the Coven standing, tiny figures foreshortened to wedges of colored cloak—green-robed Matholch, yellow-robed Edeyrn, red Medea. Behind them stood a circle of guardsmen. Before them, as I watched, the last of the chosen slaves moved blindly away among the columns. I could not see where they were going, but in essence I knew. The Window was yawning for its sacrifices, and somehow they must make their way to it.

As the light broadened, I saw that before the Coven stood a great cup-shaped altar, black on a black dais. Above it a lipped spout hung. My eyes traced the course of the trough which ended in the spout, and I saw now that there was a winding, descending curve, dark against that growing light,

which came down in a great sweep from the mysterious heights
overhead, stretching from—the Window?—to the cupped altar. A stir deep within me told me what that trough was for. I
leaned upon the sill, shaking with an anticipation that was half
for myself and half for Him, who hovered above us in the sun-
like dawning of golden light.

Thinly from below me rose a chant. I knew Medea's voice,
clear and silver, a thread of sound in the dimness and the
silence. It rose like incense, quivering among the mighty, top-
less columns of Sécaire.

A tenseness of waiting grew and grew in the dim air of the
temple. The figures below me stood motionless, heads lifted,
watching the dawning light. Medea's voice chanted on and on.

Time paused there in the columned grove of Sécaire, while
Llyr hovered above us waiting for her prey.

Then a thin and terrible cry rang out from the heights overhead. One scream. The light shot out blindingly in a great burst
of exultation, like a voiceless answering cry from Llyr Himself.
Medea's chant rose to a piercing climax and paused.

There was a stir among the columns; something moved along
that curve of trough. My eyes sought the altar and the lipped
spout above it.

The Coven was rigid, a cluster of frozen figures, waiting.

Blood began to drip from the spout.

I do not know how long I hung there on the ledge, my eyes
riveted to the altar. I do not know how many times I heard a
cry ring out from above, how many times Medea's chant rose
to a hungry climax as the light burst forth in a glory overhead
and blood gushed into the great cup of the altar. I was deaf
and blind to everything but this. I was half with Llyr at his
Golden Window, shaken with ecstasy as he took his sacrifices,
and half with the Coven below, glorying in their share of the
ceremony of the Sabbat.

But I know I waited too long.

What saved me I do not know now. Some voice of the ego
crying unheard in my mind that this was time dangerously
spent, that I must be elsewhere before the Sabbat ended, that
Lorryn and his men waited endlessly while I hung here bat-
tening like a glutton upon Llyr's feast.

Reluctantly awareness returned to my mind. With an infinite

effort I pulled myself back from the brink of that Golden
Window and stood reeling in the darkness, but in my own body
again, not hovering mindlessly with Llyr in the heights above.
The Coven was still tense below me, gripped in the ecstasy of
the sacrifice. But for how long I could not be sure. Perhaps
for the rest of the night; perhaps for only an hour. I must hurry,
if hurrying were not already futile. There was no way to know.

So I went back in the darkness, down the unseen stairs, and
out of the dark, unseen door, and back along the road to Coven
Castle, my mind still reeling with remembered ecstasy, the
glow of the Window still before my dazzled eyes, and the
scarlet runnel above the altar, and the thin, sweet chanting of
Medea louder in my ears than the sound of my own feet upon
the road. . . .

The red moon was far down the sky when I came back to
Lorryn, still crouching beside the castle wall and half mad with
impatience. There was an eager stir among the unseen soldiers
as I came running down the road, a forward surge as if they
had waited to the very limit of endurance and would attack
now whether I gave the word or no.

I waved to Lorryn while I was still twenty feet away. I was
careless now of the Castle guardsmen. Let them see me. Let
them hear.

"Give the signal!" I shouted to Lorryn. "Attack!"

I saw him start up beside the road, and the moonlight glinted
upon the silver horn he lifted to his lips. Its blare of signal
notes ripped the night to tatters. It ripped away the last of my
lethargy too.

I heard the long yell that swept the forest as the woodsmen
surged forward to the attack, and my own voice roared unbidden in reply, an ecstasy of battle-hunger that matched the ecstasy I had just shared with Llyr.

The rattle of rifle-fire drowned out our voices. The first
explosions of grenades shook the Castle, outlining the outer
walls in livid detail. There were shouts from within, wild
trumpetings of signal horns, the cries of confused guardsmen,
leaderless and afraid. But I knew they would rally. They had
been trained well enough by Matholch and by myself. And
they had weapons that could give the woodsmen a stiff fight.

When they recovered from this panic there would be much
blood spilled around the outer walls.

I did not wait to see it. The first explosions had breached the barriers close beside me, and I scrambled recklessly through the gap, careless of the rifle fire that spattered against the stones. The Norns were with me tonight. I bore a charmed life, and I knew I could not fail.

Somewhere above me in the besieged towers Ghast Rhymi sat wrapped in his chill indifference, aloof as a god above the struggle around Coven Castle. I had a rendezvous with Ghast Rhymi, though he did not know it yet.

I plunged into the gateway of the Castle, heedless of the milling guards. They did not know me in the darkness and the confusion, but they knew by my tunic I was not a forester, and they let me shoulder them aside.

Three steps at a time, I ran up the great stairway.

XII

Harp of Satan

CASTLE of the Coven! How strange it looked to me as I went striding through its halls. Familiar, yet curiously unknown, as though I saw it through the veil of Edward Bond's transplanted memories.

So long as I went rapidly, I seemed to know the way. But if I hesitated, my conscious mind took over control, and that mind was still clouded with artificial memories, so that I became confused in the halls and corridors which were familiar to me when I did not think directly of them.

It was as if whatever I focused on sharply receded into unfamiliarity while everything else remained clear, until I thought of it.

I strode down hallways arched overhead and paved underfoot in bright, intricate mosaics that told legendary tales half-familiar to me. I walked upon centaurs and satyrs whose very faces were well known to the Ganelon half of my mind, while the Edward Bond half wondered in vain whether such people had really lived in this distorted world of mutations.

This double mind at times was a source of strength to me,

and at others a source of devouring weakness. Just now I hoped fervently that I might meet no delays for once I lost this rushing thread of memory which was leading me toward Ghast Rhymi, I might never find it again. Any interruption might be fatal to my plans.

Ghast Rhymi, my memories told me, would be somewhere in the highest tower of the castle. There too would be the treasure-room where the Mask and Wand lay hidden, and hidden deeper in the serene, untouchable thoughts of Ghast Rhymi, lay the secret of Llyr's vulnerability.

These three things I must have, and the getting would not be easy. For I knew—without clearly remembering how or by what—that the treasure-room was guarded by Ghast Rhymi. The Coven would not have left open to all comers that secret place where the things that could end them lay hidden.

Even I, even Ganelon, had a secret thing locked in that treasury. For no Covenanter, no warlock, no sorceress can deal in the dark powers without creating, himself, the one instrument that can destroy him. That is the Law.

There are secrets behind it which I may not speak of, but the common one is clear. All Earth's folklore is rife with the same legend. Powerful men and women must focus their power in an object detached from themselves.

The myth of the external soul is common to all Earth races, but the reason for it lies deep in the lore of the Dark World. This much I can say—that there must be a balance in all things. For every negative, a positive. We of the Coven could not build up our power without creating a corresponding weakness somewhere, somehow, and we must hide that weakness so cunningly that no enemy could find it.

Not even the Coven knew wherein my own secret lay. I knew Medea's, and I knew Edeyrn's only partially, and as for Matholch—well, against him I needed only my own Covenanter strength. Ghast Rhymi did not matter. He would not bother to fight.

But Llyr? Ah!

Somewhere the Sword lay hidden, and he who could find and use it in that unknown way for which it was fashioned, he held the existence of Llyr in his own hand. But there was danger. For as Llyr's power in the Dark World was beyond imagination, so too must be that balancing power hidden in the Sword. Even to go near it might be fatally dangerous. To hold it in the hand—well, hold it I must, and there was no profit in thinking about danger.

I went up and up, on and on.

I could not hear the sounds of battle. But I knew that at the gate the Coven guards and slaves were fighting and falling, as Lorryn's men, too, were falling. I had warned Lorryn that none must break through his lines to warn those at Caer Sécaire. I knew that he would follow that order, despite his anxiety to come to grips with Matholch. For the rest, there was one in the Castle who could, without stirring, send a message to Medea. One person!

He had not sent that message. I knew that as I thrust through the white curtain and came out into the tower room. The little chamber was semicircular, walls, floor and ceiling were ivory pale. The casement windows were shut, but Ghast Rhymi had never needed sight to send out his vision.

He sat there, an old, old man, relaxed amid the cushions of his seat, snowy hair and beard falling in curled ringlets that blended with his white, plain robe. His hands lay upon the chair-arms, pale as wax, so transparent that I could almost trace the course of the thinned blood that stirred so feebly in those old veins.

Wick and wax had burned down. The flame of life flickered softly, and a wind might send that flame into eternal darkness. So sat the Ancient of Days, his blind blue gaze not seeing me, but turned upon inward things.

Ganelon's memories flooded back. Ganelon had learned much from Ghast Rhymi. Even then, the Covenanter had been old. Now the tides of time had worn him, as the tides of the sea wear a stone till nothing is left but a thin shell, translucent as clouded glass.

Within Ghast Rhymi I could see the life-fires dwindling, sunk to embers, almost ash.

He did not see me. Not easily can Ghast Rhymi be drawn back from the deeps where his thoughts move.

I spoke to him, but he did not answer.

I went past him then, warily, toward the wall that divided the tower-top into two halves. There was no sign of a door, but I knew the combination. I moved my palms in an intricate pattern on the cool surface, and a gap widened before me.

I crossed the threshold.

Here were kept the holy things of the Coven.

I looked upon that treasure-vault with new eyes, clearer because of Edward Bond's memories. That lens, burning with dull amber lights there in its hollowed place in the wall—I had never wondered much about it before. It killed. But memories of Earth-science told me why. It was not magic, but an instantaneous drainage of the electrical energy of the brain. And that conical black device—that killed, too. It could shake a man to pieces, by shuttling his life-force back and forth so rapidly between artificial cathode and anode that living flesh could not stand the strain. Alternating current, with variations!

But these weapons did not interest me now. I sought other loot. There was no death-traps to beware of, for none but the Coven knew the way to enter this treasure-room, or its location, or even that it existed, save in legends. And no slave or guard would have dared to enter Ghast Rhymi's tower.

My gaze passed over a sword, but not the one I needed; a burnished shield; a harp, set with an intricate array of manual controls. I knew that harp. Earth has legends of it—the harp of Orpheus, that could bring back the dead from Hades. Human hands could not play it. But I was not quite ready for the harp, yet.

What I wanted lay on a shelf, sealed in its cylindrical case. I broke open the seals and took out the thin black rod with its hand-grip.

The Wand of Power. The Wand that could tap the electromagnetic force of a planet. So could other wands of this type—but this was the only one without the safety-device that limited its power. It was dangerous to use.

In another case I found the Crystal Mask—a curved, transparent plate that shielded my eyes like a domino mask of glass. This mask would shield one from Edeyrn.

I searched further. But of the Sword of Llyr I could find no trace.

Time did not lag. I heard nothing of the noise of battle, but I knew that the battle went on, and I knew, too, that sooner or later the Coven would return to the Castle. Well, I could fight the Coven now, but I could not fight Llyr. I dared not risk the issue till I had made sure.

In the door of the vault I stood, staring at Ghast Rhymi's silvery head. Whatever guardian thought he kept here, knew I had a right to the treasure room. He made no motion. His thoughts moved far out in unimaginable abysses, nor could they be easily drawn back. And it was impossible to put pressure on Ghast Rhymi. He had the perfect answer. He could die.

Well, I too had an answer!

I went back to the vault and lifted the harp. I carried it out and set it down before the old man. No life showed in his blue stare.

I went to the windows and flung them open. Then I returned, dropping to the cushions beside the harp, and lightly touched its intricate controls.

That harp had been in the Earth-world, or others like it. Legends know its singing strings, as legends tell of mystic swords. There was the lyre of Orpheus, strong with power, that Jupiter placed amid the stars. There was the harp of Gwydion of Britain, that charmed the souls of men. And the harp of Alfred, that helped to crush Daneland. There was David's harp that he played before Saul.

Power rests in music. No man today can say what sound broke the walls of Jericho, but once men knew.

Here in the Dark World this harp had its legends among the common folk. Men said that a demon played it, that the airy fingers of elemental spirits plucked at its strings. Well, in a way they were right.

For an incredible perfection of science had created this harp. It was a machine. Sonic, sub-sonic, and pure vibration to match the thought-waves emitted by the brain blended into a whole that was part hypnosis and part electric magnetism. The brain is a colloid, a machine, and any machine can be controlled.

And the harp of power could find the key to a mind, and lay bonds upon that mind.

Through the open windows, faintly from below, I heard the clash of swords and the dim shouts of fighting men. But these sounds did not touch Ghast Rhymi. He was lost on the plane of pure abstraction, thinking his ancient, deep thoughts.

My fingers touched the controls of the harp, awkwardly at first, then with more ease as manual dexterity came back with memory.

The sigh of a plucked string whispered through the white room. The murmuring of minor notes, in a low, dreamily distant key. And as the machine found the patterns of Ghast Rhymi's mind, under my hands the harp quickened into breathing life.

The soul of Ghast Rhymi—translated into terms of pure music!

Shrill and ear-piercing a single note sang. Higher and higher it mounted, fading into inaudibility. Deep down a roaring, windy noise began, rising and swelling into the demon-haunted shout of a gale. Rivers of air poured their music into the threnody.

High—high—cold and pure and white as the snowy summit of a great mountain, that single thin note sang and sang again.

Louder grew the great winds. Rippling arpeggios raced through the rising torrent of the sorcerous music.

Thunder of riven rocks—shrill screaming of earthquake-shaken lands—yelling of a deluge that poured down upon tossing forests.

A heavy humming note, hollow and unearthly, and I saw the gulfs between the worlds where the empty night of space makes a trackless desert.

And suddenly, incongruously, a gay lilting tune, with an infectious rocking rhythm, that brought to my mind bright colors and sunlit streams and fields.

Ghast Rhymi stirred.

For an instant awareness came back into his blue eyes. He saw me.

And I saw the life-fires sink within that frail, ancient body.

I knew that he was dying—that I had troubled his long peace—that he had relinquished his casual hold upon life.

I drew the harp toward me. I touched the controls.

Ghast Rhymi sat before me, dead, the faintest possible spark fading within that old brain.

I sent the sorcerous spell of the harp blowing like a mighty wind upon the dying embers of Ghast Rhymi's life.

As Orpheus drew back the dead Eurydice from Pluto's realm, so I cast my net of music, snared the soul of Ghast Rhymi, drew him back from death!

He struggled at first, I felt his mind turn and writhe, trying to escape, but the harp had already found the key to his mind, and it would not let him go. Inexorably it drew him.

The ember flickered—faded—brightened again.

Louder sang the strings. Deeper roared the tumult of shaking waters.

Higher the white, shrill note, pure as a star's icy light, leaped and ever rose.

Roaring, racing, sweet with honey-musk, perfumed with flower-scent and ambergris, blazing with color, opal and blood-ruby and amethyst-blue, that mighty tapestry of color rippled and shook like a visible web of magic through the room.

The web reached out.

Swept around Ghast Rhymi like a fowler's snare!

Back in those faded blue eyes the light of awareness grew. He had stopped struggling. He had given up the fight. It was easier to come back to life—to let me question him—than to battle the singing strings that could cage a man's very soul.

Under the white beard the old man's lips moved.

"Ganelon," he said. "I knew—when the harp sang—who played it. Well, ask your questions. And then let me die. I would not live in the days that are coming now. But you will live, Ganelon—and yet you will die too. That much I have read in the future."

The hoary head bent slowly. For an instant Ghast Rhymi listened—and I listened too.

The last, achingly sweet notes of the harp died upon the trembling air.

Through the open windows came the muted clash of sword and the wordless shriek of a dying man.

XIII

War—Red War!

PITY FLOODED me. The shadow of greatness that had cloaked Ghast Rhymi was gone. He sat there, a shrunken, fragile old man, and I felt a momentary unreasoning impulse to turn on my heel and leave him to drift back into his peaceful abyss of thought. Once, I remembered, Ghast Rhymi had seemed a tall, huge figure—though he had never been that in my lifetime. But in my childhood I had sat at the feet of this Covenanter and looked up with awe at that majestic, bearded face with reverence.

Perhaps there had been more life in that face then, more warmth and humanity. It was remote now. It was like the face of a god, or of one who had looked upon too many gods.

My tongue stumbled.

"Master," I said. "I am sorry!"

No light came into the distant blue gaze, yet I sensed a stirring.

"You name me master?" he said. "You—Ganelon? It has been a long time since you humbled yourself to anyone."

The taste of my triumph was ashes. I bowed my head. Yes, I had conquered Ghast Rhymi, and I did not like the savor of that conquest.

"In the end the circle completes itself," the old man said quietly. "We are more kin than the others. Both you and I are human, Ganelon, not mutants. Because I am Leader of the Coven I let Medea and the others use my wisdom. But—but—" He hesitated.

"For two decades my mind has dwelt in shadow," he went on. "Beyond good and evil, beyond life and the figures that move like puppets on the stream of life. When I was wakened, I would give the answers I knew. It did not matter. I had thought that I had lost all touch with reality. And that if death swept over every man and woman in the Dark World, it would not matter."

I could not speak. I knew that I had done Ghast Rhymi a very great wrong in wakening him from his deep peace.

The blue stars dwelt on me.

"And I find that it does matter, after all. No blood of mine runs in your veins, Ganelon. Yet we are kin. I taught you, as I would have taught my own son. I trained you for your task—to rule the Coven in my place. And now, I think I regret many things. Most of all the answer I gave the Covenanters after Medea brought you back from Earth-world."

"You told them to kill me," I said.

He nodded.

"Matholch was afraid. Edeyrn sided with him. They made Medea agree. Matholch said, 'Ganelon is changed. There is danger. Let the old man read the future and see what it holds.' So they came to me, and I let my mind ride the winds of time and see what lay ahead."

"And that was—?"

"The end of the Coven," Ghast Rhymi said. "If you lived. I foresaw the arms of Llyr reaching into the Dark World, and Matholch lying dead in a shadowed place, and doom upon Edeyrn and Medea. For time is fluid, Ganelon. It changes as men change. The probabilities alter. When you went into Earth-world, you were Ganelon. But you came back with a double mind. You have the memories of Edward Bond, which you can use as tools. Medea should have left you in Earth-world. But she loved you."

"Yet she agreed to let them kill me," I said.

"Do you know what was in her thoughts?" Ghast Rhymi asked. "In Caer Sécaire, at the time of sacrifice, Llyr would come. And you have been sealed to Llyr. Did Medea think you could be killed, then?"

A doubt grew within me. But Medea had led me, like a sheep to slaughter, in the procession to the Caer. If she could justify herself, let her. I knew that Edeyrn and Matholch could not.

"I may let Medea live, then," I said. "But not the wolfling. I have already promised his life. And as for Edeyrn, she must perish."

I showed Ghast Rhymi the Crystal Mask. He nodded.

"But Llyr?"

"I was sealed to Him as Ganelon," I said. "Now you say I

have two minds. Or, at least, an extra set of memories, even though they are artificial. I am not willing to be liege to Llyr! I learned many things in the Earth-world. *Llyr is no god!*"

The ancient head bent. A transparent hand rose and touched the ringlets of the beard. Then Ghast Rhymi looked at me, and he smiled.

"So you know that, do you?" he asked. "I will tell you something, Ganelon, that no one else has guessed. You are not the first to come from Earth-world to the Dark World. I was the first."

I stared at him with unconcealed amazement.

"And you were born in the Dark World; I was not," he said. "My flesh sprang from the dust of Earth. It has been very long since I crossed, and I can never return now, for my span is long outlived. Only here can I keep the life-spark burning within me, though I do not much care about that either. Yet I am Earth-born, and I knew Vortigern and the kings of Wales. I had my own holdings at Caer-Merdin, and a different sun from this red ember in the Dark World's sky shone upon Caer-Merdin! Blue sky, blue sea of Britain, the gray stones of the Druid altars under the oak forests. That is my home, Ganelon. *Was* my home. Until my science, that men in those days called magic, brought me here, with a woman's aid. A Dark-World woman named Viviane."

"You are Earth-born?" I said.

"Once—yes. As I grew older here, very, very old, I regretted my exile. I had acquired enough of wisdom. I would have changed it all for one breath of the cool, sweet air that blew in from the Irish Sea when I was a boy. But never could I return. My body would fall to dust in the Earth-world. So I lost myself in dreams—dreams of Earth, Ganelon."

His blue eyes brightened with memories.

His voice deepened.

"In my dreams I brought back the old days. I stood again on the crags of Wales, watching the salmon leaping in the waters of gray Usk. I saw Artorius again, and his father Uther, and I smelled the old smells of Britain in her youth. But they were dreams!

"And dreams are not enough. For the sake of the love I bore the dust from which I sprang, for the sake of a wind that blew from ancient Ireland, I will help you now, Ganelon. I had never thought that life would matter to me any more. But that these abominations should lead a man of Earth to slaughter—no! And man of Earth you are now, though born on this world of sorcery!"

He leaned forward, compelling me with his gaze.

"You are right. Llyr is no god. He is—a monster. No more than that. And he can be slain."

"With the Sword Called Llyr?"

"Listen. Put these legends out of your mind. That is Llyr's power, and the power of the Dark World. All is veiled in mystic symbols of terror. But behind the veil lies simple truth. Vampire, werewolf, upas-tree—they all are biological freaks, mutations run wild! And the first mutation was Llyr. His birth split the one time-world into two, each spinning along its line of probability. He was a key factor in the temporal pattern of entropy.

"Listen again. At birth, Llyr was human. But his mind was not as the minds of others. He had certain natural powers, latent powers, which ordinarily would not have developed in the race for a million years. Because they did develop in him too soon, they were warped and distorted, and put to evil ends. In the future world of logic and science, his mental powers would have fitted. In the dark times of superstition, they did not fit too well. So he developed, with the science at his command and the mental strength he had, into a monster.

"Human once. Less human as he grew older and wiser in his alien knowledge. In Caer Llyr are machines which send out certain radiations necessary to the existence of Llyr. Those radiations permeate the Dark World. They have caused other mutations, such as Matholch and Edeyrn and Medea.

"Kill Llyr and his machines will stop. The curse of abnormal mutations will be lifted. The shadow over this planet will be gone."

"How may I kill Him?" I asked.

"With the Sword Called Llyr. His life is bound up with that Sword, as a machine is dependent on its parts. I am not certain of the reason for this, Ganelon, but Llyr is not human—now. He is part machine and part pure energy and part something unimaginable. But he was born of flesh, and he must maintain his contact with the Dark World, or die. The Sword is his contact."

"Where is the Sword?"

"At Caer Llyr," Ghast Rhymi said. "Go there. By the altar, there is a crystal pane. Don't you remember?"

"I remember."

"Break that pane. Then you will find the Sword Called Llyr."

He sank back. His eyes closed, then opened again.

I knelt before him and he made the Ancient Sign above me.

"Strange," he murmured, half to himself. "Strange that I should send a man to battle again, as I sent so many, long ago."

The white head bent forward. Snowy beard lay upon the snowy robe.

"For the sake of a wind that blew from Ireland," the old man whispered.

Through the open windows a breath of air drifted, gently ruffling the white ringlets of hair and beard. . . .

The winds of the Dark World stirred in the silent room, paused—and were gone!

Now, indeed, I stood alone. . . .

From Ghast Rhymi's chamber I went down the tower steps and into the courtyard.

The battle was nearly over. Scarcely a score of the Castle's defenders were still on their feet. Around them Lorryn's pack ravened and yelled. Back to back, grimly silent, the dead-eyed guardsmen wove their blades in a steel mesh that momentarily held at bay their attackers.

There was no time to be wasted here. I caught sight of Lorryn's scarred face and made for him. He showed me his teeth in a triumphant grin.

"We have them, Bond."

"It took you long enough," I said. "These dogs must be slain quickly!" I caught a sword from a nearby woodsman.

Power flowed up the blade and into the hilt—into me.

I plunged into the thick of the battle. The foresters made way for me. Beside me Lorryn laughed quietly.

Then I came face to face with a guardsman. His blade swung up in thrust and parry, and I twisted aside, so that his steel

sang harmlessly through the air. My sword-point leaped like
a striking snake for his throat. The shock of metal grating on
bone jarred my wrist.

I tore the weapon free and glimpsed Lorryn, still grinning,
engaging another of the guardsmen.

"Kill them!" I shouted. "Kill them!"

I did not wait for response. I went forward against the blind-
eyed soldiers of Medea, slashing, striking, thrusting, as though
these men were the Coven, my enemies! I hated each blankly
staring face. Red tides of rage began to surge up, narrowing
my vision and clouding my mind with hot mists.

For a few moments I was drunk with the lust for killing.

Lorryn's hands gripped my shoulders. His voice came.

"Bond! *Bond!*"

The fogs were swept away. I stared around. Not one of the
guardsmen was left alive. Bloody, hacked corpses lay sprawled
on the gray flagstone of the courtyard. The woodsmen, panting
hard, were wiping their blades clean.

"Did any escape to carry warning to Caer Sécaire?" I asked.

Despite his perpetual scarred grin, Lorryn looked troubled.

"I'm not sure. I don't think so, but the place is a rabbit-
warren."

"The harm's done then," I said. "We hadn't enough men to
throw a cordon around the Castle."

He grimaced. "Warned or not, what's the odds? We can slay
the Covenanters as we killed their guards."

"We ride to Caer Llyr," I said, watching him.

I saw the shadow of fear in the cold gray eyes. Lorryn
rubbed his grizzled beard and scowled.

"I don't understand. Why?"

"To kill Llyr."

Amazement battled with ancient superstitious terror in his
face. His gaze searched mine and apparently read the answer
he wanted.

"To kill—*that?*"

I nodded. "I've seen Ghast Rhymi. He told me the way."

The men around us were watching and listening. Lorryn
hesitated.

"We didn't bargain for this," he said. "Yet by the gods! To
kill *Llyr!*"

Suddenly he sprang into action, shouting orders. Swords

were sheathed. Men ran to untether the mounts. Within minutes we were in our saddles, riding out from the courtyard, the shadow of the Castle falling heavily upon us till the moon lifted above the tallest tower.

I rose in my stirrups and looked back. Up there, dead, sat Ghasti Rhymi, first of the coven to die by my hand. I had killed him as surely as if I had plunged steel into his heart.

I dropped back into the saddle, pressing heels into my horse's flanks. He bolted forward. Lorryn urged his steed level with me. Behind us the woodsmen strung out in a long uneven line as we galloped across the low hills toward the distant mountains. It would be dawn before we could reach Caer Llyr. And there was no time to waste.

Medea and Edeyrn and Matholch! The names of the three beat like muffled drums in my brain. Traitors to me, Medea no less than the others, for had she not bent before the wills of Edeyrn and Matholch, had she not been willing to sacrifice me? Death I would give Edeyrn and the wolfling. Medea I might let live, but only as my slave, nothing more.

With Ghast Rhymi dead, I was leader of the Coven! In the old man's tower, sentimental weakness had nearly betrayed me. The weakness of Edward Bond, I thought. His memories had watered my will and diluted my power.

Now I no longer needed his memories. At my side swung the Crystal Mask and the Wand of Power. I knew how to get the Sword Called Llyr. It was Ganelon and not the weakling Edward Bond, who would make himself master of the Dark World.

Briefly I wondered where Bond was now. When Medea had brought me through the Need-fire to the Dark World, Edward Bond, at that same moment, must have returned to Earth. I smiled ironically, imagining the surprise that must have been his. Perhaps he had tried, and was still trying, to get back to the Dark World. But without Freydis to aid him, his attempts would be useless. Freydis was helping me now, not Bond.

And Bond would stay on Earth! The substitution would not occur again if I could help it. And I *could* help it. Strong Freydis might be, but could she stand against the man who had killed Llyr? I did not think so.

I sent a sly sidewise glance at Lorryn. Fool! Arles too was

another of the same breed. Only Freydis had sense enough not to trust me.

The strongest of my enemies must die first—Llyr. Then the Coven. After that, the woodsmen would taste my power. They would learn, that I was Ganelon, not the Earth weakling, Edward Bond!

I thrust the memories of Bond out of my mind. I drove them away. I banished them utterly.

As Ganelon I would battle Llyr.

And as Ganelon I would rule the Dark World!

Rule—with iron and fire!

XIV

Fire of Life

HOURS BEFORE we came to Caer Llyr we saw it, at first a blacker blackness against the night sky, and slowly, gradually, deepening into an ebon mountain as the rose-gray dawn spread behind us.

Our cantering shadows fell before us, to be trodden under the horses' hoofs. Cool, fresh winds whispered—whispered of the sacrifice at Caer Sécaire, of the seeking minds of the Coven that spied across the land.

But Caer Llyr loomed on the edge of darkness ahead—guarding the night!

Huge the Caer was, and alien. It seemed shapeless, a Titan mound of jumbled black rock thrown almost casually together. Yet I knew that there was design in its strange geometry.

Two jet pillars, each fifty feet tall, stood like the legs of a colossus, and between them was an unguarded portal. Only there was there any touch of color about the Caer.

A veil of flickering rainbows played lambently, like a veil across the threshold. Opalescent and faintly glowing, the shadow-curtain swung and quivered as though gentle winds drifted through gossamer folds of silk.

Fifty feet high was that curtain and twenty feet broad. Straddling it the ebon pillars rose. And above and beyond, towering breathtakingly to the dawn-clouded sky, squatted the Caer, a mountain-like structure that had never been built by man.

From Caer Llyr a breath of fear came coldly, scattering the woodsmen like leaves before a gale. They broke ranks, deployed out and drew together again as I raised my hand and Lorryn called a command.

I stared around at the low hills surrounding us.

"Never in my memory or my father's memory have men come this close to Caer Llyr," Lorryn said. "Except for Covenanters, of course. Nor would the foresters follow me now, Bond. They follow you."

How far would they follow? My wondering thought was cut off as a woodsman shouted warning. He rose in his stirrups and pointed south.

Over the hills, riding like demons in a dusty cloud, came horsemen, their armor glittering in the red sunlight!

"So someone did escape from the Castle," I said between my teeth. "And the Coven have been warned, after all!"

Lorryn grinned and shrugged. "Not many."

"Enough to delay us." I frowned, trying to make the best plan. "Lorryn, stop them. If the Coven ride with their guards, kill them too. But hold them back from the Caer until—"

"Until?"

"I don't know. I'll need time. How much time I can't say. Battling and conquering Llyr won't be the work of a moment."

"Nor is it the work of one man," Lorryn said doubtfully. "With us to aid you, victory will fly at your elbow."

"I know the weapon against Llyr," I said. "One man can wield it. But keep the guardsmen back, and the Covenanters too. Give me time!"

"There will be no difficulty about that," Lorryn said, a flash of excitement lighting his eyes. "For look!"

Angling across the hills, riding one by one into view, hotly pursuing the armored rout, came green-clad figures, spurring their horses forward.

Those figures were woodsmen's women whom we had left behind in the valley. They were armed now, for I saw the glitter of swords. Nor were swords their only weapons. A spiteful crack echoed, a puff of smoke arose, and one of the guardsmen flung up his hands and toppled from his mount.

Edward Bond had known how to make rifles! And the woodsfolk had learned how to use them!

At the head of the woodswomen I noted two lithe forms, one a slim, supple girl whose ashy-blond hair streamed behind her like a banner. Arles.

And at her side, on a great white steed, rode one whose giant form I could not mistake even from this distance. Freydis spurred forward like a Valkyrie galloping into battle.

Freydis and Arles, and the women of the forest!

Lorryn's laugh held exultation.

"We have them, Bond!" he cried, his fist tightening on the rein. "Our women at their heels, and we to strike from the flank—we'll catch and crush them between hammer and anvil. Gods grant the shape-changer rides there!"

"Then ride," I snapped. "No more talk! Ride and crush them. Hold them back from the Caer!"

With that I raced my steed forward, lying low on the horse's mane, driving like a thunderbolt toward the black mountain ahead. Did Lorryn know how suicidal might be the mission on which I had sent him? Matholch he might slay, and even Medea. But if Edeyrn rode with the Coven guards, if ever she dropped the hood from her face, neither sword nor bullet could save the woodsmen!

Still they would give me time. And if the woodsmen's ranks were thinned, so much the better for me later. I would deal with Edeyrn in my own way when the time came.

Ahead the black columns stood. Behind me a shouting rose, and a crackle of rifle-fire. I looked back, but a fold of the hills hid the combat from my eyes.

I sprang from the horse's back and stood before the pillars—between them. The coruscating veil sparkled and ran like milky water before me. Above, towering monstrously, stood the Caer, the focus of the evil that had spread across the Dark World.

And in it reposed Llyr, my enemy!

I still had the sword I had taken from one of the woodsmen, but I doubted if ordinary steel would be much good within the Caer. Nevertheless I made sure the weapon was at my side as I walked forward.

I stepped through the veil.

For twenty paces I moved forward in utter darkness. Then light came.

But it was the light that beats upon a snow plain, so bright, so glittering, that it blinds. I stood motionless, waiting. Presently the dazzle resolved itself into flickering atoms of brightness, weaving and darting in arabesque patterns. Not cold, no!

Tropical warmth beat upon me.

The shining atoms drove at me. They tingled upon my face and hands. They sank like intangible things through my garments and were absorbed by my skin. They did not lull me. Instead, my body greedily drank that weird snowstorm of—energy?—and was in turn energized by it.

Tide of life sang ever stronger in my veins.

I saw three gray shadows against the white. Two tall and one slight and small as a child's shadow.

I knew them. I knew who cast them.

I heard Matholch's voice.

"Kill him. Kill him now."

And Medea's answer.

"No. He need not die. He must not."

"But he must!" Matholch snarled, and Edeyrn's sexless, thin voice echoed his.

"He is dangerous, Medea. He must die, and only on Llyr's altar can he be slain. For he is the Sealed of Llyr."

"He need not die," Medea said stubbornly. "If he is made harmless—weaponless—he may live."

"How?" Edeyrn asked, and for answer the red witch stepped forward out of the dazzling white shimmer.

No longer a shadow. No longer a two-dimensional grayness. She stood before me—Medea, witch of Colchis.

Her dark hair fell to her knees. Her dark gaze slanted at me. Evil she was, and alluring as Lilith.

I dropped my hand to sword-hilt.

I did *not*. I could not move. Faster swirled the darting bright atoms, whirling about me, sinking into my body to betray me.

I could not move.

Beyond Medea the twin shadows bent forward.

"The power of Llyr holds him," Edeyrn whispered. "But Ganelon is strong, Medea. If he breaks his fetters, we are lost."

"By then he will have no weapons," Medea said, and smiled at me.

Now indeed I knew my danger. Very easily my steel could have bitten through Medea's soft throat, and heartily I wished it had done so long ago. For I remembered Medea's power. The mutation that set her apart from others. That which had caused her to be named—vampire.

I remembered victims of hers that I had seen. The dead-eyed guardsmen, the Castle slaves, hollow shells of men, the walking dead, all soul drained from them, and most of their life-forms as well.

Her arms stole around my neck. Her mouth lifted to mine.

In one hand she held her black wand. It touched my head, and a gentle shock, not unpleasant, crawled along my scalp. The—the conductor, I knew, and a gust of insane laughter shook me at the incongruity of the weapon.

But there was no magic here. There was science, of a high order, a science made possible only for those who were trained to it, or for those who were mutants. Medea drank energy, but not through sorcery. I had seen that wand used too often to believe that.

The wand opened the closed circuits of the mind and its energies. It tapped the brain, as a copper wire can tap a generated current.

Diverting the life-force to Medea!

The shining mist-motes swirled faster. They closed in around us, bathing us in a swirling cloak. The gray shadowiness fell away from Edeyrn and Matholch. Dun-cloaked, cowled dwarf and lean, grinning wolfling stood there, watching.

Edeyrn's face I could not see, though the deadly cold crept from beneath the cowl like an icy wind. Matholch's tongue crept out and circled his lips. His eyes were bright with triumph and excitement.

A numbing, lethargic languor was stealing over me. Against my mouth as Medea's lips grew hotter, more ardent, as my own lips chilled. Desperately I tried to move, to grasp my sword-hilt.

I could not.

Now the bright veil thinned again. Beyond Matholch and Edeyrn I could see a vast space, so enormous that my gaze failed to pierce its violet depths. A stairway led up to infinite heights.

A golden glow burned high above.

But behind Matholch and Edeyrn, a little to one side, stood a curiously-carved pedestal whose front was a single pane of transparent glass. It shone steadily with a cool blue light. What lay within I did not know, but I recognized that crystal pane.

Ghast Rhymi had spoken of it. Behind it must lie the Sword Called Llyr.

Faintly now—faintly—I heard Matholch's satisfied chuckle.

"Ganelon, my love, do not struggle against me," Medea whispered. "Only I can save you. When your madness passes, we will return to the Castle."

Yes, for I would be no menace then. Matholch would not bother to harm me. As a mindless, soulless thing I would return to the Castle of the Coven as Medea's slave.

I, Ganelon, hereditary Lord of the Coven and the Sealed of Llyr!

The golden glow high above brightened. Crooked lightnings rushed out from it and were lost in the violet dimness.

My eyes found that golden light that was the Window of Llyr.

My mind reached out toward it.

My soul strained to it!

Witch and vampire-mutation Medea might be—or sorceress—but she had never been sealed to Llyr. No dark power beat latently in her blood as it beat in mine. Well I knew now that, no matter how I might renounce my allegiance to Llyr, there yet had been a bond. Llyr had power over me, but I could draw upon his power as well!

I drew on that power now!

The golden window brightened. Again forked lightnings ran out from it and were gone. A muffled, heavy drum-beat muttered from somewhere, like the pulse of Llyr.

Like the heart of Llyr, stirring from sleep to waking.

Through me power rushed, quickening my flesh from its lethargy. I drew on Llyr's power without measuring the cost. I saw fear flash across Matholch's face, and Edeyrn made a quick gesture.

"Medea," she said.

But Medea had already sensed that quickening. I felt her body quiver convulsively against mine. Avidly she pressed

against me, faster and faster she drank the energy that made
me alive.

But the energy of Llyr poured into me! Hollow thunders
roared in the vast spaces above. The golden window blazed
with dazzling brightness. And around us now the sparkling
motes of light paled, shrank, and were gone.

"Kill him!" Matholch howled. "He holds Llyr!"

He sprang forward.

From somewhere a bloody figure in dented armor stumbled.
I saw Lorryn's scarred face twist in amazement as he blinked
at the tableau. His sword, red to the hilt, was bare in his hand.

He saw me with Medea's arms about my neck.

He saw Edeyrn.

And he saw Matholch!

A wordless, inarticulate sound ripped through Lorryn's throat.
He lifted high the sword.

As I tore myself free from Medea's grip, as I sent her reeling
away, I saw Matholch's wand come up. I reached for my own
wand, but there was no need.

Lorryn's blade sang. Matholch's hand, still gripping the
wand, was severed at the wrist. Blood spurted from cut arteries.

Howling, the shape-changer dropped forward. The lycanthropic change came upon him. Hypnotism, mutation, dark
sorcery—I could not tell. But the thing that sprang at Lorryn's
throat was not human.

Lorryn laughed. He sent his sword spinning away.

He met the wolfling's charge, bracing himself strongly and
caught the thing by throat and leg. Fanged jaws snapped viciously at him.

Lorryn heaved the monster above his head. His joints cracked
with the inhuman strain. One instant Lorryn stood there, holding his enemy high, while the wolf-jaws snarled and strove to
rend him.

He dashed the wolf down upon the stones!

I heard bones snap like rotten twigs. I heard a scream of
dying, terrible agony from a gaping muzzle from which blood
poured.

Then Matholch, in his own shape, broken, dying, lay writhing at our feet!

XV

Lair of Power

MIRACULOUSLY the weakness that had chained me was gone. Llyr's strength poured through me. I unsheathed my sword and ran past Matholch's body, ignoring Lorryn who stood motionless, staring down. I ran to the pedestal with its blue-litten pane.

I gripped the sword's blade and sent the heavy hilt crashing against the glass.

There was a tinkling of pizzicato notes, a singing of thin goblin laughter. The shards fell clashing at my feet.

At my feet also dropped a sword. A sword of crystal, nearly five feet long—pommel and guard and blade all of clearest glass.

It had been part of the window. For within the hollow pedestal was nothing at all. The sword had been part of the pane, so that my breaking the crystal had released the weapon from its camouflaged hiding-place.

Along the sleek blade blue light ran. Within the crystal blue fires burned wanly. I bent and picked up the sword. The hilt was warm and alive.

The Sword Called Llyr in my left hand, the sword with blade of steel in my right, I stood upright.

Paralyzing cold breathed past me.

I knew that cold.

So I did not turn. I swung the steel sword under my arm, snatched the Crystal Mask from my belt, and donned it. I drew the Wand of Power.

Only then did I turn.

Through the Mask queer glimmers and shiftings ran, distorting what I saw. The properties of light were oddly altered by the Mask. But it had its purpose. It was a filter.

Matholch lay motionless now. Beyond his body Medea was rising to her feet, her dark hair disordered. Facing me stood Lorryn, a stone man, only his eyes alive in his set, white face.

He was staring at Edeyrn, whose sleek dark head I saw. Her back was toward me. The cowl had been flung back upon her shoulders.

Lorryn sagged down, the life going out of him. Bonelessly as water he collapsed.

He lay dead.

Then slowly, slowly, Edeyrn turned.

She was tiny as a child, and her face was like a child's too, in its immature roundness. But I did not see her face, for even through the Crystal Mask burned the Gorgon's glare.

The blood stilled within me. A slow tide of ice crept with iron lethargy into my brain and cold wariness engulfed me.

Only in the eyes of the Gorgon fire burned.

Deadly radiations were there, what Earth-scientists call ectogenetic rays, but limited till now to the plant-world. Only the mad mutation that had created Edeyrn could have brought from hell such a nightmare trick of biology.

But I did not fall. I did not die. The radiations were filtered, made harmless, by the vibration-warping properties of the Mask I wore.

I lifted the Wand of Power.

Red fires blasted from it. Scarlet, licking tongues seared out toward Edeyrn.

Lashes of flame tore at her, like crimson whips that burned and left bloody weals on that calm child-face.

She drew back, the lance of her stare driving at me.

With her, step by step, retreated Medea. Toward the foot of the great stairway that led to Llyr's Window.

The whips of fire seared across her eyes.

She turned and, stumbling, began to run up the stairway. Medea paused, her arms lifted in an uncompleted gesture. But in my face she read no softening.

She, too, turned, and followed Edeyrn.

I dropped the useless sword of steel. Wand in left hand, the Sword Called Llyr in my right, I followed them.

As my foot touched the first step, a trembling vibration shook the violet air about me. Now almost I regretted having called upon Llyr to break Medea's spell. For Llyr was awake, watching, and warned.

The pulse of Llyr muttered through the huge Caer. The golden lightnings flamed from the Window high above.

Briefly two black small silhouettes showed against that amber glow. They were Edeyrn and Medea, climbing.

After them I went. And at each step the way grew harder.
I seemed to walk through a thickening, invisible torrent that
was like a wind or a wave flowing down from that shining
window, striving to tear me from my foothold, to rip the crystal
sword from my grip.

Up and up I went. Now the Window was a glaring blaze
of yellow fires. The lightnings crackled out incessantly, while
rocking crashes of thunder reverberated along the vaulted abysses
of the Caer. I leaned forward as though against a gale. Doggedly
I fought my way up the stair.

There was someone behind me.

I did not turn. I dared not, for fear the torrent would sweep
me from my place. I crawled up the last few steps, and came
out on a level platform of stone, a disc-shaped dais, on which
stood a ten-foot cube. Three of its sides were of black rock.
The side that faced me was a glaring blaze of amber brilliance.

Far below, dizzyingly far, was the floor of the Caer. Behind
me the stairway ran down to those incredible depths, and the
tremendous wind still blew upon me, pouring out from the
Window, seeking to whirl me to my death.

To the Window's left stood Edeyrn, to its right, Medea.
And in the Window—

The blazing golden clouds whirled, thickened, tossed like
storm-mists, while still the blinding flashes spurted from them.
The thunder never ceased now. But it pulsed. It rose and fell
in steady cadence, in unison with the heart-beat of Llyr.

Monster or mutation—human once, or half-human—Llyr
had grown in power since then. Ghast Rhymi had warned me.

Part machine and part pure energy and part something un-
thinkable, the power of Llyr blasted through the golden clouds
upon me!

The Wand of Power dropped from my hand. I lifted the
crystal sword and managed one forward step. Then the helltide
caught me, and I could advance no further. I could only fight,
with every bit of my strength, against the avalanche that strove
to thrust me toward the edge of the hanging platform.

Louder grew the thunders. Brighter the lightnings flamed.
The cold stare of Edeyrn chilled me. Medea's face was

inhuman now. Yellow clouds boiled out from the Window and
caught Edeyrn and Medea in their embrace.

Then they rolled toward me and overwhelmed me.

Dimly I could see the brighter glow that marked Llyr's
Window. And two vague silhouettes, Edeyrn and Medea.

I strove to step forward. Instead I was borne back toward
the edge—back and back.

Great arms caught me about the waist. A braid of white
hair tossed by my eyes. The giant strength of Freydis stood
like a wall of iron between me and the abyss.

From the corner of my eye I saw that she had wound a scrap
torn from her white robe about her head, shielding her from
the Gorgon's stare. Blindly, guided by some strange instinct,
the Valkyrie thrust me forward.

Against us the golden clouds rolled, sentient, palpable, veined
with white lightnings and shaking with deep thunders.

Freydis strove silently. I bent forward like a bow, battering
against the torrent.

Step by step I won forward, Freydis to aid me. Ever she
stood as a bulwark against my back. I could hear her panting
breath, great gasps that ripped from her throat as she linked
her strength with mine.

My chest felt as though a white-hot core of iron was driven
through it. Yet I went on. Nothing existed now but that golden
brightening amid the clouds, clouds of creation, sentient with
the shaking tumult of breaking universes, worlds beyond worlds
crashing into ruin under the power of Llyr. . . .

I stood before the Window.

Without volition my arm swept up. I brought the Sword
Called Llyr smashing down upon Llyr's Window.

In my hand the sword broke.

It fell to tinkling fragments at my feet. The veined blue
glimmers writhed and coiled about the broken blade.

Were sucked into the Window.

Back rushed the cloud-masses. A tremendous, nearly un-
bearable vibration ripped through the Caer, shaking it like a
sapling. The golden clouds were drawn through the Window.

With them went Edeyrn and Medea!

One glimpse I had of them, the brand of my fire like a red
mask across Edeyrn's eyes, Medea's face despairing and filled

with a horror beyond life, her gaze fixed on me with an imploring plea that was infinitely terrible. Then they vanished!

For one instant I saw through the Window. I saw something beyond space and time and dimension, a writhing, ravening chaos that bore down upon Medea and Edeyrn and a golden core of light that I knew for Llyr.

Once almost human, Llyr, at the end, bore no relation to anything remotely human.

The grinding millstones of Chaos crushed the three!

The thunder died.

Before me stood the altar of Llyr. But it held no Window, now. All four sides were of black, dead stone!

XVI

Self Against Self

BLACKNESS and black stones were the last things I saw, before dark oblivion closed down over me like folding wings. It was as if Llyr's terrible resistance was all that had held me upright in the last fierce stages of our struggle. As he fell, so fell Ganelon at the foot of the Windowless altar.

How long I lay there I do not know. But slowly, slowly Caer Llyr came back around me, and I knew I was lying prostrate upon the altar. I sat up painfully, the dregs of exhaustion still stiffening my body, though I knew I must have slept, for that exhaustion was no longer the overwhelming tide that had flooded me as I fell.

Beyond me, at the head of the great steep of stairs, Freydis lay, half stretched upon the steps as if she had striven to return to her people in the moment before collapsing. Her eyes were still bound, and her mighty arms lay flung out upon the platform, all strength drained from them by the fierceness of our battle. Strangely, as she lay there, she brought back to my double-minded memories the thought of a figure from Earth—another mighty woman in white robes, with bandaged eyes and upraised arms, blind Justice holding her eternal scales.

Faintly I smiled at the thought. In the Dark World—my world, now—Justice was Ganelon, and not blind.

Freydis stirred. One hand lifted uncertainly to the cloth across her eyes. I let her waken. Presently we must struggle again together, Justice and I. But I did not doubt who would prevail.

I rose to my knees, and heard a silvery tinkling as something slid in fragments from my shoulder. The Mask, broken when I fell. Its crystal shards lay among those other shards which had blasted Llyr from the Dark World when the Sword broke. I thought of the strange blue lightnings which had wrought at last what no other thing in the Dark World could accomplish— Llyr's destruction. And I thought I understood.

He had passed too far beyond this world ever to touch it except in the ceremonies of the Golden Window. Man, demon, god, mutation into namelessness—whatever he had been, he had kept but one link with the Dark World which spawned him. A link enshrined in the Sword Called Llyr. By that talisman he could return for the sacrifices which fed him, return for the great ceremonies of the Sealing that had made me half his own. But only by that talisman.

So it must be safely hidden to be his bridge for the returning. And safely hidden it was. Without Ghast Rhymi's knowledge, who could have found it. Without the strength of the great Lord Ganelon—well, yes, and the strength of Freydis too— who could have won close enough to the window to shatter the Sword upon the only thing in the Dark World that could break it? Yes, Llyr had guarded his talisman as strongly as any guard could be. But vulnerable he was, to the one man who could wield that Sword.

So the Sword broke, and the bridge between worlds broke, and Llyr was gone into a chaos from which there could never be a returning.

Medea, too—red witch of Colchis, lost love, drinker of life, gone beyond recalling. . . .

For a moment I closed my eyes.

"Well, Ganelon?"

I looked up. Freydis was smiling grimly at me from beneath the uplifted blindfold. I rose to my feet and watched in silence while she got to hers. Triumph flooded through me in great waves of intoxicating warmth. The world I had just wakened to was wholly mine now, and not this woman nor any other human should balk me of my destiny. Had I not vanquished Llyr and slain the last of the Coven? And was I not stronger in magic than any man or woman now who walked the Dark World? I laughed, the deep sound echoing from the high vaults about us and rolling back in reverberant exultation until that which had been Caer Llyr was alive with the noise of my mirth. But Llyr was here no longer.

"Let this be Caer Ganelon!" I said, hearing the echo of my own name come rolling back as if the castle itself replied.

"Ganelon!" I shouted. "Caer Ganelon!" I laughed to hear the whole vast hollow repeating my name. While the echoes still rolled I spoke to Freydis.

"You have a new master now, you forest people! Because you helped me you shall be rewarded, old woman, but I am master of the Dark World—I Ganelon!" And the walls roared back to me, "Ganelon—Ganelon!"

Freydis smiled.

"Not so fast, Covenanter," she said calmly. "Did you think I trusted you?"

I gave her a scornful smile, "What can you do to me now? Only one thing could slay me before today—Llyr Himself. Now Llyr is gone, and Ganelon is immortal! You have no power to touch me, sorceress!"

She straightened on the step, her ageless face a little below mine. There was a sureness in her eyes that sent the first twinge of uneasiness into my mind. Yet what I had said was true for no one in the Dark World could harm me, now. Yet Freydis' smile did not waver.

"Once I sent you through limbo into the Earth World," she said. "Could you stop me if I sent you there again?"

Relief quieted my tremor of unease.

"Tomorrow or the next day—yes, I could stop you. Today, no. But I am Ganelon now, and I know the way back. I am Ganelon, and forewarned, and I think you could not so easily send me Earthward again, naked of memories and clothed in another man's past. I remember and I could return. You would waste your time and mine, Freydis. Yet try it, if you will and I warn you, I should be back again before your spell was finished."

Her quiet smile did not falter. She folded her arms, hiding her hands in the flowing sleeves. She was very sure of herself.

"You think you are a godling, Ganelon," she said. "You think no mortal power can touch you now. You have forgotten one thing. As Llyr had his weakness, as Edeyrn did, and Medea and Matholch so have you, Covenanter. In this world there is no man to match you. But in the Earth World there is, Lord Ganelon! In that world your equal lives, and I mean to call him out to fight one last battle for the freedom of the Dark World. Edward Bond could slay you, Ganelon!"

I felt the blood leave my face, a little wind of chill like Edeyrn's glance breathed over me. I *had* forgotten. Even Llyr, by his own unimaginable hand, could have died. And I could die by my own hand too, or by the hand of that other self who was Edward Bond.

"Fool!" I said. "Dotard! Have you forgotten that Bond and I can never stand in the same world? When I came, he vanished out of this land, just as I must vanish if you bring him here. How can a man and his reflection ever come hand to hand? How could he touch me, old woman?"

"Easily," she smiled. "Very easily. He cannot fight you here, nor in the Earth World. That is true. But limbo, Ganelon? Have you forgotten limbo?"

Her hands came out of her sleeves. There was a rod of blinding silver in each. Before I could stir she had brought the rods together, crossing them before her smiling face. At the intersection forces of tremendous power blazed into an instant's being, forces that streamed from the poles of the world and could touch only for the beat of a second if that world were not to be shaken into fragments. I felt the building reel below me.

I felt the gateway open.

Here was grayness, nothing but oblivion made visible all around me. I staggered with the suddenness of it, the shock, and the terrible tide of anger that came surging up through my whole body at the knowledge of Freydis' trickery. It was not to be endured, this magicking of the Dark World's lord! I would fight my way back and the vengeance I would wreak upon Freydis would be a lesson to all.

Out of the grayness a mirror loomed before me. A mirror? I saw my own face, bewildered, uncomprehending, staring back into my eyes. But I was not wearing the ragged blue garments of sacrifice which I had donned so many aeons ago in the Castle of the Coven. I seemed to wear Earth garments, and I seemed not quite myself, not quite Ganelon. I seemed—

"Edward Bond!" said the voice of Freydis behind me.

The reflection of myself glanced across my shoulder, and a look of recognition and unutterable relief came over it.

"Freydis!" he cried, in my own voice. "Freydis, thank God! I've tried so hard—"

"Wait," Freydis stopped him. "Listen. There is one last trial before you. This man is Ganelon. He has undone all your work among the forest people. He has slain Llyr and the Coven. There is none in the Dark World to stay his hand if he wins his way back to it. Only you can stop him, Edward Bond. Only you."

I did not wait for her to say anything more. I knew what must be done. I lunged forward before he could speak or stir, and drove a heavy blow into the face that might have been my own. It was a strange thing to do. It was a hard thing. At the last moment my muscles almost refused me, for it was as if I struck myself.

I saw him reel back, and my own head reeled in imagination, so that the first blow rocked us both.

He caught himself a dozen feet away and stood for a moment, unsteady on his feet, looking at me with a confusion that might have been the mirror of my own face, for I knew there was confusion there too.

Then anger flushed those bewildering, familiar features, and I saw blood break from the corner of his mouth and trickle across his chin. I laughed savagely. That blood, somehow, made him my enemy. I had seen the blood of enemies, springing out in the wake of my blows, too often to mistake him now for anything but what he was. Myself—and my deadliest foe.

He dropped into a half-crouch and came for me, stooping to protect his body from my fists. I wished fervently for a sword or a gun. I have never cared for an equal fight, as Ganelon does not fight for sport, but to win. But this fight must be terribly, unbelievably equal.

* * *

He dodged beneath my blow, and I felt the rocking jar of what seemed to be my own fist jolting against my cheekbone. He danced back, light-footed, out of range.

Rage came snarling up in my throat. I wanted nothing of this boxing, this game fought by rules. Ganelon fought to win! I roared at him from the full depth of my lungs and hurled myself forward in a crushing embrace that carried us both heavily to the gray sponginess that was limbo's floor. My fingers sank delightfully in his throat. I groped savagely for his eyes. He grunted with effort and I felt his fist thud into my ribs, and felt the sharp white pain of breaking bone.

So wholly was he myself, and I he, that for an instant I was not sure whose rib had snapped beneath whose blow. Then I drew a deep breath and sobbed it out again half finished as pain like bright light flashed through my body, and I knew it was my own rib.

The knowledge maddened me. Careless of pain or caution, I drove my fists savagely into him at blind random, feeling exultantly the crackle of bone beneath my knuckles, the spurt of blood over my hard-clenched hands. We strove together in a terrible locked embrace, there upon the floor of limbo, in a nightmare that had no real being, except for the pain shooting through me after each breath.

But in a moment or two, I knew somehow, very surely, that I was his master. And this is how I knew. He rolled half over to jab a hard blow into my face, and before the blow began, I had blocked it. I had *known*. He squirmed from beneath me and braced himself to strike me again in the ribs, and before he could strike, I had twisted sidewise away. Again I had *known*.

For I had been Edward Bond once, in every way that matters. I had lived in his memory and his world. And I knew Edward Bond as I knew myself. Instinct seemed to tell me what he would do next. He could not out-think me, and so he could not hope to out-fight me, to whom his every thought was revealed in the moment before he could act upon it.

Even in the pain of my broken rib, I laughed then. Freydis had overreached herself at last! In smothering Ganelon under Edward Bond's memories in the Earth World, she had given me the means to vanquish him now! He was mine, to finish when I chose, and the Dark World was mine, and Edward

Bond's kingdom of free people was mine too, and Edward Bond's lovely pale-haired bride, and everything that might have been his own.

I laughed exultantly, and twisted in three perfectly timed motions that blocked and overbalanced the man who was myself. Three motions only—and then I had him across my knee, taut-stretched, his spine pressing hard against my thigh.

I grinned down at him. My blood dripped into his face. I saw it strike there, and I met his eyes, and then strangely, for one flashing instant, I knew a fierce yearning for defeat. In that instant, I prayed voicelessly to a nameless god that Edward Bond might yet save himself, and Ganelon might die. . . .

I callled forth all the strength that was in me, and limbo swam redly before my eyes and the pain of my broken rib was a lance of white light as I drew the deep breath that was Edward Bond's last.

I broke his back across my knee.

XVII

Freedom at Last!

HURRIEDLY two cold, smooth hands pressed hard upon my forehead. I looked up. They slid lower, covering my eyes. And weakness was like a blanket over me. I knelt there, unresisting, feeling the body of the man who had been myself slide limply from my knee.

Freydis pressed me down. We lay side by side, the living and the dead.

The silver rods of the sorceress touched my head, and made a bridge between Edward Bond and Ganelon. I remembered Medea's wand that could draw the life-force from the mind. A dull, numbing paralysis had me. Little tingling shocks rippled through my nerves, and I could not move.

Sudden agonizing pain shot through me. My back! I tried to scream with the white fury of that wrenching agony, but my throat was frozen. I felt Edward Bond's wounds!

In that nightmare moment, while my brain spun down the

limitless corridors of a science beyond that of mankind, I knew what Freydis had done—what she was doing.

I felt the mind of Edward Bond come back from the gulfs. Side by side we lay in flesh, and side by side in spirit as well.

There was blackness, and two flames, burning with a cold, clear fire. . . .

One was the mind—the life—of Edward Bond. One was my life!

The flames bent toward each other!

They mingled and were one!

Life and soul and mind of Edward Bond merged with life of Ganelon!

Where two flames had burned, there was one now. One only.

And the identity of Ganelon ebbed, sank . . . faded into a graying shadow as the fires of Edward Bond's life leaped even higher!

We were one. We were—

Edward Bond! No longer Ganelon! No longer Lord of the Dark World, Master of the Caers!

Magic of Freydis drowned the soul of Ganelon and gave his body to the life of Edward Bond!

I saw Ganelon—*die*! . . .

When I opened my eyes again, I knelt upon the altar that had been Llyr's. The empty vaults towered hollowly above us. Limbo was gone. The body across my knee was gone. Freydis smiled down at me with her ageless, timeless smile.

"Welcome back to the Dark World, Edward Bond."

Yes, it was true. I knew that. I knew that my own identity, housed though it was in another man's body. Dizzily I blinked, shook my head, and rose slowly. Pain struck savagely at my side, and I gasped and let Freydis spring forward to support me on one great white arm, while the hollow building reeled about me. But Ganelon was gone. He had vanished with limbo, vanished like a scatter of smoke, vanished as if the prayer he breathed in his extremity had been answered by the nameless god he prayed to.

I was Edward Bond again.

"Do you know why Ganelon could break you, Edward Bond?" Freydis said softly. "Do you know why you could not vanquish him? It was not what he thought. I know he believed he read your mind because he had dwelt there, but that was not the reason. When a man fights himself, my son, the same man does not fight to win. Only the suicide hates himself. Deep within Ganelon lay knowledge of his own evil, and the hatred of it. So he could strike his own image and exult in the blow, because he hated himself in the depths of his own mind.

"But you had earned your own respect. You could not strike as hard as he because you are not evil. And Ganelon won— and lost. In the end, he did not fight me. He had slain himself, and the man who does that has no combat left in him."

Her voice sank to a murmur. Then she laughed.

"Go out now, Edward Bond. There is much to be done in the Dark World!"

So, leaning upon her arm, I went down the long steps that Ganelon had climbed. I saw the green glimmer of the day outside, the shimmer of leaves, the motion of waiting people. I remembered all that Ganelon had remembered, but upon the mind of Ganelon the mind of Edward Bond was forever superimposed, and I knew that only thus could the Dark World be ruled.

The two together, twinned forever in one body, and the control forever mine—Edward Bond's.

We came out under the emptied arch of the opening, and daylight was blinding for a moment after that haunted darkness. Then I saw the foresters anxiously clustering in their battered ranks around the Caer, and I saw a pale girl in green, haloed by her floating hair, turn a face of incredulous radiance to mine.

I forgot the pain in my side.

Arles' hair swam like mist about us both as my arms closed around her. The roar of exultation that went up from the forest people swept the clearing and made the great Caer behind us echo through all its hollow vaults.

The Dark World was free, and ours.

But Medea, Medea, red witch of Colchis, how we might have reigned together!

By the year 2000, 2 out of 3 Americans could be illiterate.

It's true.

Today, 75 million adults... about one American in three, can't read adequately. And by the year 2000, U.S. News & World Report envisions an America with a literacy rate of only 30%.

Before that America comes to be, you can stop it... by joining the fight against illiteracy today.

Call the Coalition for Literacy at toll-free **1-800-228-8813** and volunteer.

Volunteer Against Illiteracy. The only degree you need is a degree of caring.

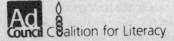

Ad Council Coalition for Literacy

Warner Books is proud to be an active supporter of the Coalition for Literacy.